Monsters Stir in the Depths. An Army Marches on the Stronghold. Will Our Hero's be Devoured by Their Demons or Will They Receive...

DELIVERANCE

THE DELIVERANCE TRILOGY: BOOK THREE

H. L. WALSH

Deliverance

The Deliverance Trilogy: Book Three

H. L. Walsh

H. L. Walsh Books

Kansas City, Missouri

Copyright © 2024 by H. L. Walsh

First Edition

Walsh, H. L.

Deliverance: The Deliverance Trilogy: Book Three/ H. L. Walsh/
H. L. Walsh Books, Kansas City, Missouri USA

ISBN: 978-1-7340922-4-0

Cover Design By: MiblArt

Map Design By: Najlakay

List of books by H. L. Walsh

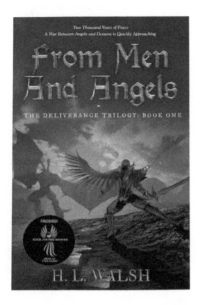

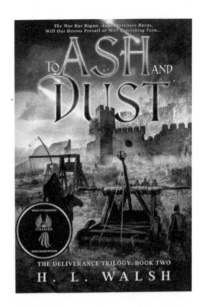

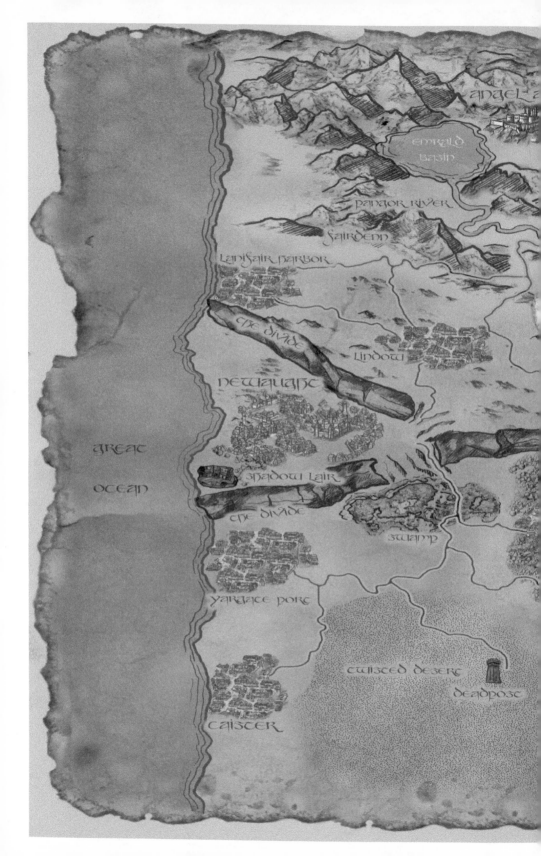

ARMY
UNRELENTING MOUNTAINS
BRIGHTWOOD
WHITESHADE
PANGOR RIVER
ANGEL TERRITORY
ANGELCROSS
UNEXPLORED REGION
THE DIVIDE
THE DIVIDE
RARGOD
RAGEWOOD FOREST
DEMON TERRITORY
RAGEWOOD
DEMON COMPOUND

Prologue

Leviathan walked the glorious halls of the shining city. She wandered, not really walking anywhere in particular. Only wishing to clear her mind. The subject of her mussing was Lucifer. The Chief of Seraphim in charge of heaven's operations. God had been all but absent in the last few years. Most angels thought he was planning something big. Something that would change everything.

So wrapped up in her rumination, she barely registered the magnificent ball room she wandered through. The vaulted, domed ceiling adorned with gold filigree starting at the peak, twisting and looping down the pillars in an elegant dance.

Lucifer had come for her help, but what he asked was troubling. He asked for half of the flaming swords God, only about a year before, had created. God had put Leviathan in charge of their security. The swords were only a few days old, and many of them were just starting to communicate. They were vulnerable and easily swayed. She was supposed to keep them away from everyone and teach them what their purpose was. She was to help them grow, understand, learn, and even name themselves.

Most angels didn't know the swords existed. They would be powerful weapons in the hands of the wielder. Lucifer had ordered her to give him hundreds of them. It contradicted God's decree. It had been more than a year since God told her that.

Lucifer had said God would be pleased if she followed his order. After all, God put *him* in charge. However, something was wrong with his order. She was now wandering the empty halls of heaven, wrestling with the problem. If she followed Lucifer's order, she would essentially betray her God, her creator. Although, if she didn't follow his order and it turned out God had ordered it, that would be a betrayal all its own.

"Leviathan!"

Her head snapped up. She had left the grand halls and was walking along the parapets of the magnificent golden walls. Below her, the city glinted in the ever-present light. The pearly gates shone in the distance.

"Leviathan," Michael alit next to her on the high wall. "You seem troubled. Is something wrong?"

She pondered that for a minute. Did Michael even know about the blades? He was an archangel, but only a handful of God's most trusted were told. She didn't know if he was one. She decided not to tell him any particulars.

"God has entrusted me with a task and I just received an order that is in contrast to His request."

Michael's eyes widened, and he was at a loss for words. He opened his mouth and shut it several times before settling on what he wanted to say. "If God gave you an order, then you should follow that above all."

"I normally would agree, but God didn't order this. He simply asked me to do it. The second was an order by someone who I believe to be the voice of God."

"Lucifer." Michael's countenance darkened and his brow furrowed.

Leviathan knew what was coming next. While God had been absent, Michael had been speaking against Lucifer in private. He believed Lucifer to be planning a coo. He hadn't been as secretive about his feelings as he thought, however. Every angel was aware of how he felt.

Leviathan's silence had spoken volumes to him.

"Don't you see? He's slowly weaseling his way into your mind!"

"God wouldn't have put him in charge of heaven if he didn't fully trust him. God is infallible."

"Or he was testing him, and Lucifer is failing. Satan sits beside him whispering in his ear stroking his ego and it's finally gotten to Lucifer. Mark my words, there will be a war in heaven in the next millennium. Ensure you are on the correct side or you will regret it."

Michael unfurled his wings and, with a powerful flurry, he was over the wall and out of Leviathan's sight.

She sighed and turned back to leave the parapets and wander the halls once again.

Leviathan had made a terrible mistake. She had not given Lucifer the blades four years prior. He had cast her down from her lofty position, stripping her of her authority. However, his anger had subsided only a few years later.

He came to her in the Hall of Blades. She was still the caretaker of the blades. He could not take that from her. God Himself directed it.

The hall wasn't anything overly gaudy. It was an open room with a high ceiling and white pillars. There were rows of hundreds of pedestals with a single stand on each. The blades were set on the stand horizontally for easy access. They were magnificent.

Today he came to inspect the blades as he did every year. They had developed quickly, to her satisfaction. When God returned, he would see her devotion and her good work here. He would set things right. So she had devoted herself to the task.

Lucifer had brought his aid, Satan. Despite God's command to keep the blades existence a secret, Lucifer told him of their existence years ago. Although, this was the first time he'd come to the hall himself.

Satan walked the halls, nodding appreciatively. "Have they learned battle tactics?"

"Battle tactics?" Leviathan's eyes widened. "What would they need those for?"

"God has created sentient weapons," Lucifer retorted. "What else would he create them for if not a war?"

"A war?" Leviathan all but shouted. "With whom?"

"God hasn't said, though I have my suspicions." Lucifer turned to her and narrowed her eyes. "If you haven't taught them battle tactics, you are too shortsighted to be their teacher anymore. Satan will hereby replace you in that role."

"But Lucifer, God has-"

"Lord Lucifer," Satan interrupted her.

"Lord?" Leviathan's brow furrowed at the new title. *Have I been down here so long that I missed his appointment to Lord of heaven?*

"Lord... Lucifer." Leviathan didn't like how that sounded. It sounded blasphemous. God was the only Lord in heaven. "I will teach them battle tactics if you require, but please leave me in charge of their education and development." She didn't say what she was thinking. *They are all I have.*

Lucifer was silent, no doubt mulling her request over. "Fine, but choose three hundred of the blades and give them to Satan. After five years, we will see whose blades have the better knowledge and disposition."

Leviathan nodded, tears welling up in her eyes. She hated the idea of her blades in someone else's hands, but three hundred was better than all, right? She prayed she was doing the right thing.

"Bow before your Lord," Satan snapped, grinding his teeth together viciously.

Had his teeth become more jagged since she had last seen him? and his incisors were much longer? Leviathan didn't move. She was not supposed to bow to anyone but God himself.

"Satan, calm yourself," Lucifer put a hand out. "Leviathan doesn't know of the new heavenly order."

"God has decreed Lucifer to be the embodiment of his will, his voice, and should be given every honor bestowed upon God himself."

She snapped her head to look at Lucifer, eyes widening.

He nodded slowly.

She hesitantly bowed before Lucifer.

"Very good." Lucifer put a hand under her chin and lifted her head. "I apologize for my anger before. It was out of place for one so loyal if a bit short-sighted. Please, if you do these things I request, I will elevate you past your former status and set you on my left hand at the throne of heaven."

Leviathan tried not to show her shock at the mention he had taken the throne. God must have really elevated Lucifer. Michael and Gabriel wouldn't have stood for it under any other circumstances. Maybe they were the reason war was on the horizon. If they had grown jealous of Lucifer, they might be planning to overthrow him. Michael had warned her years prior to this. She would stand by Lucifer during this time. Then she would have the favor of him and God to elevate her back to her rank and beyond. She wouldn't be this pitiful outcast anymore.

Lucifer and Satan left, and she quickly got to work. She handpicked the blades she thought wouldn't be as adept at military strategy and war tactics and lay them in a line carefully. It's not that she didn't care for these blades. In fact, many of them were her favorite to sit and chat with, but she needed to succeed. If Satan failed, she would be elevated and he would stay in his role. If she failed, she would have no purpose anymore. No job, an outcast, outliving her usefulness.

What would become of her then? She apologized to each blade, letting them know they would always have a place in her heart. She laid Fang down as the two hundred and ninety-ninth blade.

I am to be taught by someone else? Fang asked.

Leviathan smiled sadly. *Yes, my child. Everything changes at sometime but I will always love each of you.*

Why me?

She was the first to ask and Leviathan paused, unsure of what to say. *Because I believe you have many talents and an innocence you will never lose.*

The blade radiated warmth and happiness at her words. Tears slipped down Leviathan's cheeks. She moved on, one more blade to choose.

One more blade to betray. The thought hit her so hard her knees collapsed. Is that was she was doing? Was she betraying these beautiful minds? These wondrous blades? Each with their own thoughts and personalities? No, she couldn't be. Lucifer and Satan would protect them just as she would. They would never hurt her young charges. It simply saddened her to give them up. She wasn't losing them, though. She would see each of them again. When she excelled at her task with the blades she had left, she would regain all of her charges. Lucifer wouldn't be able to refuse her the request if she succeeded.

She stopped at a pedestal. Hope kept to himself and mostly didn't participate as much with the rest of the group. He might be an excellent candidate. She shook her head after a moment's thought. He was too smart. He probably wouldn't take part in the drills, but his mind would easily learn the strategies and maneuvers. She would keep him and turn him into her best tactician.

She moved down the row and settled on one of her most ridged blades. He was always questioning her during their session and didn't conform as quickly to her teachings. She pulled the blade from his holder. She would miss their philosophical debates, but Satan wouldn't have the patience to deal with him, and he would most likely be the undoing of the haughty angel.

Satan would be back soon to ferry the blades to where he planned to teach them. She hastened down the row and set the final blade down on the ground. Her assurance. Her wonderful, abstinent, eristic blade. She thought she might miss him the most.

She turned and walked away from Reckoning, unwilling to watch her precious blades be taken from her.

Fire raged in the shining city, burning through the buildings, smoke and soot blackening the gold of the streets and walls. Michael and Gabriel led their forces against that of Lucifers. Leviathan was ready to present her best blades against Satan's. She was ready to win her place back. If only they had waited another month.

She expected to give the blades to Lucifer's force, but no one came. They were more than willing to take hold of Satan's blades, however. She fumed. His blades would have been inferior to hers. Michael landed in front of her, startling her from her enraged thoughts. She immediately lifted Fury, ready to defend her charges to the death against the traitor.

"Leviathan, hurry," He didn't seem to think his insurrection would have turned her against him. "We must arm the ranks of heaven to do battle with Lucifer and Satan."

"No, you will not take my blades, traitor." She spat at him.

"What? No, I'm not the traitor." He seemed genuinely confused.

"No traitor would see himself as being in the wrong." She shook her head. "I cannot arm you and yours. You would tear heaven apart with your war. Lucifer was given the throne-"

"Then you are with him and Satan. You have armed them against the hosts of heaven."

"Yes, God has left us and appointed Lucifer to the throne. I will stand by him."

"Then you will be punished as harsh as Lucifer when God returns."

What was he talking about? God had put Lucifer on the throne. Michael would be the only angel punished when He returned. Lucifer would be vindicated. Everything would go back to normal.

Michael lunged for a sword, but she cut him off with Fury. He backed up, and they faced off, each waiting for the other to make the first move. Another angel, Erela, landed next to Michael. He motioned for her to circle around Leviathan. She couldn't stop them now. Not without help.

Satan appeared as if out of nowhere and drove his blade through the female angel. She was dead before her body hit the ground. He turned toward Michael, but he had already gained a blade while Leviathan was distracted.

"Come Leviathan, you're needed in the throne room." Satan ordered her.

"But what of the blades? I must protect them."

"I will stay and deal with Michael. Lucifer needs you."

"Leviathan, don't." Michael reached out as if to stop her. "This sword tells me of your compassion and faithfulness to them. Tells me of your loyalty to God despite your actions today."

Her steps faltered, and she turned to look at Michael.

"Lucifer and Satan have been lying to you and twisting your mind. They deceive you even now. God didn't put Lucifer on the throne. He did that himself."

"This isn't true, Leviathan," Satan didn't turn to look at her, but kept his gaze fixed on Michael. "Michael and his group have been planning to overthrow Lucifer for years."

His words lined up with what Leviathan understood to be true. Even five years prior before Lucifer took the thrown Michael had been planning to overthrow him. It was by his words that she had denied Lucifer's command and why she was where she was. If only she hadn't listened to him then.

The clash of swords broke her out of her thoughts.

"Leviathan, go!" Satan shouted through gritted teeth.

"No, help me overthrow these usurpers," Michael pleaded.

Leviathan took to the air, her mind made up. She would help keep Lucifer in power. When God returned, he would sort this out.

She flew over many fires in the shining city. Many angels fought in the streets and she noticed a difference between the two forces. Lucifer's forces appeared to be changing. Many of their wings starting to grow claw like protrusions at the joints.

What could it mean?

Michael's forces outnumbered Lucifer's by at least two to one. Michael had amassed a larger force than she thought. Which would be why Lucifer needed her help. Despite her low standing in the angelic ranks, she was still a powerful angel. More powerful than most. She could help protect the throne room better than Satan would have. In fact, now that she was thinking about it, he may have just sacrificed himself to save her. He wouldn't have been able to hold his own against Michael unless he had something to help him gain the upper hand. He would most likely perish before their force could come to his aid.

She almost turned around to help him, but then his sacrifice would be in vain. She prayed Satan would survive, and she prayed even more for her precious charges. The swords were still, in many ways, innocent and easily persuaded.

"Traitor," A blur collided with her in midair and they tumbled toward the ground.

Leviathan quickly regained her lift and stopped her fall, spinning wildly to find her assailant.

Anahita, a young angel who always looked up to her, had attacked her.

"How could you?" Ana growled.

"What? How could *I*? How could *you*?"

That gave the girl a pause. "You are supposed to be wise, but siding with the usurper?" The girl shook her head.

"The usurper? Is that what they are calling Lucifer? You who would try to dethrone him? I think Michael would be more aptly named the usurper."

"If you will not see reason, then I have a duty to stop you."

Ana dove toward her and Leviathan caught her as she barreled into her shoulder first. Leviathan used her weight against her and reversed direction, throwing her toward the ground. They weren't far above a rooftop and Ana impacted the building. She didn't get up and Leviathan rushed down to check on her.

She was still breathing, but a large bump was forming on her head. One of her wings appeared broken, but she didn't seem like she was in any immediate danger of expiring. Leviathan didn't want to kill her. Once the error of her actions was explained, they could acquit her of the crimes under the excuse of ignorance.

She left Anahita laying there. She was out of the way and would most likely be safe until she woke up or someone retrieved her. Leviathan would personally return to help her if she could.

She landed at the entrance to the throne room. One of the immense doors was ajar. She slipped in and the sounds of fire and battle faded behind her almost instantly. The scene in the massive space of the throne room was in stark contrast to what was happening outside. The silence was defining.

The throne room was in the shape of a cross. The longest part of the cross was the front of the room. Leviathan strode over the glass floor toward the throne. In the centers of the room was a dais with a throne set atop it. A throne only worthy of the king of kings. It was straight-backed with two arm rests and not a scrap of material on it. The arms were solid gold and the tall back was framed in gold and made of silver. Gems of all colors inlaid in the gold trim. There were several angels there already armed with the blades. Lucifer was sitting on the throne. Even though he was supposed to be there, it still looked wrong.

"Leviathan," Lucifer's voice boomed in the near silence of the room. "So glad to see you. I'm happy to hear from Satan you have joined us. Michael and Gabriel turned so many of the angels against me, I could use your help more than ever."

Leviathan knelt before Lucifer. "Of course, Lord Lucifer, I'm happy to serve. How many angels have joined the traitors?"

"About two-thirds of the hosts of heaven."

His reply floored her. That many angels would dare to rise against him. What lies had Michael spread to convince them all?

"My lord, how can we win?"

"Trust in me, my plans will work. We must strike soon before they can arm their troops."

"Shouldn't we ask God for his help?"

"Where has God been for the past ten years? Why would he come back now? No, I *am* God now. *I* will save you."

His words were like a punch in the gut to her. How could he believe he was God? Michael and Gabriel were right. She should have trusted them.

A noise from behind her made her turn. She immediately had to pull fury and defend herself from another blade. She recognized the blade as Storm. It pained her to fight against one of her charges, but she didn't have a choice. She defended herself from the onslaught of the angel.

She pushed the angel back and disengaged with him. Ishim stood, holding Storm at the ready. She opened her mouth to reason with him and tell him her realization, but he charged her before she could get the words out.

I'm not against you! They've lied to me. She called mentally, blocking his attacks one after the other.

All help from Lucifer's forces stopped in their tracks at that call. They turned against her and would have cut the two down if not for the arrival of Michael's angels. Ariel landed and engaged with Azazel. Leviathan recognized Reckoning in his hands.

How do I know that? How can I trust you when you have betrayed us? Ishim pressed.

Leviathan pushed the attack, so Ishim didn't kill her before she could convince him. Splitting her concentration between her mental conversation and fighting caused her to lose her footing. She fell toward the angels, splaying her hands out in front of her. They collided and fell in a tangle of limbs, wings, and swords.

Leviathan pushed herself up, trying to untangle herself. Her hand slipped on something slick, and she fell again. A gurgling sounded from below her as she did. She pushed herself back off Ishim.

Fury protruded from his chest just below his neck. Storm fell from his limp hand and clattered lightly on the ground; the sound muted in the vast space. His stare pierced her soul as surely as her sword had pierced his body. With his dying breath, he whispered one word that shook her to the core.

"Traitor."

The room closed in on her and she ran. All angels stood stunned at the sight of one slain within the holy of holies. The crimson blood, a reminder of the price of the sin that had caused it. Until this day, heaven had seen no casualties since its creation. She shouldered past Ariel and slipped out of the throne room, taking off as soon as she was outside. She had to get away. The situation had devolved quickly. She had been so sure at the start, and now she had murdered as a traitor. What would God say when he returned? She would be put to death, or worse, cast out of heaven, for eternity.

Tears streamed down her face. She wiped them away with her sleeve and it caught on something. She slowed her headlong flight and unhooked her sleeve from a horn protruding from her head!

She had grown a horn! She looked down at her bloody hands. Claws had grown from the tips of her fingers. Tears once again sprung to her eyes. What had she become...

"My child," a soft voice called to her. "What have you done?"

"Lord, I have made a mistake." She cried into her hands. Her heart was breaking. She feared if she gazed upon God in this state, He might well strike her down. Maybe it's what she deserved.

"I know," His voice was sad. "I also know they deceived you. However, you must accept the consequences for your actions. But fear not, you will have a chance to redeem yourself. Make sure you do not live in seclusion and miss your chance once again."

Leviathan swam the depth of the oceans. She had seen more of the world God created than any being in existence. He had cursed her for her part in the rebellion and sent all of those who sided with Lucifer and Satan to earth. Not long after, Satan corrupted the humans he had created, and he and Satan were cursed once again. Change into something unnatural.

Leviathan had been turned into a beast as well. However, her lithe body was something to behold. She was the biggest creature in the seas and the most powerful. She could travel miles in only a few moments. For the first few hundred years, she had been angry, destroying the human's feeble attempts to sail the seas. After a couple hundred more years, they had stopped trying, spoiling her fun. So she left to see the world.

Satan and Lucifer had set her in charge of the sea.

So original. She rolled her eyes.

She was a lord of hell, or whatever they called themselves. It was all just a title. Her curse stopped her from ever walking on dry land again. Satan and Lucifer had appointed four others as lords of hell. They called themselves the Seven Lords. She took that as her cue to disappear into the depths.

The Angels had sent expeditions to kill her. In the last five hundred years, she had done nothing to them. Even today, she had minded her own business hunting a whale, and they stuck a harpoon in her. She had seen their ship coming, but had thought little about it. Then she gave the angel with the ship a chance to leave. He had instead tried to kill her and they forced her to defend herself.

She had heard about the largest battle in history from Asmodeus. He had asked her to return. To help them in the open waters. She had decided it might be in her best interest to do so, not to help the demons, but to be close to the happenings of the world. God had told her she could redeem herself as long as she didn't seclude herself too much.

Now a second expedition was chasing her. She could easily outpace them and lead them on a merry chase. Unless she destroyed the ship, she wouldn't make it back in time for the battle. However, she decided not to kill them or let them catch her. She headed out into the open sea. They would have to turn back, eventually. She just had to hope she didn't lose her chance to be redeemed.

Three months into the chase, Leviathan finally decided they would not stop chasing her and headed back toward civilization. She could have taken them to the other side of the large continent that made up the world, but then they would have probably only restocked and continued the hunt. Their own stubbornness would kill them here.

By the time she returned, the battle was long over and she heard Michael and Gabriel could only imprison Satan and Lucifer. She hoped she hadn't missed her redemption, but the last battle had ended in a stalemate once again.

Leviathan had stayed near the mainland, watching and waiting for her chance at redemption. For nearly two thousand years, she hadn't heard from either demon or angel. No connection from either and no news. But now, demons were moving again. Several had been traveling into the Neutral Territory, and even one of the Blade-Bearers had visited Newaught. She didn't know the full plan of either group, but something was brewing and Newaught would be the start of it. She would wait in the waters around Newaught until it did.

Only a couple years of waiting in the depths of the river in the Great Divide and she had sensed so much. A nephilim, different from the normal variety bred by Azazel and his demons, had entered Newaught. This one was special. She didn't know why, but within weeks of his arrival, more demon and angels than had been in the city in several millennia had converged. Even Lilith had crawled out of her slimy hole.

A death pulse hit her. One of the first she had felt since before the time of peace. There was no way to tell if it was the pulse of an angel or demon. She turned around carefully in the cramped riverbed and hastened toward the ocean. It was time to return to open waters.

It wasn't long before she could see the top of the wall around Newaught. She didn't know if she could spot anything important, but she had to try. If the war was starting, she would need to gather information. She noted a demon in the sky and homed in on it with her extraordinary vision. Something was on its back. Before she could make out what, the demon climbed sharply and was hidden from her view by the clouds.

Another death pulse emanated from the sky. What could have been on the back of the demon? A human? If so, they just sealed their own fate.

She spotted the demon falling end over end. Suddenly, its wings extended. How could that be? She was sure it was dead. She swam closer as the demon fell. It wasn't a human, but the nephilim. He had pulled open the demon's wings. If he actually survived this fall, she would eat her own tail. Or at least the tail of a whale. She was pretty hungry since spending the last few years in the river eating the small fish there.

The demon and human disappeared behind the wall, hiding the result from view. Most likely, he was dead. She turned to hunt for her next meal. She would have to find a demon and ask them what happened.

Malach!

The mental shout took her by surprise. She knew that voice! If she could shed tears in this form, she would be sobbing. One of her precious blades. Reckoning by the sound of it. To mentally shout loud enough for her to hear it this far out was a testament to his mental strength.

Malach wake up!

The anguish in his voice was evident. She didn't remember any demons named Malach. Ok, there was one, but he died in the early years of the war. Why would Reckoning be shouting his name? She had to find out what was happening. The informant in Yargate port might have some answers. With any luck, she would be able to get him to pull out the accursed harpoon still stuck in her side from that brainless angel. He had hit her directly behind her head and she couldn't get to it. Her attempts to remove it had only driven it farther in. As if one harpoon could have held her.

As she swam, a shark came into her field of view and she bolted forward, snatching it in her maw. A little snack along the way would suit her just fine. It would tide her over until she could understand what was happening in the world at large.

Chapter 1

Malach Tresch sat on a grassy hill. The shade of a singular tree shielding them from the light of the sun on a breezy spring morning. Beside him stood Reckoning, who took the form of a tall lanky man. Scars lined his body from the abuse he had taken for over four hundred years. He normally took the form of an angel blade. His presence as a man reminded Malach they were not in the real world. Instead, they were in the mind of his mother, Serilda. She was captured and put into a trance-like state. Malach and Reckoning hoped to save her and bring her back to the land of the living before she perished.

They had been on this hill for what felt like hours. They had tried descending the hill on several occasions, in different directions, always finding themselves returning up the hill instead. Neither understood how they had gotten turned around. Malach didn't know how long it had really been. The sun hadn't appeared to move even slightly.

Malach flopped down onto the grass. "How are we supposed to find her if we can't even leave this hill?"

"Patience, Malach, we'll simply have to figure out the puzzle your mother has laid before us." Reckoning sat beside him. "She no doubt set this trap for her captors. If we are lucky, she may even be along shortly to check and see what she has caught."

"I know, I just hate waiting while everyone else might need our help," Malach stared up at the waving branches, the leaves movements causing them to blur together.

The light of the sun that periodically made its way through the foliage didn't hurt his eyes. In fact, it didn't even make him squint. He supposed it wasn't terribly odd since they were in his mother's mind and his eyes weren't actually his eyes. He allowed his muscles to relax, really relax, for the first time since they had left the angel army camp just over a month ago.

"You know you gave up any opportunity to help the others when we entered your mother's mind," Reckoning didn't look at him. "We agreed in our current circumstances this was the best course of action."

They had been captured, or recaptured as it was, by Azazel, one of the seven lords of hell. While awaiting torture for information about the angel army, they had mounted a rescue attempt. If they were successful, Serilda could hopefully release him from his shackles and they could get themselves out of the compound they were being held in.

Malach had experienced the time difference when you were in someone's mind world. One could spend days inside someone's mind only to discover a single night had passed. It was how Elzrod, his two-thousand-year-old mentor, and Storm, his angel blade, had trained him so quickly.

Malach sighed, "I know. I didn't think it would take so long."

Reckoning crossed his legs and placed his hands on his knees. "Time doesn't work the same here."

"Wait." Malach sat up but noticed Reckoning's eyes were closed. *Is he meditating?*

"Wait, what?" Reckoning asked without opening his eyes.

"I know that there is a time difference, but I thought it was uniform."

"Only within the same mind," Reckoning lifted one finger. "From mind to mind, it's different, and I have never entered a trance state. I don't know how it might affect the time difference."

"So what you're saying is, we have no idea how long it's been out there." He flopped back down on the soft grass.

"Correct. I suggest you take this time to relax, reflect, and prepare yourself for what comes next."

"Why? What comes next?"

"I'm not certain, but whatever it is, it most likely won't be pleasant."

Malach was forced to agree with him. Most of his life since leaving Brightwood hadn't been pleasant. A demon attack pushed him out of his comfortable life and forced him to move to a new city. Then, he was informed his parents weren't who he thought they were and thrust into a war. Not to mention slogging through the mountains in winter, being all but dunked in freezing water, attacked by gigantic spiders, betrayed by the woman he loved, and captured by demons. All within a few months.

There *were* some positives in the middle of the bad. He had rescued Reckoning from the first demon who attacked him, found out both his parents were alive, rescued his father, met Michael the Archangel, and killed more demons than most angels had along the way.

All he wanted to do was take his family back home and live his life without ever seeing another demon. Although, what he wanted and what was required of him were very different. He had never given his word he would return and help the angels fight their war. However, they have given him so much help along the way and those around him wouldn't so readily abandon them. There would be no way he could leave and keep his conscious clear. No, if they made it back alive, he would have to stay and help fight.

He glanced back over at Reckoning, who hadn't moved an inch since he sat down. Maybe he was asleep. Malach waved a hand in front of his face.

"What do you need, Malach?"

"How long do you think we will have to wait?"

Reckoning sighed and opened one eye. "As long as-"

"Traitor!"

Malach jumped to his feet, reaching instinctively for Reckoning's handle, which was no longer on his hip. He spotted movement out of the corner of his eye and he turned to see his mother charge toward Reckoning. He moved in her way, catching her slight form before she could reach her intended target.

"Mom, wait!" He had a hard time holding her. She was much stronger than she appeared and he remembered her will would constitute her strength in her mind. He spun her around and hugged her, pinning her arms to her side. Pairing his effort with his will, he lifted her feet off the ground.

Her head came back and would have broken his nose if they were in the real world. Dazed and stunned, he let the squirming woman go. He held his throbbing nose, knowing the pain wasn't real but unable to convince his brain of that fact.

"Malach, step away from Angel Cleaver and help me expel him." Serilda commanded.

Malach turned to his mother. "Mom, you don't understand. I liberated Reckoning from the demons. He is no longer Angel Cleaver."

Serilda barked a mirthless laugh. "That's what I thought about Oathbreaker when she first brought me here. She told me Reckoning was still a traitor playing you and your father."

Malach turned back to Reckoning.

His calm demeanor was ambiguous, giving Malach no indication of how he felt.

"Reckoning?" Malach wanted him to defend himself. To deny the claims.

"I am no traitor," Reckoning bowed his head. "But I can say nothing that will convince you of my innocence. Any defense I offer will be assumed lies. I will say, Oathbreaker has become an exceptional liar over the last few hundred years. I'm not sure you can trust anything she says."

"We can't trust anything you say either," Serilda poked a finger at him.

"Mom, please, Reckoning has helped me through a lot." Malach extended both hands toward her palms up. "Even before he knew I was your son. He has been a guide through a lot of difficult circumstances. Without him, I wouldn't have made it to you."

"He was leading you into this trap!" His mom swiped her hand as if to wipe away his argument. "Don't you see? You will never make it out of this alive? They will torture us until our bodies die of dehydration."

"Then why hasn't he done something already? Why didn't he turn on me the instance we got here?"

Serilda held her head in her hands as if she was in pain. "I don't know! It must be a ploy. Some trick to lower our guards."

"Mom," Malach took a step toward her. "There is no ploy, Reckoning, and I came to save you, to rescue you."

"That must be it!" Serilda suddenly stood straight. "You two aren't real!"

"What?" Malach brow knitted together. "No. I mean, our bodies in this world aren't real, but we *are* here."

Reckoning placed a hand on Malach's shoulder, and he almost jumped out of his skin. "Malach, no doubt Oathbreaker has broken her mind and shown her many visions she thought were real. It might be hard convincing her we are who we say we are."

As if to prove Reckoning's words true, Serilda screamed at the sky. "Oathbreaker! Show yourself, you wretch! You take the form of a child, but you are nothing more than a snake! God will have his vengeance on you on judgement day and I will laugh as you burn in hell with the demons!"

Malach had never seen his mother like this, and it shocked him into silence. She had always been calm, gentle, and caring. Now she hurled curses at the being who once was her greatest companion. Oathbreaker had done just as her name suggested. She had betrayed the Angels and Serilda and therefore had broken her oaths to them. He could only guess what torment she had been through. What she was still going through now.

"Mom," Malach took a few more steps and laid a hand on his mother's shoulder to calm her.

She recoiled from his touch as if it burned her.

Pain tore at his heart.

"Leave me alone," she backed away from him. "You are not real. You are here to torture me, nothing more." She turned and ran down the hill, disappearing as she went.

Malach fell to his knees, and tears rolled down his cheeks.

Reckoning knelt beside him. "She will come around. It will just take time."

"Tell me you will not betray me. Look me in the eye and tell me you're not a traitor."

Reckoning locked eyes with Malach, and he could see his words of mistrust had stung. "Malach, I am no traitor. I never was and never will be."

Malach nodded, fully believing he was telling the truth. "I'm sorry I doubted you."

"Thank you, though I don't blame you. Things are rarely as black and white as you try to make them."

Malach sat down. "I know. It would be easier if they were, though."

"Malach, we need to prepare for Oathbreaker's arrival. No doubt she has power over your mother's mind but she will not have such an easy time breaking you or I. We must protect your mother even if she doesn't want our help."

"How do we do that?"

"When Oathbreaker returns, she will no doubt change this scene to something far more sinister. Serilda no longer has the willpower to stop her. When that happens we will hopefully be drug along and using our will, fight and expel Oathbreaker. At that point, if your mother trusts us, we will start searching for a way out."

"Any idea how to go about doing that?"

"Yes, actually. Do you remember me telling you that one angel who tried to save those in the trance made it back? However, his mind broke and he couldn't form full thoughts nor tell us how he had made it back."

"Yes, but how does that help us?"

"Your mother cared for that angel for years until one day he disappeared. She might have gleaned something from the angel that could help us escape."

"Great, so now what do we do?"

Reckoning sat back down on the grass, crossing his legs and setting his hands on his knees. "We wait."

Amara rode hard as the sun was setting on the desert. She scanned the rolling dunes for any sign of life. Her half insane father was somewhere out there and she needed to find him before something happened to him. He was the key to her past, and she had paid a hefty price to save him.

The sun beat down on her head. The dry hot wind splitting her lips. She licked a drop of blood from them and tried not to focus on the pain. Sand was all she could see in every direction. It was only broken by the occasional scraggly brown bush or boulder peeking out like some bur-rowing creature poking its head out to check for danger.

Amara had betrayed her friends to the demons to save her father and Lawdel, the man who had actually raised her. She didn't even know her real father was alive until the Demon had told her. He had left her in the streets and Lawdel had saved and raised her. But her biological father would have all the answers she ever wondered about. The only problem, he had lost his mind, presumably during the years of torture, and had taken to writing symbols on the wall to retain his memory.

She had tried to take him out of the compound quickly so she could come back and save Malach and her friends, but her father wouldn't leave until he copied down everything on the walls. Somewhere in the middle of the night, however, he had left. She hadn't found out until that morning.

The gate guards had told her he had headed toward the twisted de-sert and she had collected a horse and supplies to follow. As she was leav-ing, she had spotted Daziar and an angel attacking the compound. Guilt and hope simultaneously cut her to the bone and lifted her spirits, leaving her feeling conflicted. She almost turned her horse around, but remembered Azazel still had assassins in Caister. They would kill Lawdel if she did.

Not to mention she would be even farther behind her father. She doubted he would survive long on his own. Much less in a desert. She ex-pected to find him trudging along half dehydrated, sorely unprepared for the harsh sun and conditions of the desert.

She left, praying to whatever god was out there, Daziar and his group would be successful in their rescue attempt. She never expected to see them again after what she had done. Some part of her hoped she would never have to face them, but another part of her missed them terribly.

She hadn't seen a soul since she left the compound and now it had all but disappeared behind her. She turned to check behind her for any kind of pursuit. A small dot on the horizon still marked the demon compound, but a dust cloud almost fully obscured it from her view.

The dust cloud was big enough to be produced by several horses and could only be one of two groups. Either Malach and his group had escaped or Azazel had sent soldiers after her. She had been free to leave, but she killed two guards, hoping to give the escapees a better chance. Either way, she didn't want the group to catch her.

With darkness steadily falling, they might not have seen her yet. She pushed her horse harder. She would travel through the night to make sure they did not catch her.

The slight indentations in the sand she was following blurred at the speed she pushed her horse to. She could just make them out, but they were getting harder and harder to follow the looser the sand got. One good blast of scorching desert wind could erase them altogether. Luckily for her, they had been going in a straight line since she first picked up his trail.

About an hour passed, and the dust cloud behind her was growing smaller. She turned forward after checking on her pursuers for the twentieth time and panicked when she could no longer find the tracks in the sand. She pulled her horse to a stop so suddenly it almost threw her from the saddle. Her horse stood there blowing hard and she could see froth at the sides of its mouth.

She glanced behind her at the dust cloud. No time to waste. She turned her horse and started moving back toward where she had lost the trail. Not far back, she found the tracks. They had taken a sudden southern turn. She glanced up and spotted a lone silhouette far in the distance. It must be her father.

She glanced in the direction of the dust cloud. It was getting harder to see in the failing light, but it was steadily getting bigger. She dismounted and got a length of rope and her blanket out of her pack. Tying it quickly onto the back of her saddle, she let the blanket drag the ground behind her horse. If the group behind her was tracking her the same way she had been tracking her father, she intended to make it much harder.

She mounted back up and kick her horse into a trot, watching behind her she made sure the blanket hid her tracks well enough. It did, but left a trail all its own. It was the best she could do, however, and the group might miss it in the dark.

She made her way much slower than she wanted to, leaving a drag trail behind her. Unfortunately, moving any faster caused the blanket to catch the wind, and she doubled back to sufficiently covered the tracks. She monitored the dust cloud and the silhouette. The latter tried to double back again, no doubt catching sight of her heading his way. He didn't seem to understand she could see him the whole time. Even if she couldn't, his tracks were conspicuous enough she would have been able to follow them with her eyes closed.

The dust cloud behind her was almost impossible to see now, and soon she wouldn't be able to track their progress. Her chances of going undetected were going up by the minute.

She had almost caught up to the silhouette she thought was her father. She pulled in the blanket. If they were still tracking her by this point, the blanket wouldn't do her any good.

She kicked her horse into a gallop. Her father had turned south again, and she cut the corner on and intercept course with him. As she came up on the man, she recognized his emaciated form and pulled her horse up in front of him.

He fell to the ground, breathing hard. "Don't kill us!"

"Father, I don't intend to kill you. I've been trying to track you down to save you." She dismounted. "Don't you see? I've done all this to protect you!" She had to force her voice down so it wouldn't carry across the open desert. "I'm going to get you to Ragewood and go back to save my friends."

"But you're *her* daughter." He peered up at her, fear in his eyes. "She always wanted to kill us after we sired you."

"Why?" Amara pulled him to his feet. "Why would she want to kill you? Who is my mother? Who are you?"

"We are pris-"

"No, what is your real name?"

"We...I...don't know." He sat down in the sand and unfolded the parchment and started studying the mess of symbols. It was all that was left of his memory.

Amara sighed. She searched the horizon for the cloud of dust from her pursuers. There was no sign of them. She caught movement out of the corner of her eye and snapped her head to the side to see what it was. She could barely make out a team of horses pulling a cart with other people on horses around it. From what she could tell, they hadn't seen them, nor had they seen the track's end. They didn't even slow down. She spotted something on the cart and squinted to make it out through the gloom. It was a pair of white wings! Malach and his group had made it out of the compound! She silently wished them good luck and sat down on the sand with her father.

"Doesn't look like we are going anywhere tonight."

Her father glanced up from the symbols. "Huh?"

"Those were my friends,"

Her father continued to give her a confused look.

"I betrayed them to keep you alive and to take you from the compound."

"That was stupid." He stated and continued studying his symbols.

"I didn't have a choice." She lowered her head into her hands and rubbed her face. "They would have killed Lawdel as well, the man who raised me after you left me to die."

"There's always a choice," her father mumbled.

"Sure, I could have let Azazel kill you and Lawdel or betray Malach and my friends to save you!" She shouted, her anger boiling over. "My plan was to take you straight to Ragewood and then return to rescue them. However, you had to take a whole day to copy your symbols and then left in the middle of the night. It took me all day to find you out here."

"Hmm," He grunted. "They made it out despite you."

"Argh," she growled, reaching her hands out as if to strangle the man.

"Ah, here we are, our name!" He exclaimed, sitting up straight. "Our name is Raziel, Archangel and Keeper of Secrets." He read it as if he were reading from a textbook, detached and impersonal.

"You're what?" Amara jumped to her feet, mouth agape.

"We are Raziel!" He smiled at her.

"But what was the second part?"

He frowned and lifted the symbols to his face. "Raziel, Archangel and Keeper of Secrets."

"No, no, you're not." Amara told him. "Or you are not my father."

His brow furrowed from behind the parchment he was studying. "It says here we sired a little girl and..." He paused, tracing a finger along the paper. "Left you on the street in front of a house in Caister. We watched a man pick up the baby and disappear into the sewers." His eyes appeared over the top of the paper. "Was that you?"

"I was told they found me on the streets. Lawdel would have taken me into the sewers."

"Then you are our daughter." He smiled at her.

"How?" Amara sat down hard.

"Well, the Witch came to us after we were captured while we were asleep-"

"No!" Amara shook her head and put up her hands to stop him. "I don't want to know that."

"But you asked."

"I meant, how am I a descendent of an angel? I'm small, I have no extra strength, no powers, I can't be part angel."

"We recorded nothing about strength or power. Nor anything about size, but you are our daughter. And our record says we are an arch-angel."

"Who is my mother?" She said it more absent-mindedly, but Raziel disappeared behind his paper of memory.

"She is The Witch," He mumbled. "We seem to have no name recorded. She is just The Witch. We know she tortured us for many, many years, but we do not know her name or significance in the war."

Amara sighed. She had a lot to think about, but fatigue was setting in now that the excitement was over. They needed to set up camp and settle in.

Pulling out Raziel's pack, she searched through the things he brought and, to her astonishment, he had everything he needed to survive for many days. Shelter, food, water, it was all there. She had brought enough supplies for the both of them, assuming he would overlook it. He was still poring over his symbols as she started setting up camp. She didn't want to be too visible in case Azazel sent his men after Malach. She didn't think he would do anything, but she had no wish to see the demon again, except at the end of her blade.

She lay awake late into the night, unable to sleep with all the thoughts and implications swirling around her head. Who was her mother? She thought she would find out from Raziel, but he knew nothing more than what he wrote in those weird symbols of his. And who was she? She had always thought she was just another human, just another thief. Now she was an angel. Was it even possible? She was told by two beings she was Raziel's daughter and his story lined up with what she knew of her own.

She needed to talk to Lawdel and sort this out. Maybe there was another baby? Maybe she wasn't Raziel's daughter at all. Maybe he wasn't an angel either.

She glanced over at his sleeping form. His back was to her and his skin exposed. Two jagged scars ran down his back where his wings had been. This frail, emaciated man had once been a powerful angel. There was no denying that. No wonder the demons kept him for so long. If his title was to be believed, he was the Keeper of Secrets. Most likely dangerous secrets. Secrets that could turn the tide of the war. Those secrets must be how the demons had defeated the angels two thousand years ago.

She sighed again and rolled over. She needed sleep. It was going to be a hard few days. Now she that knew Malach was safe, she would take Raziel to Caister.

To the Shadows.

To Lawdel.

Chapter 2

Honora sat in the back of the cart as they rolled along. The sand had gotten softer and softer as they traveled deeper into the desert. All night, she waited for some horror to materialize out of the darkness and end their frenzied flight. However, as first light crested the horizon, there were no monsters to be seen.

Ariel held up his hand to call a halt.

The horses were breathing hard, and the froth at the corners of their mouths belied their exhaustion. Most of the riders were all but asleep on their mounts. Only Ana and Ariel were unaffected by the lack of rest and hard pace. Ana put and hand on Honora's shoulder. She would take care of the three unconscious people in the cart.

Two of them were her best friends. Daziar, strong and tall, had taken a sword in his shoulder while trying to fight off a demon. She wasn't there when it happened, but she was told Azazel, one of the seven lords of hell, had given him the grievous wound. He had woken up during the night and was able to eat and drink a little. Ana said that was a good sign, but he wasn't out of the woods yet. His strength wouldn't return for a long time.

Her other friend, Malach, lay in the cart with a similar, although less serious, shoulder wound, but it wasn't the reason he didn't wake. He was in a trance-like state induced by his Angel Blade, Reckoning. The sentient blade and he had gone into Malach's mother's mind to pull her from her own trance. The trance was supposed to be a way to protect the bearer from years upon years of torture. Oathbreaker, once called Fang, had tricked Serilda to torture her in ways only a being so twisted could imagine.

She was the person laying in the cart.

Honora and Ana had covered her with a blanket since her clothes were so tattered they barely covered any of her body. Honora remembered Serilda from her childhood before Malach's parents were assumed dead. She had been gorgeous and graceful. Her body, fit and lean, had been the envy of most the women and all the men of Brightwood. A warrior's body, the men had said when they thought the women weren't listening. It pained Honora to see her like this. If she survived, Honora doubted she would ever be the same again.

Her beauty was still evident, even now. Even now, with her face looking gaunt and stretched. Even now, with her body covered in scars. Honora hoped Malach would bring her back. Until then, they could only do their best to keep her alive. She seemed to grow weaker by the hour, however, and Honora wondered if it was a fool's hope.

Ana told her if Serilda died, so would Malach, even though his body was much stronger than hers. His mind was deep within Serilda's and if Reckoning and Malach didn't bring her out of the trance, their consciousness would be lost. Malach's body would still function for days after. However, he would never wake until he expired from lack of water. Reckoning would be lost as well. His form, for angel blades could change into almost any weapon, was permanently fixed.

She turned away from them, tears welling up in her eyes. She wiped them, but her gaze now fell on a bundle wrapped at the front of the cart. Her tears flowed once again, unbidden. Elzrod's body. He had given his life to save Ariel from Azazel, and another angel blade turned evil. Fury had deceived them and Elzrod had paid the price.

Elzrod had been Malach's mentor from Newaught. Those days seemed like ages ago, though in reality it had been less than a season prior since they had entered Newaught through one of its massive gates. Elzrod was part of the city guard, but really he was a Blade Bearer, sent by the archangel Michael to find Malach. He had told Malach of the real fate of his parents. They were not dead, only captured and shortly after, they had rescued Ariel.

It was on the same mission they had rescued Fury and Ariel had taken him as his blade, allowing Malach to keep Reckoning. In the end, Fury had played them. As Ariel was about to land the blow to end Azazel's life, Fury had incapacitated him somehow. Elzrod had taken the thrust meant for Ariel and Ariel was able to defeat Azazel, who had retreated.

A hand rested on her shoulder and gently helped her out of the cart. Her father wrapped his arms around her, giving her a measure of comfort as he always had. They had been on a mission of their own when they arrived at the demon compound. Auron, a man they had met in Newaught, was forced into the demon army and his wife held captive. Through a series of fortunate events, they freed him from his conscription and mounted a rescue mission to not only save his wife but the other prisoner who were taken for the same purpose. Prinna had led her own escape with the help of Malach. Once reunited, Auron and Prinna had taken most of the former prisoners to Ragewood city where they would, hopefully, be safe.

Honora pushed slowly out of her father's arms, composing herself. They would need her to help with those who had smaller, nonlife-threatening wounds while the rest setup whatever shelters they had. After a quick search, she found Marena had tended to most of the wounds. Marena would need help with her own, however, and Honora spotted her and Togan nearby.

The towering blacksmith was standing over the woman trying to clean and dress Marena's wounds while she gave him instructions, and

Honora could tell it wasn't going well. He was used to hammering stubborn metal into shape, not gently tending to wounds.

Marena grimace as he clumsily wiped at a cut on her shoulder.

"Togan," Honora put her hand up to stop him. "I'll take it from here. We want Marena to get better, not worse."

Togan let out a sigh of relief and relinquished the cloth to her. "Thank you. I have no skill as a healer."

Honora smiled a thin smile at him. "That was pretty obvious."

"Togan," Ariel walked up to the now idle man. "Help me get Elzrod out of the cart and prepared for a pyre. We may not be able to stand vigil, but at least he can have a warrior's send off." He turned to Honora. "Use as little of that water as you can. We will need every drop before we are on the other side of this desert."

Honora nodded and concentrated on cleaning the cut with as little water as possible. "How did you manage to get cut back here?"

"I got careless and while firing on the archers on the wall. A soldier snuck up behind me." Marena sighed, careful not to move. "I would be dead if Togan hadn't deflected his sword."

"You two are a good team," Honora finished cleaning the wound and pulled out some mostly clean bandage. She wetted the cloth and shook the sand off. She laid the cloth across the wound and took another strip, tieing it around the woman to hold the bandage in place. It wasn't pretty, but it would do.

"What about you?" Marena asked. She pulled her shirt back on and turned to face Honora.

"What do you mean?" Honora put her supplies back in the bag of healing supplies.

"Do you have someone like that?" Marena asked.

"Oh," Honora studied her feet. "I don't do any fighting if I can help it. I've never killed anyone."

Marena put a hand under her chin and gently lifted her head. "That's nothing to be ashamed of, and don't let anyone tell you otherwise."

Honora nodded, but dropped her gaze again.

"If anything, you are better than the rest of us."

Honora snapped her gaze back up. Marena had to be making a joke and her expense. "That's not funny."

"I'm not joking. I envy you, you have a rare strength. It's easy to conform to what everyone else is doing. War is a part of our normal. We are trained, almost from birth, how to fight and kill. It's rare to find someone who won't take a life. I think one day, when this is finally over, we will need people like you to teach us how to be at peace."

"Really? You think so?" She had never thought of it that way.

"I do." Marena nodded. "I think if we live to see the end of the demons, people like you will teach true peace."

Honora pondered her words. She had always thought of herself as weak, but Marena thought the opposite. She would have to think more on it later.

"Thank you, Marena." Honora bobbed her head at the woman.

"No, thank you, you patched me up and I'm sure I will be good as new soon." Marena nodded her thanks.

Honora moved around the camp, helping where she could. Togan and Ariel had built a small funeral pyre even as the others reverently moved Elzrod's body. They would light it soon, sending the valiant warrior to his final rest.

She sat for a while, trying to quiet her mind, or at least sort through the turmoil of her thoughts. Realizing she had been staring at Ariel and Ana for the last several minutes, she tore her gaze away, only to turn back, wondering what they were doing. Ariel was looking at her injured wing. As Honora understood it, she had sustained the injury while fighting Azazel. The Angel hadn't complained once about it since they had escaped. Guilt stabbed at her gut. She had forgotten all about the angel's wound.

Ana's wings resembled tendrils of light more than actual wings. Honora wouldn't have known they were hurt if the one didn't hang at such an awkward angle. She had no idea how that even worked or if there was anything she could do to help, but she wanted to offer. Maybe she could learn something which might prove useful in the future.

"Ariel, do you need any help with Ana's wing?" It dawned on her at that moment that touching an angel's wings might be something very personal. "I mean, if it's ok with Ana."

"Oh, it's fine," Ana waved a hand in dismissal. "It's nothing different from an arm or a leg and Ariel could use some help."

"How did you know what I was thinking?" Honora raised an eyebrow at her.

"You humans are all the same," Ana shrugged, as if that explained it all. "I just correctly read your hesitation and gave a good guess from past experience.

"If you've been asked the same question as many times as we have over our lifetime, you recognize when it's about to be asked." Ariel smiled warmly. "We appreciate the concern for our privacy."

"Not to be rude, but can we get on with this?" Ana grit her teeth. "The pain is getting worse."

"Yes, of course," Ariel turned back to the wing.

"Is it broken?" Honora moved around behind the beautiful angel.

"I think it's out of joint." Ariel told her. "If you will brace her here and hold her wing here, we will get it in place again."

Honora nodded and braced her back against Ana's and held onto her wing, as Ariel had directed.

Ariel jerked the wing, almost pulling her and Ana off their feet.

A wet pop came from the wing and Honora winced as Ana tensed.

"Done," Ariel declared after checking the wing. "Any other injuries that need to be taken care of?"

"No, but we need to get these three into shelter." Ana motioned to the three in the cart. "They won't survive the day in the direct sun."

"What supplies and shelter did we manage to procure before our flight?" Ariel asked.

"We have tents, but not enough. I believe we have enough food and water to make it to Caister, however." Ana reported.

"Cover the cart with the tents. Then we can set up some people on top and some below to maximize our shelter." Ariel pointed to the cart. "You and I will stay awake to stand guard in case of pursuit."

Ana nodded and set off to do as he ordered.

"Honora, please gather everyone for Elzrod's funeral." Ariel turned and walked toward the pyre.

She did as she was asked and not long after; they lit the small pyre and gave Elzrod the best sendoff they could. Ariel decided they could risk staying to see their old friend off. Once the fire burned out, Togan and Ariel wrapped the remains and buried them so the animals didn't carry them off.

They retired to the makeshift shelter, and it didn't take any of them long to fall asleep. All of them were exhausted. Even with Togan snoring within seconds of his head hitting the sand, Honora was unconscious almost as quickly.

Ana and Ariel sat up on the driver's bench, scanning the horizon for any sign of enemy pursuit. Ana kept an eye out for anything coming from Deadpost, the small enemy resupply and lookout tower in the middle of the Twisted Desert. They expected nothing to come from that direction, but neither angel was ready to rule it out.

"Why don't you take a beat?" Ariel suggested, breaking her out of her thoughts.

"I'm fine," she replied. She hadn't lost as much sleep as he had, nor was she injured as badly. If anyone should rest, it should be him. He was the ranking angel, however, and if he ordered her to, she would have to comply.

"The last few days had been a trial," He started again. "I need you well rested for the journey. You are our only air support. Besides, there's no need for us both to be awake."

"Then, with respect, *you* should rest. You have been through more sleepless nights than I."

Ariel took a deep breath and then let it out slowly. "I...I couldn't if I wanted to. Between my own grief at the loss of Elzrod and the grief I feel from Storm, I would have no chance."

"I knew Elzrod as well." She lowered her gaze.

"I'm sorry. I didn't mean to say that you weren't grieving his loss as well."

"No, you're right, I might not sleep, but I can at least meditate and clear my mind." Ana sighed. "I didn't know him as well as I should have. He was a great man."

"Yes, he was, but don't feel guilty. Your path in this war simply took you in a different direction than his."

"I guess," Ana stood. "I'll be meditating then if you need me."

Ariel nodded his understanding, and she moved into the back of the cart. She checked on each of the unconscious people, carefully squeezing water into their mouths to keep them hydrated.

A thought hit her. She decided she would meditate and try her idea. After laying down, she cleared her mind. She preferred this position over a seated one. That way, when she finished meditating, she could simply fall asleep. That, of course, came with the danger of falling asleep prematurely, but she didn't really have a problem with that.

She sought her angel blade to run the idea by him first. Out of the darkness walked a young boy. He wasn't really a boy, being thousands of years old, but he liked to appear in that form. Hopes point, Hope for short, was shy. Which didn't fully make sense to her, but that's who he was. Since the fall, he had been her blade. They had shared many, many experiences, battles, and momentous events, but he never changed. He would rather her sit in a musty library reading books through her eyes and meditating on everything learned from it. She could only do that for so long, however, and he had to deal with her dragging him all over the world.

The young boy could have been her little brother if you took out the fact he wasn't the same type of being as her. He had short blond hair which was never well kempt and had bright blue eyes similar to her own. You would never know they weren't related if you first met them in the mental world.

"This is a mistake," He mumbled, scowling at her.

"How so?"

"You don't know what will happen."

"Neither do you."

"I know it could be dangerous."

"Oh, live a little." Ana threw up her arms. "You only want to do what is safe, familiar."

"And you seem to want to throw your life at whatever idea pops into your daft head."

They had this conversation many, many...many times. "I do not."

"What would this gain you? Gain the group?" He arched an eyebrow.

"Uh, I could keep him up to date with what's happening and we wouldn't have to update him when he wakes up."

"So your impatience is driving you to recklessness."

"No, I could also help him and train him so that he is better prepared for his next fight with a lord of hell."

"Just admit you enjoy this human."

"I don't know what you are talking about?"

"You have never gotten close to any humans, ever. You always told me they died too quickly for you to bother becoming friends with them."

"I never said that." Her brow knitted together. She had cared about many humans over the years.

"Close enough. Yours were prettier words dressed up by your sense of propriety, but the underlining meaning was the same."

"No, I felt like I was protecting us from getting too close to them. Not that I didn't care about them."

"So, what makes this one different?"

"Nothing, I just want the mission to succeed." She shrugged.

"No," He arched his eyebrow again.

"Fine, I think he could actually make a difference in the war. I think he might be a suitable candidate for the next generation of Blade-Bearers."

"And that's it? No other feelings?"

Ana gave the boy a withering look.

"Fine, but if he dies while you're connected, I don't know what will happen," Hope reiterated.

"He's stable. There's little chance of that."

"There is still a chance." He crossed his arms.

Ana just shook her head in response.

She mentally reached out to Daziar's mind. She intended to train him while he recovered. It would be a long time before Daziar could use his sword arm. If he was to be of any use to them, he couldn't wait until he recovered. And he still needed practice defending his mind. If he was going to become a threat to the demons, he would paint the proverbial target on himself.

She didn't know why she expected him to become a Blade Bearer, but she had a feeling he and Malach would be. The female human who was with them through their journey might have been a new Blade Bearer as well. However, her betrayal seemed to have revealed what side she was truly on.

There had been ten Blade-Bearers chosen after the demon's slew so many angels in the last battle. Serilda was now the last known surviving member of those ten. If this war went on much longer, she suspected Michael would choose another ten, maybe more. Michael had chosen the first ten in God's name and God had blessed them with the capability to control the blades, among other abilities.

She focused her mind once again on reaching Daziar and realized she had been blocked. He had a mental barrier in place. Pride in the young man made her smile. Even injured, he had a basic barrier up. It had stopped her while her mind wandered.

She brushed past it easily now that she was concentrating and entered his mind. He was in a memory, and it took her a minute to orient herself. They were back at the demon compound and she was now watching herself, Skie, and Daziar, fight Azazel.

They had their back against the wall. The Ana of his memory held her spear at the ready, not a hair out of place, too perfect for it to be real. She could swear Skie was just a little larger. Daziar charged Azazel almost twice as fast as he was in reality, but instead of being stabbed through the shoulder, he ducked the demon's sword and plunged his knife in once, twice, three times and twisted.

Azazel fell gasping.

Ana crossed her arms at the fantasy playing out before her. The real knife Daziar held would never have killed the demon, even if Daziar ducked the sword. He was playing back *this* scene, changing facts to favor his victory. Living in this fantasy, he would never see the error of his actions. Azazel died and Daziar hefted Oathbreaker, turning to gloat. The copy of herself praised Daziar and his cunning and prowess. She almost vomited.

"He really fantasizes about you." Hope stood beside her, crossing his arms in the same fashion as her.

"Yeah, you want to have some fun with him?"

"Of course," Hope grinned, a mischievous light coming into his eyes.

Ana overpowered Daziar's will within seconds, restarting the fantasy with slight changes. The knife was a more realistic size. Daziar was not as fast, and Azazel was much smarter than the version Daziar created.

This time, he charged, and she allowed him to duck the stab, only to be impaled by Azazel's claws. The next few iterations of the scene went similarly, only with slight changes. Daziar met his fate repeatedly in different ways. Once she even had Azazel unhinge his jaw, which he obviously couldn't do in the real world, and bite Daziar's head clean off his shoulders.

The sheer impracticality of the last scenario broke Daziar out of his fantasy turned nightmare. He noticed the real Ana and Hope for the first time. The scene vanished, and he ground his teeth together as he walked over.

"I assume you think that was funny?" He asked as he approached them.

Hope let out a repressed giggle but made no attempt to disguise it.

Ana couldn't hold back her mirth at his anger. She belly laughed until tears streamed down her face.

Daziar cleared his throat.

She quelled her laughter. "I was just bringing a little realism to your perfect fantasy."

"Biting my head off is what you consider realism?"

"That was my idea," Hope replied, grinning sheepishly.

Ana hadn't even realized it wasn't her idea until he had taken credit for it. After being bonded for thousands of years, sometimes thoughts bled over without the other realizing. She smiled down at the boy fondly.

"It wasn't funny, and it was just as much of a fantasy as what I was enjoying. Can't I recover in peace?" Daziar asked.

Ana turned serious. "Unfortunately not."

"What's wrong?" Daziar asked, his scowl deepened. "How long has it been since I woke up?"

"Nothing worse than when you passed out last, and you have been out less than a day." Ana informed him.

"Then why are you in my mind?"

"We are here to train you." Ana replied. "The injury to your shoulder is going to leave you with little strength in it for many months if you ever regain full use of it. However, I fear we will need you back to full fighting form the moment you awaken."

Daziar stared at her for a second, as if trying, and failing, to understand what she was saying. "You're telling me I might never use my right arm again?"

"I'm sorry Daz, yes, you might never use that arm again." Ana nodded.

"However," Hope spoke up. "You might have use of it within a week. We don't know."

Ana gave him a sidelong glance. "Most likely it will be months before you can use it," she reiterated. "Hope is giving you the best possible outcome."

"What's wrong with that?" Hope held up his hands and shrugged.

"If my shoulder won't work for a month, or possibly never, how can I be in fighting form when I wake up?" Daziar's brow furrowed.

Hope threw up his arms and walked out into the darkness.

Ana sighed. "Sorry, he doesn't have much patience for people. Books he can spend years on end with. People, it only takes him a few minutes to give up."

"Is there a way I can will my arm to heal?" Daziar raised an eyebrow.

Ana chuckled, "No there isn't, I'm going to teach you to fight with your left arm."

"Your what?"

"Since you won't be able to use your right arm, I will teach you to use your left."

"Uh, huh." Daziar nodded once, obviously skeptical. "I've never even held a sword in my left hand."

"Yes, until now you have been able to get by with little skill and a lot of brute force." Ana crossed her arms. "Much like how you approach life. That will need to change."

"What do you mean? I have plenty of skill."

"You have plenty of *strength* and you beat your opponents into submission. Most don't have a choice but to defend themselves until you wear them down." Ana called up memories of his training, then battles, then his most recent defeat. "Until you came up against an opponent who was stronger, faster, and made you look like a novice in comparison."

"Ok, I see your point," Daziar ground his teeth together.

Ana clasped her hands behind her and started pacing in front of him, her gaze never leaving his face. "Now, let's start with the weapon. That unruly broad sword needs to go."

"That was my great-great-grandfather's weapon, the man for whom my namesake is. He fought beside the angels long before the time of peace." Daziar put up his hands as if she were about to physically take the sword from him.

She stopped pacing for a moment, overpowered his will and called up an image of his ancestor. The sword Daziar wielded was in his hands.

"You knew him?" Daziar's mouth dropped open.

"Yes, he was a powerful and skilled warrior. His cunning on the battlefield was only matched by the amount of food he could make disappear in one setting." Ana smiled to herself. "He also makes you look like a child next to him."

Daziar studied his ancestor. The man was twice his size in almost every aspect except for height. The family broad sword appearing to be much smaller in his hands. His muscles bulged and rippled, his hulking build gracefully flowing through the movements. He wielded the blade on a battlefield Daziar didn't recognize.

"He also is much older than me in this memory you have of him. I could learn to wield the sword as he did, maybe even better." Daziar crossed his arms.

"Possibly," she admitted. "Not with one hand, though. Also, did you notice? The sword was forged for him? The sword you wield was never meant for you. With a hundred years of training, you could be a match for the man. However, you would always be at a disadvantage against the same sword held in a larger man's hands."

"What are you saying?"

"Let's find a weapon to complement your build, size, and situation."

"What would you suggest?"

"Glad you asked." Ana willed a table into existence and filled it with weapons.

She motioned for him to follow her over to the table and picked up a sword. "This is very close to what you've been wielding, resized specifically for you."

"Then why do we need all these other weapons?"

"Because you are very narrow minded." Hope walked up behind the table. "Why do you use a sword?"

"Uh, because I've been trained with a sword."

"Why were your trained with a sword?"

Daziar scowled, no doubt thinking hard. "I don't remember."

"This is why." Ana waved her hand over to a scene that was just unfolding.

A young boy sat on his father's lap. Snow falling outside the window and a roaring fire in the hearth. It was him before he was old enough to train. His great-great-grandfather's sword lay across their laps as young Daziar stared at it in wonder.

"Your great-great-grandfather once killed a demon with this very blade." He heard his father say, and he watched his small eyes grow to twice their normal size. He smiled at his own innocent admiration of the sword. His heart sank as he remembered this same spectacular sword was now broken and would most likely never be whole again.

"You grew up hearing of your ancestors' exploits with this sword." The scene changed to one of him picking out his training weapon. "So when the time came, you had no chance to pick anything other than the sword." The slightly older Daziar picked up a wooden training sword far too large for his size.

"I picked the sword only because my ancestors used the sword." Daziar stated, more to himself than to her or Hope.

"So, let's find a weapon for you."

Ana opened her eyes to the real world. She spent most of the day in Daziar's mind. Only leaving a few times to check on his wounds and care for Malach and Serilda. Daziar had worked to keep her out of his mind every time she tried to connect with him, and it was getting more difficult. It still didn't take her long, but she couldn't just brush past his defenses as she did before. She still held one of his memories as motivation. Although, it would be more accurate to say she had blocked one of his memories. One day, he would turn the tables on her infiltration and take it back. She had no doubt.

The memory was one he held dear but not one that would harm him to not remember for a bit. It was a memory of him and Honora after a day of horseback riding. Malach had been out hunting with Skie, and it was just the two of them watching the sunset. He had leaned over and kissed her just as she turned to say something to him. Having experienced the memory from his perspective, she could say without a doubt Honora had actually returned the kiss.

You are jealous. Hope's voice sounded in her head.

I am not, she retorted.

Remember, I can feel everything you do. You are developing feelings for this one.

I am not. I'm fond of him, that's all.

When you are ready to admit your own feelings, I get to say I told you so.

Ha! That won't happen.

Ariel and Serilda. Hope stated, as if that was enough to prove his point.

Daziar's making progress. She changed the subject. *He picked the sickle sword of all weapons.*

Only because he thought it was cool. Hope replied, and Ana got a mental image of his skeptical look.

You have to start with something. The movements and fighting style will be different enough. Hopefully, he won't get confused with his right-handed sword stances. However, they will be familiar enough he will pick it up quickly.

I agree, Hope admitted. *I think it will be a suitable weapon for him. With his strength, he will be quite deadly once he learns the skills involved with that weapon. Maybe we will even teach him a little patience during this whole thing.*

Optimistic, aren't we?

Maybe a little.

Ana busied herself with getting the cart ready to leave. The sun hadn't fully fallen, but already the temperature was cooling. Soon they would move again. They would need to make most people walk, keeping the cart in reserve for the wounded. The wheels of the cart already had problem sinking into the sand without any extra weight.

Others started stirring as she moved around the cart. Ariel still sat up on the driver's bench. He hadn't once called for her during the day, presumably he had seen nothing alarming.

"Spot anything worth noting?" She climbed up on the seat next to him.

"There was someone off to the south headed toward Caister, but either they weren't interested in us or didn't see us."

"Someone in pursuit of us?"

"I don't think so." Ariel pursed his lips. "I'm not sure who else would be out here, though."

"I don't know, but if they aren't bothering us, I don't really care."

"Agreed."

"Time to go. I'll walk, you drive. Honora will watch over the wounded. She's lighter than me."

"Good thinking."

Ana helped everyone get moving and soon Ariel snapped the reins to get the horses plodding along. She walked along beside the cart, monitoring the horizon. It wouldn't be long and Deadpost would appear on the horizon. Hopefully, they could pass the outpost tonight and get far enough away to have a good lead if the enemy tried to pursue. Only time would tell.

Chapter 3

Amara and Raziel plodded along, the sun beating down on their heads. Raziel hadn't stolen a horse like she had, so they loaded all the supplies onto hers and both walked. The heat caused the air to wave in front of them and it made her eyes water.

At first, she had stripped down to her shorts and crop top, but Raziel had corrected her thinking. According to him and his symbols, keeping a layer between your skin and the sun kept it from scorching the moisture straight from your body, not to mention any exposed skin would burn. She almost didn't trust what he said since he couldn't even remember his own name without looking it up, but he apparently had survived the desert a few times in his life span.

Around midday, she spotted the group that had passed them the night before. She turned farther south just in case the group noticed them. She was pretty sure that was Malach's group, and she still didn't fancy facing their judgement. They never moved. Not even forward, and she wondered if they were even alive. Maybe they were injured worse than she thought. She contemplated turning to go check on them when she caught sight of movement on top of the cart. A figure turned toward them. If they had someone on watch, then they were most likely just resting. The watch didn't hail them or try to get their attention, but she could feel their eyes on her.

Only an hour later, they passed behind a dune and out of the figure's sight and she breathed a sigh of relief. Raziel seemed to be blissfully unaware of just about everything. The heat, the figure watching them, and her unease. He just kept following her and the horse wherever she turned.

After pushing them for another hour, she stopped for food and a rest. She consulted the map stolen from the demon compound and guessed they would see Deadpost by the end of the day. She hoped they would be far enough out of the way the soldiers wouldn't spot them, or at least wouldn't bother with chasing them.

She noticed on the map there were some labels on Caister and Newaught. The Dark Hallow were marked in both cities. Could that mean the group of assassins was working with the demon army? It would make sense they would want to recruit them for the war. There were also symbols of ships at Caister labeled "Navy". She didn't know what each symbol represented, but there seemed to be a specific number. She traced a line from Caister up into Angel territory. The same ship symbols littered Yargate Port and Lanifair harbor. Did that mean the demon army controlled those ports? So many questions ran through her mind. Not that the answers would help her at all. However, knowing The Dark Hallow had a presence in Caister might help the Shadows chapter there. She would have to show this to Lawdel and the master when they arrived.

She rolled the map back up and put it back into her saddlebag.

Raziel took her cue and put his things away as well.

"Did you find out the identity of my mother?" She asked as they walked.

"No."

Ever the long-winded answers I see, she thought to herself. *Who am I?*

She thought she would find answers when she rescued her father. Instead, she once again found more question. She was part angel, which meant she was a nephilim like Malach. But why didn't she have the abilities of a nephilim; the height, the strength, the agility? Why was she a normal, mundane human? Who was her mother? The one Raziel called the witch. Was she someone Amara even wanted to know? Or was she this awful human being Raziel made her out to be?

Amara shook her head. She might live the rest of her life never knowing. As they plodded along in silence Amara over thinking every mistake, every question, every action that led her to this point. She wished she was with Malach. That she had never betrayed him. Or better yet, that she had never met Azazel on the road to Newaught. Maybe she should have called Azazel on his threats or told Malach. If she had, maybe he could have helped her get her father back and keep Lawdel safe. Although, the opposite could be true as well. If she had told him and they were unable to save Raziel or protect Lawdel, she could have lost both her fathers simultaneously.

A tear slipped down her face. If only she had realized Azazel had been real down in the spider caves. Another tear fell. Maybe things could have been different. Her knees buckled. She would never see Malach again. She would never see any of them again. This was all her fault. She could have done so much better. She *should* have done so much better.

She *would* do better. The tears slowed, replace with determination. She would never let anyone use her again. She would never again let anything like this happen.

"Are you ok?" Raziel asked from behind her.

"No," she wiped the tears from her eyes. "But I will be. I will be stronger from now on, I will be smarter, I will do better."

"Ok," Raziel shrugged. "But we need to keep moving if we are going to get out of the desert."

Amare stood and walked forward with renewed purpose. Azazel would pay for what he had made her do. She would hunt him, kill him. However, she needed to gain the tools and the skills to do that first. She knew where she could find those. Lawdel would help her and keep Raziel safe. Then she would seek out the Dark Hallow and find one who could train her to kill. One who would train her in the art of the assassin.

Honora climbed up onto the cart bench next to Ariel. The only light around them was the half-moon shining down on them. They were on the move again. Serilda was getting worse. Her body was shutting down. Even with their best efforts, if she survived another week, it would be a miracle. She didn't know how to break the news to Ariel.

"She only has days to live, doesn't she?" He didn't take his eyes off the horizon.

"Yes," she bowed her head.

He nodded and sighed. "I'm surprised she has made it this far. I only wish I could help."

"If you can, I don't know how."

"You don't know how many times I've considered entering Serilda's mind to help bring her back."

"If you did, you would just be risking your and Storm's life."

"Maybe, or maybe we could help them escape."

"You can't know that."

"Is it worth living if they both die?" Ariels voice had been slowly raising throughout their exchange and now he was almost shouting. He seemed to realize this and visibly deflated.

She opened her mouth to protest on reflex, but closed it. She couldn't answer this question for him. He had to answer it on his own. After an uncomfortably long pause Honora spoke. "I think the people you help would say it is. I think both Serilda and Malach would want you to live."

"I know," He grumbled. "I'm sorry. I didn't mean to shout at you. I'm just…."

"It's fine," Honora put a hand on his arm. "There's no need to apologize." Honora decided maybe she should change the subject. "So tell me about these Lords of Hell."

Ariel turned his head toward her. "You're just trying to take my mind off things, aren't you?"

"Yes, but I *do* want to know more about the origins of angels and demons and about the lords of hell. I feel like they are going to play a major role in the war soon."

He sighed again. "Your right. The fact Azazel has already made his presence known means the rest of the surviving lords will follow shortly."

"Then we need to be brought up to speed."

"It's not like we are going anywhere soon." Ariel motioned to the surrounding desert. "We'll start at the beginning. You've probably been taught there has always been war and they would be correct. However, before God created man, He created angels."

"I've heard all of this before." Honora shrugged. "Lucifer convinced some angels they were better than God or something and God banished them to earth. Then when they started harming humans, he sent the angels to battle them."

"Ah, but what you don't know is the first two angels to be convinced by Lucifer, and he himself, were cursed beyond the rest. Lucifer and Satan were cursed to share a body and Leviathan was cursed to live in the sea."

"And the rest of them were cursed to look hideous." Honora nodded knowingly.

"Actually, the only curse on them is that they have to roam the earth." Ariel shrugged. "No one really knows why they started looking like monsters. The current theory is, for our kind, the outside reflects the inside."

Honora nodded slowly. "So how did the lords of hell come to be?"

"As you can imagine, being cursed to live in another form, as Satan and Lucifer were, would take some time to adjust. The lords were picked out of the strongest demons to command the rest."

"So why seven?"

"I'm not sure. Although, there are eight if you count both Satan and Lucifer. Possibly, it was simply the number of leaders needed to command the demon legions. However, they could have had other reasons for the amount of lords chosen. If you ever have the unfortunate chance to talk to one of them, you might ask about the reason for their number. However, you would have to have leverage over them to extract any information."

"Are there still sev- eight of them?"

"No, we have been able to kill a couple of them throughout the years. Beelzebub was killed a few thousand years ago and more recently I hunted down Mammon and slue him. That was within the last thousand years. I fought with several others, but I've never been able to do more than wound them. Nobody has seen Leviathan since the beginning of the war. We have sent a few expeditions out over the years hoping to find and slay her, but-"

"Wait, Leviathan is female?" Honora interrupted.

Ariel chuckled. "Just like there are female angels, there are female demons. There are a lot less of them, however."

"That's because they were too smart to follow Lucifer against God." Honora mumbled.

Ariel guffawed. "Your probably right." He got his laughter under control before continuing. "As I was saying, we've sent out expeditions, and they never returned. We assumed them lost after the fourth ship and never sent another."

"So, if Lucifer and Satan are still alive, why haven't we heard anything about them?"

"All I know is Michael and Gabriel told us they managed to bind him around the time we started this uneasy peace. It's most likely the only reason the demons hadn't attacked this whole time."

"Do you know where he is bound?"

"No, only Michael and Gabriel know. They never told us the location to minimize the chance of the enemy finding out."

Honora paused for a moment, trying to process everything she had just been told. "So, when the battle begins, we are going to have to contend with the rest of these lords?"

"Possibly, but Asmodeus thinks he is well above this war and Belphegor is lazy. He, most likely, had a hand in creating the canons but he wouldn't be caught *walking* anywhere much less fighting a battle. Then of course Leviathan can't set foot on land, not that she has feet anymore. We will most likely only have to contend with Azazel in the last battle and the handful of demons still alive. The only reason the rest would come out of hiding is if Satan and Lucifer were released. Mostly, we will be killing humans." Ariel fell silent at his last words.

"War is terrible. But we have to go through it to get to the peace on the other side. This battle will end it all, right?"

"I hope so," Ariel shook his head. "I'm tired of fighting. Tired of losing everything I hold dear, only to continue to live on. Unfortunately, if we don't kill all the Lords, they will come back with another army. Maybe thousands of years later, but none the less the surviving angels will be right back in this same situation."

"Then why didn't Michael and Gabriel kill Satan and Lucifer? Instead of trapping him?"

"They said the devils together were too powerful. They bound him and left to regain their strength. I believe they planned to return with reinforcements to destroy them. However, before they could, the demons led an army against them."

"Then why not now?"

"We will need them in the last battle here. We're outnumbered and with the advancement of canons the demons have the upper hand. I don't even think the surviving angels outnumber the surviving demons anymore. If Michael and Gabriel were to leave with the power needed to slay the two, we would surely lose everything else. I would think the best course of action would be to wait until we know the outcome of the battle and if we survive, then deal with those two."

"Ugh," Honora ran her fingers through her hair roughly. "Why does war have to be so complicated?"

Ariel chuckled. "Because each side wants to win. If not, we wouldn't have a war."

"Then what do we do?"

"Survive. And get back to the army to do our part to have the outcome we desire. Quiet now, I can see Deadpost looming on the horizon. Our voices will carry on the wind if we aren't careful. Spread the word to the rest if Ana hasn't already."

"Horizon?" Honora asked. "It's dark, how can you see it?"

"Angel." Ariel said it with a question in his voice as if it should have been obvious.

"Oh, right," Honora climbed down from the slow-moving cart and found Ana. "We need to spread the word to be silent. Ariel has spotted Deadpost on the horizon."

"I see it too. I will spread the word. Stay with the cart." Ana moved soundlessly to each person in the group, letting them know to be quiet while Honora returned to the cart.

"What of Furry and Oathbreaker?" She whispered.

"There's not much we can do about them." Ariel shrugged. "I'm not sure how the demons have been blocking our communications or we would have a chance to do the same. Either way, if there is a demon there, then he will see us long before we travel past. Oathbreaker and Fury would only communicate our numbers and strength."

"Then why are we even getting close to Deadpost?"

"Because we do not have the supplies to go farther south. It would add too much time to our route, and the weakest among us would surely perish. As it is, we will be lucky if we don't lose them by the time we reach Caister."

Honora sighed. *Why can't something be easy for a change?* Then to Ariel. "I'm going to go check on Malach and Serilda."

She climbed into the back of the cart. She squeezed a little water into their mouths, careful not to waste any or to allow too much water. Daziar stirred a little when she dripped water into his mouth and she thought he might wake, but he just turned his head and started snoring. She turned him on his good side, not wanting his snoring to give them away, but careful not to aggravate his wound.

"You're a pain in my butt even when you're asleep," she muttered.

She sighed again. Both of her childhood friends lay here fighting for their lives and she couldn't really do anything except give them a little water to keep them alive. If only she could heal them. With all the crazy and amazing things she had seen lately, she only wished she had some magic power to heal each of them.

She studied Malach and Serilda. If only there was a way to bring them back to consciousness. She checked Malach's wound, but not much had changed. It was, however, smaller than the day before. His healing abilities were such a blessing. If only Daziar had the same, he would already be awake and out of danger. Ana had said he might not regain the ability to use his arm right away, but no one was worried about Malach's arm.

"Demon!" Ana shouted.

"Hold!" Ariel commanded. "Let him come to us. We have the numbers, but only if we force him to land."

Ariel snapped the reins, making the horse move faster. "If he's smart, he will wait until he can muster his battalion to attack. He is baiting you, Ana."

The former prisoner and slowest among them mounted up on the few horses they had stolen, and the rest of the group jogged beside the cart. The demon circled the tower slowly. A light appeared at the top of the tower and swung their direction. The sand lit up around them. They weren't getting out of this without a fight.

The demon turned toward them.

"Ana, how's your wing?" Ariel asked.

"Sore, I might be able to keep myself in the air long enough to bring the demon down, but not much longer." Ana flexed her wings, flapping them slowly.

The demon didn't dive at them. Instead, he flew well over their heads, too far for Ana to be able to get to him in her current condition.

"Why isn't he attacking?" Marena asked.

An explosion rocked the cart and sand pelted Honora's exposed skin.

"He's dropping explosives!" Ariel shouted. "We saw this tactic at the battle of Fairdenn! Everyone spread out. If we stay together, we'll be a singular target. Ana, if he gets close enough to the ground, take him down."

Everyone ran in different directions, trying to spread out as much as they could. A second explosive landed close to Togan, knocking him from his feet. Marena helped him up, and he didn't seem badly injured. She thought the demon would have headed back to the tower to resupply, but he didn't. Two explosions hit the ground, one on either side of the cart, jarring it violently. Honora covered her head as the sand pelted her again.

"Keep going! Don't move in a straight path!" Arjun bellowed out of the darkness to Honora's left.

The cart veered right sharply, throwing Honora to the side. She crawled to the front of the cart and pulled a bow from the supplies. Anger boiled in her belly. She might not be able to kill a human, but a demon was a different story. Demon wings caught the light of the moon and she fired her arrow. It wasn't even close. Not only did it miss its mark well to the left, but it hadn't gotten near the height it needed to hit the demon.

Another explosion rocked the cart. This time, from her kneeling position, the concussion knocked her over the rail. The sand scratched her hands painfully as she landed. No time to dwell on the pain. She picked herself up and started running before she had fully gotten her bearings. Moving was more important than the direction at the moment. The light from the tower helped her realize which direction she had been running, and she adjusted her course.

She was well behind the group now and she watched as the explosions lit up the night periodically. A thought dawned on her. She could stay in relative safety if she stayed away from the cart. She felt a pang of guilt as she thought it, but it wasn't like she could do anything, even if she was on the cart. But she might be able to help if someone was injured by the explosions.

She gathered her courage and charged forward to catch up. She couldn't just let them take all the risk and she would need to be close if she was going to be able to help. An explosion lit up the silhouette of a horse and rider rearing and falling. She turned toward it.

She surveyed the scene as she arrived. Gore coated the side of the fallen horse from the explosion. It was already dead, but its rider was still alive. The horse pinned him, and half his face was red and angry from the burns. It was one of the former prisoners. She didn't even know his name.

"Leave me," He pushed her away. "I'm dead and you are an easy target if you stay here."

"Quiet, only your leg is pinned, and your wounds look superficial." She positioned herself to push on the horse's corpse, trying to lift it enough to free the man's leg.

He shut his mouth and pulled, pushing on the horse for more leverage. The shifting sand allowed him to inch his leg out slowly. He looked up and his eyes widened. He sat up and pushed her with all his strength, propelling her to the side. An explosion deafened her, and the force sent her forward onto her face. Her arms burned; her ears rang.

She picked herself up and looked behind her. The horror she turned back to would haunt her for the rest of her life. She ran again, trying to put as much distance between her and the remains as she could. There was nothing more she could do for him.

Her eyes adjusted to the dark once again, and she spotted the demon banking back toward the tower. Lights flickered at the base of the tower. No doubt the soldier leaving to chase them down.

Honora took her chance and ran for the cart. Ariel could only go so fast in the sand and most of their people, even those on foot, had outpaced him. Ana and Skie were the only ones who had stayed nearby.

Honora finally caught up to the cart and hopped in. She quickly checked on the three laying in the cart. All three were still breathing, and she sighed with relief. Daziar's wound was oozing blood once again, however, and she would have to change the bandage. She took a length of rope and strapped each of them down to the cart. Hopefully, it would help keep them secure.

The demon was much lower in the sky as he returned, no doubt hoping to raise his chances of hitting his targets. It was a mistake. Ana took to the sky with a whirlwind of wings and sand. Honora grabbed another arrow and nocked the bow she had somehow held on to through the entire ordeal.

Ana slammed into the demon. Hope, in spear form, only just deflected at the last second. Several objects fell from the demon's pack. They hit the sand without exploding. Togan appeared out of the dark with Marena behind him. They collected the objects and ran for the cart.

Honora lowered her bow and helped them offload the round explosives onto the cart and secure them.

"These might come in handy later," Togan handed her two of the round balls. They had fuses coming out of them, similar to the explosive described to her at the battle of Fairdenn.

She quickly put them away in the middle of the supplies, so they were less likely to explode. She turned her attention back to Ana and the demon. Ana had gotten the upper-hand, forcing the demon into the sand. Her spearpoint followed him down as the sand sprayed up, blocking them from view.

Ariel halted the cart, drawing Storm and, changing her into a battle axe, he charged for the battle with Skie on his heels.

Honora vaulted into the bench and took the reins just as Arjun appeared out of the darkness and did the same. "I'll take these. You take care of those in back."

She relinquished the reins and once again climbed into the back. This was chaos. She glanced back and spotted Ariel, Skie, and Ana heavily engaged with the demon. She nocked and drew the arrow again but couldn't get a clear shot as they fought. The demon took to the sky, retreating toward the tower. Honora let the arrow fly and missed the main mass of the demon. However, she caught a wing; the arrow causing enough damage that he couldn't outpace Ana.

She caught him by his heel and used his momentum to slam him into the ground. She then reached out and twisted his wing viciously, and the demon bellowed. Skie clamped down on his other wing, using her weight to hold him. Ariel tossed Ana her spear. She must have lost it somewhere in the fight. Letting go of the demon's wing with one hand caught Hope and rammed him home into the demon's back. She let go of the demon and he crawled away. Ariel walked up behind him and swung Storm in a long, deadly arc, severing the demon's spine.

Ariel put a foot on the demon and ripped Storm free, and Ana removed Hope. The demon was dead for sure. Ariel retrieved the demon's pack of explosives where it had fallen, and they started running for the cart. Arjun slowed the horse to let them catch up.

"Keep moving!" Ariel shouted, handing the explosives to Ana.

Arjun snapped the reins again, doing as he had been told.

Ana jumped with the aid of her wings and covered the distance between her and the cart. She stowed the bag of explosives on the cart and continued running next to it. Ariel caught up and fell in beside them.

"Don't stop for anything we have riders coming up behind us." Ariel commanded. "Everyone, fall in beside the cart if you can hear me!"

All but the dead prisoner materialized out of the darkness to join the cart. Two horses remained; both being ridden by former prisoners. Marena had her bow in her hand, but she wouldn't be able to make a decent shot on foot. If they swapped, Marena would be of more use to the group.

Ariel had apparently realized the same thing. "Marena, swap places with Honora. Secure the wounded as best you can and be ready to fire at the front runners. Togan, do you have a source of fire handy?"

Honora vaulted off the cart and hit the ground running.

"I got flint." Togan huffed as he ran. "If Marena can light a torch, I'll have that."

"Do it, take the explosives in the demon's pack and when they get close, leave the horseman a present."

"Ye'sir!" Togan all but bounced with excitement. No doubt the big blacksmith had been waiting for his chance to use the explosives.

Marena handed him the pack and used his flint and a knife to light one of the few torches they had. She handed it down to him, careful not to get it too close to the pack. No one wanted the explosive going off prematurely.

Honora chanced a glance behind her to see that the front cavalry were outpacing them at an alarming rate. It wouldn't be long before they caught the group. There were only about five riders in front with a long string of riders out behind them. Those on foot were even farther behind them. These first five would die quickly.

Honora heard the twang of Marena's bow string and the first rider tumbled from his horse, rolling as his momentum carried him end over end. He didn't rise. A hiss sounded next to her, and she jumped thinking she had run over a snake's den in the dark. Togan dropped an explosive, and the hiss receded behind her.

Boom!

The explosive detonated harmlessly but startled one horse, throwing its rider from the saddle. Although, he quickly regained control and remounted. He was soon back on their trail.

"Give it a count of ten, love, then light the next," Marena called, calculating the distance for Togan.

Another twang of Marena's bow and another horse lost its rider. "Make it fifteen."

Togan counted under his breath and he huffed and puffed along behind Honora. When he reached fifteen, he lit another explosive and dropped it behind him. This time, the explosion killed the horse and rider instantly, leaving only a smoking crater. Seconds later, small pattering noises reached Honora's ears, and she shuddered at the implications.

The front runner slowed, falling behind and keeping out of bow and explosive range. Ana turned and charged back at them, snagging Togan's torch and explosive. She lit it and sent it flying back at the riders, who had now grouped up. The explosion killed several of them and injured many more.

With their demon commander and many of their best riders slain, the survivors decided this group wasn't worth dying for. One called for a retreat and those who were able turned toward the tower. Several of them dismounted and carried the injured back on their horses.

"Keep moving," Ariel called, keeping the horses at a steady pace, although allowing them to slow slightly.

"That was easier than I thought it would be," Ana stated, as she caught up with the group.

"Easy?" Honora gaped at the angel.

"Easier," Ana corrected. "The human soldiers gave up much quicker than I thought they would."

"It probably had something to do with the explosives you were lobbing at them." Marena sat down in the cart.

"That should be the worst of it," Ariel let the horses slow. "We need to get a few more miles in tonight, but we are going to need to rest the horses soon."

"They need water as well," Honora walked up to check on them.

"Unfortunately, we don't have any water for them." Arjun replied.

"If we get to Caister tomorrow as planned, they might make it." Ariel told her.

"Are there any oases on the map?" Ana asked.

"None," Togan shook his head. He had been carrying the maps since they had lost Elzrod.

"Maybe Ana could fly up and see some water from the sky?" Marena asked.

"She can try once we've stopped for the night," Ariel told them. "Right now, we are still too close to Deadpost. I don't want a group of soldiers sneaking up on us while we are resting."

No one disagreed with Ariel's plan. It was only a few more hours when the light of the sun started rising behind them. The tower of Deadpost still loomed behind them now visible, which made everyone uneasy. They had enough problems with water; they didn't need to be chased till the horses died of dehydration.

Ariel called a halt, and they dragged the makeshift cover together. Honora checked one more time on the wounded before Ana took over for her. She crawled beneath the cart and didn't even care about the sand. It was already everywhere from the night before. She laid down and was asleep before the sand had settled under her.

Chapter 4

Fury and Oathbreaker had been in contact since well before Ariel and his half-breed son had arrived at the compound. Fury had first contacted them when Azazel had carried her with him to visit the young-unwitting traitor. He had assured them his capture by the Angels at Newaught hadn't turned him to their side. He had been acting the entire time. Rather well if he was to be asked.

Oathbreaker had only trusted him after he proved himself by interfering with the execution of Azazel. As a bonus, they had killed the old man. It was far pastime for his generation to have ended and Elzrod always irked her.

Now, Fury and Oathbreaker were captured by the angels. That wasn't supposed to have happened, but they were still in demon territory. There was still a good possibility of rescue. She had glimpses of what was happening by infiltrating a former prisoner's mind. Somewhere in his bloodline there was demon blood, which allowed her to see things periodically. If she could connect to a demon, she could attack this prisoner's mind, starting with his dreams. She and Azazel had practiced and perfected it over the years.

Since there were no demons nearby, her abilities were limited. She deduced from the former prisoner they would go past Deadpost. She and Fury decided it would probably be their best chance of rescue. Most demons had already traveled with the army into Angel Territory, and there were a few left behind. One of whom would be stationed at Deadpost.

Not long after they discovered they were heading that direction; she contacted the demon. She didn't care to remember his name. He was such a low demon; it didn't matter. He would, however, be able to muster the troops at Deadpost and recapture the prisoners. Then she could finish what she started with Serilda.

As she understood it, the half-breed boy and Reckoning had delved into Serilda's mind to help her find her way back. Fools, no one had ever done that. The imbecile of an angel, Raziel, was the only one to make it back, and he would never be the same. Now she would have the chance to destroy all three of them.

"How did you make it out?" Fury broke into her thoughts.

"What are you rambling about?" She turned her ire on him.

"The bearer and the blade start the trance state and cannot leave until they both decide to." Fury explained his confusion. "How did you leave her mind?"

"You were there when the angels attempted to liberate those in the trance, correct?"

"Yes, I was still with them. They weren't able to rescue any as far as I know. Raziel and his blade were the only ones to return."

"I was able to find Raziel's blade, Serenity, before he was destroyed." Oathbreaker said, the last part with pleasure coloring her voice.

"Destroyed? As far as I knew, we weren't able to be destroyed."

Oathbreaker sneered. "There are a lot of things you don't know. Serenity and I had a nice, long chat. I was finally able to extract information out of him. He told me while the bearer cannot leave the trance state without us, we can leave the trance state without them. It's difficult, but it is possible."

"How?"

"There is a place within their mind you can find an escape. You could lead them there, but without you, their mind is too weak, too easily distracted."

"You mean the door?" Fury knew about the door, though he had never seen it himself.

"Yes. Their minds alone have no chance of getting to it. However, your mind is more powerful, more focused than theirs. You can reach that door and leave without them."

"That make sense. So why can't another team of bearer and blade rescue the stranded human?" Fury asked.

"Have you never entered a trance state with a bearer?" Oathbreaker rolled her eyes at his naivety.

"No, I have never trusted a bearer that much or been with one that long."

Oathbreaker sighed. "The door is in a part of the mind which is not normally used. Oddly enough, that place is in a similar location for both human and angel bearers. Since it is in such a spot, it takes a large amount of concentration to reach it. Neither humans nor most angels can reach it on their own. Do you remember the sessions with Leviathan in heaven before the rebellion?"

"The ones where we would meditate for hours?"

"Yes, those insufferable sessions taught us how to block out everything."

"I remember Leviathan was one of the few angels then who could sit like that for hours, ignoring hunger, sleep, and discomfort."

"I believe she could leave without one of us supporting her. Conversely, most blades would have no issue leaving on their own."

"That explains how to leave, but what about the fact a blade and bearer team can't retrieve those stuck in the trance?"

"That is much harder to explain. I haven't been able to deduce why. For all I know they can, only no one has figured out how." Oathbreaker's mental concentration changed. "We are coming up on Deadpost. I can see the cart through the demon's eyes."

"Good, I'm ready to be rid of our captors."

"The imbecile is going to drop explosives on us," Oathbreaker all but shouted.

"He's what?"

"You heard me. The oaf is going to blow us sky high."

"You said that we can be destroyed. How?" There was a haste to Fury's voice.

"Not with those paltry explosives." She assured him.

Fury's relief flooded through their connection.

"At least I don't believe so."

The cart shook and jolted beneath them.

"You don't believe so?"

"Larger explosives have proven useful in torturing a blade physically, but nothing we've tested has done more than slight damage."

"Then how can they be destroyed?" Fury's voice was once again calm.

"That is a closely guarded secret. I wouldn't share that with you, even if you were authorized to know."

"You have heaven's anvil?" Fury whispered reverently.

"Shut up." Oathbreaker snapped, confirming his suspicion. "Do not even entertain the idea of it in case the angels catch wind. We want them to think we are only turning the blades we capture."

Fury was quiet, and another explosion shook the cart.

"I've lost connection with the former prisoner I was gaining information from." Oathbreaker reported. "It seems he's dead."

"Not to worry, we will be rescued soon."

"Don't be so sure."

Another explosion.

"What do you mean?"

"Quiet," Oathbreaker snapped. "I've been thrown from the pile of supplies. I'm close to the wounded, including Malach and Serilda. If I can reach one of them, I can enter Serilda's mind again and gain the information Azazel wanted. You will be in charge of our rescue if that happens."

"Fine, just warn me before you-"

"I'm touching Serilda, good luck and hail Lucifer." Oathbreaker's presence in Fury's mind disappeared about the same time the demon's death pulse hit him.

He cursed. No rescue would be forthcoming until they reached Caister.

Malach had truly lost all track of time in his mother's mind. She had come back to the grassy hill several times since her first visit, but never believed their pleas of authenticity. Reckoning stated, however, her continued reappearance in this plain of reality showed Serilda was questioning where or not to believe them.

They waited. Reckoning spent the time retelling parts of the angels' history. He mentioned he was even originally under the charge of two different angels who were now Lords of Hell, Leviathan and Satan. How Reckoning had been able to keep his morality and virtue under such circumstances was beyond Malach, although Reckoning still held to the belief Leviathan wasn't inherently evil, only led astray by those who were.

The ground shook here and there recently. Malach nor Reckoning fully understood why, but Reckoning hypothesized either something was happening in the real world or Serilda's mind was becoming unstable as she faded from lack of nutrition. Either way, they were running out of time.

Malach stood. "I can't sit here any longer. We need to find the way out. How does one normally leave the trance?"

Reckoning explained the door to Malach and how a blade and bearer would normally find it.

"Then we need to find this door. Can we will ourselves there?" Malach asked.

"This differs from your training sessions with Elzrod. That was built between your two minds, on a neutral ground of sorts." Reckoning explained, not getting up from where he was sitting on the grass. "Our will has a lot less power here. I don't believe we would have a chance of reaching the door without your mother's help. There was only one instance of an angel and blade escaping another's mind, and I don't know the full extent of that encounter. Possibly he did this by some other means, which is possibly why his mind was scrambled. We don't want a similar fate."

"No, I just wish she would believe us." Malach scratched his head irritably.

"I'm starting to believe you."

Malach whirled to see his mother standing behind him. "Mom, I-"

She put up a hand to stop him. "As you have deduced, we're running out of time. I'm willing to believe you two are real. However, I will not reveal any information, so don't ask me. Also, if you are real, I still don't trust Reckoning. Oathbreaker told me he is a traitor."

"He's not a traitor," Malach sighed and shook his head. "I think I would know. He has been in my head for the past few months."

"And Fang, Oathbreaker, was in mine for *years* before she betrayed me." Serilda replied. "I believed she was recently turned, but I found out Satan planted the seeds of evil in her before the rebellion in heaven. She was captured and turned during mine and your father's missions. We rescued her at that time, but when Reckoning and her were captured again, about four hundred years ago, she was simply returning to report her findings of the angel army. Now she wants more information. My point is you can't trust your own feelings. She tricked me for hundreds of years."

"But you will work with us to get out of here, right?" Malach extended a hand toward his mother.

She took it gently and wrapped him in a hug. "Yes, son."

Malach's anxiety melted away as he wrapped his arms around his mother. For the first time in almost ten years, he embraced her. It was just how he remembered it. Her warmth, how she smelled, and the comfort she brought him. Tears slipped down his cheeks. He loved her, and he had missed her more than he could ever explain. More than he had admitted to anyone, even himself. His mother was there and everything would be alright.

"I hate to break up your reunion," Reckoning prodded with a soft tone.

"Then don't," Malach grumbled.

Serilda squeezed him, chuckling softly.

"As pointed out earlier," Reckoning continued anyway. "We have little time. We need to find a way out. Oathbreaker made it out on her own, so it stands to reason that Serilda can as well, and hopefully take us with her."

"The door we need to find is accessible to us, just as it is accessible to her. I haven't been able to will myself there yet, but I searched Oathbreakers' mind while she tortured me."

Reckoning smiled. "You were always stronger than anyone gave you credit for. Oathbreaker shouldn't have underestimated you."

"No! I shouldn't have." A voice boomed from above. Oathbreaker descended from the sky to land softly on the grass.

"This is Oathbreaker?" Malach guffawed. "She just a little girl!"

Serilda, still holding onto Malach, reached out and grasped Reckonings arm. The entire scene changed around them. They were in the cottage back in Brightwood.

"How'd we get here?" Malach asked, peering around at the sparsely lit room.

"This is my safe room. A place I've been building to keep Oathbreaker out while she was gone. I've been able to take control of my mind once again. We should be safe for a few minutes."

Reckoning opened his mouth to say something when the door slammed open.

All three turned to watch a slightly younger Serilda enter, carried by a still winged Ariel. His wings were midnight black, and Malach thought the color suited him. He wondered if the black color was because he was doing under cover missions or if it happened when he left the angel army with Serilda. He would have to ask later.

The pair were clearly in love, giggling like children and kissing each other. They had still been like that years later, when Malach had been young. It made him smile. However, he didn't really want to see where the night took them.

"I told you I would carry you across the threshold," Ariel smiled in triumph.

"And I told *you,* you would have to fight for the privilege." The younger Serilda slapped his chest playfully.

They giggled and quipped their way through the house to their room, Reckoning moving out of their way instinctively. The door to their room mercifully shut, blocking any sounds coming from within.

"Um, sorry Malach," Serilda grinned sheepishly.

"That was...awkward." Malach just stared at the ground.

Reckoning cleared his throat loudly. "Might I remind everyone we are on a timetable?"

"Yes," Serilda all but jumped on the change in topic. "I found Oathbreaker's secrets while she was in my mind. She found where the door was and she didn't believe I could get there. I don't think I could have either. However, she was always thorough, and she found a way to move it into one of my memories. We need to search through my memories to find a door out of place. Once there, we should be able to leave."

"You're saying, if she had left the door where it was, we most likely wouldn't be able to escape since you wouldn't be able to focus long enough to reach it. However, in trying to make it harder for us to escape, she instead made it possible?" Reckoning grinned. "Interesting. I'll have to find out how she moved it if I have the chance to question her."

"You can continue that line of thought later," Malach stopped him before they lost him to his thoughts. He turned to Serilda. "Which memories should we start with?"

"My worst memories," Serilda's face sobered, and she took a long deep breath. "Malach, before we go, you are going to see some things I never wanted you to. Some are going to be...terrible."

"Mom, I have seen some pretty terrible things already," Malach assured her, remembering the horrors of the battle of Fairdenn.

"Yes, but you will see *me* do some of these things..." Serilda's voice trailed off, and she turned away from him.

"Mom," Malach put a hand on her shoulder. "It's going to be ok."

"I just don't want you to think any less of me,"

"I could never."

The cottage shook, similar to when the demon had attacked Malach back in Brightwood that fateful night. Although, no demonic howls accompanied the shaking of the house.

"She found us," Reckoning reached out to Serilda and Malach. "We need to go."

Serilda took Reckoning's hand and Malach took both of theirs, making a triangle. The cottage disappeared, and they were standing in a city street covered in a light dusting of snow. It was dark out and there was no one around. There was a small lump against the wall a short way down the street.

Malach glanced at his mother. However, she was staring at the lump down the street. She walked down the street to it and reached out as if to pick it up, but she stopped a few inches shy of touching it. Malach walked up to her, not fully understanding what was happening.

"What is it, mom?"

"It's...me."

Malach's gaze jumped to the lump once again. He spotted movement under the cloth, and it fell away from a young girl's gaunt face. He glanced from his mother to the girl and could see the resemblance.

"This is the first day I met Azazel." She all but whispered.

A cloaked figure appeared at the end of a street, as if conjured by her words. Malach assumed this was Azazel and his conjecture was confirmed as he got closer to the girl. He sat down with his back to the wall and pulled young Serilda into his lap, holding her close and covering her with his cloak. Slowly, she stopped shivering.

"Why are you out here, little one," Azazel cooed.

Malach threw up a little in his mouth, but he swallowed the bile.

Young Serilda said nothing.

"Do you have a family?"

She shook her head.

"Now you do." Azazel stood, effortlessly carrying young Serilda off the street.

"I never thought this kind of man would turn out to be a lord of hell. Nor that he would be capable of the things he's done." Serilda bowed her head, her hands balled into fists.

"No door," Reckoning walked up behind them. "We need to move on."

"Yes, thank you Reckoning." Serilda said automatically, her lack of tone revealing her thoughts were in a far-off place.

"What's next, mom?" Malach touched her arm.

She glanced up and shook her head as if to clear it. "My first kill."

She reached out and touched both Malach and Reckoning, and the scene changed again. They were in a desert. There were pairs of young kids sparring and Malach remembered this sight from his own training. They were in the courtyard of an outpost with a single tower. It reminded him of the demon compound, but this was not near the size of that tower. Also, there was no tree line in sight. It must be Deadpost.

"Ciarán!" a voice called.

All the pairs of sparing children stopped and turned toward the tower. Azazel, in his most human form, walked out of the tower. One girl quickly made her way forward and bowed in front of Azazel.

"Ciarán," Azazel, address the girl. "Come, I have something important for you to see."

Serilda and Malach followed.

The girl looked a lot like his mother, but Azazel called her Ciarán. Reckoning was not paying attention to the scene. Instead, he searched for the door. Malach felt a little guilt. They should help Reckoning search, but Serilda seemed to need to concentrate on the memory and Malach desired to know his mother's history.

Reckoning caught Malach's gaze and waved him off, motioning for Malach to pay attention to the memory.

Malach turned back to the scene unfolding before him. He trusted Reckoning not to leave any place unsearched.

Ciarán followed Azazel up the slightly curved stairs as they slowly wound their way around the tower. It reminded him all the more of the tower in the demon compound. they must have had the same architect. Azazel stopped at one of the doors and produced a key from somewhere in his robes. He inserted the key, opened the door, and entered. Ciarán followed wordlessly, even as Malach followed Serilda.

"Mom, who is this?" Malach asked, unable to contain his curiosity any longer.

"This is me. Azazel gave me a new name when he took me in. Ciarán means 'little dark one'. This is the day he took me out of the general training and made me his hidden hand." She never took her eyes off the prisoner in the room. He was bound, bloody, and just barely conscious. "This was the day everything changed."

Azazel handed her a dagger; It had a meandering, double-edged, black blade. "Kill him." He commanded simply.

Ciarán's head snapped up from where she was studying the blade to stare at him wide-eyed.

Azazel walked out of the room. Malach heard the door lock behind them.

Ciarán whirled and ran to the door, casting the dagger aside. She pushed on the door wildly. However, it didn't budge. After a moment of trying to wrench the door open, she resorted to beating on it. She finally turned and worked to slow her breathing.

"Kill him and I will let you out," the door muffled Azazel's voice.

Ciarán turned around, searching for the dagger she had abandoned in her rush to escape. The prisoner had come to enough to work his way toward it. She snatched it up before he could reach it. She backed away, holding the dagger out between them, but tripped and fell on her butt.

The prisoner seemed to have used all his energy and slumped to the ground, breathing heavily.

Ciarán backed up until she was sitting with her back against the wall.

Malach felt sorry for the girl. The first time he had killed a man, he hadn't had a choice either. His fear and panic made him forget almost everything about how to fight. In fact, he had been a little older than his mother when he was first set upon by the highwayman. He had more or less stumbled into killing him. He had been so scared he ran after stabbing the man, letting him slowly bleed out on the road. David Wervine had come back with him, and they had buried the man. David had talked with him about self-defense and how he had done the right thing. He hadn't *felt* like he had done the right thing then. However, if he hadn't killed the highwayman, he probably would have *been* killed.

His mother wasn't defending herself. Azazel was forcing her to take a life in cold blood. To kill this prisoner with his hands bound. It was cruel of him to make her kill in this way.

Time seemed to speed up, the sun going down and back up within seconds. Ciarán stayed in the same position for most of the night, but in the wee hours of the morning, she had fallen asleep. The prisoner stirred, startling her awake, and she cut her hand on the knife as she grasped for it frantically. Blood flowed freely from the cut and she cried out in pain.

"Kill him and I will let you out," Azazel's voice said again.

Most of the day passed within seconds, and Ciarán still hadn't moved. The blood on her hand had started to dry, but now was slowly oozing. She would need to clean and bandage it, or it would continue to bleed. He glanced over at his mother, who was looking at the scar on her hand. No doubt the evidence of the cut from that day.

Ciarán got to her feet and walked over to the prisoner. Her stomach growled loudly. She peered down at the bloody mess of a man and then back at the knife.

As if Azazel heard her stomach growl, which he very well could have, he egged her on. "Kill him and I will have them throw a feast in your honor."

Ciarán looked at the knife again. She stood over the man who had passed out face down. She pulled his head back, laying the knife across his throat. Sweat beaded on her forehead and the man made a slight choking sound. She slid the knife across his throat, parting the skin. Malach knew from experience she hadn't cut deep enough.

The prisoner thrashed, trying to throw her off of him, and she stabbed down with the knife. It went into his back and might have pierced a lung, but it was anything but a clean kill. He twisted, pulling the knife from her grasp, and rolled. He rolled onto the knife and the tip appeared out of his chest.

Everything in the room stopped. Ciarán lay on the floor on one side of the room while the prisoner writhed in pain on the other. The door open and Azazel walked in.

"Well, close enough." He frowned at the prisoner, drew his sword and stabbed him through the heart, ending his pain. He turned to Ciarán and reached out a hand to help her up. "Come, we will go have a feast to commemorate your first kill."

She took his hand, and he lifted her to her feet. They left the room, and the scene seemed to freeze in place. Serilda was staring at the man on the ground.

"Who was he?" Malach asked.

"I never found out."

"No door here." Reckoning interjected softly.

"So, you have figured out my secret!" Oathbreakers' voice boomed in the quiet space. She strolled into the prison. "You won't find where I hid the door."

"There's three of us," Malach reasoned, not listening to what she was saying. "We could take her. Kick her out of your mind."

Reckoning held out a hand to stop him. "Malach-"

"Yes, come kick me out." The little girl smirked.

"Malach, she has more power here than either of us. She can't be kicked out of Serilda's mind. Since she is part of this trance, she must leave via the door."

"This is so confusing." Malach scratched his head vigorously.

"Oh, Malach, you have no power here. You couldn't hurt a fly without my or Ciarán's permission."

"My name is not Ciarán!" Serilda turned to Malach and Reckoning.

A split second before she touched his arm, he understood what she was going to do.

"No mom, wai-"

The scene changed around Him and Reckoning, however, Serilda and Oathbreaker did not make the trip with them.

Chapter 5

Amara and Raziel walked through the main gates in Caister. Amara fully expected to be stopped. She expected they would be flagged as fugitives, expected they would have to contact the Shadows of the Earth, the thief's guild she had grown up in.

As it was, they were well into the city, and nobody had stopped them. As far as she knew, she was still wanted in Caister for past crimes. She had seen wanted posters on the walls with her face on them, but most were old and worn from the elements. Her appearance had changed in the past few months. Her body was now fit and strong instead of lean. The scar from her plunge over the flume still marred the left side of her head. Marena had helped her shave and style her hair, and she quite liked the look. The left side was fully shaved, other than the recent growth, with the rest brushed over to the right. Marena had braided it in various places, keeping it out of her way during any action. She had adorned the braids with various metal beads. She appeared to be a warrior rather than a scared child. Though her actions told a different story. She was no fierce warrior. She was a betrayer.

She was still afraid the city guard would recognize her. However, not one guard had given her a second glance. Although many people had given the scared, rugged, rag wearing Raziel multiple, sometimes fearful, glances. He was the best camouflage she could have hoped for.

They arrived at the sewer entrance, which would lead them to the hidden Shadow's lair. Amara pulled open the cover and Raziel turned his nose up at the smell that wafted out of the opening. Amara gestured for him to go first, and he shook his head vigorously.

"Oh, come on, you lived in a room for years that was covered in your own blood. A little smell won't hurt you." She put her fist on her hips and tapped her foot.

"At least it was all mine. None of this is mine." He replied weakly.

"You won't be touching it."

"No, we don't think so."

"Get down there now or I'll leave you to wander the streets alone."

"Sounds like a good plan to me. I was going to leave you, anyway." He turned around to leave.

She reached out and grabbed the back of his shirt, pulling him back. "Get down there now. I need more answers out of you, and this will be the safest place to do it."

"But it smells," He whined, drawing out the last word like a pouting child. "If we go, could we have some cheese?"

"What?" Amara was so confused at the sudden change in his demeanor. "Uh, Sure."

He whooped and climbed down the ladder.

Amara just shook her head and followed him down. At least she knew where her love of cheese came from.

At the bottom of the ladder, they didn't step down into sludge, which would normally cover the floor. The Shadows engineer had masterfully rerouted the sewers to keep this area free of the waste and the smell to a minimum. It still smelled terrible, but all the fumes wouldn't poison them.

Amara led Raziel down the twists and turns of the sewers toward the lair. Before they had gotten close enough to see anything of the Shadow's lair, cold steel pressed against her throat. She heard Raziel make a whimpering noise behind her. The same thing had happened to him.

"I got closer than I expected," she smirked. "Your security is getting lax."

"There are less of us than when you were here, little one." Lawdel appeared out of the shadows in front of her and nodded to the two thieves holding knives to their throats.

The pressure of the knifes edge lifted, and she scratched lightly at the irritation the knife had caused. "What's going on?"

"The Dark Hallow," Lawdel replied. "They have a new leader, and he is working on wiping us out."

"That's the same group trying to take over the jobs in Newaught." Amara's brow furrowed.

"They started by taking our jobs from us and starving our income, then they started killing us if they caught us on the street alone."

Raziel gasped. "That's horrible."

"Let's get farther in and I'll tell you everything." Lawdel motioned her to come with him. "Who's your friend?"

"We are Raziel, Archangel and Keeper of Secrets," Raziel piped up from behind her and beamed.

Lawdel's eyebrow when up and he turned to look at Amara for confirmation.

"He has no actual idea what that means," Amara grumbled. "He's lost his mind a little."

"Is it even true, then?" Lawdel asked as they started walking.

"As far as I can tell," Amara shrugged. "I...I rescued him from a demon prison."

Lawdel's eyebrows slowly returned to their normal position on his face, but as they dropped, so did his jaw. "You have changed so much since leaving here. You'll have to tell me everything soon. For now, do you think he can help us out of this predicament?"

"I doubt it," Amara replied, shame keeping her silent about her journey up to this point. She wanted to tell Lawdel everything like she used to, however she feared his disappointment in her for what she had done. "Like I said, he's not all there, and he had all but accepted he was just a prisoner. I don't think he has any fight left in him."

"Huh," Lawdel grunted. "That's unfortunate. We could have used an angel on our side. Many of our fingers have become spies instead of thieves. They've heard whispers: The Dark Hallow has the backing of the demons. None of them can prove it, though."

There goes my plan to learn from one of the Dark Hallow. She pursed her lips. "So, what is the plan? The master has a plan, right?"

"The plan is to leave."

"What?" Amara was so shocked at the idea of them leaving Caister she stopped in her tracks. "You're going to give up without a fight?"

"No, this is a tactical retreat." Lawdel turned to her and motioned her to continue walking. "We are joining and combining with the Shadows chapter in Newaught. All the chapters are working their way there."

"Yargate? And Ragewood too?"

"Yes, all of us. The master has been in contact with the others, and this is happening in all the cities in varying degrees. The Yargate chapter was almost wiped-out last week."

"When is this move happening?"

They walked into the main room of the Shadows lair. It was the place where they took all their meals, had all their meetings, and spent most of their time. The only other room that was close to the same size was the kitchen.

Amara stopped in her tracks at the scene unfolding in front of her. Men were carrying boxes out to the main table, which was already stacked high with them. They were not uniform boxes but a mismatch of large and small. Bags of grains and other food items lay below the table.

"Three days." Lawdel put a hand on her shoulder. "We have two loads of things almost the same size as this up in an abandoned warehouse already waiting in carts."

Amara didn't know what to say. This had been her home and to see it like this, soon to be abandoned, was just wrong. How could they just leave?

"Amara, come with us." Lawdel squeezed her shoulder gently. "You obviously need help, and we can bring you back into the fold, help you get back on your feet. Once we get through this thing with the Dark Hallow, we can come back here and pick things up again."

She nodded slowly, "I will. I'll come with you and help defend the Shadows against this threat. Can I talk to you in private?"

Lawdel's brow knitted together in concern. "Of course. Do you want your friend to come along?"

"Um, no, I think I've had enough of his company for a minute." Amara studied Raziel as he glanced around with a blank expression, seeing it all, but none of what he saw moved him to any emotions, at least outwardly.

Lawdel pulled a man she didn't know aside and talked to him quickly. He nodded and headed over to Raziel. Raziel focused on the man and he led the angel away toward the kitchen.

"He's a flight risk." Amara warned.

"I figured as much." Lawdel nodded. "I have encountered people like him before. They tend to wander, either because they don't know any better or because they have some misguided idea. Do you know how he ended up like that?"

"No," Amara studied the ground. "I think possibly the years of torture?"

Lawdel nodded slowly. "Come, we can talk in the meeting room."

They moved to the smaller meeting room where she had first met the master of the Shadows chapter. Lawdel moved to sit down at the table and she followed suit. She took a long breath to calm her nerves. She didn't know how Lawdel would react to Raziel being her father. For that matter, she hadn't fully accepted it.

"Raziel is my father," she heard herself say.

"Pardon?" Lawdel just blinked at her.

"He's my father."

"How do you know?"

"A demon told me, and Raziel all but confirmed it."

"Tell me everything," Lawdel interlocked his fingers with his pointers pressed against his lips.

She told him everything that had happened since she left Caister. How she had met Malach, fought at the battle of Fairdenn, followed him across the entire known world, and eventually betrayed them all to save Lawdel and Raziel.

At the conclusion of her story, Lawdel rubbed his eyes with one hand. "Your betrayed the only people you have ever called friends to, *possibly*, save me and Raziel." He heaved a heavy sigh. "Girly, you shouldn't have done that."

"What was I supposed to do? Let you and my biological father die?"

"Yes!"

Amara threw up her hands. "I didn't want you to die!"

"I can take care of myself, girl, been doin' it longer than you've been alive. And as for your father, what good is he doing you? He can barely remember his own name from what you've told me."

"I...well I thought..."

"Not everyone needs you to protect them. It sounds like Raziel might have been happier dying, might have been a mercy. I, on the other hand, have survived several attempts on my life in the last few weeks. If the Dark Hallow *is* backed by the demons, then this Azazel character has been trying to kill me long before you made the deal with him."

"Then what was I supposed to do?"

"What you promised!" Lawdel stood, toppling his chair. "You followed this Malach guy through war and giant spider caves, and it sounds like he saved your life as much as you did his. Then, the first time you run into something you can't handle, instead of seeking help from those who trust and love you, you stab them in the back. I thought I taught you better than that." Lawdel was breathing hard.

He's...angry? He's angry at me for betraying them... Amara couldn't believe it. Her first reaction was to be angry right back at him, but realized he was right. She had tried to do everything on her own without the help of those who cared about her. In the end, she had hurt everyone who loved her. How stupid was she? She sat back heavily in her chair; the revelation weighing on her heavily. "You hate me then." She mumbled.

The bluster escaped Lawdel in a heavy sigh and he rubbed his face again, deflating and righting his chair to sit. "I love you, little one."

Her head snapped up at the words. He had never said those words to her. Ever.

"I love you like I would my own daughter, if I had one. That's why your mistake hurts me so much."

"What a moron I've been," Amara studied the wood table, refusing to meet Lawdel's eyes.

"You're not wrong there," Lawdel took another deep breath. "But there is nothing you can do about that now. The only thing you can do is learn from your mistakes moving forward. Loyalty to your friends and loved ones is the most precious thing in this world."

"I know that now." Amara still didn't look at Lawdel.

"Let's get you some food and water." Lawdel stood. "I know you've been traveling through the desert, but when you feel you're up to it, I'm sure we could use your help."

Amara stood without a word, dwelling on what Lawdel had said. The full weight of her betrayal and his words fully on her shoulders once again. She would learn from her mistakes; she would do her best to apologize and make up for what she had done.

"Lawdel."

"Yes?"

"The people I betrayed..."

"Yeah?"

"They're headed this way. They will no doubt be barred entry to the city, at best, and captured once again, at worst..." her voice trailed off. "Is there a way we could help them?"

"When will they arrive?"

"Probably tonight sometime. They weren't far behind us and I think they were traveling by night."

"I'll post someone outside the city to wait for them for the next two nights. They can lead them in through the sewer dump pipes that lead into the ocean."

"Thanks."

"You know that won't be enough for them to trust you again, but I'll make sure they know you provided for them."

"Thanks," she repeated.

Lawdel lead her into the kitchen, and she sat down at the same table as Raziel. He was stuffing food into his mouth as if he hadn't eaten in days. She didn't know why. They had plenty to eat during their travel through the desert. She sat down and had a meal before deciding to take a trip to the market to replenish her throwing knives. She had a feeling she would need every one of them in the coming days.

She found a cloak to hide her from the prying eye of the guards. This time, she wouldn't have the distraction of Raziel to save her. She left, nodding to each of the guards as she did.

She walked the streets as the sun started to set. Even though daylight was fading, the market near the docks would be open for a few more hours. She had borrowed money from Lawdel to restock the knives she had lost along the way.

She pulled out the pendant Raziel had left on her when he had abandoned her all those years ago. She had forgotten to ask him about it while they were making their way across the desert. Not that he would remember much about it, anyway. He didn't even remember the woman's name who had birthed his daughter.

She studied the pendant in the waning light. It was blood red with swirls of lighter shades in it. She had noticed a few weeks ago that if she put it in direct sunlight; it seemed to suck the light in and grow darker, making it look like the swirls were moving. She had always thought her mother must have given it to her because she loved her, but according to Raziel, her mother had planned to make her into something evil.

She sighed and let the pendant drop to swing it in time with her steps. She didn't put it back in her shirt, letting it dangle. It was about time she showed it off. Besides, it would draw attention away from her face if someone noticed her.

A crowd blocked her entrance to the market. She pushed her way through but came up short when she noticed a structure which hadn't been there the last time she was in the city. Massive gallows towered over the crowd. Five nooses hung from a heavy wooden beam, three of them taught with the bodies which hung limp from them. She stood frozen in her tracks by the macabre sight. Sure, they had gallows before, but it hadn't been directly in the center of the city. If you wanted to go witness the hanging of a criminal, you would have to leave the city proper. Also, they had never left the bodies for more than a day. By the sight, and smell, of these three, they might soon fall from the decay.

On the far edge of gallows, two men stood. While on the other side, a town crier shouted about the latest unfortunate soul to feel the bite of the rope. The man condemned to die had his hands bound behind him and his head bowed, the noose already tight around his neck.

"...this man is charged with aiding the angels in their war!" The town crier shouted. "He has killed several city guards and officials and has been sentenced to hang by the neck until death. Brandon, do you have any final words?"

The man's head bolted up, tears, saliva, and mucus mingled on his face. "I didn't do nothin'!" He shouted in desperation. "I only stole an apple! Never killed no one! Please! Help me!"

Amara wanted to turn away, but she couldn't stop watching.

"Not the most dignified death, is it?" A man standing next to her spoke conspiratorially.

"This is awful." Amara felt tears welling up in her eyes.

"The worst part is, he probably didn't do any of the things they are charging him with." The man continued. "They've been doing these hangings weekly these days and they most likely have run out of the real criminals to hang. This poor fella was probably just a simple thief. Though in death, it would seem he's a coward as well."

"How can they do this? Why are they doing this?"

"Set an example most likely," the man shrugged. "Though you didn't hear that from me. I don't fancy being the next sad sap to take that short drop."

The man pushed past her and continued through the crowd toward the market. Amara felt as if she had to watch the end of this for the sake of the man. He was still blubbering on about how he didn't deserve death.

"I heard he beat his wife." She overheard a woman in the crowd say.

"Yeah, well, I heard he help massacre a small town in the name of Angels." The man spat on the ground. "Good riddance to him and any who fight the demons."

Amara turned her attention back to the puddle of a man and noticed a wet spot moved down his trousers. She hoped if she ever faced her death this way, she would have a bit more courage than him. The hooded executioner stood with his hand on one of five release levers, shaking his head as the condemned continued to beg for his life. Finally, the executioner had heard enough and pulled the lever.

The man shrieked and flailed, catching a foot on the platform. This one, unfortunate act slowed his descent enough that the fall couldn't do its work. Amara couldn't watch anymore and covered her ears to the sounds. Keeping her head down, she moved through the crowd. The sight and sounds she had heard forever burned into her memory. She moved down an alley, trying her best not to think of what had just happened. She finally got her breathing and shaking under control enough to leave the alley.

She entered the market and headed for a weapons vendor, trying to keep her mind busy, wiping moisture from her eyes every time the emotions threatened to overwhelm her. She bartered with him for a time and found some knives to match her current ones. The second vendor she bartered with didn't give her the same deal as the first. She didn't have enough money to buy the full complement.

His eye caught hold of the pendant, still swaying slightly. "I'll trade you the entire set for your pendant." He bartered.

She glanced down at it and lifted it up. What good had it done to her? Given to her by a father who didn't remember her and a mother who didn't care about her. Wouldn't it be better to trade it for something useful?

"I will buy the set of knives for her." A cloaked but distinctly feminine figure set a bag of gold coins on the table.

Amara put the pendant away quickly, hiding it from the newcomer.

"I would like the girl to decide." The merchant frowned. Clearly, he desired the pendant more than the gold he asked for.

"I won't trade the pendant." Amara decided, mostly because the man's actions meant it was worth much more than he was offering for it.

The merchant grumbled and swiped the bag of coins off the table, laying the knives out.

Amara collected them and turned to the woman. "Thank you. If you will follow me. I will get the coin to pay you back."

"No need," the woman replied. Her voice was as sweet as honey. "I like a strong woman who can defend herself. But could you answer me one question?"

"Of course, and thank you." Amara nodded and collected her knives, stowing them in her bag, not wanting to reveal the location of the rest of her hidden knives.

"Where did you get such a beautiful pendant?"

"My father gave it to me before he left me on the steps of a house when I was a baby." Amara explained. She didn't think telling the woman that bit would hurt anything.

The woman guided her out of the crowd, into the shelter of an awning. She lowered her voice conspiratorially. "Was your father the angel Raziel?"

The city of Caister was in sight. The lights of the city had reached their eyes long before they had arrived. They had doused all their own lights, not wanting to telegraph their location. Ariel assumed they could get into the city through the main gates, but now realized the error of his oversight. The city was under demon control, after all. They would be on the lookout for the escaped prisoners.

They had left the group on the other side of a dune, a mile out from the city. He and Ana had gone on ahead to scout a possible path in. They had to find a way in tonight or they would risk losing the horses to dehydration. They would need to sell them to get the money to sail to

Lanifair. If they could find a ship, willing to take them in the middle of a war.

Arial and Ana snuck around the wall. They had approached it from the south and thinking to find a way in from the sea. They had reached the wall but weren't even half the distance to the water when a man materialized out of the darkness. Hiding from an angel was an impressive feat. This man was a master of stealth.

Ariel drew Storm in battle ax form and Ana leveled Hope's spear point.

The man didn't react, nor did he appear worried. "I was sent to help you and your group into the city."

"Sent by who?" Ariel asked, not letting his guard down yet.

"Amara," the man replied. "She sends her apologies for her disloyalty and asks for your forgiveness. She also requested I lead you into the city as an act of good faith."

"We can't trust her." Ana gave Ariel a sidelong glance.

"What choice do we have?" Ariel asked, narrowing his eyes but not taking them off the man.

"We can find our own way in."

"Before daylight? And how do we manage smuggling the horses and cart in? We need them to fund our passage on a ship."

"I think this is a mistake." Ana relaxed her grip on Hope. "But I'll trust your judgement."

"Fine, what do you propose?" Ariel lowered his ax, addressing the man.

"Gather your people and meet me here. I will send my associates out to collect your cart and horses. I hear you might have wounded?" The man crossed his arms.

"Yes, three, unable to move on their own." Ariel told him.

"Can they be carried?"

Ariel turned to Ana and raised an eyebrow.

"Two are uninjured and can be carried without risk." Ana drew a curious look from the man, but she continued without explanation. "Can you send out a litter so we can carry the final one? I'm afraid his wound will open if he is handled too roughly."

The man nodded and melted into the shadows.

Ariel shook his head, and the glanced at Ana. "If more of these people are as stealthy as him, we need to be on guard for an attack."

Ana nodded once.

They made the long roundabout trek back to the group and informed them of what had transpired. Not long after, men dressed in merchant garb walked up to them. They carried water and a litter between them. Ariel was encouraged by Skie's lack of aggression toward the newcomers, as they handed out water to the group. They moved Daziar onto the litter carefully.

When they moved Serilda, a long sword, half wrapped in cloth, fell from the cart and Ariel's heart sunk. Oathbreaker landed in the sand. Serilda and Malach's path just got much harder. There was nothing he could do about it now, and he didn't want to say anything about it in front of the strangers in their midst. He carried Serilda as Ana hefted Malach's limp form and the others picked up the swords and supplies.

They all followed the mysterious man down in the same roundabout path Ariel and Ana had walked only a few hours before. Instead of leading them back to the wall, however, he continued toward the sea.

They passed under the shadow of a lighthouse who beacon was blazing. Luckily, its light was pointed out toward the sea and didn't illuminate the area around the lighthouse much. The man led them down a steep set of steps carved into the coastal cliff face. They gave way to the sandy beach where the water lapped gently against it. In any other circumstance, the scene would have been one he would have wanted to take Serilda to on a romantic evening out. As it was, he was carrying her much too light, limp form, turning the scene at hand into something surreal and forlorn.

They moved along the beach, keeping to the shadow of the cliff side and heading toward the city. Just before they reached the walls, the man turned and disappeared into the side of the cliff. Ariel assumed there was a cave the man had moved into, but it was bizarre to watch him walk into what appeared to be solid rock.

Ariel found the cave the man had walked into. It had a trickle of rancid smelling liquid slowly running down toward the ocean. That couldn't be good for the environment.

The smell only got worse the farther in they traveled. They approached a grating with large, heavy metal bars. It allowed the waste to move through it but wouldn't admit even the smallest person in their group. The man produced a key from his cloak and inserted it into a lock. He pushed the bar, and the door glided open on oiled hinges. They must use this path to smuggle things into the city often. The tunnel they entered was less than ideal. Sludge slowly pushed its way down toward the opening while the foul-smelling liquid flowed much faster on either side of it. The amorphous nature of the more solid waste caused the liquid to splash and splatter against the lower half of the tunnel. Their legs were soon soaked through and Ariel, though he had been in worse, wanted nothing more than a bath. He would have to burn the pants he currently wore. There was no cleaning them now.

There were more gratings they traversed on their journey, but soon, they stopped at a ladder. It would be a challenge to get Daziar, Malach, and Serilda out without farther injury. Arjun climbed up the ladder to confirm there was no one around the exit.

The man got Ariel's attention.

"Go south to the poor district. There, ask for Jorah, she will take care of your injured. My men will meet you there in the morning with your horses and cart."

"Thank you for your kindness." Ariel nodded at the man, since his arms were full.

"I will pass your thanks to Amara," the man replied.

"Tell Amara I have forgiven her for what she has done. I can't promise everyone else in our party has, but I wish her the best."

The man sighed. "I think there is a lot more hardship to come for us."

He didn't elaborate on his words, however, and Ariel didn't press him. "Good luck and may God be with you and yours."

The man backed into the shadows and all but disappeared. Ariel could just make out the slightest silhouette as he stole away from the group.

Just as the man had instructed, they made their way to the poor district. The houses were run down and Ariel felt eyes watching them from behind cracked shutters. He expected someone to try to take advantage of them with their wounded, but none did. It probably helped that Ana hadn't hidden her wings. However, they would have to leave quickly before someone told the authorities.

An old lady stepped out from behind a door and motioned for them to get inside.

"Jorah?" Ariel whispered.

She nodded and motioned more insistently.

They all filed in quickly.

Once they were inside, she shut the door behind them. "For hell's sake, girl, hide those wings before they get you killed. And what's that smell?"

Ariel barely contained his mirth at Ana being called a girl, despite the grim situation they were in. And surprisingly, Jorah took Skie in stride, barely giving her a second glance.

The room was lit with a single candle set atop a small square table, allowing the shadows to dance along the walls. It was sparsely furnished with only one bed, one chair, and the table the candle sat on. Against the far wall was a set of bookshelves which had only a few items sitting on them. Ariel wondered how they were going to all fit and still have room to tend the wounded.

Jorah answered his question before he could even voice it. She pushed the bookshelf aside, and it glided on hidden tracks to reveal a spiral staircase. "Please, get down the stairs quickly."

They moved to do as she bade. She followed, sliding the shelf back in place behind them. Ariel ducked through a low doorway but was able to stand to his full height once inside the room. It was sparsely lit but compared to the light of the previous room; it was as bright as day.

Joran motioned for them to lay the wounded on three of the six beds lining the walls. She moved to a set of shelve which were in stark contrast to the one upstairs. These were packed with all manner of herbs and plants. Ariel eyed her suspiciously. Not all the plants on her shelves were for healing, more than a few were poisonous. She started crushing and mixing things into a bowl. None of the ingredient she used gave Ariel any pause, but he had to turn away to set Serilda down on one bed.

Jorah walked over to Daziar and unwrapped the bandages on his shoulder. "Who wrapped this?"

Honora stepped forward. "I did, after she sewed it up." Honora motioned to Ana.

"Good. Was it kept clean?" She asked.

"As best as we could manage in the desert." Ana replied.

Jorah grunted, then said, "This poultice will pull out anything that might have gotten in the wound and help him heal. Do you know if there was any internal damage?"

"No," Ana shook her head. "I didn't have the equipment or the environment to go digging around in his shoulder."

Jorah nodded slowly. "Probably a good thing you didn't try. I won't open him back up to dig around in there. Not much I could do, even if I could find something. It looks like it's healing nicely, though. Now I see an old injury on the other boy but it's all but healed. What is wrong with him?"

Ariel took over the answers before Ana or Honora could speak. He wanted to control the information given to the healer. "They are unconscious. As I understand, there isn't anything we can do to wake them up. However, is there anything you can do to help keep them alive longer?"

Jorah narrowed her eyes at Ariel, but turned and studied the two, shaking her head slowly. "How did they end up in this state? Maybe if I know more about it, I can help treat it."

"It's something to do with the mind, not the body,"

"Are they able to drink anything?" She turned to Honora and Ana.

Ariel nodded as they looked at him, giving them permission to answer her question.

"We've been able to have them drink a little water," Ana spoke for them. "Their basic functions, like swallowing, seem to work well enough. We've been careful, so as not to choke them but haven't had a problem."

"Good. I might add certain herbs to help give their body's nutrients." Jorah's face screwed up as if she was thinking hard. She walked over to her shelves, slowly picked and pulled things off them. "If any of you need rest, use the beds. Just make sure you stay out of my way."

"Yes Ma'am," Ariel replied. He moved to the corner next to the doorway and sat cross-legged. He would be out of the way, but could observe the entire room. Ana moved down the row of bed and assumed a similar position as he had on the floor. Others took their chance to sleep, moving to the beds. Honora followed Jorah around, asking her questions about what herbs she was using, what would help, and why. Ariel hoped she would pick up some excellent knowledge from the old healer. She was going to need it all, and more, soon.

Jorah was gruff on the outside, but she didn't seem to mind Honora's endless questions. He decided to meditate and give his body some rest. The last several sleepless nights had taken its toll. He didn't give himself the luxury of being unconscious, however. Someone needed to stay vigilant in case they were double-crossed or found. Ana hadn't gone into sleep either, opting for a deep meditation which would keep her mind and body ready to spring into action should the need arise. He closed his eyes and cleared his mind.

Ana took her chance to reach out to Daziar's mind. She had left him last time working through forms with his new weapon. If she had a chance, she would procure a sickle sword for him to use as soon as he was physically able. She also wanted to take this time to inform him of their journey so far.

Ana's mental probe hit a stone wall. She smiled to herself. He was getting much better at defending his mind.

She set to work, testing his defenses, pushing and pulling, looking for any weakness in his wall. To her shock, she couldn't find one. He had put up a complete defense and wouldn't be swayed. Until this point, she easily skirted around his attempts, much like a thief when there was an unlocked door. Now she would have to tear it down.

Hope entered her mind. "He's a swift study."

"Yes, but he won't have the power to stop me." She grinned, self-assured.

"Do you want my help?"

A battering ram appeared beside them, a construct of her will. "No, I'll make quick work of this."

She didn't.

Sweat poured down Ana's brow, stinging her eyes. She realized the sweat wasn't just in the mental world but in the real one as well. She had been at it for a long time. Hope sat on a small patch of grass he had constructed, leaning up against a tree reading some book or another, not paying any attention to her struggles.

"Do you want help now?" He asked, turning the page to his book.

Ana growled.

"Well, either admit defeat or accept help. The boy has bested you and by now he knows it." He turned the page again. "You're only embarrassing yourself."

Ana growled again and slammed the battering ram one last time against the wall. She took a deep breath and let the anger leave her. "I guess this is what I was teaching him, and he has learned well."

"And remember, it's easier to keep someone out than to break in." Hope closed his book with a snap and it disappeared.

"I don't need your pity."

"I was simply pointing out-" Hope stopped mid-sentence, studying the wall.

A door materialized and opened. "You knocked?" Daziar beamed.

"Stop gloating," Ana scolded, crossing her arms. "Next time I will have Hope help me."

"Bring it on,"

"Oh, dear," Hope shook his head and stood. "You two were made for each other." He brushed past Daziar without another word.

Ana followed.

They walked into the training arena Daziar had constructed. Ana asked him to move through his fighting stances. She adjusted a few of his movements along the way, but he was coming along nicely.

After they finished, Ana quickly updated him on the events of the real world.

"Traitor," Daziar spat after hearing Amara had helped them again. "Malach should have let her be executed after I turned her in."

"How could you say that?" Ana furrowed her brow. "She has helped him so much along the way. She was trapped in what appeared to be an impossible situation and made a choice. Even though we believe it was the wrong choice, we couldn't have known what would happen. You are trying to justify your wrong actions from the past using someone else's wrong actions for proof. Two wrongs don't make things right."

Daziar took a deep breath and let it out slowly.

Ana recognized it as an action to calm himself down. It was something she had done a lot over the decades.

"You're right," Daziar nodded, pursing his lips. "That wasn't fair of me to say. I have no idea what would have happened if Malach and Elzrod hadn't saved her."

His admission almost floored her. He had admitted he was wrong. "Who are you and what have you done with Daziar?"

He grinned. "I've replaced him with an improved version, one humbled by a wise teacher."

"Good, but let me know when this wise teacher is around. I'd like to thank her." Ana punched him in the arm lightly. "Let's get to training."

Chapter 6

Malach and Reckoning sped through the dark city streets of Ragewood. Serilda had sent them here when Oathbreaker had found them in her last memory. Malach and Reckoning were now chasing his mother. Or, more accurately, a memory of his mother. They ran through the street while she raced along the rooftops at a blinding speed. His mother, Ciarán, was fast to the point of recklessness. Reckoning watched for the door while Malach kept track of his mother. She was on a mission. Most likely to assassinate someone. He understood the choice his mother had to make all those years ago. To kill the unarmed prisoner. Azazel had used it to push her farther into darkness. However, Malach hadn't expected his mother to embrace that darkness.

Finally, mercifully, she slowed. Ciarán stopped at the edge of an inn's roof to survey the area and then swung down with the grace of an acrobat. She landed softly on a windowsill on the second floor, pushing on the roof overhang to steady herself. Slipping a knife into the window, she opened it without a sound.

The surrounding scene changed, and they launched into darkness. Malach's eyes adjusted. He could make out the shape of Ciarán and the furniture in the room. There was a bed in the center with a sleeping form in it. Ciarán walked up to the form and, without hesitation, expertly slid a knife into the person's back and up underneath the ribs. It was a skilled move and only one used by an assassin because of the chance of failure. The man didn't jerk, gasp, seize, or even moved a muscle. A shadow moved behind Ciarán and Malach, all but jumped out of his skin.

The man pressed a knife against Ciarán's back. "Don't move. Disarm, slowly."

Ciarán gingerly pulled her knives out of their sheaths and dropped them on the floor.

"And your boot knife."

She leaned down and pulled a small knife out of her boot and dropped that on the floor.

"Now, we are going to have a nice chat about who sent you and what you know." The man maneuvered Ciarán over to a chair and sat her down. He backed up a step and the dim light filtering in through the window hit his back. Black feathery wings lay flat against the angel's back. Another step back and his father's face was illuminated.

"Nothin'." Ciarán crossed her arms like a pouting child.

"Then why are you in my room trying to kill me?"

"I's gonna steal all your money."

Malach cringed at her overly heavy accent and slang. She hadn't had the accent in the last memory. What happened?

"Nice try, but you are too skilled and too eager to kill me for your ploy to work. A thief might have tried to kill me, but they would have gone for my throat, not my heart. You, my dear, are an assassin. Which brings me back to my original questions. Who sent you?" Ariel held up one finger. "How much do you know?" He held up a second finger.

"Don't know what you're talkin' bout." Ciarán jutted out her chin in defiance.

"Fine, this is how it will go, then. I can't let you go and I don't want to kill you. So, you will travel with me back to Angel territory and be imprisoned for the remainder of this war or your life, whichever ends first." Ariel opened his wings suddenly, an impressive sight, to be sure.

Ciarán didn't move, didn't react, just stared back at Ariel.

"You've seen angels before? and you knew I was an angel before you arrived." Ariel nodded; his suspicion confirmed. "Did Azazel send you?"

Ciarán's eyes widen ever so slightly, betraying the information without ever saying a word.

"How did he know I was here?"

Nothing from Ciarán.

Ariel turned around and picked up a pack in the corner of the room.

Ciarán bolted for the window.

Ariel turned, dropping into a defensive stance. However, instead of attacking him, she sailed out the window, headfirst. Ariel ran to the window, so did Malach, and they peered out to see if Ciarán had survived her fall.

They both dodged as one, though Malach didn't have to, as a small knife cut the air where Ariel's head had been. Ariel watched Ciarán run down the street and when she turned down an alley, the scene changed.

Once again, Malach and Reckoning were running, keeping pace with Ciarán's headlong sprint. Mostly, because it was less jarring than the jumps in scene as her perspective changed. She barreled around corner after corner, trying to lose the pursuer she assumed was following her. Only he wasn't. Finally, she stopped and ducked behind a crate in an alleyway. She slowed her breathing quickly, listening.

"You failed me, Ciarán."

The voice made her jump, and Malach's blood ran cold.

Azazel stood in the alleyway on Ciarán's side of the crate.

"Lord Azazel," Ciarán bowed quickly. "He was an angel. He knew I was coming long before I entered his room. I barely escaped."

"Excuses," Azazel spat. "Come, you will be punished for this."

"Please, not my baby."

Baby? Malach's jaw dropped, and eyes widen.

"Your baby?" Azazel laughed, soft but maniacal. "Don't you mean our baby?"

"Please, don't harm him." She moved to Azazel, groveling at his feet. "I'll do anything."

"It's too late for that." He reached down and picked her up by her throat. "You should have killed the angel or died trying."

The scene dimmed around them as if someone was covering the only torch in the room.

"Ciarán is losing consciousness," Reckoning explained, reading Malach's confusion.

The scene faded to black.

The next thing they saw was Ciarán laying in a bed, curled in a ball. Tears streamed down her face. She had been crying for a while. She was broken. Broken beyond anything Malach had experienced.

"He killed my baby boy," Serilda walked up behind Malach.

He turned to see a mirror image of the one laying in the bed, only older. The pain was just as evident, just as real. Fresh tears of a wound reopened. Malach could feel a portion of her pain radiating through his mind, sharing the emotion.

"That was my punishment for failure."

"Mom, I....I'm...sorry." Malach didn't know what to say.

Serilda shook her head. "That was a long time ago. I've imprisoned Oathbreaker for now and I know where the door is located."

"Then we need to hurry," Reckoning spoke up.

Serilda took hold of Malach and Reckoning and the scene once again changed. The northern mountains rose up around them, familiar to Malach. They were in the woods around Brightwood. A version of Serilda in the not far distance past walked through the woods following one of the game paths Malach used to hunt with his father. They followed her through the woods, walking single file.

Malach couldn't shake the thoughts of his brother. His dead brother. He knew his mother had lived a much longer life than most due to her being one of the first Blade-Bearers. Because of that fact alone, he wouldn't have been able to meet his brother, even if he had lived to a ripe old age of eight hundred. However, knowing Azazel took his brother before he even had a chance at life made him furious. He would kill Azazel for this.

"Serilda," Reckoning moved past Malach. "Where is the door?"

"In this memory." Serilda held up a hand to calm him. "Oathbreaker stopped me from jumping to the exact moment, so we are going to have to move through the memory in normal time."

Malach spotted a shadow moving through the trees in front of the Serilda of the memory. He almost called out to warn her, but remembered she wouldn't be able to hear him. Azazel moved out of the trees in front of her, and she drew a knife. The same knife, in fact, that he gave her to kill the prisoner.

He chuckled at her response. "Where is your blade, Ciarán?"

"I bet you already know," Serilda replied. "Give Fang and Reckoning back and I might spare your life."

"You have a son," Azazel ignored her last command.

"Don't you dare touch him!"

"I won't," He smirked. "If you and Ariel surrender to me as my prisoners."

"No, I'll kill you before I give into anything you want," Serilda shouted. "And I will not let you kill another child of mine."

"I will be back in three days' time with an army of demons. You know I can. You and Ariel will surrender to me or I will kill young Malach." Azazel spread his wings and took to the sky, angling away from Brightwood.

Serilda in the memory collapsed to her knees, her hands trembling. She took a few moments to bring her body back under her own control.

Once she had, she stood and sprinted back toward the cottage.

"Who's Raziel?" Amara asked, unfortunately not before the shocked expression on her face gave away what she truly knew.

"I'm your mother," the woman beamed, eyes tearing up. "I've been looking everywhere for you! Ever since that angel stole you from me."

"W-What?" Amara took a step back.

"Please come with me and I will tell you everything!" The woman couldn't stop smiling. "I've finally found you!"

Amara didn't know what to think. This woman claimed to be her mother and also knew about Raziel. Alarm bells rang in Amara's head and she became wary and suspicious.

"How did you know who I was in the market? And what makes you think I'm your daughter?"

"Amara, I've been searching for you for seventeen years. I've searched everywhere, cobbled together information from all the cities in demon territory, and a few in Angel Territory. I recently found a contact in the Shadows who told me of you. The baby who was left on the streets and raised by Lawdel. The time frame fit, and I sought you out."

"Raziel says you're a witch." Amara squinted at the woman as if that would allow her to see through any ruse.

"I was with the demons until Azazel double crossed me. I... well, I did some pretty terrible things back then."

"How can I trust anything you tell me?" Amara narrowed her eyes. "I don't even know your name. I have no proof you're my mother and I have no proof you're anything different from what Raziel says you are."

"I'm so sorry Amara. My name is Lilith. I know you have no reason to trust me, but I'm not asking you to. I'm just asking for a chance to get to know you." Lilith's face creased with concern and worry.

Amara wanted this to be true. She wanted her mother to come looking for her all her life. to sweep her away from the street life and to love and care for her. Lilith's story lined up. She knew about Raziel. She had been with the demons at the time, and she would have had no idea where Raziel would have taken her. But she was with the demons, presumably for many years. To show up now, on the precipice of war? She had no idea if she could trust the woman or what she said.

"I...well, I can't give you much time. I will be on my way to Newaught in two days." Amara didn't want to tip her off to the Shadows' movements, but as long as she kept the details to herself, she wouldn't put anyone at risk, right?

"I was headed there myself in a week's time." Lilith beamed. "I would love to travel with you and have a chance to get to know you. I can move up my timeline if you could wait for a day or two longer."

"I don't know. I'm traveling with a group." Amara turned away, unsure of what to say.

"Go talk to your people and if they are willing, I would travel with you. If not, let's meet at Newaught. Please, you're my only daughter and I want to reconnect with you."

"Alright, would it be ok if I met you here tomorrow, midday?"

"Yes! Thank you so much, Amara. You don't know how much this means to me." Lilith started walking away, turning to beam at Amara once again. "I will see you tomorrow. I'm so excited to get to know you."

Amara still didn't know what to make of Lilith. Was she her actual mother? She needed to run the name by Raziel and find out what he knew. Or, more accurately, what he wrote in his strange symbols. Then, if Lilith was her mother, what about the things she had done while in the demon army? She believed people could change, but it didn't happen overnight. Could Lilith be lying to her about her change? If so, why? These and many other questions swirled in her head as she walked back to the Shadow's lair. She checked around her by habit before entering the sewers, but she was so deep in her own thoughts, she wouldn't have noticed anyone watching her.

She walked past the guards, nodding to each of their hiding spots and continuing on without a word. Lawdel was carrying a heavy box to the stack in the main chamber. They must have moved a load out to the warehouse while she was gone. The stack was lower than when she had left.

Raziel walked out of the tunnel Lawdel had come from carrying a much larger crate with little effort.

"Amara!" Lawdel noticed her for the first time. "Having an angel around is quite handy. Wish we had ten more of him. We would have this move finished tonight."

"I'm glad he's helpful. It's about time. Although, I need to borrow him." She pointed at Raziel as he sat down on the large crate.

"Just bring him back when you're done." Lawdel shrugged. "At this rate, we could leave a day early."

Amara grinned at Lawdel's excitement. "Of course, I will send him back here to help when we are done talking." She turned to Raziel. "Raziel, could I talk with you for a minute? We will need your book of memories."

Raziel blinked at her for a few seconds with a vague, far away expression.

"It's on the table in the meeting room," Lawdel walked away from the two.

"Thanks," she called after him.

She steered Raziel toward the room. They found the book where Lawdel said it would be. She picked it up and handed it to Raziel.

"Oh! We think these are our memories." Raziel took the book from her, eyes wide with excitement.

She rolled hers at him. "What do your memories say about Lilith?"

He snapped his head up at the mention of the name and...smiled? "Lilith is such a pleasant woman."

"What?" Amara's jaw just about hit the floor. She couldn't believe what she was hearing. This woman, who claimed to be her mother, was supposed to be this horrible witch of a woman, and now that she said her name, Raziel's whole demeanor changed. "You said she was a witch."

"No, we said your mother was a witch." Raziel held up a knowing finger. "Lilith is wonderful."

"Lilith is claiming to be my mother,"

"Oh yes, she is!" Raziel nodded, as if all the things he was saying made complete sense.

"So you are saying that the witch is my mother and Lilith is my mother?"

"Oh yes, now you understand." He smiled at her again. Then his smile disappeared, reappeared, and disappeared again. "Lilith was nice to us over the years. Coming and giving us food and talking with us for hours. The Witch was horrible; hateful, painful, and always brought the demon with her. *They* are your mother."

Amara shook her head, trying to figure out how the two women could both be her mother. Or was Raziel just so crazy he had confused the two women and, in his mind, they were the same person? No, that didn't make sense either. "Ugh. " She rubbed her eyes, her head aching. Then it dawned on her. "You said the witch always came to you with a demon, right?"

Raziel nodded, frowning. "I knew when she came with the demon, it would hurt."

"But when Lilith came, she was never with a demon, correct?"

"Oh no, never." He shook his head, smiling fondly. "We enjoyed those times."

"So," she couldn't believe she was about to ask this. "Which of them came to you when you know I was conceived?"

"The witch. The demon told her to and was present for it."

Amara shivered, fighting the urge to throw up. "Then Lilith is not my mother."

"No, she is."

"Augh," Amara turned away from him. This was maddening. How could both women be her mother? A thought hit her. "Are Lilith and the Witch the same person?"

Raziel's brow furrowed. "Their very different."

"Their actions are different. Other than how they acted, was anything else different? Did they look different, talk different, or have different mannerisms?"

Raziel sat down and opened his book of memories. Amara would have to wait for her question to be answered. Her current theory was that Lilith and the witch were the same person. Raziel only saw them as two different people, since they treated him differently. The only difference would then be the demon. It would match with Lilith's story. She would have been biding her time until she could leave. The demon must have forced her to do those things to Raziel. The only other thing she could think of was Lilith had an identical sister. She would ask Lilith tomorrow to find out.

A few long minutes later, Raziel looked up from his book. "No,"

"No, what?" Amara pushed.

"Hmm?" Raziel asked.

"You said 'no'. What do you mean?"

"Oh, no other difference between Lilith and The Witch." He nodded once as if he was right and just proved it.

Amara doubted he even knew what he thought he was right about. Her last proof would be Lilith's own story. If it matched up with Raziel's, then she would know she could trust her. Then she would finally know her mother. She sat down hard in the chair across from Raziel, the weight of the realization buckling her knees.

"Thank you Raziel," Amara mumbled, mind numb. "Please return to Lawdel and continue to help with the move. You can leave your book here."

"Ok, we will do that." Raziel set his book down and walked out of the room.

Oh, to be that naive. Amara wished, in some ways, she could be like that. Not have a care in the world, nothing phasing her, and nothing weighing her down. Obviously, she wouldn't want to go through what he had, but in some ways, she envied him.

There wasn't anything she could do about it until tomorrow, when she met Lilith again. She stood and headed to the main room. There was work to do and she would help. Hopefully, it would help take her mind off things.

Ariel awoke suddenly. He hadn't realized he had fallen asleep. Daziar sat up in his bed, back resting against the wall with a pillow cushioning him. He was trying to drink water and eat food simultaneously.

"Don't eat so fast, boy," Jorah scolded, trying to slow him down. "You'll throw up if you keep up that pace."

Daziar slowed down a bit, but the look on Jorah's face told him she wasn't satisfied.

Ana sat against the wall, smiling in Daziar's direction. Ariel had seen that look several times in the past, including when Serilda looked at *him*. He didn't know how Daziar had captured her heart, but he wasn't overly surprised. They had been spending a lot of time with each other over the last few weeks. Even though she hadn't told him, he knew she had been training Daziar while he was unconscious. It didn't bother him. In fact, he thought it was a good idea.

She caught his gaze and turned away from him quickly, her cheeks growing a slight shade of pink.

Ariel grinned.

Most of the group had left to sell the Horses and cart and buy supplies. Ana had requested a sickle sword for Daziar and Ariel had agreed to it. Daziar's sword would need replaced if he was going to be of any use to them. Ariel had taken the time to add a few weapons to outfit their party. They would have to fight their way back to the angel's stronghold. He hoped they would have enough money to pay for passage on a ship. Once at Lanifair Harbor, if Gabriel still held the port city, they would be able to acquire horses from the angel army.

He stood and stretched, reflexively trying to stretch his wings, which were no longer there. He walked over to check on Serilda and Malach. Serilda looked better. With the medicine Jorah was giving her, she might last a few more days. Malach was starting to look gaunt, and the color had returned to his face. Perhaps they would get out of this alive after all.

Jorah poked Daziar's finger with a needle, watching for any reaction from him.

"I still can't feel my fingers," Daziar answered her unasked question.

Jorah frowned. "You might never feel them again. It's hard to say." Jorah let go of his hand and it fell limp to the bed. "I've seen this type of injury make a full recovery and I have seen people never get feeling back in any part of their arm. Only time will tell. Until then, you might want to tie your arm down until you get used to using it without any feeling. Be careful of your stitches. You may not know if you rip them if you have no feeling there."

"Oh, I can feel *them*." Daziar smiled ruefully. "The place with the most pain is, of course, the one thing I can feel."

"I will get you an herb blend for the pain. Make it into tea and drink it when the pain gets unbearable." She handed him a large bag of herbs. "They're pre-measured into little bags. You can simply drop one into hot water and wait a few minutes before drinking it."

Daziar nodded.

Jorah turned to Ariel, and he got to his feet. "The other two are stable, but the woman won't last more than another day or two. Her body is already failing her. Even if she wakes up now, she may not survive. The boy is healthy, however. If I knew more about their condition, I might be able to do more."

Ariel rubbed his face and sighed, fighting back the feeling of helplessness threatening to consume him. "I'm afraid I can't divulge that information, nor would it give you any new option to care for them."

Ariel! We're back. Reckoning's voice sounded in his head. He was still carrying the blade as the small needle Malach had turned him into, to conceal him from the demons.

Malach gasped and sat up straight in bed as if waking from a bad dream. He moaned, which was more of a croak, and immediately laid back down, holding his head. Ariel moved quickly to his side.

Reckoning what happened? Ariel demanded. Jorah moved to Malach, pushing Ariel out of the way.

Ariel turned to look at Serilda. No change.

We were attacked by Oathbreaker and Serilda willed Malach and me through the door.

You found the door without Oathbreaker's help?

Yes, and no.

Tell me what happened.

I promise I will tell you everything, but right now Serilda is fighting Oathbreaker. She could use any moral support we can give her.

"Jorah," Ariel turned to her. "Serilda may wake any moment. We need to be ready to keep her alive if she does."

Jorah raised a brow at him as if to ask how he knew, but she didn't question him. Instead, she turned to Ana. "You, angel girl," she barked. "Tend to the boy."

Ana frowned but did as she was bidden.

Jorah moved to her herb shelves and starting pulling and mixing things together. Ariel didn't watch her. Instead, he moved to his wife's side and took her small, fragile hand in his. "Come on darling, fight this, fight her."

Serilda's eyes opened slowly, and she looked at him. He almost didn't believe his own eyes.

She was out.

She was alive.

She coughed violently.

Jorah appeared on the other side, lifting her head and putting a cup to her lips. It was a second before Serilda was able to drink a few sips. Her cough lessened significantly.

She turned to Ariel and smiled. "It's good to see you again, my love." She coughed again, but waved off Jorah. "It won't do any good. I'm past the point of recovery."

"Don't say that." Ariel squeezed her hand gently, tears forming in his eyes. "You're strong. You can recover from this."

"You and I both know I won't recover from this." She smiled at him. "I'm old Ariel. The blessing of the Blade Bearer has slowed my aging process, but I'm at the end of my life. You need to let me go."

"No!" Malach stood shakingly, pushing off help from Ana. "You can't die. We did all this to rescue you."

"Malach," Serilda's head lulled to the side so she could see him. "I love you two so much. Thank you for everything you've done, but I'm not long for this world."

"Darling..." Ariel's voice trailed off, thick with grief.

"My angel," she smiled at Ariel again. "You were the best thing that ever happened to me. You saved me, pulled me from the depths, and showed me how to live." She turned again to Malach. "My baby boy, I wish we had more time together. I wish I could have watched you grow into the warrior you are. The man you are."

"Mom, no." Tears flowed freely from Malach's eyes.

Ariel wiped his own away. "Serilda, I promise I will look after him."

"I know." She lifted her hand out of his and caressed his cheek. Her face turned serious. "Azazel and Lilith know where Satan is being held. They are looking for a key. You need to find it first."

"Where is he being held? Where do we look for the key?" Ariel asked.

"Return to Michael. He will know where the prison is and where to start looking for the key. Malach, you are strong. You have a role to play in the war. Don't give up hope when I'm gone. If the angels don't win, then all we have done is for nothing. And Malach, live your life to the fullest, love dangerously, and let no one dictate your actions."

"Mom, don't leave me again." Malach sobbed.

"You're strong. You will make it through this. And when you come to the end of your long life, I will be waiting to welcome you into heaven."

"Mom, no..."

Her hand slipped from both his and Ariel's and she closed her eye. "I love you both. Goodbye..."

Malach let out a wail that tore at Ariel's heart. The pain his son was feeling was almost as terrible as the pain of losing his wife, his best friend, his greatest ally. He dropped his head into his hands and wept.

Chapter 7

Kragen sat in his hidden room. He had found it while setting the explosives and made it his for the time being. It was well out of the way in the depth of the angel's stronghold. His nearly seven-foot frame barely fit when he laid down in the small square room, but it was enough. He ran a hand through his jet-black hair. He hated this part of his missions. The waiting. The boredom. There wasn't much to do until they gave him the signal. When his master appeared with the rest of the army.

He had caught glimpses of the mountains, and the snow was melting along the lowest regions. No doubt the lowlands were already clear, and the army had moved to Fairdenn. It would be a few more weeks before the passes would be traversable.

The angel army was already moving people behind the walls of the stronghold to prepare for their enemy's arrival. Little did they know, they wouldn't be safe inside, either. As they moved people into the stronghold, they had sent those not fit to fight down into the lower rooms. However, the room he was in seemed forgotten about. It was at the end of the lowest hall, halfway hidden by a wall hanging. It might have at one time been a storage room, but had long been out of use.

At first, the room had only been a place to rest and eat in seclusion, but now he spent most of his time here. He ventured out to check on the explosives he had set covering different sections of the stronghold each day, adjusting them if he needed. The rest of his day was spent sleeping or moving through his fighting stances to stay in shape and practice for when the battle started. His Zweihänder was too long to swing, but he could drift through the forms. In a way, the slow movements were a better workout than moving through them at full speed.

He would be ready. The refugees would be the first he would kill. Not because they were any threat to him. No, they would be no challenge. The reason he would kill them was their constant noise. At all times of the day and night, they were talking, coughing, laughing, shouting, and keeping him awake. He hated them with a passion. Plus, he had to shoulder through their numbers everyday rubbing against their stinking, smelly bodies. Most of them were walking corpses, anyway. Bodies, not healthy enough to be of any use, just waiting to die. Well, he would bury them. The rooms that they lived in would also be their tombs. Only after he had sated his blood lust on them first. He would get his pleasure before burying the rest alive in these accursed halls.

It wouldn't be long now. He could all but feel the Lords, Lucifer and Satan, growing stronger. They would be found and liberated from their imprisonment soon. Then they would defeat the Angel army and setup their kingdom where he would have his reward.

"Fury!" Oathbreaker shouted.

"I'm here." Fury walked out of the darkness.

"Why have we not been rescued?" Oathbreaker fumed, pacing back and forth in front of Fury.

"The oaf of a demon got himself killed shortly after you entered Serilda's mind." He clasped his hands behind his back calmly. "There doesn't seem to be any demons left in Caister. Although, I felt Leviathan well out in the depths. I believe they intend to take a ship to Lanifair Harbor. We should be able to contact her when we are out in open waters. What happened in Serilda's mind?"

"The little excrement of a son, and his pet, helped her escape out of the purgatory I put her in."

"I didn't think that was possible."

"It shouldn't have been," Oathbreaker ground her teeter together.

"How did they do it?"

"I moved the door," Oathbreaker said under her breath, as if she was just realizing her own mistake.

"You what?"

"I moved the accursed door!" Oathbreaker shouted.

"You moved it?" Fury raised an eyebrow at her. "Why? I thought you said she couldn't get to it."

"I don't think she could have, but with help, I didn't know that for sure. Instead, I moved it so they wouldn't be able to reach it. I underestimated Serilda's continued will, and she read my mind. They found where I hide the door. But I still killed Serilda."

"That wasn't the plan,"

"I know that!" Oathbreaker turned on him.

Fury didn't flinch at her ranger. They were on neutral ground. There was nothing Oathbreaker could do to hurt him here.

"Then why did you change your full-proof plan for one that was less effective?"

"I made a mistake!" She roared. "Don't you think I know I botched this?"

Fury smiled. "Yes, but I wanted to make sure *you* knew."

"If I could, I would tear you to pieces right here!"

"But you can't and we both know it."

"I hate you. When we are out of this, you'll pay."

"*I* think, when we're out of this, you'll be humiliated. The demons will no longer hold you in such high regard. Azazel might even take a new blade. He might even be taking a new blade as we speak."

"ARGH!" Oathbreaker raged at him, objects appearing in their mind's eye for her to toss around. To Fury, she appeared to be a little girl throwing a temper-tantrum after her parents told her she couldn't go out and play. It was almost comical.

Fury would have to be careful when they were back with the demon army. Despite her most recent failures, Oathbreaker had a lot of power and sway, and he had just enraged her. He would need to play his hand carefully when they arrived. Playing up her failures and his successes. However, he might, just might, be able to seize enough of her power to climb the ladder a bit.

"When I am back in contact with Azazel, you will pay. I will send you to a small little dungeon and leave you there for a few millennia. And when you go insane, I will have them chip away at you for the next few millennia. Then, when you are a small, pathetic shell of what you once were, I will have you broken. And then throw you away for the rust to take you!"

"We will see soon enough." Fury shrugged. "But know this: your threats will become one of our realities in the end."

"Yes, you will see, as soon as they find a ship to sail them to Lanifair Harbor," Oathbreaker cut the connection between them.

Fury smiled. He had done enough damage for now. Contrary to what he told Oathbreaker, he had already connected with Leviathan. She had reached out to him and he told her about Oathbreaker's failures. That information would precede their arrival, paving the way for his rise through the ranks. With any luck, Azazel would choose him to be his traitor blade. One thing nagged at the back of his mind. Leviathan had been silent. Even though she made the connection, she hadn't said a word, only listened.

Lilith was waiting for her in the alley they had agreed on the day before. Amara didn't trust her even after talking with Raziel. Her theory was Lilith might have been put into a situation where she fell in with the demons either by accident or by force. Similar to her own experience. Or maybe she had changed somewhere along the way and escaped. Either way, it explained her two-faced appearance, which caused Raziel's confusion. The question was how to get that information out of her without tipping her hand.

"Good morning, Amara! Thank you for trusting me enough to meet me again. No doubt you talked with Raziel and he has told you a lot of bad things about me. I would like time to explain before you make your judgement." The words spilled from Lilith's mouth, obviously having been thought through and rehearsed repeatedly.

It made Amara feel better, knowing Lilith was just as nervous as she was. Amara simply nodded. Letting Lilith talk might just be the best thing she could do. She would get her side of the story without ever having to ask a question or give away any information.

"Then I will start at the beginning," Lilith replied. "I was the first woman to walk this earth."

Amara jaw dropped and she look at the woman who was her mother in wide-eyed wonder.

"Yes, I do mean the first woman. But I rebelled against my husband. Who was right and who was wrong doesn't matter now, but God cursed me for my rebellion. Never to have a child with a human being and to wander for eternity. Some would consider immortality a blessing, but it has only led to pain. So I turned to the demons to get my revenge on those who I thought had wronged me. Raziel changed that. I met Raziel when he was captured by Azazel. Azazel tasked me with his torture and information retrieval, and my heart broke. I realized the cost of my revenge and was not willing to pay it anymore. But I couldn't let Azazel or the others know until I was ready to get away with Raziel."

It was all making sense now. Lilith wasn't a perfect person, but who was? The important part is she had changed.

"I bid my time, waiting for the right moment to leave. Raziel seemed to understand and played his part well during the times I was forced to act against him. During this time, I conceived you with Raziel. I didn't know I could be pregnant. In fact, it was quite the shock when I realized it. The only thing I can think of is he is an angel, not a man. I guess he tired of waiting for me to get him out because after you were born, he used our plan to escape, and he took you away. At first, I was elated. Thinking I could find him and we could be together as a family, but he wasn't at our pre-arranged meeting place. When he was caught by Azazel and you weren't with him, I didn't know what had happened. I've spent every day since searching for you, but I never thought he would have hidden you in demon territory. I assumed he would have taken you back to an angel-controlled city. He wouldn't tell me anything. He seemed to have grown to hate me and I thought I had lost everything I held dear."

She must not know he thought she was two different people. She must not know he's lost his mind. Amara thought. She didn't want to interrupt, but everything was making sense.

"Only a couple months ago, I saw your wanted poster and just knew it was you. I'm not fully sure how I could recognize you, but it had to be you. I found you had been sent to Newaught, but I couldn't find you anywhere. It was like you had disappeared. A few weeks after your trial I located you, but before I could approach you, the demons attacked and you and that Malach boy the demons were after disappeared. I tried to find where you had gone, but finally gave up after the trail went cold. I returned to Azazel, hoping to take Raziel away from him only to find out you had already rescued him. The next morning, I set out to follow you here, and I guess you know the rest."

"So you don't have any ties with the demons anymore?" Amara asked.

"None, any remaining ties I burned when I left to find you."

"What about the thief you talked to? Who told you about me?"

"Oh, I found him through an old contact and he told me about your history. Which is how I knew you were my daughter. The timeline matches up."

"Well, I would be happy to get to know you, but I am leaving for Newaught."

"I'll come with you!" Lilith brighten visibly. "I was hoping to get out of demon territory completely, but Newaught would still be better than staying *here.*"

Amara thought about that for a minute. If she allowed Lilith to go with them, how would Raziel feel about it? Would he see her as Lilith or The Witch? And would the Master even let her travel with them? "I'm not sure if the Master would let you travel with us."

"Please ask him for me. If he doesn't, I will travel to Newaught on my own. Anything to be with you! I had almost lost hope of ever finding you and I won't leave you now that I have." Lilith all but begged her.

"Alright, I promise I will ask him." Amara smiled. She seemed like a mother who had finally found her only daughter. Not just that, but likely the only daughter she would ever have? The thought struck her then. "Why do you think I'm as small as I am?"

Lilith seemed caught off guard at the sudden change in subject. "Wha... um... I'm not sure what you mean."

"I mean, I'm the daughter of the first woman and an angel. The other Nephilim have height, strength, and power. I don't seem to have any of that. I'm just a normal girl."

Lilith grew silent, and tears formed in her eyes.

Amara was afraid she had said something wrong. "I'm sorry. I didn't mean to offend you."

"No," Lilith smiled a sad smile. "You didn't. It's only... I tried to have kids after God cursed me. But they all died. I could still conceive, only none would grow to full term. It's still hard for me to think of the babies I've lost."

"I'm sorry," Amara's heart broke for the woman. How terrible would it be to lose a single child, much less lose every child? Hoping against hope that the next one would be different until you finally gave up trying because they all perished.

"You were my last hope to have a child of my own." Lilith looked up at her and wiped the tears away quickly. "No, man could give me a child and no angel would touch me. I tried with Azazel," her face twisted in disgust. "but even those children perished before being born or shortly after. Raziel thought it would be different with him. He thought his divinity would counteract the curse and produce a healthy child. He convinced me to try once again. When you didn't grow as fast as I thought you should, I feared the worst. I feared I would lose yet another child, but Raziel helped me to be strong. When you were brought into this world, you screamed and wailed. I knew you were strong. I knew you were a survivor. And you are, you did. Here you are, standing before me against all odds." Tears were once again streaming down her cheeks. "The only reason I can think for you not having the power of a Nephilim is, the curse countered Raziel's power that would have been passed to you, just as his power counteracted the curse. You were left somewhere in the middle."

Amara nodded slowly, having to wipe away tears of her own. She had no idea what this woman had gone through. And she hopefully never would. This strong woman who stood in front of her no matter what obstacles had tried to stop her. She remembered her pendant then. She pulled it out of her blouse.

Lilith's eyes grew wide at the sight of it.

"Did you give this to me?" Amara asked.

"The pendant," her mother smiled. "I never knew where it went until I saw you with it yesterday. I assumed someone stole it from me, but I didn't know Raziel gave it to you."

"So it *is* yours!" Amara smiled excitedly. "I always assumed it was. I took it as proof my parents cared about me when they left me in the streets."

"Oh, darling," Lilith smiled. "We *did* care about you. I don't know why Raziel took you that night, but I wish things could have been different."

"Oh, I know the answer to that."

Amara and Lilith talked until late into the evening. Amara told her about Raziel's metal breakdown and confusion. And Lilith told her about many things she had seen and experienced.

"Umm, did you want your pendant back?" Amara asked, pulling it out. "I've been carrying it so long as a sign that my parents did love me, but Raziel stole it from your so it's only right to give it back, right?"

"A thief with a heart of gold." Lilith said a bit absent-mindedly, her eyes fastened on the pendant. She shook her head as if to clear her thoughts. "But I want you to keep it. I would have given it to you when you came of age, anyway. And, well, here we are."

"Alright, if you're sure."

Lilith seemed to break out of her trance fully. "Yes, I'm sure. I'll tell you the story of it one day, but for now, it will be a symbol of my love, even if we get separated." She clapped her hands, suddenly making Amara jump. "Now it's getting late, and you ought to be getting back to wherever you are staying. The streets are getting more and more dangerous at night."

Amara reluctantly agreed, not wanting to leave her mother now that she had truly found her. She returned to the Shadow's lair late that night with a silly grin plastered on her face and a spring in her steps. She couldn't remember ever being as happy as she was now. Her father and her mother were both back in her life within a matter of days. She hoped against hope that Raziel would remember the woman as Lilith and not the Witch when he saw her again. However, they had talked about many scenarios and how they would have to keep him calm if he didn't. Lilith told her he might have days where he thought of her one way and then, without warning, think of her totally differently. They would have to ride his moods and help him through the darker days, but they would be together. As a family.

Lawdel sat in the main hall, arms crossed, waiting for her. "Where have you been? I've been worried this Lilith character killed you or carted off with you."

Amara laughed, genuinely laughed for the first time in weeks. "She wouldn't hurt me. She's genuine. My *mother* has been looking for me all these years! Only had no way of finding me until I rescued Raziel."

Lawdel pursed his lips, deep in thought. "This all seems too convenient."

"What?" Amara couldn't believe her ears. "Convenient? What part was convenient? Was it the part where she was cursed? The part where she lost her only daughter? Or was it possibly the part where I had to betray my friends to rescue Raziel? What part of this tail is convenient?"

"The part where she finds you just as this war starts." Lawdel replied without missing a beat. "Think about it Amara. Why Is she finding you now? She says it because she couldn't before, but what if she's tracking you down because she needs something? She allied with the demons. Maybe she's trying to get information out of you or recapture you and Raziel?"

"The demons were done with Raziel or they wouldn't have let him go so easily." Amara crossed her arms. "And they don't need me for information. I don't have any, nor was I privy to anything important during my time with the angel army. That doesn't make sense. She doesn't want anything other than what she says she wants. To get to know her only daughter. You didn't see the pain in her eyes when she was talking about the children she had lost. She's been searching for me for years. She wanted to travel with us to Newaught."

"You didn't tell her about us, did you?" Lawdel mirrored her, crossing his arms and frowning at her.

"No," Amara protested. "I told her I was traveling with others, but I didn't tell her who."

Lawdel shook his head. "Look, all I'm saying is, be careful. I'm happy you've found your parents, but I'm not sure you should just trust them without question."

"I *did* question her!" Amara held out her hands, imploring him to believe her. "I talked with Raziel and got his point of view and then talked with her and her story lined up. She told her story freely without me giving away any information." Another thought hit her. "Your jealous."

"What?" Lawdel scoffed. "No, not at all. I'm happy for you."

"You're afraid they are going to replace you." Amara continued, as if he had said nothing. "Lawdel, you don't have to worry. You will always be my father. The one who saved me from the streets and raised me. Raziel could never replace you. Besides, he's a bit crazy if you haven't noticed."

"I'm happy to hear you say that little one." Lawdel's stance relaxed even though he didn't uncross his arms. "As one who cared for you all your life and has over a hundred years more experience than you, I can tell you most of the time when people who haven't talked to you in years finally show up it's usually because they want something. I hope for your sake I'm wrong, but for my sake, please promise you will be cautious."

Amara sighed. Lawdel cared for her, and she knew he was just trying to look after her. She also would not get away from this conversation without promising to be careful. "Fine, I promise, I'll be careful. But that doesn't mean I'm going to stop talking to her."

"Good, I wouldn't try to keep you from her," Lawdel smiled at her, his feature softening. "Let's go talk to the master about this Lilith traveling with us. I don't think he will mind as long as she doesn't see anything she shouldn't, like our entrances."

"Thank you, Lawdel!" Amara beamed excitedly as they walked through the tunnels. "I'll make sure she meets us at the gates of Caister and we will separate at the gates of Newaught."

"We won't be going to the gates of Newaught." The Masters' voice said from the kitchens they were passing.

Amara jumped. *Does he always have to lurk like that?*

"We'll be using the secret external entrance." The Master held some pastries in his hands as he appeared in the doorway. "One I believe you are most familiar with."

"Yes, Master," Amara nodded quickly. "I've used it on a few different occasions. Most recently, to escape Newaught when the demons attacked."

"I, however, do not see an issue with your traveling companion," The Master took a bite of a pastry.

"Thank you!" Amara bounced up and down. Then, remembering her place, stilled her legs and nodded reverently. "I mean, thank you Master, this means a great deal to me."

Satisfaction radiated from the master. She thought he might be smiling even though she couldn't see his face under the robe's hood.

The Master rarely showed his face to anyone, and she had never heard his name used. Everyone referred to him as The Master. She wondered if that might change when they arrived at Newaught. After all, there would be several masters present, each representing their respective chapters. They would have a hard time if they continued referring to each as only "Master".

She dismissed herself from the two men and all but skipped down the hall to her room. They had housed Raziel in the room next to hers and she could hear him snoring lightly as she got closer. For the first time in her life, she would have both parents. She would have a family, a real family.

Lawdel and The Master watch Amara leave, bouncing along down the hall in her excitement. "Who *is* this Lilith woman, Lawdel? I sense she is either in trouble and would bring it down upon us, or she is the trouble."

"I'm afraid you are correct." Lawdel set his jaw, turning back to The Master. "If I may ask, why did you allow her to travel with us?"

"Keep your friends close Lawdel," The Master replied cryptically, "and your would-be assailants closer."

"You hope to find out if she's plotting against us or if she's simply in need of help," Lawdel guessed. "That's risky."

"But it could reap significant benefits." The Master raised a wise finger as if he knew what the future would hold. "Goodnight Lawdel, Sleep with one eye open tonight. Trouble is brewing."

Before Lawdel could fully comprehend what The Master's words meant or ask him questions, he walked off down the hall, disappearing into the darkness. His ominous words playing back in Lawdel's mind.

"Trouble is brewing."

Chapter 8

Amara woke up to screams. People were running past her room. She sprung out of bed, grabbing her cloth and armor and pulling them on as she reached for her weapons. A man she didn't recognize entered her room with his dagger drawn. He was dressed very similar to the assassin she had fought and killed in Newaught when she had first arrived. Raza, the master of the Shadows chapter in Newaught, had told her he was an assassin from the Dark Hallow. No doubt this man was from that same group.

He leered at her.

She feigned fear and confusion, well the confusion wasn't fully fake.

"What do we have here?" He gloated. "A poor little lamb. Don't worry, it won't hurt for long."

She used his assumptions of her being helpless against him. Playing the part of a defenseless woman, she whimpered and turned away from him. She reached down and pulled a knife out of the leather armor still on the floor next to her bed. She felt the man's presence loom up behind her. Turning, she plunged the dagger into the side of the man's neck. Blood spurted from his neck in waves. He clamped a hand over the wound as he fell back in shock.

The man cursed at her, calling her all manner of names. He lunged at her; his movements now sluggish. She fell backed against the wall and kicked his face as he scrabbled forward, clawing at her legs. Blood gushed from his nose, covering her in gore. His eyes rolled back into his head. He went limp and fell on top of her. She shuddered, struggling out from under his soon to be stiff corpse. She slipped into her leather armor, her blood slicked fingers fumbling with the laces.

They really need to make these easier to get on.

She finally secured it and ran for the door. Pandemonium reigned in the halls of the Shadows lair. Figures all dress in black ran hither and thither, some brandishing knifes, other daggers, and still others running with no visible weapons.

Raziel burst through the door beside her, taking it off its hinges and crushing a cloaked figure who had been diving at her. The man in the dark robe hit the wall with a sickening crunch and didn't move. Raziel pulled a short sword from her assailant's now limp hands and brandished it.

"Stay behind me." He commanded and pulled her along as he started through the crowd.

Me? Did he just say me? *Not* us?

Raziel fought with the strength and prowess only an angel could muster. Killing as many cloaked figures with his bare hands as he did with the short sword. He seemed to be fully aware of his surrounding, who was evil and who was good, who to kill and who to rescue. Had he been faking his confusion and insanity this whole time? Or would this clear-headed angel disappear once this was over?

Lawdel fell in behind them, covering their flank. "When did he become a functioning being again?"

"Just now," Amara shouted back over the din of battle. "Don't know why."

"Don't question it, just thank your lucky stars." Lawdel parried a blade thrown at them and Amara returned one of her own to the man who had thrown it. He didn't fare as well as they had taken the knife in his belly. "Good throw."

"I'm going to have to buy more knives after this, *again*!" Amara growled in frustration.

"Just be thankful you will be around to buy them," Raziel replied.

Amara and Lawdel looked at each other and shrugged.

"I don't know why I'm not confused," Raziel said, as if reading their mind. "I remember everything from the beginning of time, but I don't know if it will last. Amara protected that amulet with your life. Do not give it to anyone, especially Lilith. I will explain more when we are out of this." He parried a blade and killed a man by jabbing two fingers into his chest.

Amara didn't understand what was happening or why he had mentioned her amulet. Besides, it was Lilith's in the first place, right? And how had he killed with only his fingers? She and Lawdel ducked, a blade aimed at their necks, and both stabbed the bearer. Raziel barreled forward, smashing through anyone in his way. Amara and Lawdel rallied behind him, trying to keep up with his headlong charge. Many of the Shadows followed, seizing their chance of escape. Soon, they reached the exit to the warehouse.

"Should we go back for any survivors?" Amara asked, not wanting to abandon any of them to the enemy.

"If they don't reach an exit, they won't survive long enough for us to rescue them." Lawdel replied, winded from their run. "We all have standing orders if the chapter were to fall to head to Newaught and meet here."

Footsteps running toward them sounded from the dark corridor.

"Get up and get the horses hooked to the carts." Lawdel commanded one of the Shadows who was with them. "That goes for the rest of you, too. Raziel and I will hold them off."

"Lawdel," Raziel address him as the men were climbing out of the tunnel. "I must inform you I have no idea how long I will be lucid. I might, at any time, revert to my confused state, leaving you exposed."

"Thanks for the warning." He turned to Amara. "You stay here and watch him. Replace him if you need to."

Amara nodded, and they all turned toward the tunnel.

Two Shadows' members appeared out of the darkness running head long and looking behind them.

Lawdel and Raziel let them pass and Lawdel shouted after them. "Get up there and get ready to ride. We will be up shortly."

The Master strode forth out of the shadows of the tunnel. For the first time, Amara realized the similarity between his cloak and the Dark Hallows cloaks. No, that couldn't be right. The Master had always been kind to her. It had to be a coincidence. He walked up to them as if he was in no hurry.

"I retrieved as many of the stragglers as I could. Everyone else either made it to another exit or is dead." A note of sadness creeped into The Master's voice.

Amara shook her head. Of course, The Master was no traitor. How could she even have thought that?

"Come, we must leave this city." The Master pushed past them and started up the ladder.

They followed him up the ladder, sealing the hatch behind them as best they could. The men were actively hitching the horses to their respective carts. Amara never knew the Shadows Chapter here had been this rich. She always had what she needed growing up, but she had assumed they were a poorer chapter. Three carts stood pulled each by a team of four horses. Two of the carts were full of crates, and the third was about half as full. Standing off to the side of the carts were several horses for the rest of them to ride. Some would be horses owned by members, but only the best handlers and fingers had their own. The Master must have purchased the rest. She mounted up on a horse not already taken and waited for the signal to leave.

Raziel wandered over to her. He meandered as if he was once again confused as to where he was. "Amara, I'm fading fast. You have to listen to me." He said in a rush. "You need to keep the amulet I gave you safe."

"You said that before. Why do I need to keep it safe?"

"It...It's important." He was clearly fighting hard to think straight. "We...I know it's...used for something that will turn the tide of the war. I....we... we are so sorry for leaving you on the streets. We love you..."

Tears sprung into Amara's eyes. "I forgive you, and I love you, too."

Then Raziel, the true Raziel, was gone. In his place stood the confused, unstable shell of an angel. Amara sighed. She had witnessed her father as his true self and that was a blessing, but it made this all the worse.

"Were you talking to us?" Raziel asked. "Why do you love us? Do we know you? Where are we?"

"Yes," Amara smiled. "I love you because you are my father."

"That's nice," Raziel looked around himself absently.

"Why don't you get up in the cart in the back and hold on tight? We're about to leave."

"Ok," He turned and wandered down the row of carts running his hand along the horse being harnessed and the wood railing alike.

Lawdel moved his horse over to hers. "I'm so sorry, little one."

She leaned into Lawdel and he caught her, making sure she didn't slide out of her saddle and she cried. "He loved you a lot. He wanted you to know that before he left. Even over the information that could turn the war. You can take solace in that."

Amara swallowed her tears, forcing herself to calm down. "I know. I just wish I could have had more time with him. I mean the real him."

"I know, little one, I know."

"My mother!" Amara sat straight up in the saddle. "How will she know where to find me now?"

"You can't seriously think she wasn't behind this attack?" Lawdel gawked at her.

"Why would she ever attack us?" Amara's eyes grew wide. How could he say such a thing?

"This is either some crazy coincidence or that women followed you back to the lair and brought the Dark Hallow down on us."

"You said they were close to finding the lair. That's why you were packing to leave." Amara set her jaw. "They simply found us before we could finish our preparations."

Before their disagreement could turn into a full fledge argument, the thumping noise came from the hatch they had seal. The Dark Hallow had caught up with them.

The Master called. "The horses are harnessed, let's move out. Hagen, did you bribe the guards on duty tonight?"

"I was only able to get the south gate guards to accept the bribe." The man driving one of the carts, apparently Hagen, replied.

"Then we ride for the south gate. No one stops, no one looks back. If you fall behind, we will regroup on the road before Newaught." The Master ordered. "Lawdel, Amara, ride ahead and have the gate open for us!"

Amara and Lawdel kicked their horses into motion.

"Tell them Hagen sent you!" Shouted Hagen.

Amara kicked her horse hard, wanting to be away from Lawdel and his accusations. She refused to entertain the idea her mother had been the one behind the Dark Hallow. However, no matter how hard she tried to deny it, doubt had already taken root.

Behind them, each of the carts began to move and in front of them, the big barn doors slide open, powered by two men guarding the warehouse. Amara took the lead and squeezed her horse through the doors. She kicked her horse into a gallop, not having to worry about people on the streets at this time of night. She took hairpin turns down back alleys, not caring if Lawdel kept up or not. Although, he was only slightly behind her as she burst through a short alley and onto the street directly in front of the south gate. The guard in front of the gate lowered spears at the two horses.

"Hagen sent us!" Lawdel shouted before they could tell them to halt.

One of the guards reacted faster than the other, lifting his spear and calling for the gate to be opened. The second guard looked between Lawdel and the first guard. Finally, he walked over to consult his fellow. Apparently, he hadn't been read into this bribe. Possibly so they could keep his portion of the money.

Regardless, the heavy gates were opened well before the carts arrived. Amara and Lawdel fell in behind the three carts as they passed, and they were out. Free of the city. Amara kept glancing behind them to confirm they weren't being followed. No sign of any pursuit.

They turned north to travel around the city along the road to Newaught. A line of horses sat waiting for them across the breadth of the road. Dark cloaked figures sat on the horse waiting for them. The Shadows outnumbered the Dark Hallows two to one, but their confidence stance made Amara uneasy. She studied their surrounding but there was nothing to hide behind except a few scraggly bushes.

The cause for their confidence became apparent as they got closer. Each of the cloaked figures pulled a bow from beneath the folds of dark material. Amara fell back to the first cart, hoping to find a bow and arrows. They would be in bow range in a few short moments.

"Do we have any bows?" She shouted to Hagen.

"They're all packed in the crates!" He shouted back.

"Which ones?"

He shrugged and shook his head.

"Argh!" *What moron packs away weapons when under threat of attack?*

"Amara!" Lawdel shouted. "Heads up!"

She turned to look ahead of her. All the cloaked figures lowered their bows, and at first Amara didn't understand why they weren't firing. They were within range. Why wouldn't they be firing? Then she realized they already had. Her head snapped up, eyes searching the sky for the deadly barbs. She couldn't see anything against the black sky. She ducked, covering her head, and hoped none of the arrows would hit her or her horse.

The projectiles whistled down, and she heard several impacts against the wooden carts and crates. Against all odds, she didn't hear one horse or human hit by an arrow. She leveled her gaze just in time to spot the second volley being released. This time, she could follow the movements of the arrows as they climb into the night sky, keeping track of their general location. Down the arrows came again, and this time they were not so lucky. An arrow took one of the riderless horses, causing it to stumble and pull on the horse it was tied to. The man on that horse was jolted from the saddle, but she wasn't able to see if he was ok. A late arrow whistled toward her head, and she ducked quickly. The arrow skimmed down the back of her leather armor and stuck fast in her saddle, the fletched end poking her in the back as she straightened.

They had closed the gap between them, and the Dark Hallows considerably. Lawdel moved his horse beside hers and reach out with a bow in his hands. "I can't control this horse and fire. Take out as many of them as you can."

She didn't question where he had gotten the bow, only took it from him and then the quiver of arrows next. The quiver had a hook on it, and she attached it to a strap on the saddle. Nocking an arrow, she quickly took aim and let it fly. It fell well short of her target. She growled at her own inexperience as the Dark Hallow took aim with their bows once again. Another arrow came from her group and struck one of them, knocking him from his horse. She glanced over and did a double take. Raziel had fired it. He stood on the top of the stack of crates and let off another arrow. It struck a second figure in the chest as well.

She observed the angle at which he was firing his arrows and tried to mimic him and anticipate the change in distance as they charged ever closer. The enemy let another volley fly. Most of the arrows seemed to be aimed at Raziel. She ducked and pulled the reins to the left in case she had made a target of herself, but only one arrow whistled past her. She glanced at Raziel and fear gripped her heart. An arrow protruded from his chest, but he didn't fall. Wait, no, an arrow aimed at his chest had been caught? Yes, he had caught the arrow.

Pulling it away from his chest, he returned it to the original owner. She turned her attention forward again, a grim grin on her face. She fired her next arrow, and it found a home in the man's shoulder next to her target. If anyone asked, she was aiming for the man she hit. Adjusting her aim, she fired and finally hit her target.

The cloaked figures had had enough. They started firing at will, some faster than others. Amara heard a shout of pain and anger come from the cart, and she caught sight of Raziel falling from his stack of crates. He disappeared behind the rail of the cart. At least he hadn't fallen to the dirt.

A lone rider galloped toward the line of the Dark Hallow and halberd held out away from his horse. Was this rider arriving as reinforcements to the cloaked figures or to aid the Shadows? Either way, he was not an immediate concern, as he couldn't hurt them currently. She turned forward just in time to take an arrow to her gut. The impact, and surprise, took her off her horse. She hit the ground with a crutch and everything went dark.

Daziar was worried about Malach and Ariel. Neither had talked since Serilda died. Both were now sitting in separate corners, and both had mentally retreated. Daziar understood now where Malach had gotten his coping skills and methods from. He was worried about them both, but he was most worried about Malach. His friend, his brother. What pain. Terrible, horrible, emotional pain. He couldn't really do anything to help but be there. Ariel, on the other hand, had lost a lot over the years. He would bounce back from this much faster than Malach, even though Serilda was his wife and partner. At least, he hoped so.

Daziar had tried to get Malach to talk, to eat, to even respond, but he had received no reaction. His body already showed signs of malnutrition. He couldn't lose much more weight, or he would be in danger of long-term effects, or so said Jorah. Honora, Ana, and even Skie try to help but none could reach him.

Daziar was getting his strength back, but just as Ana had warned, he couldn't feel his arm from the shoulder down. Jorah told him movement wasn't good for it right now. She had tied his arm to his chest so it wouldn't impede him or get injured even more. Unfortunately for him, he *could* feel his injury. Every step, every turn of his head, every slight movement set the wound on fire. Jorah stated in a week or two, the pain would lessen as long as he took care of it. He was glad Ana had pushed him to use his down time to train his off hand with the sickle sword. It would be some time before he could spar again without pain.

He was going stir crazy, and he was ready to get out of this underground hospital. Ana was donning a cloak to hide her wings, which meant she was leaving for something. He really wanted to help his friend, but there wasn't much more he could do until Malach worked through some of this on his own. That might take a while. Malach had done this same thing when his parents had been presumed dead when they were kids. He would start eating soon and when he did, Daziar would be able to reach his friend and help him. No one would be able to break through his steel exterior until he was ready.

"Ana," He walked over to her. "I'll come with you."

"I don't need any company, and you need to rest and heal. We will need your sword arm soon enough."

"I'm going crazy sitting in here. I need to get out. Besides, Jorah said the fresh air will do me good."

"I said no such thing," Jorah called from where she stood, caring for Marena's wound. "But he's probably right."

Ana sighed, "Ok but we are going to the docks to find a ship to take us to Lanifair Harbor. It's going to be a rough place, usually full of scum. Don't get us into a fight."

Daziar saluted with his good arm. "Yes, Ma'am."

Ana groaned and rolled her eyes as she turned to climb the stairs.

Daziar scrambled after her, glancing back one last time at Malach. Malach glanced up, his blood-shot eyes meeting Daziar's. He almost turned around to go to his friend, but Malach just dropped his head back down. He was not ready, but it was a good sign. He was interested in what was going on around him again. Maybe they could talk when they returned.

He caught up with Ana in time to follow her through the hidden door into the rundown hovel. This being the first time he had seen it. He could only imagine what had been going through the group's heads when they entered. It's a wonder Ariel didn't simply turn around in search of a different healer.

He followed Ana taking in the port city. They started in the poor district of the city, but soon they were walking by large houses, which then gave way to warehouses as they got close to the docks. For the next few hours, Ana met and talked with a dozen different first officers and captains of vessels. Vessels, both big enough to transport a small army and so small they would be lucky to stay afloat. No one wanted to sail anywhere near Lanifair. They learned a half dozen warships had set sail packed full of soldiers to take the harbor. With the numbers they were talking about, the demons were moving a large percentage of their army by sea. Others would travel by land, but those ships held a good portion of the fighting force.

Daziar was just about to expire from boredom when Ana got a tip from a dock worker that there might be a captain crazy enough to take them. Apparently, they had run into some trouble on their last voyage and they were hurting for money. Which was just what they wanted to hear. They quickly moved north toward the dry docks, where the worker said the ship was being repaired. The name of the ship didn't fill Daziar with confidence, but they inquired about where to find the captain of "The Mule".

Ana approached one worker. He grinned a somewhat toothy grin and pointed them to a seedy brothel set right on the docks. It might have once been a nice tavern. The name was pleasant, and the wooden sign had been well made, but everything about the place was rundown. Sea spray had crusted the chains holding the sign and cuts and gouges in the wood had made the name of the tavern hard to read. The sign read "The Stormy Cutlass", although the paint in the carved letters had faded to the point you could only faintly see the outline. Daziar peered around to the other side of the sign, but it appeared in a similar shape to the first. Ana paid little attention to the sign. She just marched right into the place.

Daziar didn't think any self-respecting woman would be found dead in a place like this. Unless, of course, they were desperate, or like Ana, confident in their ability to protect themselves. He followed Ana into the brothel, expecting trouble. He had little in the way of weapons, and he wished he had brought his sickle sword, not that it would do him much good. His off hand didn't have the strength to wield it yet and probably wouldn't for the next couple of weeks. But it would at least look fierce. Better than the hunting knife that was currently hanging from his belt.

All heads turned their way. Most studied Ana's lithe form from head to toe with unabashed stares. Several smiled, their eyes stopping in inappropriate areas of her body. They were disgusting and dirty, and not just in the way they thought. A general musk hung over the place, making it hard to breathe without gagging.

One man stood and walked over to Ana, a nasty grin on his face. His eyes never left Ana's chest. "Hey there little lady, What I wouldn't do to buy you a drink and have you sit in my lap ov- oomph"

Ana's knee had found its target in the man's groin and he double over. She grabbed a hand full of his hair and forced his head up just far enough to talk low and menacingly in his ear. "Next time you will treat me with respect and look me in the eye, not fantasize about my body." She pulled his head back, causing him to stumble backward toward the table.

His companions at the table he had been sitting at stood. "You'll regret that." The man on the floor growled.

Another group stood and Daziar readied himself to face the second group, while Ana faced the first. However, the second group didn't come after them. They moved between them and the first group.

The leader addressed them. "You will leave the lady alone. She is now under the protection of myself and the crew of 'The Mule'. Anyone who wants to harm them will have to go through us."

The man backed off and his group of lackeys returned to their seats, eyeing the new group. The leader of the group from "The Mule" turned. He motioned for Ana and Daziar to join them at the table they had vacated. They obliged and one man pulled the chair out for Ana, politely seating her in his former seat. Daziar declined the seat offered him, standing as tall and gruff looking as he could manage behind Ana.

"I'm Captain Stanton, at your service." The leader swept off his hat and bowed gracefully before taking a seat next to Ana.

She smiled at him. "I'm Anahita and this is my pupil Daziar. We were seeking you out."

The Captain's smile faltered for only a moment. "To what do I owe the pleasure of such a fine woman seeking me out?"

"We have a business proposal for you and your ship when it is seaworthy again."

"I'm listening." The captain took a seat and motioned for the barkeep to bring a round to the table.

"I and a group of my people need passage to Lanifair Harbor."

"Ha!" the captain bellowed.

Daziar glanced around to see if his outburst had called attention to their table. It would seem no one was paying attention to them at the moment.

"Lady, you know there's a war on." He noticed her serious expression. He mirrored it. "My sources tell me the war is raging the hardest in Lanifair harbor. No sailor in his right mind would take a job there right now."

"Then we have nothing further to discuss." Ana stood to leave, but the captain grabbed her arm to stop her. She eyed him as if she was contemplating taking his hand off for grabbing her. She must have decided against it because she sat back down.

"I didn't say we wouldn't take you." The captain grumbled. "It's going to cost you, though. How many are in your party?"

"Eight," Ana replied.

"Twenty gold a head."

"That's ridiculous," Daziar scoffed.

Ana held up a hand. "As passionate as my pupil is, he is also correct. At that price, I could buy a couple small vessels."

"Then why haven't you?" The captain raised a smug eyebrow.

"Because we have neither the funds nor the skilled seamen to man them. However, I'm willing to bet a few merchants would like to get their wears to Lanifair, even with the war. They would pay handsomely for you to move it, no doubt. Our small band wouldn't hinder your ship so much you wouldn't be able to take on cargo."

The captain stroked his greying beard. "Fine, but it will take me a couple days to find those jobs. If you can't wait, the price remains twenty gold. If you can, I will charge two gold a head."

"We will pay three gold a head. The extra will be for your discretion." Ana replied, holding out her hand to shake on it.

"Are you fugitives?" The captain didn't move to take her proffered hand.

"More like refugees from the powers that be." Ana smiled.

The captain chuckled. "I like that. You know that my cargo will probably be something for the demon army; weapons, food, or other war supplies, right?"

"We will not impede your other jobs." Ana assured him. "I assure you, whatever cargo you haul will not be tampered with, at least until it is no longer in your care."

He nodded thoughtfully again and then took her hand and they shook.

"I will check in with you at high noon every day at the dry dock," Ana instructed, standing. "When you are ready to depart, I will bring my people."

Captain Stanton nodded his understanding and Ana and Daziar headed for the door.

Daziar glanced at over at the group of miscreants who had accosted them on the way in. They were no longer in their seats and his stomach fell. He quickened his pace to walk beside Ana.

"I saw," she said flatly before he could say anything. "We will head to the market. In the crowd, they wouldn't dare attack and risk the city guard coming down on them. They are not assassins. We'll try to get you a weapon and then try to lose them. If we cannot, they will attack us when we return to the poor district, where no one will bother checking on the screams. We'll be ready then."

Ana was right, of course. They encountered no problems as they left the docks and arrived at the market. Daziar hadn't thought the market vendors would still be there as the sun set and darkness fell on the market. He was only partially correct. Many of the stalls where already closed, and any wears locked up or carried away. There were a few stalls still open, and they perused them as if looking for supplies. They wound through the market, purposefully turning this way and that to lose any tails they might have, until finally Ana pulled him down a dark alley and pushed him behind garbage that smelled of old rotting meat.

"You couldn't have picked a better place?" Daziar whispered, working to calm his breathing.

"Shhh," Ana shushed him watching the street they had just turned off of.

Two men walked by and Daziar recognized them from the brothel. He ducked farther behind the garbage and out of sight. He and Ana waited, listening for any signs they had been spotted.

After a few minutes, Ana chanced a glance out. "They're gone." She whispered and continued down the alley, away from the market.

They made for the poor district, hoping they might have lost the men tailing them. They were almost there when they heard a shout from behind them. Four men sprinted toward them.

"Run!" Ana pushed Daziar ahead of her and they ran.

He pumped his legs in the opposite direction of their destination. No matter what, they couldn't lead this group to their wounded. He faintly heard Ana's light footfalls behind him and he took a hard right down another alleyway. He doubted they could shake this group a second time, but he didn't want to give them an easy target if they had projectiles.

"Ariel is on his way." Ana shouted. "We just have to stay alive until then!"

Chapter 9

Ariel had never felt such pain as he was feeling right now. When the demons had sawed through the bone of his wings, it had been something he could all but block out through the pain management techniques learned through hundreds of years of war. No, all his other injuries paled compared to this emotional pain. Sure, he had lost before, good friends and comrades. This, however, he could not have prepared for. Even if he had several thousand more years, he wouldn't have been ready. The love of his life had been taken from him. They had ripped her away. Taken before her time.

Ariel.

He had never thought he would want to stop living. Without Serilda, was there a reason to live? Could he go on fighting a war that would most likely kill him and everything lovely in this world? He looked up and spotted Malach. Of course, his son. He must protect Malach at all costs. He would need a father more than ever.

Ariel.

Could he take him away from the war? Between the two of them, they could make a life together east of the mountains in the unexplored regions. He and Serilda had explored some of that region unofficially. They were trying to start their family, but it was too inhospitable for them to feel safe having a baby. Even if he could find a safe place for them, eventually, Malach would die, too. Ariel never aged. Malach would die one day, whether from the perils of the wilderness or from old age, and then he would have to face his demons. He might even live to be the last angel alive. No, the only way to assure Malach had a long, happy life was to win this war and achieve peace.

Ariel!

The mental call finally snapped Ariel out of his despondency. How long had Ana been calling for him? He pushed his sorrow away, but the ache in his heart and the pain of loss remained, no matter what he did.

ARIEL!

Yes, Ana, I'm here, sorry for the-

It's ok Ariel, but we need your help now. We've picked up a group of degenerate scum and they are now chasing us. I do not want to give up the location of Jorah's house. Daziar is unable to fight and I'm afraid when it comes down to it, he cannot defend himself. There are too many for me to defend the both of us effectively.

Malach and I are on our way.

Ariel stood. Malach lay curled in the corner. How could he have been so selfish? He had been so caught up in his own pain; he hadn't even noticed his son was hurting just as much. How terrible a father he was. He had left him on his own all those years ago. Now he hadn't even been trying to help him through one of the hardest things he had ever faced.

"Malach," He walked over to his son.

Malach didn't stir, but Ariel noticed his body lightly convulsing with his sobs. Ariel's heart broke. He kneeled and pulled him into his arms, holding him close.

"Malach, it's ok son," Ariel tried to soothe him, but there was no conviction in his voice. "No....no it's not ok. None of this is right, none of this is ok. Your mother should have lived longer. Right now, unfortunately, we can't break down. We can't stop and grieve for her. Ana and Daziar are in trouble, and they need us."

Malach glanced up at him.

Skie lifted her head from his lap at the movement.

"A group of men are chasing them right now. I know it's hard, but we have to put our feeling aside for now and go aid them or Daziar most likely will die."

A hard light came into Malach eyes and his tears dried up. He wiped his eyes, cleared his throat, and swallowed. "Then let's go."

Ariel nodded, "Good man."

The two of them stood and walked purposefully toward the exit. Skie followed in their wake.

"Stay here," Ariel told the wolf. "You will draw too much attention. He had expected Malach to protest, but he just nodded.

Skie flopped her body to the ground and Ariel could have sworn she huffed as she did.

"Where are you going?" Honora stepping into their path.

"Daz needs help. We are going to kill some people." Malach replied.

Ariel studied his son. He had spoken with so little emotion; it scared Ariel. He had heard that tone many times. Soldiers who had lost a comrade would snuff out their emotions. They usually became unpredictable in battle. They would eventually break down and experience anger, fear, and grief all at once. He had witnessed one such man actually cry so hard he cried tears of blood.

Honora turned to Ariel wide eyed.

Ariel put up a hand to calm her. "I will keep him safe and help him through this."

She nodded, calming down and stepping back to allow them to leave.

Malach and Ariel charged up the stairs. *Ana, where are you?*

Daziar pulled in air in ragged breaths. He wasn't used to long-distance running, not to mention his wound, and after the first few minutes of the chase, he was breathing hard.

"Ariel and Malach will be here soon." Ana turned the corner in front of him and he followed her blindly.

"You said that before and yet I can't help but notice," Daziar panted. "We are still running." He was running out of stamina rapidly.

"Someone ought to teach you some manners," Ana quipped back.

"Many have tried."

He skidded to a halt directly behind her and peered around her to see why they had stopped. Ahead of them were several men with weapons drawn, brandishing them at the pair. Ana and Daziar turned to find their retreat cut off by the rest of the group.

"What now?" He asked Ana under his breath.

"Do your best to survive. Hopefully, Ariel and Malach will find-"

A shout of unadulterated rage cut her off. A blur slammed into a man. Malach rolled over the man's dead body. Daziar hadn't even seen how he had killed him. Malach hit the second man before their confusion had worn off. Ariel's axe landed a deadly blow on a third man. Daziar turned in time to see Ana engage with the other group. She moved through them like water against rocks. Sliding around between them; twisting, sidestepping, keeping her weapon moving at all times. One man grabbed at her to stop her long enough to land a blow. Instead, she just shrugged out of her cloak. Her beautiful wings unfurled, making her, in Daziar's opinion, the most ravishing woman in the known world and probably the unknown world.

He was forced to turn away from the sight of her lithe, graceful movements to defend himself against a much more revolting sight. He caught the boarding axe with his knife above his head and stared directly into the fat, ugly face of the wielder. His breath smelled of rank fish. He pushed the axe back, throwing the man off balance. He followed up with a kick to his chest. Before the man hit the ground, Malach was on top of him stabbing down; once, twice, thrice. The man was dead, and Malach charged away to help Ana.

Two of the remaining men broke away from the fight and re-treated down an alley off the main street they were on. They were headed toward the docks. Most likely to take refuge in the ship with the rest of their crew. Malach charged after the men, dropping Reckoning at Daziar's feet and pulling the sickle sword from Daziar's belt. Their eyes locked for a second and he didn't recognize his friend. Something dark had replaced him. All the light had gone out of his black eyes. He shivered as Malach moved on to chase the men.

"Malach, let them go!" Ariel shouted after the already retreating form of his son.

"Ariel, they've seen my wings," Ana was pulling her cloak back on, hiding her wings beneath the heavy folds once again. "They need to be dealt with."

"He left Reckoning." Daziar picked up the blade in knife form. "What does that mean?"

Nothing good. Worry was evident in the blade's voice.

"Whatever he's planning, he didn't want Reckoning talking him out of it." Ariel scowled.

He's going to kill those two men, and not quickly. Reckoning replied. *I tried to talk him out of it, but he isn't in a good place right now.*

"We need to make sure he doesn't get into more trouble." Ana ran after Malach.

"Daz, get back to Jorah's house and get yourself to safety. I'll take Reckoning and we will be back soon." He snatched Reckoning from Daziar's outstretched hand.

Even though Daziar wanted to follow the two angels, he did as he was told. He glanced back to watch the two angels go after his best friend. What good was he in this state? He was the reason they couldn't fight. He was the reason Malach and Ariel had to come to their rescue. He was useless. He couldn't even help his friend in his time of need. Daziar trudged back toward the healers, head hung in defeat.

Ariel was worried. He had misread his son's mood and emotions. He was out for revenge, and it didn't matter who was to blame. Malach was going to kill these men, and it would not be pretty. Ariel caught sight of movement as someone disappeared around the corner of a building ahead. Maybe they were catching up to Malach. He had a chance to stop this before Malach did something he would regret. He turned the corner and tripped over something that gave slightly when he kicked it. It was the body of one of the men. The body was sprawled awkwardly, his head spun around to face the wrong direction. A wound where a blade had pierced his shoulder still drooled blood, his heart no longer pumping. At least this man had had a quick end.

Ana held a hand out to help him up, and they continued their hunt.

"Where is your captain?" Malach's voice carried on the wind from somewhere on the docks.

Ariel and Ana double their efforts, climbing the ramps up to the dock without pause.

Malach was holding a clearly dislocated arm behind the man's back and had him bent over the railing. The man didn't utter a word, no doubt in too much pain. Malach slammed a foot down onto the man's ankle and Ariel heard a sharp snap. and knew the man would never walk right again.

"Where is your captain?" Malach shouted again.

"North docks on the ship called the Leviathan!" The man screamed.

Malach cut the man's whimpering short with a twist of his head and pick up the corpse.

"Malach!" Ariel called. "We need to go."

"They must pay," Malach growled, walking north toward the north docks. "They will pay."

"Malach," Ariel rushed forward.

"They deserve to die,"

"No, they don't," Ariel pushed him back. "You are misplacing your anger and pain. Don't let it rule you."

"Out of my way." Malach pushed past him.

"Malach,"

Malach turned on him. "People like this are who kill people I love. I won't rest until they are all dead."

"Then you will never rest." Ariel let out a long breath. "There are always these kinds of people out there. Seeking them out just because they might hurt someone you love will only get you killed one day. Once you're dead, who will be here to protect the people your care about?"

Malach set his jaw, scowling at his father. "Then what am I supposed to do? Watch as, one by one, those I care about either die or betray me?"

"No, Malach live for those who care about you and defend them when the need arises. But don't seek danger or you invite more death on yourself and those you protect."

"Fine, then what do we do?"

"Nothing, yet."

Malach tossed the corpse over the railing where it splashed in the shallows below. "That's your grand plan?"

"Yes," Ariel snorted and gave Malach a half-smile. "We will join the fight against the demons soon. We'll be needed to win this war once and for all."

"Fine, but I don't do this for your God or for the angels. I fight only to kill those who have hurt me or would hurt those I love." Malach pushed past him again, but this time to head back toward the poor district.

Ariel reached out to stop him, but Ana put a hand on his shoulder. "Leave him for now. He is in pain, but he will come around. He will believe again, someday."

"What do I do until then?" He couldn't believe how much Ana had grown in wisdom from the time of her creation. So much so he was now turning to her for advice. He remembered when she had sought him out after the fall of the demons and he had counseled her on her misplaced trust in Leviathan, who she looked up to as her mentor.

"Be there, like you were for me after the fall."

"That's it?"

"That's it. Be there to temper his anger, to be the one he can talk to, and to help him see the correct path forward. One day he'll talk to you about his belief and when he does, you can lead him towards what is true and right."

Ariel nodded. They followed Malach as they trudged back to their hideout.

Amara fought her way out of her unconsciousness. Her memories slamming back into her mind before her body was fully under her control again. She had been shot. But she wasn't going down without a fight. Strong hands grabbed her, holding her down. They would kill her. She thrashed harder, flexing her abs to bring her feet into the fray. Pain screamed in her gut, stopping her from moving her feet.

"Girl, stop your thrashing!"

She knew that voice. She finally opened her eyes. Lawdel was using most of his weight to hold down her shoulder and arm. On the other side, Hagen held her other arm.

"You're a strong one, little lady." Hagen grinned at her.

They released her arms. She reached down and felt bandages around her stomach. It hurt, but not as bad as she thought it would have been. Mostly when she moved or flexed her muscles.

"It didn't pierce deeply enough to do any major damage," a female voice told her.

She raised her head. Above her, silhouettes of trees passed in front of the night sky. They were already at the tree line? And who told her about her injury? She knew that voice as well.

"Lilith?"

"Shhhh, you're fine," Lilith replied, and she felt a hand gently press on her shoulder to keep her in place. "I'm here to help you."

"How are you here? Where did you come from?"

"It was just a right place at the right time kind of thing. I couldn't sleep. I was too excited to know we were going to spend a lot more time together, and I spotted you and Lawdel racing toward the south gate. Something was wrong, so I ran to my room, saddled my horse, and left through the east gate. Paid a pretty penny for it, too. It was worth it. I came up just at the time you were fighting the Dark Hallow. I didn't have any long-ranged weapons, so I couldn't help until I was upon them. By then you had already taken the arrow and fallen from your horse. Once their line was broken, they fled like cowards. We were able to retrieve you and the others who had fallen. Some were not as lucky as you."

"Raziel?" A spike of fear ran through her.

"He's fine. Still crazy and has a new hole in his thigh, but it will heal soon, and he'll be fine."

"He had a lucid moment in all the fighting, two actually."

"Really? What did he say? Did he mention me?" Lilith's eyes widened, but she smiled broadly.

"Um, no." She lied. "Mostly we were fighting, but he asked for my forgiveness for abandoning me and told me he loved me. It meant a lot."

"That's wonderful dear. I'm so happy you got to have that moment with him. You got to see your real father. This man who has replaced him is just a shadow of what he used to be."

Amara thought she looked a bit relieved. Why would she be relieved?

Raziel hadn't talked about her? Wouldn't she want him to talk about her? This coming on the heels of Raziel's warning made her think

Lilith might not be everything she was claiming. Maybe Lawdel had been right?

"Little one!"

Speak of the devil. Amara thought, relieved someone else was there other than Lilith.

"Your one lucky lady!"

"She also had a delightful piece of armor to stop the arrow from going too far into her gut," Lilith reminded him.

"Thank you Lawdel. Your gift has saved my life several times in the few short months I've had it. I never thought it would stop an arrow, though."

"What kind of armor would it be if it didn't do the basics?"

"I need to go check on my other patients." Lilith told Amara. "I'll be back to change your bandages soon. Oh, also now you're awake, you shouldn't go back to sleep for some time. You hit your head pretty hard and falling asleep could be dangerous. Lawdel will be here to keep you company." Lilith leaped off the cart, causing it to sway under Amara.

"Girly, I have an apology to give you. I shouldn't have questioned you about Lilith."

"Lawdel-"

"No, I know what you are going to say. You were right. I was just being a paranoid, old fool,"

"Lawdel-"

"And Lilith really came through for us. Without her, we would have lost more people to the Dark Hallow."

"Lawdel, would you listen to me?"

"Fine, what's wrong?"

"I think Lilith can't be trusted."

"Hell's bells girl, I just told you I trusted her, now *you* don't trust her? You're confusing my old brain."

"Lawdel, you were right. There are too many coincidences. On top of the ones you mentioned earlier, she just happens to be taking a walk through the dark alleys at night? We rode down all the seedy alleys in the south part of town. We barely touched any main roads. Also, why did she leave through the east gate and not follow us through the south?"

"Amara, there's not much south a Caister. I'm not even really sure why they have a south gate. Besides, she knew we were headed for Newaught, so she would have assumed we would have doubled back."

"Ok, I'll give you that. Even so, things aren't adding up. Also, Raziel, during one of his lucid moments, told me not to trust her with my amulet, even though it is supposedly hers."

"That is odd, but how do you know he was understanding what he was saying? I mean, even his lucid moments might have been confused."

"I don't know." Amara closed her eyes and rubbed her face with both hands. "All I know I that until I figure it out, I can't fully trust her."

"It sounds like a wise plan." Lawdel replied. "When did you grow into such a shrewd young woman?"

"The more I see of this world, the more I realize how much evil it contains." Amara sighed. She had lost any innocence she had held since leaving Caister. She had thought she knew how the world worked growing up on the streets. However, once shoved out into the world at large, she learned she had known nothing. All the rules changed. Monsters were real and not all were giant malformed creatures. She was worried Lilith might be one of the more elegant monsters.

Chapter 10

Kragen was in the dudgeon. He had gotten careless and complacent and an angel had discovered him. Raphael tracked him back to his closet and later that night, a small force had taken him. Lucky for him, they knew nothing except he was a Nephilim and he wasn't supposed to be there. They assumed he was a spy sent to find out information and report back. They hadn't caught him checking on the explosives.

They had stripped him of his weapons and armor. However, these angels were soft. Their questioning didn't even touch the training he had received to withstand interrogation. He lied to them, giving them only some of the truth so they wouldn't question him deeper. After only a few hours of questioning, they tossed him in this cell, no doubt patting each other on the back for getting answers out of a weak-willed spy. Kragen didn't mind. Sitting in here waiting for his master signal or sitting in the closet it made little difference. The only downside; he now had to escape and couldn't check the explosives. If one was found, he wouldn't know until the time came to detonate it.

Now he needed to make sure he didn't get complacent here waiting for his master's signal. As he had in his closet. He would need to keep up his strength in preparation for the battle. The one where Lucifer and Satan would be free to kill the remaining angels.

Honora stood on the deck of "The Mule", rubbing Daziar's back as he heaved over the railing. Nothing came out any longer, for he had lost everything in his stomach long ago. He was not meant for sailing in open waters. Although the crew and the captain had mentioned they weren't in open waters, they were just off the shore, just deep enough they didn't risk running aground on any reefs or large rocks. They assured Daziar it could get much worse. Their words didn't help Daziar at all. He just leaned against the railing, dry heaving and generally being miserable.

The weather had been fair so far. Sunny, with the occasional cloud blocking the direct rays every so often. Even Malach's countenance had brightened. She was happy he was once again eating, although still grieving the loss of his mother. He had even confided in her, he would have given his own life to save Serilda. She was told that was part of grief. A type of bargaining. She would be happy when the old Malach was back. Amara's betrayal and the death of his mother so close together had taken its toll on him. He appeared to have aged a hundred years in only a couple of weeks.

Ariel helped Malach as much as his duties would let him. He was the leader of this group, silently voted by every member still alive. Which meant he had to plan their next moves. Between that and keeping the peace on the vessel that seemed to grow smaller by the hour, he stayed rather busy.

Everyone else was growing ever restless. After their flight, the few days of waiting in the healer's "dungeon" had everyone itching for action. Now, stuck on this vessel, the pent-up energy only grew. Honora hoped their journey would take even less time than they told her. Three more days on the ship and someone was likely to start a fight.

Honora sighed heavily. *Guess who will have to patch them up?*

"Am I frustrating you?" Daziar asked, voice slightly muffled as he held his hand over his mouth.

"No," Honora replied as sweetly as she could manage. "I was just thinking about the current state of our group."

"How many people do you think you are going to have to patch up before the next three days are over?"

"Hopefully none," Honora frowned. "You feel the nervous energy too?"

"Yeah, you would have to be blind, deaf, and mute not to. Everyone is restless cause we haven't had to fight for our lives in days and no one knows what we will find at Lanifair."

"I know, large war ships have sailed. If they made it to the harbor, the enemy has likely taken the city. With their new weapons, it feels like they are unstoppable." Honora stared out ahead of the ship as if she could catch a glimpse of Lanifair.

"Gabriel wouldn't let the city fall easily. But I fear she will be fighting that battle on two fronts."

"You mean Fairdenn?"

"Yeah," Daziar wiped his mouth again, the heaving seeming to subside for now. "Last we knew, Fairdenn was in the enemy's hands, since we failed to protect it. Ariel said they would have moved the main army over land, even with the warships. Fairdenn would be the only place able to house such an army."

"So you think they would hit the city from land as well as from the sea? Isn't that a little overkill?"

"If you could choose between attacking on one front and attacking on two, which would you do?"

"Oh, since you put it that way..."

"When we arrive at Lanifair, there will likely be soldiers everywhere. If we have an altercation like the one in Caister, we will be caught for sure."

"So then, what's the plan?" Honora was getting worried.

"Ariel is creating one right now. I've been too sick to follow up with him or-" suddenly he gaged and turned to heave over the side of the ship again.

"I'm sure they don't need your input." Honora patted his back. "You need to take care of yourself."

"I know," He heaved again. "I'm useless right now to just about everyone."

"I didn't say that," Honora replied, rubbing his back to comfort him.

"*I* did. I can't feel my arm, I can't fight, I can't plan, I can't even keep my lunch down right now." He spat over the side.

"You'll get back to being able to do all those things. Just trust that others will pick up the slack for now."

"I trust others to pick up the slack, but I don't like that they have to. I feel useless."

"Ana has been training you, right?"

"You know about that?"

"Yeah, she told me," Honora nodded. "And I shouldn't tell you this because your ego will reach the stars, but she said the way you've learned to handle your new sword, you will be a master someday if we all survive this. But you have to get through the trials and training. You will only come out stronger on the other side."

"Really? She said that?" Daziar's eyebrows shot up. "The only thing she just tells me is I need to work on this or that. She never says that I'm doing good or encourages me much."

"Yeah, she did. She also said that she wants you to be the next generation of Blade-Bearers if God chooses another group."

"What?" Daziar's surprise changed, and he turned and heaved over the rail again.

"Don't tell her I told you, but I felt like you needed the encouragement. You might not be able to help now, but by the end of this war, you will be better than before."

"Thanks," He spat over the rail again. "Thanks Honora, I really did need that."

"Now don't go getting yourself killed cause you think you're better than you are."

"No, I think I've learned my lesson about that. Rushing things got me into this mess. It's a lesson I won't soon forget."

"Good." Before she could stop herself, she leaned over and pecked him on the cheek. "I can't have you dying on me. Especially if you want to court me someday."

Daziar stared at her, stunned, but as he opened his mouth to say something, he leaned over and heaved again.

"I'll leave you to that. I have a few other sick people to check on."

Daziar watched her go. Just when he thought he had figured her out, she went and did *that*. And said something like that to boot. He was just settling into the idea of gaining Ana's affection and now Honora wanted him?

Ugh, women. He rolled his eyes, causing a wave of nausea, and over the side he went again.

But Ana had told Honora he was doing well. He couldn't let it go to his head, though. He had to keep training hard, gain strength in his off-hand, and achieve the finesse and agility needed to wield the sickle sword. It differed from his grandfather's sword, lighter, balanced differently, and had only one edge. The basics were the same, but the deeper he got into training, the more it differed from the hand and a half blade.

No, he couldn't focus on the two women in his life. He needed to focus on his training and making sure he survived this war. Then he could worry about love.

Leviathan had heard the call of her blades. Fang, now Oathbreaker and Fury, called for her aid. The only problem, they were against the angels. Fury and Oathbreaker had turned to the demon's side, technically her side, but her part in the fall was greatly exaggerated and largely in part to her own ignorance instead of a conscious decision to betray God. He knew that, too. The almighty had told her when he cursed her, she would have one chance to redeem herself. This might be that chance. She loved Fury and Oathbreaker like her own children. Or as she imagined she would have if she had her own children. But they turned from the light and she wouldn't be swayed to betray all she held true to save them from the consequences of their actions.

She had already betrayed the demons, slaying one of the lower ranks, and sinking the three ships that set sail to take Lanifair Harbor from Gabriel. There was no turning back now. However, the ships were not her chance at redemption, for she was still the terrible beast. But now she headed toward an Angel controlled vessel. An angel who would most likely try to kill her. The last time she had encountered Ariel, he had not been the most forgiving, nor willing to listen to her side of events. Although for the first time since her banishment on earth had begun, she felt hope. This could be her chance. Her chance to follow God once again and to fight for what was right.

Her excitement crescendo, and she breached the water at her top speed. Her whole, massive body was almost fully free of the water when she came crashing back down, causing an enormous wave to form. The lookout would have seen her and, no doubt, wet himself, but she didn't care. She was going to talk with Ana for the first time since the fall. Nothing could quell her excitement.

Amara was back in the tunnels of the Shadows' lair for the Newaught chapter. They were ancient tunnels, carved long ago, and all but forgotten in recent years. She wondered briefly if any of the angels knew about this place and what it used to be. Maybe they also knew why it was abandoned. It could have something to do with the monster in the chasm. She would ask Lilith to see if she had any knowledge of it.

Their trip didn't take near as long as hers had. Her first trip here was filled with pain, adversity, and danger. This time, it had been as easy as riding in the cart for days. Lawdel nor Lilith would let her up for more than an hour at a time, nor would they let her ride a horse. Even though the wound in her gut was already starting to feel better.

She had introduced Lawdel to Demien, and the two hit it off rather well. Their topic of choice, at least when she was around, was how stubborn and strong-willed she was during her upbringing and training. She had rolled her eyes and sought better company.

Which had brought her to the chasm. The gaping maw of darkness opened before her was vast. Only a few weeks after she had left, two Shadows' members explored the depths and found a monster. The news hadn't surprised her. She had always felt a presence, even as she did now. The confirmation of the monster, however, seemed to have an effect on the Shadows' members.

The chasm room connected most of the tunnels in the underground network. It was the largest of the rooms. Ornate columns ladened with filigree cascaded from the top of the cavern, most disappearing into the darkness. Although a few stood on the platform near her. When she was here a few months earlier, there was always someone moving from one tunnel to another. There should be even more people now the Chapters had converged. However, the room was void of everyone but Amara and the occasional lost member of a visiting chapter.

Amara sat in silence, studying the darkness. Her amulet slipped out from under her shirt as she peered down into the ink. She was certain she felt an all but imperceptive tug on the amulet. Clutching it, she backed away from the edge. She peered at it, inspect it for any change. The swirling pattern in the stone was moving? Even more so than it had appeared to in the sunlight on the cliff side when she last studied it closely. This time, there was no sun playing tricks with the light. It was actually moving.

"Have you figured out what that is?" Lilith walked up behind her.

"No, do you know?"

"Michael and Gabriel created it just over two thousand years ago. It was then entrusted to Raziel to keep it, along with all his other secrets. Not long after, Raziel lost his mind trying to save an angel from a trance. In his addled state, he wandered too far from the safety of the angel's stronghold. Demons captured him and his amulet was taken. Not knowing what it was or its significance, Azazel gave it to me for safekeeping. Raziel took it back from me and gave it to you."

"Have you known this the whole time?"

"Yes, but it wasn't until this moment that I was certain it was the key." Lilith moved forward quickly and ripped the amulet from her neck. She cocked her arm and threw it out into the chasm with all her might.

"Wha...Lilith, why?"

"Because my lords Lucifer and Satan yearn to be free once again."

"What? I thought you were done with the Demons. I thought you wanted to spend time with me."

"Ha! You were a means to an end. You weren't supposed to exist in the first place. I slept with Raziel to solidify his trust in me. I never thought I would conceive a child with him."

"Then everything you said was a lie?"

"Not all of it. I have been looking for you for most of your life. Although, it wasn't for you. All I wanted was to find the amulet to discover if it was the key to my lord's prison."

Something stirred in the darkness.

Lilith turned toward the chasm. "It would seem I was correct."

Amara turn toward the chasm as well just in time to see the outline of a massive wing appear and disappear in the same breath. "You monster."

"I've been called worse."

"How could you? I trusted you. All I wanted was to be a family, to know my parents!"

"You witless simpleton. Who would ever care about you? Especially after your betrayal."

Tears sprung to Amara's eyes. Lilith was right. She had betrayal those who loved her most. She was pushing everyone away and would soon be alone.

The ground shook, and small rocks rained from the ceiling.

"Oh, I also forgot, thank you for letting me come along with you to Newaught. It was because of you I could show the Dark Hallow your secret entrance. They will arrive shortly. I will make sure the masters know of your most current failure." Lilith laughed.

"No!" Amara bolted forward and tackled Lilith, however instead of hitting the solid ground like she had planned, the floor seemed to disappear and they plummeted into the chasm.

"Amara!" She heard Demien and Lawdel both shout behind her. At least someone would know her last act was killing the evil that was her mother.

Demien and Lawdel were in the cafeteria, still swapping stories about Amara, when the ground shook underneath them. A few fist size chunks of rock broke loose from the ceiling and came thumping down onto some of the long tables. Both men ducked and covered their heads so they didn't get killed by the falling rocks. When it was over they glanced around. Fortunately, the room was all but empty and no one had been injured.

"Is this normal?" Lawdel raised a brow at him.

"The small amounts of shaking yes, the chucks of rock hurtling down at our heads? Hardly." Demien furrowed his brow. "The monster in the chasm is most likely the culprit. We need to check it out."

"After you," Lawdel replied with a wave of his hand.

Demien took off down the tunnel, toward the chasm. As they entered, they watched as Amara and Lilith fell off the side of the cliff. "Amara!"

Only seconds later, a giant form shot from the chasm and headed toward one of the walls of the chamber.

"Did you see that?" Lawdel turned to him eyes wide.

"Yes," Demien drew out the word, before adding. "I think our chasm fiend is no longer in the chasm."

"Not only that, it was holding Amara and Lilith."

Before Demien could say that he hadn't seen the monster holding them, it slammed into the rock at the far end of the chamber. To Demien's utter shock, the wall crumbled outward. Light stung his eyes, and he was forced to look away. The silhouette of the monster was burned into his retinas. Was the monster a dragon? Like in the myths? Demien always thought those to be tall tales, but it had resembled the stories rather exceptionally.

He turned back, and the monster was gone. In its place, a large hole let in the sunlight. Through the hole he could see an opposing cliff wall. Who knew that wall was so close to the great divide? The original creators of this tunnel system must have cut to close to the canyon.

"We need to go after them." Lawdel pointed to the hole.

"And how do you propose we do that?" Demien gestured to the chasm in front of them. "It's not like we can sprout wings and follow."

"What's the quickest way to the surface?"

"The carts." Demien ran for the carts, but before they could get there, sounds of fighting reached their ears. "Amara will have to wait. Our duty compels us to fight beside our brethren."

"I cannot abandon her!"

"Even if you made it to the surface in time to see which way the dragon went, do you think you could keep up with it? No, we are needed here. Once the danger is delt with, we will both go to aid Amara."

Lawdel growled but turned away from the carts. Cloaked figures filed out of the tunnel in front of them. The Dark Hallow had arrived.

The lookout all but fell out of the crow's nest, hollering about some sea monster or another. Malach wished he would just shut up. Someone else would go find out what all that commotion was about. He just wanted to stay below deck and be alone. He didn't want to fight; he didn't want to talk; he didn't want to do anything. He almost didn't want to live. It should scare him, but it didn't. And that should probably have scared him more. He had a hard time feeling much of anything, though.

Reckoning tried to help, but he was also dealing with his own grief over the loss of his dear friend. Ariel was the same way. He was trying to be strong, but Malach could see the pain just below the surface. Why were they even fighting anymore? Obviously, the Demons were evil. That was a given. However, to those who fought against the angels, weren't they just as evil? Killing people to forward their own goals? Who was right and who was wrong? Did it even matter?

"Malach," Ariel came below deck. "Leviathan is coming."

"And?"

"We must fight."

"Why?"

"Because we must keep evil at bay." He seemed to understand what Malach was struggling with.

"But who is evil here?" Malach met his father's eyes. "Who hasn't committed atrocities against the other side? Why do we fight the demons? We've lost so much. Let others fight."

"Malach, that is the depression brought on by your grief talking." Ariel walked over and sat down beside him. "You know just as well as I, the angels are good. I'm not going to say that every action taken by every angel has been right. However, if the demons win, this world will literally become hell on earth. We must not allow that to happen. You know your mother wouldn't have wanted you to give up. She fought for this for almost two millennia after the demons did terrible things to her."

"I saw her memories. The ones with Azazel, and others."

"Oh...I'm sorry. How bad were they?"

"Some worse than others."

"Then you know why we fight. You know why she fought." Ariel put a hand on his shoulder. "The only chance for peace is under the rule of the angels and God. If the demons win, there won't be peace for long. Their regime would continue to sow pain, destruction, and death. Whereas the angels' rule would sow the seeds of peace and justice."

Something in Malach's head clicked. Purpose blossomed anew, and that purpose pulled him from the mire of despair. He set his jaw. "Very well, but I don't fight for the angels or for a God who would let these things happen to good people. I fight against the demon, for their evil is much greater than anything on this earth."

Ariel nodded slowly. "I can accept that." Ariel stood and pulled Malach up with him. "No matter what happens, know that you will always be my son and I will always love you. I am proud of you and your mother would be as well."

"I know." Malach locked eyes with his father, but he felt no conviction behind the words he was saying. "I will see this war through to whatever end comes. However, I make no promises after it is over."

"Then let's go fight Leviathan."

Malach sighed. Forcing his limbs to follow his father.

Up on deck, men were scrambling for the ballistae mounted to the two ends of the ship. Ana stood on the rigging, peering out into the open ocean. Even Daziar, still looking a little green, stood with his sword on his belt.

Malach and Ariel walked to the captain.

"What is the situation?" Ariel more demanded than asked.

"A sea monster has been spotted and then confirmed." The captain replied. "Your angel friend up there says it is Leviathan."

Malach shouldn't have been surprised the captain had figured out Ana was an angel. It was hard to keep secrets on such a small vessel for any amount of time. They had only been at sea for two days, and the captain was astute to figure that out so quickly.

"Very well. What is your complement of weapons?"

"Two ballistae that you see and bows and arrows to outfit a small army. Have all your people grab one with a few quivers."

"Aye, captain." Ariel turned and Malach followed.

One of the men on deck was handing out bows and arrows. Ariel and Malach filed by picking up theirs. They then took their place below Ana.

"Is it Leviathan?" Ariel called up, not looking her way but searching the calm waters.

"I'm certain. She is approaching swiftly."

"She will try to destroy the ship first! We must fend her off! If she gets us in the water all with be lost!" Ariel shouted to the surrounding men.

A long ridged dorsal fin crested out of the water.

"She doesn't look that big." Daziar swallow his words as the fin continued to rise and grow as the beast got closer.

"You just had to say something, didn't you?" Honora retorted.

"Sorry,"

The man on the ballista at the bow of the ship took aim. When the monster was in range of the large weapon, he fired. Only a few moments after, the one on the stern let loose its bolt as well, sending a second shudder through the ship. Neither hit its mark, and the crewmen scrambled to load the two weapons again.

"She wants to parley!" Ana shouted to Ariel.

"That beast can parley?" The captain's jaw dropped.

"We will hear her out," Ariel turned toward the captain. "I didn't like our chances in this fight, anyway. Keep your ballistae trained on her, but do not fire unless I give the order."

"I don't like it, but I'll do as you say." The captain nodded his men to follow Ariel's command.

No later had they finished speaking than Leviathan breached the surface of the water so close Malach could have jumped to her snake-like boy. The dorsal fin they had been watching was still more than a hundred yards from the boat. They all realized they would have been at the bottom of the sea if they hadn't decided to talk with the creature who now towered over them.

Malach found he could no longer move his body. His feet might as well have been part of the deck and his hands bound to his sides. The only thing he still had control over were his eyes.

Malach studied the Leviathan and found her quite majestic. Terrifying beyond belief, but she had her own grace and beauty about her. She had a long snout with huge teeth lining her mouth. No doubt she could fit most of the boat into it without issue. Her body was like that of a serpent, long and thick, like a tree trunk. He would never have been able to fit his arms around even the thinnest part of her body. She didn't have scales as he had imagined, but her skin appeared leathery and thick. Their arrows would be lucky to pierce her hide and the ballistae would be only a nuisance to her.

I am here to be of any assistance I can. A booming voice equal to that of Leviathan's size sounded in Malach's head, and he winced involuntarily.

And yet last I knew your title was Lord of Hell. How could we ever trust what you tell us? Ariel replied calmly.

Just last week, I sunk three demon-controlled warships in full sail to aid the attack on Lanifair harbor, which I believe is still controlled by Gabriel. I would aid your journey in speed and strength to her aid.

You've betrayed your word and your duty before. We have no reason to believe your words. You could lead us directly to the three warships you claim to have sunk.

If I wanted you destroyed, I would have simply done it myself. Even through the pride of an angel, you should be able to see that, Ariel.

Ariel huffed under his breath next to Malach.

Malach's limbs were slowing loosening and his nerves were calming. He smiled at Leviathan's words. Most of the angel *did* have an overabundance of pride. He wondered if that had always been the case.

Why would you aid us? Are you not the enemy of God and the angels? What do you stand to gain?

Redemption.

We cannot be your judge.

God will judge.

We will need time to converse and decided if we will trust you or not.

I will wait.

Ariel turned and motioned for Ana to come down. He then turned and walked back to the captain. However, before they could start talking about Leviathan, the lookout shouted from the Crow's nest. "Monster!"

They all turned to the man.

"Yes, we see the Leviathan," Malach shouted in response.

"No, Dragon!" The man pointed toward the distant shoreline.

Malach searched the land for any sign of what the Man had shouted about.

Satan and Lucifer are free. We must hurry. The Leviathan stated.

"In the sky," Ana pointed. "Satan and Lucifer are coming."

Chapter 11

Amara assumed her life was over. She had pushed Lilith over the edge of the chasm, and at the bottom, their deaths. At least her last act would be to take this monster with her. But the end didn't come. One moment they were falling, the next they were going back up. She opened her eyes and saw a large, clawed hand around her and Lilith. The bony claws pressed against her back and forced her against her mother.

"Foolish child," Lilith hissed. "My lords wouldn't let me fall. They will reward those who are faithful to them."

Amara couldn't look at the woman and turned away in time to see the cave wall rushing to meeting them. She recoiled away from the inevitable impact. Lucifer, or Satan, or whatever was carrying them slammed into the cave wall and, to her utter shock, it gave way. Daylight hit her and she shut her eyes even tighter. One thing was certain she would die this day. They would land, and either this monster or Lilith would kill her. She opened her eye finally to see not land like she had thought she would but water. They were headed out to sea. Why were they going out there? Was there an Island no one knew about? And what was carrying them? Lilith had said *lords*, but there was only one creature, as far as she could tell.

They were being jolted and jostled around, so getting a clear view of the monster was difficult. Amara thought she could see two long necks. It had large, leathery wings, much like that of a normal demon. However, they were much larger to carry the enormous bulk. There were three legs in addition to the one which held them. They were as thick as a tree trunk and scales covered every inch of them, overlapping and providing all but impenetrable armor.

Suddenly, the beast jerked them forward and let them go. Air rushed past Amara and stole her scream from her mouth. Although, as quick as the panic of free fall set in, she was plucked out of the air once again. This time, the claws pushed in under her ribs and she felt a painful pop. If she didn't have the leather armor on, the claw surely would have pierced her stomach. When she was able to focus, she glanced up and screamed again. A large snout filled with teeth and slit eyes like a serpent stared directly into her eyes.

"This is the infelicitous spawn."

"The what?" Amara pushed on, the claw digging in painfully to her rib.

"And semiliterate as well, it would seem."

"My Lord, with all due respect," Lilith's voice came from Amara's left. "Most people no longer talk as you do."

A fowl-smelling roar blasted into Amara's face, causing her eyes to water and hair to fly back more than it already was.

She gagged as the smell pushed its way into her nose and down to her lungs.

"Do you think my speech is inappropriate?" The terrible face left Amara and moved to her left.

"Not at all, my lord. I was simply explaining she was not used to such talk as she has never heard those words. I would never imply you were anything less than perfect."

"Good, I am, of course, as wise and as all-powerful as God himself."

"Of course, my lord,"

The head moved back into Amara's field of view. "You will see firsthand the power of Lucifer and Satan. Leviathan has betrayed us and we will have our revenge. Then you will know our perfection and bow before us. All will, when we extirpate God."

Before Amara could retort and imply his ego might be large enough to crush God to death. Satan, or Lucifer, let her go. She plummeted quickly and hit the water almost instantly. It was like the time she had been running from Lawdel when she was a kid and turned a corner, only to run into the wall. Except worse. The water felt solid and her recently injured rib screamed at her for relief. She tumbled and rolled, sinking farther into the water. When the pain of the impact wore off, she realized she had no air. Panic gripped her. Which way was up? She needed air now! It hurt to move, but she swam anyway. She picked a direction and pushed with all her might. Through instinct or dumb luck, she didn't care which, her head breached the surface. She breathed deep and coughed hard. She had breathed in a mixture of water and air in her haste to fill her lungs. When she had no air to cough anymore, her body forced her to breathe in even though the water was still obscuring her airways.

She battled her way through the cycle of coughing and breathing, coughing and breathing. Until she finally was able to catch her breath once again. How much time had passed? She glanced around her, seeing a ship not far away and next to it, the sea boiled.

Ana was right. Malach could just make out the speck in the sky she was pointing at. Although, as they watched, that speck grew quickly. Soon they could make out more of the thing headed their direction.

Malach had heard tales of dragons before and he had dismissed them as myths. He had also heard tales of the Leviathan he hadn't believed at the time either. Now, however, it seemed he was wrong on both accounts. What flew toward them fit the myth's description in every way but one. This dragon had two heads.

"It's holding something in its claws," Ariel said, more to himself than to anyone else.

I've betrayed them. Leviathan sounded resigned. *They've come to kill me. Leave at once and you might survive. I will hold them here as long as I can.*

"Captain, get your ship underway," Ariel commanded without hesitation. "Full speed ahead."

"Aye," the captain turned to his crew. "Flank speed, fast as ya like!"

The crew was already in motion before the captain finished his command. Apparently, 'fast as ya like' was as fast as they could. The fear was palpable, and it only got worse as the dragon closed in. Just before it hit the Leviathan, it dove toward the ocean and deposited two human forms into the sea. Malach watched them skip like stones on a pond, but ducked as the two-headed dragon skimmed the sails and barreled into the Leviathan. The two titans plunged in to the ocean, causing an enormous wave to crash against the ship. Malach thought they were going to tip over. Everyone on deck took hold of whatever they could to keep them from tumbling overboard. One crewman wasn't fast enough, and he slipped over the side and into the water with little sound. No one seemed to notice but Malach.

"Man overboard!" He shouted before the ship had fully righted itself. The sails were furled, and Malach ran to the railing.

The sailor was swimming frantically toward the ship. Two men were already throwing ropes to help him. One of the two forms the Devil had dropped was also swimming madly toward them, the other was either dazed and confused or resigned to their fate because they made no move toward the ship.

"What is that daft man doing?" One of the crew pointed out the second figured still treading water.

"If he doesn't get moving, he's getting left behind." a second grumbled.

"Three men in the water," a third crew man reported to the captain.

The first man arrived at the ship and held on to the first of two ropes. Two crew men hauled on the rope, pulling him up as he climbed. Malach moved to the rope and waiting for the signal to pull the second man up. Daziar got behind them both, his single uninjured arm on the rope.

"It's a woman!" The crewman in front of Malach called. "Haul!"

Malach and Daz pulled with the crewman and as the woman's head crested the railing.

Malach stopped.

"Mal, pull!" Daziar protested from behind.

Malach dropped the rope, causing the man in front to lurch forward, which pulled the rope from Daziar's hand. The crewman held on for only a moment longer before the rope slipped from his grasp as well. Amara fell back into the water.

Malach stood there, dazed. Frozen for the second time in the same hour. This time it wasn't fear that stopped him. He never expected to see her again. How in the world had she ended up in the clutches of Satan...Lucifer...ugh, it was too confusing. The devil. How had she ended up in the claws of the devil? She was supposed to be in Caister far away from this war and from him.

The sails were trimmed, and the ship lurched under him, but he barely felt it.

"Malach," Daziar grabbed his shoulder and pulled him around. "Snap out of it."

"Why does she have to be here?"

"I don't know, but you need to snap out of it and help out or we will never find out why she's here."

"Your right, I'm sorry," He shook his head to clear it. He needed to be in the present with a clear head. So much had happened, and he realized he was actually happy to see her. Despite all the other feeling that surrounded the young woman. He would have to sort it all out later.

He moved to the rope and heaved until Amara's hands latched onto the railing and the crewman hauled her over onto the deck. She was gasping for breath and the saltwater clinging to her spilled slowly onto the planking. Malach turned from her to look for something to take his mind off the young woman.

They were already out of range of the battle between Leviathan and the devil. They thrashed around in the water and it looked like Leviathan might have the upper hand. Coils of leathery flesh and muscle wrapped around the dragon's scaly armor and pulled it under the water. Malach didn't know how long the devil could hold his breath but he hope Leviathan might be able to kill the pair. Fire and steam shot out of the water, followed quickly by the heads and then the wings of the devil.

Just as Malach thought the devil would clear the water and escape, Leviathan shot out behind him and clamped its maw firmly on his tail. Both heads roared in pain, but one turned and shot a blast of fire directly into the sea monster's face. She reeled back, snout and eyes burned black, but she held on, pulling the devil back into the water.

The surface of the water calmed slowly. Not a wing or fin was visible. Nothing disturbed the top of the water. Malach rushed over to the side of the ship they had disappeared closest to. He searched the water for sight of either titan hoping to see the sea monster. But neither surfaced. The air itself stilled, and the ship slowed. All on board not actively engaged in keeping the ship moving were gathered on that same railing, searching the water.

Something caught Malach's eye, and he looked directly below the ship. He fell back as Leviathan's dorsal fin breached the surface, gouging out a rut in the ship's hull. The impact rocked the ship hard enough to knock a few of them from their feet. When Malach recovered, he watched the end of Leviathan's tail float past the railing. This would not be good.

He followed the Leviathan's body up to its apex. The devil held her with her head hanging loosely toward the water. Her eyes were burned, and he was all but certain she was blind from the fire. She was bleeding from more cuts than he could count. She was defeated.

"I will crush all those who oppose me just as I have Leviathan." One of the head shouted. The other head plunged snout first into Leviathan's neck.

She was dead. Malach knew it as surely as he knew they would not make it out of this unscathed. The devil was too powerful for even one so great as Leviathan. How could any of them hope to defeat him?

The devil dropped Leviathan's body, and it seemed to hang in the air for a second before it rushed toward them and The Mule. Everyone scattered as the weight of her body buckled the boards of the deck and continued through, splitting the ship in half.

Splintered wood and people flew in all directions. Malach hit the cold water suddenly, and it took his breath away. It took all of his self-control not to breathe in sharply. Around him, he could see the two halves of the ship sinking slowly down to the depths. Below that was the Leviathan's body. It was still sinking, but if he was judging it correctly, it was slowing down. It was a surreal scene.

His lungs burned, and he turned toward the surface. The heavy canvas sails wrapped him up instantly, and he was unable to propel himself in any direction. The white canvas only wrapped tighter around him as it dragged him farther down.

Malach, stop panicking, Reckoning commanded.

I can't move.

Can you reach me?

No!

Can you swim further down to get out of the sails?

No!

Something rushed by outside the cocoon that was soon to be his grave.

What was that? Malach asked.

I'm unsure. Remember, I can only experience the world through your senses.

The sail cinched tight, and he was dragged through the water. His lungs burned, and he wanted to breathe in so badly, but he knew it would be the end of him. He did not know what was going on, but he had little a choice but to wait and hold his breath. But darkness was creeping into his vision at the sides. The last thing he remembered was a rush of water and air around him and an impact of soft ground as the world went black.

When Malach came to, he had been unwrapped from the heavy canvas. A small fire warmed him on his right. Most of his clothes had been removed and were laid out to dry next to him. Skie laid against him, guarding him against something. He sat up to find Amara tending the fire. She glanced his way and Skie growled low.

"You're lucky I was able to get you unwrapped, before Skie got here. I haven't been able to get near you since." Nodded at Skie, who let out another growl.

"I might have forgiven you, but remember, you betrayed more than me."

Amara sighed and stared into the fire. "This is going to follow me for a while, huh?"

"You made your bed." Malach shrugged. He peered around at the darkness outside of the firelight. "I thought I felt something pulling me through the water. What happened?"

"Leviathan towed the sail you were wrapped in to shore. I just happened to be holding onto a piece of the mast it was still connected to. Skie swam the whole way here. Only arrived a few moments ago."

"Leviathan's still alive?" Malach asked. he had assumed the worst. "Where is she?"

"She was alive, long enough to get us to shore. I didn't know how to help her." Amara stared at the fire. "It's my fault she's dead, too."

"What do you mean?"

"I set Satan free."

"You what? Why?" Malach sat up.

"I didn't mean to." Amara put her head in her hands, silent tears glinting in the fire light. He allowed her time to compose herself and once she had she filled him in on her journey. He couldn't believe what he was hearing.

"Your parents are Raziel and Lilith? An angel and the first woman?" Malach stared at her. "How is any of that possible?"

"I don't know, but maybe I'm cursed too. Maybe Lilith's curse passed to me somehow."

"Amara, I'm not sure anyone could have seen that coming. I don't think it was a bad thing to want to know your mother."

She raised her head suddenly. "What about your mom? Was she on the ship?"

Malach turned to stare into the blackness. "Her wounds were too great and her malnutrition too complete. She succumbed to them in Caister." He knew his voice sounded detached and calloused, but he didn't want to let her see him cry. Not now.

"Mal...I'm sorry. You must blame me for her death. If I hadn't delayed your rescue attempt-"

"There's no telling what would have happened." Malach cut her off. "Don't get me wrong, I blamed you, myself, and just about everyone else at one point or another since she passed, but the truth is Azazel, and this war, are the only things I can truly hold accountable. If you hadn't betrayed us, your father and my mother might have died. Or they might both be alive, or we might have ended up in the same place we are now with the same outcome."

Amara nodded but stared into the fire.

Malach had a feeling she didn't believe him. That wasn't really his problem. "Have you seen any of the others? Do you know if anyone else made it out alive?"

"I saw a few people swimming around in the wreckage, but there was too much water spraying in my face to know who."

"I guess there's not much to do until morning," Malach sighed. "Then we will go search for them. The current will hopefully bring them in close to land."

"I hope they don't freeze to death before that happens." Amara shivered.

"I know what you mean. Out here, it's somewhat warm, but the water is still frigid."

Skie sat down next to Malach and finally lowered her hackles and let her hair return to normal. She didn't relax, however, and Malach wondered if she would stand sentry the entire night. He didn't think Amara would do anything to them in their sleep, but then; he didn't think she would betray them. Who knew how much he actually could trust her. He fell into a fitful sleep, not able to fully relax even though his body desperately wanted rest.

Ariel floated on a large piece of wreckage from The Mule. He and
Ana had immediately swum to it and got out of the freezing water. Once
secure they pulled as many survivors as they could up on it without it cap-
sizing. Many more survivors were left in the water, but they swam over to
other debris and climbed out onto them.

All the crew of The Mule except for a single crewman were ac-
counted for. Ariel's group wasn't as fortunate. Amara, Arjun, Malach, Marena, and Skie were all missing. One of the crew said he saw the mast land
on top of "the boy" before he lost sight of him. Ariel feared the worst. If the
mast had landed on Malach, it would have dragged him under. If he was
unable to escape its grasp... He couldn't think about that now. For all he
knew, Malach and Skie had simply started swimming for shore. Skie's powerful legs and body might have been able to carry the two far from them
before Ariel and Ana had a chance to look for them. That left Amara, Arjun
and Marena.

There had been no sign of them anywhere. Togan was beside himself with worry for the first few minutes after they realize Marena was
gone. Them he visibly fought to calm himself, taking deep breaths until he
was in control of his emotions once again.

"She's a fighter. She wouldn't let the sea beat her." He stated.

"We need to get moving toward the shore as quick as we can." Ana
worked her way to her feet somewhat unsteadily on the wreckage. "Hopefully, those missing will have done the same." She took to the air with a
rope in hand. She dropped pieces of rope to a survivor on each of the floating debris, pulling them together into a piecemealed raft. They set to work
lashing all the pieces together so they wouldn't float away as they made
their way to shore.

They fashioned some pieces of the wreckage to use as paddles, and as Ana pulled them, they paddled. Ariel estimated they would make landfall sometime late in the morning. Then they could search the coastline for the others. He sent up another silent prayer for Malach and the others and set his mind to the task at hand.

Malach woke with a start, pulling Reckoning from under his pillow. Someone squatted next to the embers and Skie sat next to them. Malach put the knife away. If Skie trusted whoever it was, he wasn't worried about them being unfriendly. The figure was larger than any normal man. They were too large to be Ana. Maybe Ariel had found them. The new logs lit, casting their light upon the newcomer. Leathery bat wings set off a warning alarm in Malach's head and Reckoning flew from his sheath again.

"I know I look like a demon," the figure had a low but distinctly feminine voice.

She turned to him, her face still in shadow. No horns sprouted from her head. In fact, if it wasn't for the bat wings, he would have sworn she was an angel.

"Who are you?" Malach asked, now more curious than alarmed.

"I am Leviathan." She stood straight and proud. "I have been redeemed." Some of the pride went out of her stance and she angle her back to show her demon wings. "Mostly, at least."

"But you died. Amara told me you pulled us from the water and died."

"I did!" Leviathan's eyes widened, and she put a hand over her mouth. That action startled her, and she started slightly, but acted as if nothing had happened. "I'd forgotten, the last thing I remember is the devil killing me, then the heaven's opened up and God told me I was redeemed. I thought my time on earth was over, but he told me I was to help you destroy the devil and cast him into his final judgement. My old body lay next to me when I regained consciousness, and I spotted the embers of your fire."

"Wait, so you talked to God?" Malach asked. "*The* God."

"Yes,"

"And he said I'm supposed to be the one to defeat the Devil himself?"

"Yes, I am here to assist you with that task."

"Ha!" Malach couldn't help himself. He could accept he had a role to play in the war, he could accept he was a strong warrior, and he could help turn the tide of the war. However, killing the Devil when both Michael and Gabriel together could only imprison him? It was absurd. "Did he happen to mention how I was supposed to accomplish this?"

"No-"

"Of course he didn't. Because he never cares enough to lay it out for anyone or help anyone. He just stays up there in his empty kingdom, on his lonely throne, and never lifts a finger to help those who fight and die in his name."

"We cannot know his will," Leviathan shook her head. "I spent thousands of years holding onto one promise he gave me and he followed through when the time came."

"He could end this war."

"And take our free will away from us."

"What does that have to do with anything?"

"You chose what side you fight for, so did everyone. If he came down and ended the war, no one would have free will. It would force them to follow him."

"Sounds like a weak excuse."

"As far as never helping the people who fight for him, how many times could you have died on your journeys and have scraped through? Also, he could have let me stay in heaven with him, but he sent me back to help you accomplish the mission he has for you. You have been given more help than you realize. He will see you through this trial as well."

Their voices had slowly raised in volume throughout their conversation, and Amara stirred. "Is someone else here?"

"Leviathan, and she says God himself wants me to kill the devil." Malach threw up his hands and walked away from the fire, leaving the two to get acquainted and for Amara to catch up.

Skie followed him.

He couldn't believe it. After all, he had been through, more was being asked of him. Was this how it would always be? Finish one task only to be hit with another even harder one? Would it only end when he was dead?

Malach, you're spiraling, Reckoning said. *This isn't healthy. Take one breath at a time. Then we take it one step at a time.*

Malach did as he was told and took a deep breath, and then another, and another. His heartbeat and racing thoughts responded, slowing down, calming his mind.

Much better, Reckoning said. *Now, first thing in the morning, we are going to see if we can find our friends. Then we'll head toward Lanifair. Once we arrive at the city, we'll find out where to go from there. Don't dwell on what you can't change, work on what you can, trust God will provide what you need when you need it.*

"I don't know if I believe that." Malach sat down on an outcropping of rock and watched the waves crash against the shore.

Skie sat down beside him. Giving him space but also being there with him.

When has he failed you through this entire journey? Reckoning asked.

"When my mother died." Malach replied, tears forming in his eyes. He wiped them away.

Yes, that was a tragedy. However, you had time with your mother you never thought you'd have, and you still have your father. Remember, no one took your mother from you but the demons.

"Fine, but I'm not saying I accept this hairbrained idea that I can kill the devil."

I understand. We'll take this one step at a time.

Malach stood and walked back toward camp as the sun crested the horizon.

"Malach!" Amara shouted.

He sprinted forward, Reckoning at the ready.

Both Amara and Leviathan were running for the shore. Leviathan took off with a powerful stroke of her bat wings.

The Devil's back! Malach thought in dismay, adjusting his angle to intersect Amara before she reached the shoreline. He searched the sky for signs of the dragon.

Malach, look where Leviathan is flying, and there's another figure ahead of her. Reckoning instructed. I think you will find a much more positive sight than the worst-case scenario your mind jumped to.

Malach did as he was bidden, and the sight before him was a welcome one. Ana, with her brilliant Angel wings, was flying slowly towards them. He looked closer and he could see she was pulling a rope. Relief washed through him. Not only because there was no Devil attacking them but also on the other end of the rope was a raft of some sort with a quite literal boatload of people on it.

Ana reacted sluggishly, trying to defend herself unnecessarily from Leviathan. However, it didn't take her too long to understand that she wasn't being attacked, and she gladly relinquished control of the rope to the newly redeemed angel. She all but feel from the sky beating her wings hard at the last minute then collapsing to the ground.

"Amara, get the fire as large as you can." Malach pointed back at camp. "They will need to warm up and dry off."

She nodded and jogged back.

Malach ran forward to help Ana.

"I'm fine, just tired." Ana called, pointing to the wreckage raft, which was almost to shore. "The others need more immediate help."

Malach changed his course and arrive in time to help his father pull the lashed together debris onto the shore. There was no time for pleasantries, only to acknowledge each other was alive. They started helping people off the raft and toward the fire. Those who still had feeling in their extremities, helping those who didn't. Soon they were around the fire, and, with the aid of the sun, their clothes were drying.

"I'm so glad you are alive," Ariel pulled Malach close. "One of the sailors said he saw you get drug down with the mainsail."

"I did."

"How did you survive?"

"Leviathan, with the last of her strength, pulled us to shore. Luckily, Amara tagged along and untangled us from the sail."

Ariel smiled. "You owe her your life once again."

"I see you have forgiven her for her betrayal."

"I forgave her a while ago. She was stuck between two hard choices. She chose her family. I can empathize with that."

"Well, looks like we are stuck with her again. Hopefully, her presence won't cause problems with everyone. Oh, and Leviathan said God told her I was supposed to kill Satan and Lucifer."

Ariel's head whipped around. "You?"

"Thanks for the vote of confidence." Malach grinned ruefully.

"No, it's not that." Ariel said quickly.

"It's ok dad, I've been having the same thoughts. If Michael and Gabriel couldn't defeat them, how in the nine hells am I supposed to?"

"First, there is only one Hell."

Malach rolled his eyes.

"Second, He never said you had to do it alone."

"I know, I already got the 'He'll equip you' speech from Reckoning."

"He's right though."

"Malach?" Togan's voice shouted from the other side of the fire. "Thank the 'eavens you're alive. 'ave you seen Marena?"

Malach shook his head. "You are the first survivors we've seen other than Amara, Skie, Leviathan, and myself. We were going to search the shore today, but your untimely arrival delayed that." He smiled but added more seriously. "Leviathan is already out searching. Hopefully, she will find the others we are missing."

Togan nodded, swallowing and fighting the tears that were in his eyes.

"I didn't see Arjun either." Malach turned back to Ariel. "Who else are we missing?"

"Other than those two, only a couple crew members," Ariel replied. "For the amount of damage sustained, we were lucky. Most weren't injured and few were lost. I'm still holding hope of those who are missing, though. With the amount of water displaced, they could have been carried far from us in short order, taking them out of our sight and putting them into a different current. We may still find them."

"I hope so." Malach stood. "I can't sit any longer. I'm going to search the shore the opposite way Leviathan flew."

"I'll join you." Ariel stretched his stiffening muscles. "I'm not near as tired as Ana."

Skie jumped up and hurried to Malach's side as he spotted the female angel passed out next to the fire. Daziar wasn't far away from her snoring loud enough to wake the dead. Malach shook his head at him. The only person still awake was Amara, who was tending the fire.

They moved along the beach, keeping an eye out for any sign of other survivors. However, after a few hours they found nothing, and were forced to turn back. Hopefully Leviathan would find the others. They turned their attention to a more immediate matter. Other than any rations they might have had on their person at the time of the attack, there wasn't any food for the group to eat. It was time to hunt.

Malach and Ariel were a deadly hunting team bringing down several rabbits within an hour, moving through the plains just above the beach. It brought back wonderful memories of a happier time. A time when Malach and Ariel had spent weeks hunting together. A few more hours and they were both carrying a full load of game and they returned to camp to clean and cook them. However, his mother wouldn't be there to welcome them home with the smell of a pie cooling in the window. Despite his melancholy, spirits amongst the group were once again high. Everyone could fill their stomachs and warm themselves by the fire. Togan was still worried for Marena, but for the most part, things were looking up again. An hour after sundown, Leviathan returned. Materializing silently out of the darkness and making almost everyone jump.

"I found tracks," she declared. "Far up the coast, only one set. A man by the size."

Togan had perked up, but quickly deflated again. No doubt hoping the tracks had belonged to Marena.

"Did you follow the tracks?" Ariel asked.

"No, but they were headed toward Lanifair Harbor."

"Then we need to continue the mission," Ana replied.

"I won't leave without Marena," Togan stated. "But I don't expect any of you to stay to help. The mission needs t' be finished, and the army needs t' know the Devil is free."

"Then this is where we part." Ariel nodded solemnly. "In the morning, we will continue toward Lanifair while you search for Marena."

"My crew and I will be heading for Newaught. We will keep an eye out for your missing people." The captain stated. "We will journey with Togan until our paths split."

That was the end of the conversation. Most weren't able to sleep even as the night wore on. They had slept for most of the day and talked late into the night. Malach moved away from the fire aways but couldn't stop himself from thinking about what Leviathan had told him. Some time, when the moon was high in the sky, he slipped into a fitful sleep.

The next day, they parted ways. Malach was sad to see Togan go, but he understood why. The blacksmith had found his soul mate, and he would not let her go without discovering her fate. He had clasped arms with Togan and the large blacksmith pulled him into a bone breaking hug. Maybe they would see each other after this all was finished.

It took them two days to reach the spot Leviathan's wings had brought her to in a few hours. The tracks in the sand had disappeared. However, farther up onto the plains, the trail was found again. They turned northward toward Lanifair. Malach knew Honora was hoping it was her father. Malach did as well. He hoped the missing crewman was alright, but Arjun was much more dear to him.

It took them almost two more days to reach the harbor on foot, but the city still flew the Angel Army flag. That was a good sign, but they still spent a few hours watching the city before Ariel attempted to contact

Gabriel. She responded instantly letting him know the city was indeed still controlled by the angels. He got an update from her and made arrangements for them to be accepted at the gate. She did inform them a man arrived a day ahead of them telling a similar tale, although he didn't tell them who. They all had high hopes it was Arjun.

They entered the city by the southernmost gate, and a contingent of soldiers was there to meet them. "Demon!" One of them shouted, spotting Leviathan's wings.

Ariel caught the spear thrown at her as it passed him. "She is no demon, despite her appearance. If anyone attacks her, they will have me to deal with. Not to mention she will probably kill you."

"Leviathan, sister!" Gabriel alit next to the group and rushed forward to embrace her. "I was overjoyed to hear the Lord had redeemed you."

Leviathan reacted slowly, as if in shock, but she finally embraced the other angel. "I didn't expect you to ever accept me again."

"I always knew you wouldn't betray us willingly, and when Michael and I locked the devil away, he confirmed my suspicions. I was forbidden to search for you, but God revealed to me you would have your chance at redemption, and here you are!" Gabriel was like a child seeing her long-lost sister. It was a beautiful reunion.

"Gabriel," Ariel cut in. "Whereas Leviathan's redemption is a call for celebration, we are carrying grave news that will affect us all. We need to catch you up on current events and send a messenger to Michael."

The smile on Gabriel's face fell slowly with each word, and she nodded gravely. "Very well. We need to get indoors. I fear there is a spy here, as in Fairdenn. As there is at the stronghold."

"There is a spy at the stronghold?" Malach cut in. "I thought I saw a Nephilim when we were there."

A couple month priors Malach had chased a man through the Angel Army camp but lost him. He had warned the angels the man might be a spy but couldn't stay long enough to search the man out himself. They must have caught him, or at least weeded him out. The first spy in the battle of Fairdenn hadn't gone down without a fight.

"Yes, he has been taken into custody." Gabriel turned to walk away. "Come, we've much to discuss." She smiled at Leviathan. "It really is wonderful to see you again, even if your wings are a little less magnificent than they once were. Perhaps those too, will return to normal in time."

"Perhaps."

They followed Gabriel as she led them to the northernmost part of the city where a large keep was set up on the ridge overlooking the port. They filed inside and to a table where they all took their ease. Food was brought out for them, and they ate and drank their fill. Malach hadn't been this full since the last time they were with the Angel Army. It was nice to have a break from the rigors of the road.

Ariel caught Gabriel up on the events of the last few months; including Elzrod's death at the hands of Azazel, Serilda's eventual death, and the devil's escape. Malach couldn't help but notice he mostly left out Amara's involvement with the last major event. However, he made sure everyone knew Leviathan was the only reason the city was still under angel control. The sinking of the warships was not only something that helped the city but also a major blow to the Demon Army, losing hundreds of troops on those vessels.

"These are mostly unfortunate events that have transpired. With the Devil loosed, the army will not wait long to attack. With their forces at sea destroyed, Lanifair is no longer a strategic location to hold. I believe we ought to abandon the city and make our stand at the stronghold."

"Would you abandon its people to the demon army?" Malach jumped up.

"Of course not." Gabriel's brow furrowed, and she studied Malach. "We have evacuated most civilians and will take the rest with us. We aren't demons."

Malach was slightly ashamed of his outburst and sat back down.

"I know of no other vessels that would be able to carry the number of troops need to make a difference to the war effort." Leviathan brought them back to the topic at hand. "I believe leaving troops here to defend Lanifair would prove to only weaken your army at the stronghold."

"Very well," Ariel spoke up. "Then it is time we leave the city. The final battle is upon us, and we will see who will take the victory."

"You forget that God has already promised that honor to us and those who stand with us." Ana smiled. "We will be victorious."

"But at what cost?" Malach mumbled.

"At the cost the Lord sees necessary," Gabriel must have heard him.

"You're telling me the Lord has seen it necessary to let people die, including my mother?" Malach worked to keep the anger out of his voice. To let a cool head prevail. However, he could not wrap his head around their theology and justification.

"We have been promised all those who follow in faith will be taken to heaven. We will be reunited with them one day," Ariel told Malach. "Don't you remember the lessons I taught you as a child?"

Malach turned away from his father. He did remember, but he had a hard time believing them even back then. Now he understood their faith, but still couldn't share it. He stood. "I wish I could share your confidence and faith, but I cannot. Nevertheless, I will stand and fight when the day comes and, by our strength, the demon army will fall."

"By God's strength," Ana corrected. "And by his goodness and mercy, you will, one day, be convinced of that fact."

"For now, we need to make the city ready to march," Ariel replied.

That proved to be almost as easy as saying it. With few non-military personnel still in the city, they simply passed the orders to the commanders, who passed it on to their subordinates. Within an hour, the troops stationed at Lanifair Harbor were ready to march. A half an hour after, they were moving.

This is the beginning of the end, Malach thought to himself. It had been a long road in such a short amount of time. He was weary. Bone tired. Tired of the fight. Tired of the politics. And tired of religion. He all he wanted was a simple life. A life apart from war and the goings on of the wider world. Perhaps he would get his wish, but if not, he would die in pursuit of it.

Chapter 12

Kragen had found his means of escape. The maid. She came down to give food to the prisoner. He was the only one there, and he slowly talked his way into getting more food. Then he talked her into staying for a short time and talking with him. Giving her ample time to spout her lies and deceit about God and how he loved everyone. He would just listen, and act interested, even offering a few questions here and there. Mostly, it made him want to throw up the food he was eating.

Through these conversations, he had found she had the key to the outside door. The guards were so confident he was subdued and safe. They thought he could never get out to harm the poor pathetic maid. The fact was, he had been working on his escape since he first arrived. Everything was in place. The hinges of the cell door were weakened with disuse, and he had no problem cutting through what was left of the bolts with a file he had in a nondescript location on his person. One good hit with the bench within his cell and he would have the hinges off and the maid would be dead.

He couldn't wait to break her little neck. Being forced to sit through her lectures on God and why they would be victorious was infuriating. It grated on his very last nerve like and off-key violin. But she was not without her usefulness. Through her, he learned that the demon army was on the move. It wouldn't be long now.

The outer door lock clicked and swung open on oiled hinges.

If only they had remembered to take care of these hinges, it would have taken me much longer to file through them. Kragen thought.

The maid walked in, holding his tray of food. "I brought you a treat today." She smiled up at him. "Apple pie. My mother baked it fresh this morning."

Kragen smiled that fake smile of his. "Thank you, Emmeline. Why don't we talk more about your big brother Daz and his friend Mal today? I'm dying to hear more about their adventures."

Daziar felt a little left out of the goings-on recently. Sure, he was present for the meeting with the angels at Lanifair, but he hadn't been given any voice in what was happening. He didn't really get any say in continuing to the stronghold. Not that he disagreed, but he had always had a say in their path and now no one asked him. He had to admit; It was simpler. No pressure on him to help make the correct decision, no blame set on his shoulders if things went badly.

"You need to continue your conditioning and training." Ana's voice came from behind him.

How in the world did she get behind him? She was just up walking with the group of angels up front. "And *you* need to give me my memory back that you stole. You promised when I repelled your mental attacks I would get it back."

Ana feigned indignation. "How dare you suggest that I've gone back on my word?"

"Oh, don't give me that," He saw right through her act. "You were just waiting for me to ask. Now that we don't have the Devil or a mob of angry sailors chasing us, you need to hand it over."

"I never took it." Ana replied. "It has been in your mind the whole time. I simply put a block around it. Since you bested me, you should be able to break through that barrier and retrieve it yourself. While you do that, I want you to go through the fighting forms I taught you in your mind's eye. When we break at midday, I want you to move through each of them once before resting. Remember, take your time and make sure you get your form correct. Slowing them down will also work your muscles harder and build them to fighting form much faster."

"Yes, I know, you've told me twenty times already," Daziar rolled his eyes.

"Only nineteen, by my count." Ana winked at him.

He did as he was told, picturing himself moving through the forms with his left hand. When they broke for midday, he followed instructions, moving off away from the group and drawing his sword. He was getting stronger. When he had first started his training in the real world, he didn't have the strength to hold the sword for long. His heart would be pounding, and he would be pouring sweat before he could move through his forms. Now, although he was soon breathing hard, he was moving through them for a second time. The sickle sword he used now felt like a part of him. Even more so than his great grandfather's sword. He only needed to build enough strength to wield it long enough not to die if they got into a skirmish.

It only took him a half hour to fully wear his arm out, doing more than Ana had instructed him. He only hoped that after all this practice, the group didn't get attacked. They most likely wouldn't encounter any strong enemy resistance until they neared Fairdenn, however, and Daziar tried not to worry about it too much.

Several days passed without event and his arm grew stronger for it. They were less than a day's march from Fairdenn when they left the road. Since the only road to the angel's stronghold passed through the city, they would have to march through the mountains well out of sight. It was possible they could return to the road farther north, but Daziar got the feeling they were in for a long, arduous trek.

Almost all the snow up to this point had melted, but Daziar spotted some patches still clinging to their shadowy shelters, fighting off the heat of the day as best they could. It wouldn't be long, and the roads would be passable by the large army and their siege weapons. For a while Daziar wondered if they were just wandering the mountain in a general direction or if the angels knew of a hidden pass. It was soon apparent, this was no mistake or happenstance. The mountains parted ahead to reveal a passable, if muddy, trail.

The contingent of troops narrowed to two or three men wide, and they continued their brisk march as the trail sloped upward. It was a hard march. Daziar had to concentrate fully on where he placed his feet, or he would drop face first into the churned mud. He now wished he had moved to the front with Malach. Their pace was slowed as the first few men started to fall. More than once, Daziar helped the man in front of him return to his feet and they were all soon covered in the muck, regardless of if they had tripped or not. The hours slipped by and Daziar wondered if this would ever end. Finally, when he thought his legs would buckle under him, Gabriel called for a halt and a rest.

Mud or not, Daziar flopped to the ground, his legs still screaming. Just as he was contemplating how it would look if he moved to the front, Malach walked back to him just as caked in mud as he was. Another mud man and Skie walked with him, and it took Daziar until they were right up on him to realize it was Ariel. Apparently, the front was not any better than his position with the men. Skie, however, was practically immaculate.

Not a speck of mud spotted her fur coat, although the fur on her belly and legs were wet. She apparently marched a little way off the path. Maybe she was the smart one.

"Hey Daz." Malach's teeth shone white through the muck as a mischievous grin spread across his face. "You got a little something on your face."

"Ha," Daziar sat up from his prone position on the ground. "Maybe I should borrow Honora's little mirror and pretty myself up a bit."

"I wouldn't mention the mirror." Malach's grin vanished, and he lowered his voice conspiratorially. "She lost it at sea. She is still unhappy about it."

"Oh," Daziar shook his head and rolled his eyes. "After all we've been through. She's upset about a little mirror?"

"Well, one's that size are pretty rare," Malach defended her.

"Still seems a little nonsensical to be worried about it. It's just a thing."

"Is that the hilt of your grandfather's sword I see hanging out of your pack?" Malach raised an eyebrow.

"That's different!" Daziar crossed his arms.

"I know, I know," Malach smiled again. "I just couldn't help but rib you a little about it. Are you hoping to have it repaired when we get back?"

"I'm not sure we will have the time for that or if it would be appropriate, as I already have a blade." Daziar frowned. "But I'm hoping to one day get it reforged into something I can use."

Malach nodded, but before they could continue their conversation, Gabriel called to reform and make ready to leave.

"Looks like we are on the move again." Malach replied. "You are welcome to join us at the front, but it's not much better up there."

"Thanks," Daziar smiled. " I think I will stay where I am. Although I don't know their names, I'm making friends back here."

"Then I will see you at the next rest," Malach promised, and jogged away.

Daziar sighed and stood. They were soon back in line, slogging through the mud. Daziar had hoped the farther into the mountains they went, the less mud there would be, but that wasn't the case for the rest of the day. As the sun disappeared behind the mountains, Gabriel called another halt. Daziar expected they would make camp on their next rest, but there was nowhere they could with the uneven ground around. The snow patches had grown as they marched upward and now it covered most of the ground.

"We rest for ten minutes and then push on the top of the rise." Ariel told the man in front of him.

"How much farther is that?" Daziar asked.

"Another mile and a half." Ariel turned to face Daziar. "Take this time to remove as much of the mud as you can. The temperature is going to drop. It will freeze to your furs and skin and could cause your body temperature to plummet. You don't want to freeze to death while marching." He turned and followed Malach after his warning.

Daziar did as he was told without complaint. It was just something they had to do. There were many of the men who didn't share the same feelings as him. He heard many complaints as they worked to clear the mud from themselves. Daziar pulled a mostly dry cloak from his pack and took his heavy furs off. He put the cloak on, then the furs on top, providing a barrier between him and the water and mud. Darkness fell and still they pushed on. Daziar took it as a sign they were worried about something. Either pursuit, although there was no sign of that, or someone had a hunch the demon army was on the move. They wouldn't be able to get any siege weapons over the mountains during the thaw, however, they could be planning to build them once they were there. Either way, Daziar pulled his cloak tighter against the cold. Others weren't as prepared as he was and as the temperature dropped, many were happy for the heat generating, arduous march. A couple of long, cold hours later, they stopped for the night.

Daziar's furs had become so stiff with the frozen mud he stood them up by a fire they quickly built and lit. After enough fires had been lit and the troops warmed up, they set to work making camp for the night. Daziar was out before his head hit his pack.

Daziar awoke sometime in the middle of the night with a painful urge to empty his bladder. He shouldn't have drunk so much water while setting up camp. Getting dressed quickly, he shook out his furs, knocking a shovel load of dried mud off them. He grabbed his pack just in case he needed something out of it and headed out into the woods for a little privacy.

He was just buttoning his pants, which was not easy without feeling in one hand, when a voice called out through the trees. He took off at a sprint, heading back for the camp. It had to have been a call from one of the troops on watch.

Something hit him square in the chest, knocking the wind out of him and throwing him onto his back. His head hit the ground hard enough to give him a headache, and he might have lost consciousness for a few seconds. Either way, his head pounded, and he had been attacked. He rolled, using the momentum to get to his feet. He almost fell over again, stumbling back to keep his balance.

"Daziar!" The deep resounding voice, like thunder rolling through the mountains, sounded from his left.

He quickly turned to find...a goat? He'd lost it. He had hit his head harder than he thought and he had lost it.

"I'm not the goat." The deep voice sounded amused.

Daziar looked past the goat to find a warrior. Dressed in full plate mail and with a broadsword on his back. A golden crown sat on his head, jewels of all colors adorning it. The man had a large silvery beard, but his hair was cut short. His muscular arms crossed in front of his massive chest. He reminded Daziar of Togan except bigger and stronger and much scarier.

Daziar drew his sword despite his fear. If this man was here to kill him, he wouldn't go down without a fight. Although judging by his size, Daziar didn't stand a chance.

"I'm not here to fight you," the man's laugher rumbling in his chest. "I'm here to bless you."

"Huh?" Daziar lowered his weapon. "What do you mean? Who are you?"

"You don't recognize me?" The man lifted one eyebrow. "Your father spoke of my deeds and showed you portraits of me. You carry the remnants of my sword, even though you should have left it where it shattered."

Daziar's mouth dropped open, and he squinted his eyes. "Great...great grandfather?"

"The one and the same." The man winked at him. "You do our name proud, grandson. Your father couldn't have known when he named you after me you would fight beside the very angels I once did."

"How are you here? I mean, you're dead." Daziar tried to put it kindly, but he didn't know how else to say it.

His great-great-grandfather laughed a deep belly laugh. "That I am. The Lord has blessed me with so many things, but this has got to be one of the best. He has allowed me to bring this news and blessing to you, the blood of my blood. You are to be the first of the next generation of Blade-Bearers. Please, hand me the hilt of my old sword."

Daziar realized he was still holding his sickle sword, and he sheathed the weapon. He unwrapped the broken blade and pulled it from the sheath. He stretched his hands out toward the man, eyes on the ground in reverence.

Is he going to repair it? Make it an angel blade? or just replace it? Daziar shivered with excitement.

"Daziar?" Honora's voice came from behind him.

Daziar lifted his head quickly. His great-great-grandfather was nowhere to be seen. He spun, spotting Honora just a few feet away from him.

"Who are you talking to?" She asked, giving him a dubious look.

She made him feel like he was going insane. "You didn't see him?"

"No," she drew out the word like she thought he might be trying to trick her.

"My great-great-grandfather was here." Daziar knew how that must sound. "I mean, God sent him with a message for me."

Honora just stared at him, mouth agape, one eyebrow slowly raising.

Daziar held up his sword as proof, but nothing had changed. How could that be? *Something* should have happened. Had Honora interrupted the process before it could be completed? Or did he hit his head too hard? It couldn't have been all in his head...could it?

"Daz, let's go back to the camp and get you to bed. You must have been sleepwalking." Honora put her hand on his should and started guiding him back toward camp.

"No..." but his voice trailed off. Had he been sleepwalking?

The weight of the hilt in his hand grew...lighter? He jerked his head down and hand up to look at the broken sword, but it was no longer broken. Instead, it had transformed into a sickle sword, much like the one in his sheath. He felt a consciousness brush against his, as if it was stretching out for the first time. He put pressure against it, not hard, but firm and gentle. This was not anything evil...or good. Something not yet fully formed.

"How do you explain this?" Daziar shouted triumphantly, hold the sword up.

"Your sword you've been training with?"

"No! That's still in my sheath." He was all but bouncing up and down with excitement. "This, my dear Honora, is my very own Angel Blade."

Malach wake up! Reckonings' voice resounded in his head.

He sat bolt up, grabbing for the blade. He had his boots laced up, his armor adjusted, and was out of the tent, ready for war in only moments. Ariel and Ana stood outside. They were...smiling?

"What's going on?" Malach asked. "Who's attacking us?"

"No one." Ariel shrugged.

"It would seem, however, we have a new Blade Bearer in our midst," Ana added.

That was why there were both smiling. "Who?"

Honora and Daziar emerged from the woods and stopped short of the small group. Honora's eyes widened at the group and Malach was sure her face was bright red, although by the light of the moon he couldn't quite see it. Daziar, on the other hand, was excited. He held his sickle sword in his good hand and practically bounced up and down as he walked forward. It was then Malach noticed the pommel of a second sword protruding from the sheath at his friend's side and it dawned on him. Daziar was the new Blade Bearer with an Angel Blade. But where had he gotten it? They didn't carry any extra blades. How did Daziar get a hold of one? And how would he communicate with it with no angel or demon blood in his lineage?

"God sent my great, great grandfather to appoint me as a new Blade Bearer," Daziar explained excitedly. "He transformed his broken sword into an Angel Blade and has made it whole once again."

"Congratulations are in order, then." Ariel clapped Daziar on his good shoulder. "What is your blade's name?"

"Its name?" Daziar frowned. "Umm, I don't know."

"Have you connected with it yet?" Ana asked.

"No," Daziar's frown deepened. "How do I do that?"

"When I try to enter your mind and you block me, you do that with your consciousness," Ana explained. "If you reach out with that same consciousness, you should now feel other minds around you."

Daziar closed his eyes.

"I never had to learn that." Malach turned a questioning gaze on Ana and his father. "Why not?"

"Because believe it or not, you grew up with that ability," Ariel replied. "It developed with you even though you didn't know it was there. When you rescued Reckoning, you used your ability without having to concentrate. Just like breathing. Imagine if you never had to breathe your entire life and then suddenly you had to start. You would have to concentrate on your lungs and make yourself inhale and exhale."

"Huh," Malach furrowed his brow. "Never thought about that."

"This is all well and good, but if you guys could shut up," Daziar didn't open his eyes. "I'm trying to focus."

"Sorry." Malach shut his mouth and tried to stay patient.

Good try, Daz, but you've got the wrong blade. Reckoning's voice sounded in Malach's head moments later.

"The new blade will have a freshness to its consciousness." Ariel coached. "Whereas ours will have more substance. Almost like a shallow well versus a deep one."

Daziar nodded slowly, but didn't say anything for a few moments. "She….she doesn't know her name."

"Then you two will need to find a name for her." Ana smiled like a parent who just became a grandparent. "May we join you?"

"She isn't ready for everyone yet." Daziar frowned. "She requests we give her a few days to acclimate to…well, to existence."

"That is understandable." Ariel put a hand on Ana's shoulder, motioning for the rest to follow. "We will give you two time to become more acquainted."

Malach held back and fell into step with Honora. Once they were out of earshot of Daziar, he asked, "What were you two doing out in the middle of the woods?"

"What? Nothing." Honora sped up. "I just saw him go into the trees alone and then heard him talking. I thought he might need help."

"Uh huh," Malach winked at her. "I'll keep your secret."

"Malach!" She pushed him. "Nothing happened."

"Incorrect." He held up a finger. "Daziar got knighted as a Blade Bearer."

"But that was it!"

"But that was it!" Honora's voice roused Amara from her sleep.

She peered out of the tent she was sharing with some of the female soldiers and spotted Malach and Honora as they walked by. Malach seemed to have gotten over his feelings for her in record time. She watched the couple pushing and picking at each other as they walked away. It was her own fault, but it still hurt. She wasn't supposed to have to see him again, but they ended up back together. A walk would clear her head, she decided and stood.

She moved toward the edge of camp, passing Daziar sitting on a log talking to...himself? Maybe she wasn't the only one getting restless around here. She walked out into the woods once she was alone and well out of earshot. She put her back up against the tree. It struck her once again how badly she had hurt everyone. How big of a mess she had made and the lives who were lost because of her actions. Tears welled up in her eyes. She was the cause of so much bad in the world. Malach and the rest had forgiven her, but how could she ever forgive herself? How could she ever hold her head high again knowing she had all but killed Elzrod and Serilda? She had at least sent them to their death.

She slid down the tree, curling her knees up to her chest. The tears flowed freely now. She hadn't been able to stop and think about everything since crossing the desert. The weight of it threatened to crush her as soundly as if a mountain was dropped on her.

"Little one, why do you cry so grievously?" A low resounding voice asked.

"Leave me alone Togan," Amara waved him away, processing only a second later, Togan was no longer with them. Her head snapped up and her hand went to her knife, remembering the last time a stranger had approached her in the woods.

"Peace." The large man in front of her held his hand out by his side, showing he was unarmed. "I didn't come to threaten you or to harm you."

Amara eyed him, still suspicious, and climbed to her feet. The man carried himself like a warrior but had no weapon she could spot. Although he could no doubt snap her in half with his bare hands. His face was kind and wore a smile that put her at ease. The crown upon his head drew her attention, but she forced her eyes back down to lock gazes with him. "The last man to approach me in the woods turned out to be a poisonous snake. How do I know you are any different?"

"The last man who approached you came to you shrouded in shadow, brandishing hate and flourishing fear. I come open and offering only advice."

The man wore only a simple leather tunic, pants, and sandals. She wondered how he wasn't freezing in the cold mountain air. His silver-grey beard and hair cut short.

"Who are you?" Amara challenged, working hard not to be lulled into complacency by his innocent appearance and fancy words.

"I'm Daziar," He replied simply as if that explained everything.

"No, you're not. I know Daziar and you are not him."

The man chuckled, low and melodious. "I am who the Daziar you know obtained his namesake. I am his great-great-grandfather, sent by God to visit you and call you to something greater."

"HA!" She clapped a hand over her mouth, stifling the rest of her outburst. She did not mean to insult him, she just couldn't help it. What he had said, God calling her? It was laughable. She had worked for the demons. There was no chance she would *ever* be trusted with anything more than running supplies if they would even let her do that. "Sorry, I think you might have the wrong person. Honora is back at camp. Or maybe one of the soldiers can help you."

"Your name is Amara, correct?"

She nodded.

"You were given the surname Westbay by a particular kind-hearted captain of the guard in Caister when you were caught in relation to the theft of the Mayor's manor." He continued.

"Uh, yes," Amara replied. "How do you know that? Did Malach tell you?"

"No," the man shook his head slightly. "God did. He knows you very well, after all."

"What?" Amara shook her head. "You definitely don't know me well enough. No one would trust me after what I've done."

"No one has held your past deeds against you except yourself."

His words cut Amara to the quick. No one *had* held them against her. Malach hadn't, Ariel hadn't, even Honora and Daziar seemed fine with her. "I don't think I'm the right person for this. I'm not special like Malach, or talented at healing like Honora. Or even as good a fighter as Daziar."

"God does not call the equipped but equips the called."

"No, find someone else." Amara backed up, bumping into the tree, then rolled around it. "I'm not ready."

"Find peace within yourself," the man called gently from behind her as she started to walk away. "God will be waiting for you to take up this task. Do not tarry too long or it will be too late."

Amara couldn't hear the man's voice anymore. She had to get away. She wasn't the right person for this, whatever it was. Devil's wings. She hadn't even heard the man out to find out what he wanted her to do. No matter what it was, she was not the right person for it. She would just mess things up again and get more people killed. She passed Daziar again, still sitting on his log.

Gathering her things out of her tent, she stuffed them into her pack. No one would stop her from leaving the camp. She would head back to the Shadows. There, she would be safe. There *they* would be safe. Safe from her. Safe from her weakness and safe from anything she could do. She stole a horse walking it far enough away from the camp the hoof beats wouldn't be heard.

Chapter 13

Malach was overjoyed that Daziar had his own blade. And a new one, untainted by the world. Daziar found it easier to talk to them out loud along with his mind and so kept up a steading stream of words in what appeared to be a one-sided conversation. Malach hadn't heard the name of his blade, but didn't want to interrupt them. He would find out soon enough.

What worried him most was he hadn't seen hide nor hair of Skie all day. It wasn't unheard of for her to go on all-day hunts or even be gone for several days. However, since they'd been on the road, she would hunt first thing in the morning and be back with Malach before noon. Now it was well into the afternoon and she was nowhere to be found. He had told himself he was being overly concerned. She was just on the trail of a deer, but for some reason, that didn't settle his mind.

It didn't help that their trail got easier. Sure, it was nice not to be slipping all over the place in the mud, but it gave him plenty of time to overthink Skie's absence. He spotted Honora up ahead and sped up to catch her.

"Hey Honora," Malach hailed as he fell in step with her. "Have you seen Skie today?"

"No, I can't say I have." Then added. "But how many times has she just disappeared to go hunting? She's probably on her way back now."

"That's what I keep telling myself, but I can't seem to make myself believe it."

"Your just worried cause we are in enemy territory."

Malach sighed. Honora just confirmed his suspicion that he was just be paranoid.

"It's hard to believe the demon army has pushed us this far back."

"I know, not a few months ago, this was all controlled by the angels. Now we have to sneak through the mountains hoping we don't run across a major enemy force." Malach forced a smile. "But since they previously controlled this land, they know it better than the demons."

"Yes, and Gabriel has taken us on the safest route back." Honora rolled her eyes.

"What's wrong with you?" Malach caught her exasperated look. "Did Gabriel do something to draw your ire?"

"No, not Gabriel." Honora sighed. "You don't know how many times I've heard those reassuring words spoken like a mantra to make me feel safe."

"That might be so, but it's also true."

"I know, I know," Honora waved him off. "How are you holding up? I know the last few days have been hard for you."

"I'm...doing better." Malach replied. "I mean, I lost both my parents when I was so young, but I had hope for a bit that I would have them back. Then I had to watch my mother die." Malach shook his head and stared at his feet. "I mean, I'm glad I got to spend some time with her and I learned a lot about her past from those few hours, but I thought...but it was stupid."

"It wasn't stupid." Honora reassured him. "You wanted your family again. I don't think anyone could blame you for that. Other than, apparently, yourself."

Malach sighed. "I guess you're right. It just feels so futile. I mean, I'm going to fight this war against the demons for revenge against them for destroying my family while simultaneously hoping to get my family back. But what happens after it's all done? Assuming we survive."

"Maybe you should make your own family?" Honora gave him a suggestive look.

Malach stopped and had to consciously close his mouth. Was she insinuating something?

She stopped and stared up at him uncomfortably close. "Malach, you've been trying to recreate your old family, but maybe you should turn to the future. There are still people here for you who love you."

"Honora-"

"Think about it Malach," She took a step back from him. "Think about the future you might have. We'll talk more about this when you are ready." She skipped away from him to join her father.

Where had that come from? Malach stood dumbfounded while the soldiers marched around him. Honora had always had a crush on him when they were younger, but Malach had never thought it would be anything more than a childhood infatuation. She had given no indication of romance between them for a while now, and he hadn't thought of her that way for longer. Had something changed? Had Malach just not seen it because of his love for Amara? The thought of his love for Amara nearly crushed his heart for the hundredth time since her betrayal. He had forced his mind to forgive her, but his heart still held a grudge. But could he find room in it for another? One who could fill it once again with the feelings Amara had? Could Honora be that person?

Daziar walked by, still keeping a steady monologue going. "Malach?"

"What?"

"I asked if you were ok," Daziar raised an eyebrow at him.

"Oh, I didn't realize you were talking to me and not your blade. I'm fine, just lost in thought."

"Well, do you want to meet my blade? She has picked a name!" Daziar all but bounced with excitement.

"Sure Daz," Malach smiled. Daziar's excitement was infectious.

"Malach meet Dawnbreaker," Daziar beamed like a proud parent. "Dawnbreaker meet Malach and Reckoning."

Malach closed his eyes and reached out with his mind. Reckoning was there in the blackness, as always. He appeared healthier than Malach had ever seen him. A form walked out of the darkness, lithe and short. And a chill ran down Malach's spine, remembering Oathbreaker and the form she took. A child with blonde hair and piercing blue eyes formed slowly. Daziar appeared a little later, seeming to take some time to project his mind into their impromptu meeting.

"Nice to meet you two." The girl clasped her hands behind her back, twisting back and forth, watching her feet.

Daziar still beamed. "Isn't she the best? We have been talking about all sorts of things."

"I hope you have been steering her in the correct direction." Reckoning fixed Daziar with a stern look.

"Oh, yes!" Dawnbreaker replied. "About mountains and trees and the open seas!"

"I've just been informing her about all the wonderful things in the world we have and will see. She said she would like to experience a lot of them *with* me, not only in my memories."

"Very good." Reckoning replied.

"You two know she will soon be used as a weapon…in a war." Malach glanced between the pair. "Has anyone thought to prepare her for that?"

"God gave me the knowledge and history of your world." Dawnbreaker spoke before either other of two men could reply. "I have been told and shown many things about war and battles. I'm prepared to be used to end lives of humans and Demons. Daz has been sharing with me the wonderful and beautiful things of this world. He is helping me to understand why the killing is necessary."

Malach could only nod and be proud of his adopted brother. He was doing a wonderful job so far, teaching this new being. He wondered if Daz would be as gentle and caring if he became a father.

"It was very nice to meet you Dawnbreaker." Reckoning filled the silence left after the other blades' response.

"Please call me Dawn."

"Dawn," Reckoning amended. "We will leave you two to your conversation."

"Going so soon?" Daziar asked.

"I believe we are being left behind as we converse," Reckoning informed them. "The last soldier in the line has passed you two."

Malach opened his eyes. Reckoning had been correct. He spotted the end of the line of soldiers walking farther and farther from them, their quick march taking them around the bend.

Daziar opened his eyes. "We are being left behind!"

"Don't worry, they just went around the bend." Malach reassured him.

The pair took off at a run to catch up to the soldiers. Once they reach the end of the line, Malach inquired about Skie only to find Daziar hadn't seen her either. He reassured Malach that the wolf would be back shortly and that there was nothing to worry about. Malach then filled him in on his conversation with Honora to get his friend's opinion and advice.

"Malach!" Daziar exclaimed, drawing the attention of the soldiers closest to them. "I always knew you two would end up together."

"Daz." Malach motioned with his hands for his friend to calm down. "I'm not saying we are going to end up together. I don't know how long it will be before I can trust someone like that again. Sure, I trust you two with my life, but I'm not sure I can trust someone with my heart."

"Malach," Daziar turned serious. "You know Honora would never betray you like Amara did. That's the beauty of it. She is safe. She will help you heal. After that, you can decide what to do."

"That's not fair to her," Malach replied. "If I use her to heal and find out that, I don't love her. Then I've wasted her time and used her for my own gain. And what if I never heal? What if I'm broken? What do I do then? If I can never love, then I wouldn't want to tie anyone down. It would be miserable for them."

"Malach," Daziar gave him a withering look. "You're not permanently broken."

"But what if I am?"

"You aren't."

"Fine, but I'll not play with Honora's heart like that and risk hurting her. Risk losing our friendship. At least until I know if I can love her more than a friend."

"Then your dilemma's solved. Next time you talk with her, tell her that. Or you might hurt her just as much with your silence."

"Wait, when did you become a good counsel for relationships?" Malach pushed his friend.

"What?" Daziar looked hurt. "Me? I've always been good with the ladies."

"Ha, if by good you mean hopeless and pathetic, then yes, you have."

"You wound me!" Daziar put a hand over his heart. "Now you need to get back upfront. You really should ask your father this stuff."

"Yeah, I talked with him about Amara before she betrayed us, and he told me to follow my heart. It might have worked for him, but it didn't turn out well for me."

"He's lived longer than just about anyone. I bet you he has some sound advice for this." Daziar put a hand on Malach's shoulder.

Malach sighed. "I'm sure you are right."

Malach decided Daziar was right. He needed to talk with Ariel. With his father. Just because he wasn't right about Amara doesn't mean he would be wrong every time.

Malach, Reckoning cut into his thoughts. *More important than your love life, you need to talk with him about your muscles freezing up on the ship and then again when you were in the water. This is something you can't ignore, or it will get you killed in the battle to come.*

Malach frowned, but he knew the blade was right. *Have you seen this before? Maybe in other soldiers over the last few thousand years.*

Yes, it doesn't get better on its own. Reckoning told him. *Ariel might know how to help you. If not, maybe he can find someone to help.*

I won't be left out of the battle.

No one is saying you will be. Now go. Reckoning pushed.

Malach rolled his eyes and trudged off to find Ariel.

Close to the front of the group he found his father walking with the other angels. Leviathan was conspicuously absent. Malach walked over to him and fell into step.

"Dad, can I talk with you about something?" He asked.

"Sure," Ariel replied between measured breaths. He didn't make any move to leave Gabriel and the other angels.

Malach tried to get his father's eye and nod away from the group, but he didn't catch the hint. "Dad, I need to talk with *you.*"

"Oh!" Ariel's eyes shot up. "Uh ok, lets, uh, head over here then."

"Thank you," Malach and Ariel left the group of angels and walked mostly out of ear shot.

"So, it's that time in your life, huh?" Ariel asked.

"What?" Malach asked confused.

"Is it Honora?" Ariel asked and then pushed on without letting Malach speak. "No matter, whoever it is she's a lucky woman. I know I wasn't around to explain a lot of this but whatever you don't know I will help you learn."

"Dad!" Malach couldn't believe he thought this talk was about *that*. "My muscles froze on the ship when the demon attacked. And then again in the water. If Leviathan hadn't saved me, I would have drowned and not totally because I was tangled in the sail. It has nothing to do with a woman."

"Oh!" Ariel eyes widened and then his brow knit together with worry. "Oh, Malach that's serious."

"Which is why Reckoning wanted me to talk with you about it." Malach stared at the ground not wanting to see what he feared in his father's eyes. Disappointment.

"Malach, you've been through a lot in the last few months and that changes a person. How couldn't it? You lost your... *we* lost your mother." Ariel put a hand on Malach shoulder and turned him stopping him.

He did something that Malach didn't expect. He pulled him into an embrace and sobbed. Malach stood there for a moment unsure of want to do and then hugged his father back tears forming in his own eye.

"Son, I'm sorry."

"For what?" Malach asked. "You haven't done anything. You tried to save Mom as much as I did."

"No, I'm sorry I didn't reach out to you first." Ariel pulled him out to arm's length and wiped his tears. "This locking up episodes are a fear response. It's something in your brain that tells you if you hold completely still you will be safe, even though your conscious self knows that's not what happening. Any no wonder you've developed something like this. You've lost so much and have faced more than you fair share of monsters. I should have known you would need help. Instead, I was complacent and made you come to me."

"Dad, it's not your fault. You lost mom too. You've been a captive for years before that." Malach tried to let his father off the hook although he wasn't sure he could believe it completely himself. "What matters is how do I get past it. How to I stop the response?"

"I, well, I don't know." Ariel replied. "I'm not the best angel to talk to about the mind. In fact, the one who *is* went a little crazy and wandered off a couple thousand years ago. No one has been able to find him since."

Malach's shoulder dropped. "I will never be rid of this?"

"The only thing I've seen help something like this is time away from war and the horrors that entails. Time to heal."

"I don't have time. We are marching toward a war where I'm supposed to kill a two-headed dragon. How can I do that when I can't so much as move my pinky when I'm in danger?"

"I don't know, but God always equips those he calls."

"I don't need your religious platitudes. I need something that will help me."

"Then you and I will spend time each day centering and calming our minds together. We can start the healing process and I can talk with some of the other angels to see if they have any actionable suggestions we could try. I know that you might not believe it, but I have faith God will provide what you need to survive. He provided Leviathan when you needed her."

"Where is she anyway?" Malach asked, only now realizing that she wasn't with the rest of the angels when he had come to find his father.

"She has been a little," Ariel gestured with his hand as if searching for a word. "Reserved, since she has been redeemed." He pointed into the sky. "See that dot?"

Malach followed where his father was pointing and spotted a speck moving through the low clouds.

"That's her. I can understand how much she must have missed flying. The freedom to soar through the sky and feel the rush of wind over your wings is like nothing else. I've only missed my wings for a few years, but she was relegated to the sea for thousands. Besides, she must feel so out of place with us. She has been alone for most of her time since the fall. And she probably feels like she isn't welcome with the angels after all that's happened."

"Is she?" Malach asked. "Welcome I mean. Do you trust her as you trust Gabriel?"

"It's not that easy Malach," Ariel turned away. "I watched her kill a friend in the throne room of heaven. In the holiest place that has ever existed. She used Fury to kill an angel, one of the first casualties of this war. How can I trust her?"

"I don't know dad but if she doesn't feel welcome, it's probably because she isn't."

"Your probably right." Ariel sighed. "I will try to help my unbelief."

Amara was leaving. She had made up her mind last night, and she was going to follow through with it. She glanced behind her to where she knew the group was still trudging their way toward the relative safety of the Angel Army. Her heart ached. Could she really turn her back on them now? After all she had done?

She turned her horse around.

No, that was why she was leaving. All she did was mess things up. They might think her a deserter, but really, she was doing them a favor.

She turned her horse back down the mountain.

It snorted in protest at its treatment.

She needed to get back to the Shadows, to Lawdel and Raziel. There, they would survive this war and live under whoever the victor was. They were thieves, and she'd grown up in Demon territory, so how bad could their reign be if they won the war?

She turned back again.

She was abandoning them to die, wasn't she? She had already decided what the outcome would be, and she was leaving. No, she was surviving, as she always did.

She turned her horse down again.

This was what was right for her. She had some good times with them, but they were on the path to their deaths. The angel army was outnumbered and now the Devil was free, not even God could stop them. If he was even there. Did he care about them? Did he even know what was happening?

That's why he sent me Amara.

The Deep voice made her start. Her horse started and shot forward. She tumbled off backward into the mud and slid down the path a few yards, limbs flailing widely. Finally, she stopped with her butt in the mud and she peered around to see who had spoken. She didn't see anyone, but she had known the voice. It had been the voice from the night before Daziar's great-great...great-great-great-grandfather or something. At least, that's what he claimed. She spotted movement in the forest.

"Leave me alone!" She shouted at it. "You already have my answer. I'm not the person for the job. Pick someone who is more fitting for the position."

Silence.

"Ugh!" she growled and slapped the mud. "Go away!"

A wolf padded out of the trees and her heart jumped into her throat. A moment later, however, she sighed as she recognized Skie. Then she tensed again. "What are you doing here? You're supposed to be with Malach."

Skie just padded up to her and sat, as if waiting for something.

"Skie, you need to leave. You'll be needed by Malach's side."

The she-wolf cocked her head at Amara. As if to say Amara was needed as well.

"No, they don't need me." Amara stood and started brushing the mud off her. "Malach doesn't need me. He has his real friends there."

Skie didn't move, just stared at her with an expectant look.

"No, I won't go back. I'm leaving. You need to go to Malach." She pointed up the trail the way she had come and then started walking away, not watching to see if the wolf was following. She found her horse, glanced back, and jumped. Skie was only a few feet behind her. She hadn't heard the wolf moving at all. She turned angrily and swiped her hand up to ward off the wolf. "Go!"

Skie sat.

"Go!" she shouted again, more insistently.

Skie scratched her ear with her back paw, studying it when she finished.

"Ugh!" Amara growled in frustration. "Do whatever you want then, but I'm not going back."

Are they better off without you? A husky female voice asked this time.

Amara spun. No one was there but Skie. She spun back to the she-wolf.

Yes, I said that.

"Since when can you talk?" Amara asked, shocked.

Technically I can't. Skie tilted her head. *But at the moment you can hear my thoughts. I'm not sure how long this will last, though, so you need to listen. I have been with the hunter for years and he has never trusted a soul outside of the valley and few even who lived there.*

"The hunter?" Amara asked. "You mean Malach?"

So you call him. Skie's head bobbed slowly. *You, thief girl, are a first for him. Not only that, but you made him happier than I've seen him his entire life. Isn't that worth fighting for? You've also made the hunter the saddest I've ever seen him, and I will never forget that.*

"See, I messed everything up."

You made a mistake, yes, but that doesn't mean you can't help make it right. What you need to understand about yourself is why you fight. When you figure that out, you will know your path.

"I fight for *me*." Amara replied. "I always have."

Did you fight for yourself when you save the hunter and his master in the city forest from the assassin? Did you fight for yourself in the battle of explosions?

"City Forest? Battle of explosions? You mean Newaught and Fairdenn?"

Skie nodded slowly again.

"Well...no..."

Did you fight for yourself when you betrayed the hunter and his pack?

"Yes, I was selfish."

No, you fought for your sire. Even though your action caused pain to my pack, your actions were for a noble cause.

"I didn't think about it like that."

Then what do you fight for? Because it is clearly not yourself, little thief girl. Or maybe the better question is, what do you want to fight for? I will return to the hunter and fight for him, his pack, and the creator. Return to us if you will or find your fight elsewhere.

Skie turned and plodded away from her, following the trail off to the side to stay out of the mud.

Amara sat on a rock, staring at nothing, searching for the answer to the wolfs question. What did she fight for? When she was in Caister, she fought for herself. She stole to eat and to live. When she was sent the Newaught, she fought for the betterment of the Shadows. However, inadvertently she fought for the betterment of the city as a whole by exposing the assassins who planned to kill the guards of Newaught. When she met Malach, she fought for him and his family, following him across the known world. Then for her family, but now? Her fathers, biological and faux, were relatively safe. Her mother didn't care about her or anyone but herself and the demon cause. Should she return and fight with Malach? Was this a lost cause?

"Why not fight for a higher cause?"

Amara groaned, not him again. She was just starting to sort through her thoughts, and he had to show up. "What, you would have me fight for God?"

"Yes, as a Blade Bearer." The man walked in front of her and squatted down.

His smile was confident and sure. It was infectious and Amara started to smile back. She quickly frowned at him again. She knew what he was doing.

"Why would I fight for a God who has done nothing for me? Never once has he helped me or cared about me. I grew up an orphan, fought for every scrap of food until I was almost eighteen. Then he allowed all these things to happen in the war. Nothing but bad things have happened in my life, the only good thing that happened I ruined. Where was he then?"

"Do you ever wonder what Lilith had planned for you as a baby?"

"N...no." She hadn't thought about it.

"She was going to kill you. She had no use for a baby in her plans and you were a burden to her."

Those words cut Amara to the core. Somewhere inside, she had known Lilith hadn't wanted her but to hear it said out loud…. It hurt.

"Raziel saved you from death at her hands. His mind was fractured even then. Have you stopped to consider how he escaped with you?"

"Your saying God helped him?" Amara asked skeptically.

"He had a lucid period and could rescue you and take you to Caister. Have you stopped to consider Lawdel finding you just in time to save you from the cold? Caister only has few cold days and rarely gets snow. But that night you almost froze."

"And where was God in that?"

"Do you think the thieves, even Lawdel, would have rescued you if it was a warm, temperate night? They would have left you for someone else since you weren't in immediate danger. You would have starved on the street without them."

"The cold night saved me?"

The old Daziar nodded.

"That doesn't mean God had anything to do with that."

"Why do you think the Captain of the Guard spared you? He could have left you to your fate and hung you the next day. Instead, he sent you on your road to Newaught."

Amara opened her mouth to answer but had no reasoning for that. It didn't make sense. The captain risked his career for a little thief girl he all but knew was guilty.

"You were well received in Newaught by the master of the Shadows chapter."

"Raza doesn't believe in your god," Amara scoffed.

"That doesn't mean she wasn't used by him. She trusted you and sent you on your mission, which led you to Malach."

"And God had nothing to do with me after that. I fought through hell to make it here and not without sacrifice."

"Oh? Is that so?"

Amara nodded confidently.

"The arrow that was meant for your heart in Fairdenn was turned aside."

"What? What arrow."

"My point," the man smiled.

"But you could say that to anyone who survived any battle." Amara pointed out.

Old Daziar nodded. "Why did Skie get in the canoe with you instead of Malach on the day you went down the flume? Why did you survive the spider caves? How did you fight off the Dark Hallow when they were sent to kill you and Raziel specifically? How did you survive when you were taken by the devil?"

Amara's head was spinning. Could it all have been just dumb luck? Could everything she had experienced by chance, mere circumstance? Or was there a design and pattern? Was God there, orchestrating the events of her life unseen by her? Tears spilled down her cheeks and the thought of someone loving her so completely he would take such a vested interest in her life.

"Now you see, through all the events in your life, He has watched over you. Now he calls you to action." The old man held out not one but two blades. "What is your answer?"

"Do I have a choice?" Amara asked.

He cocked his head and narrowed his eyes. "You always have a choice."

"What I mean is." She lifted her head and smiled at him. "How could I say no with such a debt owed?"

"You *could* say no, but I think I understand what you mean."

"Why *two* blades?"

"Fitting for one born of both demon and angel. Don't you think?"

"So it is true?" She searched his face for her answer. "Lilith is really my mother, and Raziel is my father?"

"Ever wonder why you heard Reckoning's pained cry in Brightwood?" He asked.

"Because I'm part Angel?"

The old Daziar pointed at her and smiled. "And part demon. Lilith is, for all intents and purposes, a demon. Although she doesn't share their lineage and power, she is cunning and shouldn't be underestimated. Her curse doesn't only stop her from having children, it changed her very being."

"So then, the theory was correct: she could have children with a demon or an angel?"

"Just an angel."

Amara's head was spinning.

The old Daziar offered her the two daggers again.

She put a hand out hesitantly.

"This is a big decision. Don't make it lightly. There will be no going back."

Amara slapped her hand down on top of the blades before she could second guess herself and took them.

The old Daziar was gone when she glanced back up, as if he was never there. She stood there blinking, the only evidence he was real, the two blades in her hand. She was a Blade Bearer. However, that didn't mean she was going in the wrong direction. She dropped her two old daggers into the mud and sheathed her new blade in their place. Turning, she marched down the mountain pass with a new purpose. She was going to see the Shadows about some reinforcements.

"You Imbecile!" Oathbreaker fumed, pacing back and forth in the darkness in front of Fury.

"How was I to know that Leviathan had changed sides?" Fury asked. "And I did make contact with lord Lucifer and lord Satan."

"And cost them the battle!" If Oathbreaker had the power to destroy him, Fury had no doubt he would be a pile of scrap metal. "You distracted them and the very time he had Leviathan in his death grip. Now she has been redeemed and we are still captive!"

"Maybe this is a good thing."

"A good thing!" Oathbreaker bellowed in her tiny voice.

It was all Fury could do not to let the image of this tiny girl fuming in front of him raise a smile on his face. "Yes, we have been with them for quite some time, and they are starting to relax a little. Now would be the time to gain information."

"And do what with it?" Oathbreaker stopped her pacing and glared at him. "We cannot get a message to anyone until after the battle is won, and we are liberated!"

"There was a rumor of a spy in the angel army camp when I was there last. Malach even chased what he believed was a nephilim."

"Of course!" Oathbreakers' demeanor changed suddenly. "Kragen! Azazel's finest spy."

"Then you know of him and his mission. Perhaps we could provide him with more information, or at the very least, our services as weapons, to further his cause."

"I'm so glad I remembered." Oathbreaker smiled at him, and he gave her a withering look. "Perhaps I will let you live when this is all over, after all."

"Don't overestimate your position among the demons. You are still just a weapon to them, just as *I* am."

"Don't underestimate my sway over Azazel." She grinned that creepy grin of hers that looked so out of place on the face of a child. "You best watch your tongue and your actions from here out. Do remember, I've found the secret to destroying angel blades."

"Yes, yes," Fury dismissed her, having heard this threat too many times for it to affect him anymore. "If that is true, I'm sure you will have your hands full destroying the actual angel blades when the war is won."

Oathbreaker ground her teeth together but then smiled, no doubt thinking of destroying Reckoning and Storm first. "We will have our revenge. Not only on the blades, but on those who now imprison us."

"I will enjoy feeling their flesh part beneath my edge." Fury agreed.

Chapter 14

Relief flooded through Honora as the Angel Army camp came into view. But that relief immediately turned into anxiety. The camp was less than half the size it had been the last time they were there. Most of the outlying tents had disappeared. Only the larger communal tents remained in the shadow of the mountain stronghold.

"Don't worry," Ariel said, as if reading her mind. "Fewer tents only mean they are already pulling refugees and soldiers into the stronghold in preparation for the enemy's arrival."

Honora glanced around, spotting relief wash over the others even as she felt it like cold water running through her chest.

As they moved down through the mountain pass, more details were apparent to her. The training grounds were still setup and there was a small group still training there. Smoke still rose from the Blacksmith's area like a gray column growing wider as it lazily floated up into the clouds. Also, the massive front gate was still open, allowing tiny figures to move in and out at will. More carts and people went in than out, a testament to Ariel's assessment of the situation.

As they moved down the mountain, Malach maneuvered his way over to her and her heart started pounding harder. It had only been a few days since she had, not so subtly, dropped a hint she was interested in him.

She had always been attracted to him, but he had been more interested in hunting with Skie than any girl. Now though, He had showed he was ready for a relationship. That thief had stolen his heart before she could realize it and then broke it. She understood he would need time to sort out his feeling, but she didn't want to miss her chance. And who knew? She might help him pick up the pieces along the way. She loved him much more than she realized. The realization of that hit her when he was stuck in his trance, and she didn't know if he would survive. Although, she would be lying to herself if she didn't want to help him partially for her own gain. He was strong, muscular, and a good man. He would work to make her a good life and with her father backing them, they would go far. Maybe have a few kids to grow their own family. His cottage in Brightwood could grow with them if it was still standing after the war.

He made it to her, Skie at his side.

"See, I told you Skie would be back." She smiled warmly at him.

"You were right," Malach smiled back. "Umm… can I talk to you?"

"Sure," she felt her cheeks burn a little, and they moved out of the main marching lines.

"Umm… There isn't…well there is, but…I don't know how…" Malach took a deep breath, stood up straight and said, stiff as a board. "I'm not ready to be in a relationship."

"I know." She smiled at him again. "When you are, I'll be here. I'm willing to help you pick up what Amara broke."

She slid past him purposefully, brushing her arm against his and she felt him stiffen even more. Amara had really hurt him. She would wait for him to be ready. They had time.

"Honora," Malach put a brawny hand on her arm, stopping her. His grip was firm but gentle and the power in that grasp wasn't lost on her.

"It's not that I don't find you attractive or think that I couldn't love you. I'm just not sure I can love anyone right now."

"I know." She turned to face him, peering up at him and his strong jawline. "Malach, if you ever want to talk about what happened, I'm here. If you want to order your feelings and sort everything else out yourself, I'll wait for you." She took his big hand between hers. "But if there can never be anything between us, please let me know."

"Uh, oh… of course," Malach studied his hand in hers. "I would never want to do anything to hurt you. And I…love you…in some capacity. I'm not sure what that is yet. Is that ok?"

She giggled. "Of course. I just told you I'll wait for you."

"Oh…yeah…so you did."

They stood there in awkward silence. Honora enjoying the warmth of his hand in hers while he seemed to have no idea where to take the conversation. He finally pulled his hand back slowly.

"When did we grow up?" He chuckled nervously.

"Here and there along the way." She smiled back at him. "You were always more grown up than the rest of us, though."

"I guess we better catch up to the group."

"I guess so."

They started walking.

"What, um, what are you going to do after the war?" Malach seemed to be trying to make small talk.

"I'm planning to go back to Brightwood. If it's still there. You?"

"Same. It will be different, though. My father will be there again."

"He's not going to stay with the rest of the angels?"

"Oh, umm I don't know, to tell you the truth. We hadn't really talked about it, I just assumed."

"Then, you might build your own cottage or something?"

"Amara and I had planned…." His voice trailed off.

"It's ok you can tell me."

"Well, we found this spot." Malach told her about the cliff they had found with the breathtaking view of the valley below and how they had talked about returning there after the war. "Now, though, after everything that's happened. I don't know if I ever want to go there again."

"Hang on. Why didn't we see this place on our way from Fairdenn or on this last leg of the journey? We would have gone right past it."

"When we left Fairdenn, we didn't go far enough north to see it, moving east to Brightwood. On this part of our journey, we were too far up into the mountains to the west."

"Huh," Honora really wanted to see the view just from how Malach described it. "If you ever want to go back, promise me you'll take me so I can see it?"

"Sure," Malach smiled at her. "It's weird to think about that. I was so sure Amara, and I were meant for each other. So sure we would be together through it all."

"Wait, have you seen her in the last couple of days?"

"Come to think of it, no." Malach's face screwed up into a frown. "I haven't seen her since Daziar got his blade."

"You don't think she left, do you?" Honora asked.

"I'm not sure it makes a difference to me either way." Malach frowned. "I've forgiven her for her betrayal..."

"But it still hurts." Honora finished for him.

He nodded. "It was easier when I didn't have to see her every day. In some ways I'll be glad if she left."

"Seems a bit cowardly though..." Honora studied Malach's face.

He nodded. "She will have to reconcile her actions with herself. With or without her, we have to get ready for this battle all the same. Maybe one day she will see that fighting for something other than yourself is worthwhile. Lord knows it was a lesson *I* had a hard time learning."

"What do you mean?" Honora stepped back to look at him. "You have always fought for others."

"Mostly, I've fought for those I considered my friends and family. Until...well until my mother died, I didn't fight for any other reason. Until that moment, I could have cared less if the demons or the angels won as long as those I loved were not harmed."

"Really? You would have abandoned the angels?"

"In a heartbeat." Malach replied. "That's just as selfish as what Amara did. Now I see the demons are truly evil and need to be defeated. I can see they wouldn't stop until they remove all the good from this world. Although, the angels aren't perfect. They bicker and fight like children without their father. It's like God has taken a step back and let everything take its own course. I think Michael has tried to keep them on the straight and narrow, but many look down on the humans they protect. But I guess we can worry about those problems after the demons are defeated.

"What if God hasn't taken a step back?" Honora asked. "What if He has simply allowed his creation to act with free will? Maybe He wants us to make the right choices and is nudging us in the correct directions while allowing that."

"I...I don't know. I wish He would just come down and tell us what to do."

"We know He is still active though."

"How's that?"

"Only he can appoint new Blade-Bearers, right? Then, two thousand years ago, he appointed Blade-Bearers and now he's doing it again."

"I can't argue with that logic. So why doesn't he just come down here and put an end to this?"

"Malach, our entire society is based on choice. Everyone chooses a side to live on, everyone chooses to fight or not. If that choice is taken away by force, people will revolt. No matter who wins the war, the victor will have a hard time bringing the people in line. The only way I see there being no resistance is if the victory is so complete, there is not one to incite a revolt."

"You might be right, but I don't see the angels being able to have that complete of a victory. From the reports Gabriel received in Lanifair, we are outnumbered four to one, and now the devil has been loosed."

"We will see." Honora shrugged. "My job is just to patch you big strapping warriors up when you get hurt."

"Hurry up, you two!" Daziar called from up ahead. "I want to see my family sometime today!"

"We're coming!" Malach called and ran ahead of Honora. When she didn't follow him right away, he turned around. "You coming?"

"I'll catch up."

He shrugged and continued his charge ahead. He heard him and Daziar giving each other a hard time, and she smiled. Yes, she would be happy with Malach when his broken heart healed. She believed he would be happy with her as well.

A shout from the angel army camp drew her attention away from her friends. The tiny figures had grown and at first, she thought they were pointing their direction, having spotted their group coming down the mountain pass. However, as she watched, they started running, pulling carts, and tearing down tents. She ran to catch up to Malach and Daziar.

Whispers traveled from the front of the marching troop to the back, finally reaching the trio's ears. Gabriel and Ariel had called a retreat into the mountains and quietly as possible.

Most turned and did as they were told, marching as fast as they could as to not slow down those behind them. Honora continued pushing her way forward, ignoring the rest. As she turned the corner on a rocky outcropping, the valley came fully into view. Soldiers adorned in crimson red and black armor poured into the valley. They had followed the makeshift road from Fairdenn and were quickly cutting Honora and her group off from the stronghold. There was no way they would make it in time if they were spotted, their group would be as good as dead. The demon army would take care of their little band with minimal casualties. They were pushed well back into the cover of the rocky crags and trees of the mountainside before they were allowed to stop. They were trapped on the other side of an army hell bent on destroying them and the stronghold they needed to reach.

Amara had ridden hard. Harder than she ever had. Time was slipping by and the longer she took to get to Newaught, the more people would die. She had passed Fairdenn on her journey south and had seen the empty city as a terrible sign. The demon army had been amassing there. The fact they were no longer there did not bode well for the angels. She needed to hurry.

She rode through the night, ignoring the sores forming between her legs and the bruises on her butt. She took her mind off the pain by learning to communicate with her Angel Blades. They took the form of twin girls appearing around the same age as her. They chose their names after a few hours of brainstorming with them. One would be called Ember and the other Blaze. They took the form very similar to hers, despite her informing them they could take any form they wanted. They both were short and petite with black hair. Ember wore her hair cropped short while Blaze left hers long and pulled back, tied behind her head in a high ponytail.

She talked with them mentally for hours, finding it easy to communicate with them without distracting her from what was going on around her. It was like she should have had this connection all her life, only lacking the entities to help facilitate it.

Her exhaustion forced her to stop. She all but fell off the horse and would have fallen asleep right there on the ground if she had let herself. Instead, she forced her weary body to get up and tie off the horse to a craggy bush. It might hold if the horse didn't pull much. She was in the plains now. But how? It had only been two days since she left Malach's group in the mountain pass. She had spent most of the first day getting down the muddy slopes. How had she made it this far without a break? How had the horse made it this far?

She glanced up at the sky where she presumed God resided and sent up a silent thanks. Then got to work caring for her horse. She finally rolled out her bed roll after what seemed like an eternity to her tired mind and laid down.

Her eyes opened, and she wondered for a second if she had even slept, but the sun was high in the sky now. She took a quick bite of some marching rations she had been given and saddled her horse to ride hard once again. Her horse didn't seem to appreciate being saddled so soon after being ridden so hard. Amara had a hard time keeping him still enough to saddle. It didn't help she must have picked the tallest horse in the bunch. She finally managed to saddle him and mounted up.

"No more breaks until Newaught," she told herself as much as she told the horse, and they were off again.

She caught her first sight of the city the next morning. Instead of going to the gate where there would be many questions regarding who she was and where she came from. She skirted around the city to the Shadow's secret entrance. The woods on that side of the city felt different. Something wasn't right. Maybe it was the oppression of the demons, but she felt eyes on her.

She reached the hidden door leading down into the caverns beneath the city and pulled her blades. The door was open. Something was wrong.

She barely deflected the blade aimed at her throat. She rolled off her horse and slapped it on the rump. Then turned to see where the throwing knife had come from. Nothing moved. A breeze played through the leaves on the trees, but she could see nothing out of place. A second blade sliced down at an angle, cutting a shallow gash in her arm and embedding itself into the ground. She whirled, wincing slightly at the pain.

She tracked the trajectory of the blade, but the tree was empty. Another blade bit at the back of her calf. They were coming from multiple directions and she had no way of predicting where they would come from next. Another blade embedded itself in her leather armor, piercing just enough to prick her skin. She pulled it from her armor and readied it. There was a pattern, there had to be. She just needed to find it.

She heard a faint click to her right, and a knife flew out of the brush. She side stepped it and sent her knife back in the same direction. Nothing.

Click.

She spun just in time to dodge the knife aimed at her back. Where is he? She turned a full circle. She didn't see anyone.

Click.

She dropped to the ground, not knowing where this knife was coming from. The weapon embedded itself in the ground next to her ear. She growled and pushed herself up. She was done with these games. Picking a direction, she charged out of the clearing. Trying to watch in every direction for pursuit. She ran for a half mile or so with no attack from any direction. She slowed to a stop. Waiting. Watching. Nothing happened. No attack came. She relaxed ever so slightly.

"He's protecting the entrance." She said out loud.

That would make sense. Ember replied. *From what you have told us...*

He is most likely a member of the Dark Hallow. Blaze finished for her sister.

Amara had noticed they did that a lot. Like they both knew what the other was thinking before they thought it. It was a bit annoying at first, but she was getting used to it. *How did you come to that conclusion?*

The Dark Hallow has been working to infiltrate the Shadows. Blaze stated.

And from you recounting of your flight from Caister... Ember started.

Your mother is most likely the hidden head of the Hollows. Blaze finished again.

We don't know that for sure but it makes sense. Ember added.

It makes even more sense if they are attacking now. Blade remarked.

"I showed my mother the layout of the Shadow's lair." Amara mentally kicked herself.

Yes, Ember remark quietly. *Though you didn't know what you were doing at the time.*

It's my fault, nonetheless. Amara gazed determinedly back toward the entrance. *And it's my job now to set it right. Did either of you see our assassin friend back there?*

No, Ember replied.

Neither did I, Blaze agreed.

"How was he getting around so quickly, then?" Amara asked out loud. She picked her way through the woods, careful to stay out of the clearing which held the entrance. She stopped well outside of the clearing and studied the surroundings.

There! Blaze's call made her jump. *Sorry, back to the right something glinted in a tree.*

Amara scanned back the other way and, sure enough, a glint shone through the foliage. She carefully circled around careful to keep the tree in sight. When she was behind it, she snuck up to it. She had learned how to move silently in these very woods with Malach, and the irony was not lost on her. She peered up through the lower branches but didn't see anyone.

She climbed the tree, but not far up, she found a small crossbow like contraption. It looked like it was modified to take larger ammunition than the normal bolt. A thin string was attached to the trigger. She followed it up and around a branch. This must be how he was triggering the weapons. If she searched the other trees around the clearing, she was sure she would find more of these crossbows. Now to find the person pulling the strings.

They would need to reload each crossbow manually, Ember mused.

And when they do, that's when we will strike, Blaze added.

Amara nodded and ascended higher into the tree. She climbed just far enough she would be shielded from view from the ground, but not too far as to lose sight of the crossbow.

She didn't have to wait long. A slender form scaled the tree, stopping at the branch the crossbow was affixed to. Amara's breath caught in her throat as she recognized the woman.

Xylissa.

Who is she to you? Ember asked, picking up on Amara's feelings.

Amara sent images to the twin blades of the woman. A meeting room in the Shadow's lair where three former Shadows' members conspired to kill the city guards. Then a battle on the top of Newaught's outer wall. Borden's death, Xylissa's defeat, and at last the woman railing against her, promising Amara death at the hands of the Dark Hallow.

Now, it seemed Xylissa intended to make good on her promise. Amara took a moment to calm her racing heart and take stock of the woman below her. Thin, beautiful, tall, Xylissa struck an intimidating figure. Her red hair was cut short, a scar parting her hair in an arc from her left temple to back to her ear. She wore formfitting black leather armor similar to Amara's. Knife hilts stuck out from her armor and many places, and a bow was strung across her chest. A single curved scimitar lay across her back within easy reach. From her first encounter with the assassin, she understood this wouldn't be an easy fight.

Amara didn't feel anger against the woman below her. Only pity, she had been used before by the Dark Hallows, by Lilith. Now she was no doubt being used again. Xylissa had carried so much rage and anger when they last met. That anger would now be aimed at Amara. Even with all that, she wondered what had happened to the woman to lead her down this dark path. If certain events hadn't happened, or had been allowed to happen, in her own life, might she herself turned out differently? Would she be standing next to Xylissa with a similar amount of rage?

Amara sighed. Nothing she could do about that now. She needed into the lair, especially if her friends and family were down there fighting for their lives. Xylissa planned to stop her, and she didn't think she would be able to get around killing the woman this time. But that didn't mean she had to spring Xylissa's trap a second time.

She quickly relayed her plan to the twin blades, and they agreed with her course of action.

Xylissa climbed down from the tree, having finished resetting the crossbow. Amara followed her, careful not to alert the assassin of her presence. Xylissa reset two more crossbows, checking their strings were still untangled. Amara followed Xylissa to a third tree, where the assassin climbed to a branch and sat amongst a veritable web of strings. Amara marveled at Xylissa's cleverness and ability to keep each string, and the corresponding crossbow, straight in her head.

Amara slipped back into the underbrush. Now she knew where Xylissa was watching from and could stay out of sight. She found each of the strings coming out from Xylissa's tree and cut them. Tying them each to a branch to keep them taught so the assassin wouldn't know until she pulled them that her trap had failed.

Once she was down, she took a deep breath and strode out into the clearing. This time, instead of the clicking of crossbows, all Amara heard was the rustling of branches.

Amara smiled up in Xylissa's direction. "If you want to kill me. Follow me down and fight me on even footing." With that, Amara climbed down into the Shadow's lair.

She had to hurry. No doubt Xylissa would be following. The need for revenge prompting the woman to leave her post. Amara smiled, hopefully that would free up the exit for any survivors to escape through. She just hoped the time it took her to sabotage the traps didn't make her too late to help the surviving Shadow members.

She had memorized the paths leading from this entrance to the main chambers the first time she had lived here, however short that was, and her memory didn't fail her now. The stone hallways were void of any human life as she descended. She passed the library, where stacks of books lay untouched on bookshelves. No one was there. Was she too late? She turned toward the living chambers. She found no living soul there, either. However, the signs of battle were unmistakable. Bodies littered the chambers, some still in their beds, taken by surprise.

Amara's heart broke. She moved from room to room, searching for any familiar faces among the dead. As she did, more and more of the bodies she found were members of the Dark Hallows. It would seem someone had discovered the assassins and sounded an alarm. Many of the Shadows' bodies she was familiar with, although none were more than acquaintances. The battle seemed to have ended halfway through the living chambers. Most likely the Shadows beating a hasty retreat. The bloody path of the wounded, dying, and dead leading her toward the main meeting hall.

Amara picked up her pace, now running down the straight halls and slowing at each corner. The Dark Hallow was still here or Xylissa wouldn't have been guarding the entrance. She peeked around a corner and ducked back quickly. A large enemy force was just around it. No shouts came from the group. They hadn't seen her. She cautiously peeked her head out again. There were a handful of assassins hiding behind different pieces of debris facing the barricaded entrance to the meeting hall. Neither side made any attempt to attack. The assassins waiting appeared to be more bored than excited or frightened. She felt like she would find a similar scene at every entrance.

The meeting hall would be the best place they could have barricaded themselves. There was space, food, and plenty of things to barricade the entrances. Unfortunately, they wouldn't be able to replenish their arsenal from there. She needed to communicate with the survivors in the hall and find out how she might help. Everything in her screamed to get into the hall; to see if Demien, Lawdel, and Raziel were safe. However, she wouldn't be able to do anything to help if she was dead. She moved through the tunnels checking each of the hall's entrances, but she had been correct in her assumption. Both sides guarded the barricades. There were at least five Dark Hallows members per entrance. So much for a speedy rescue.

If she couldn't contact them from any of the entrances, maybe she could find another way to help. She needed to get to the armory and see what she could use. Maybe she could pick off the Dark Hallows members one at a time. She ran out into the massive cavern that held the chasm and slid to a halt. Instead of the normal dark chasm, light spilled in from a large hole in the wall that was open to the daylight outside. She stood gaping for a few moments before collecting herself and ducking back in the tunnel she had come from.

The devil had smashed through the outer wall when he had escaped, but she hadn't expected such a large hole. It was clear there had been a cave in when he had destabilized that wall, opening it farther. She peered back out of the tunnel and took in the cavern. Many of the pillars holding up the ceiling on that side of the expanse had collapsed as well. It was a wonder the whole place hadn't come down, taking the city above with it. How much of the city was directly overhead? She would never feel safe in Newaught again, know the cave system could collapse at any time. She exited the tunnel again, this time more cautiously.

This was where Michael and Gabriel had imprisoned Satan and Lucifer? Ember asked.

Yes, until I set him free, Amara replied.

You didn't do it on purpose. Blaze reassured her. *How could you have known your amulet was the key to their prison?*

A noise coming from the opening drew her attention, and she ducked back into the tunnel for a second time. She had just made it inside the tunnel as the large two-headed dragon flew through the opening into the cavern, his wings billowing out to slow his decent his four legs extended for landing. When he hit the ground, his claws cut into the stone and sent a tremor through the rock around Amara. She ducked, shielding her head from the rocks broken loose from the ceiling. She glanced up just in time to see a large chunk fall from the opening, widening it and letting more daylight in. The chunk of rock crashed to the stone floor, causing a deafening crack that echoed around the pillars slapping her ears over and over. Amara stood when the sound had mercifully faded. She noticed for the first time the ground was covered in claw marks. The Devil was using the Shadow's lair as his base of operations. Had they been besieged since she freed the Devil? It was good she arrived when she did.

Lilith, her mother, stepped out from a tunnel to greet the Devil, but before she could, Xylissa hurried from a third tunnel and stopped short prostrating herself in fear.

"What is it?" Lilith snapped.

"My lady, uh, my Lord, I apologize for the interruption, but I think there is something you need to know."

"Spit it out, worm." One head bellowed. Amara wasn't sure if it was Satan or Lucifer. Or if it even mattered.

"A girl got passed me and is now in the tunnel system. The same girl who stopped the assassination of the guards and caught Grent and myself."

"What is her name?" Lilith asked.

"Amara Westbay, my lady,"

Xylissa's eyes never left the floor, or she would have seen anger cross Lilith's face. "My daughter is back and seems to be determined to ruin our plans."

"There is nothing that sprat can do to stop us now." The second head said. "Lilith, our time is at hand climb onto my shoulders, and we will be off to see the end of this war. Leave this worm to deal with your offspring."

"Yes, my Lord," Lilith turned to Xylissa. "Kill her and then finish the other rats. I leave this in your hands. When we return, I expect you to have full control of these facilities."

"Yes, lady Lilith," Amara could hear the smile in Xylissa's voice. "With pleasure."

Lilith climbed up and straddled one of the dragons' necks, and the Devil turned and leaped into the air, his wing beating the wind fiercely. Amara turned away as loose stones and dirt hurtled her way. By the time the wind died down, the Devil's tail was disappearing through the open wall. Amara glanced back at Xylissa. This would probably be one of the few times she would have Xylissa alone. Also, if she took her on now, she could stay anonymous and move through the facility without being hunted by every Dark Hallow assassin.

Amara stepped from her hiding spot as Xylissa was just raising her head. She jumped to her feet and launched a throwing knife in one motion. Amara deflected it with Ember and charged to bring Xylissa within striking distance. The assassin pulled her scimitar and brought it down as Amara brought her own blades up, catching it in a high cross block. Amara used her momentum and brought her knee up into Xylissa's stomach. The assassin disengaged, sucking in air to replace what Amara had knocked out of her. Amara didn't stop, driving her blades forward while she had her opponent off balance. Xylissa backpedaled, fending off Amara's attacks only by losing ground. Amara drove her back toward the chasm. It hadn't been her initial plan, but it seemed like a good idea now.

Xylissa must have noticed the peril she was in. She drew a long knife and used it to break Amara's offensive, planting her feet, and standing her ground. Amara continued her onslaught but was no longer gaining ground. Xylissa eyes veered from their focus on her to something behind her for only a moment. Amara reacted, jumping to the side away from the chasm and spun to find another opponent. This assassin was male and not much taller than Amara. Now she would have to play this more defensively. She launched a throwing knife in his direction and turned to catch Xylissa's scimitar with Ember and used Blaze to turn away the long knife plunging toward her belly. It was Amara's turn to backpedal, placing her back to the stone wall. She didn't want to get surrounded or maneuvered off the cliff.

"You little wretch. I'll skin you alive for what you did to me." Xylissa came on hard, attacking from both directions.

Amara was able to fend her off but only just. If the male assassin joined, she would be in trouble. It had been a mistake to attack Xylissa in the open.

"You cost me my position within the Dark Hallow. You put me in a hole down here in the dark for weeks."

It was all Amara could do to parry each strike as the other woman railed at her.

"All I could think about was how I would kill you when I got out. When Lady Lilith found me, she sent me to guard the entrance and who just happened to come along. You! You humiliated me."

Amara found her opening. Xylissa had put all her strength into her last swing overextending her body and unbalancing her stance. Amara ducked the crosscut and Xylissa's body follow the momentum of her blade. Amara plunged Blaze up to the blade's hilt in Xylissa's exposed side, rolling over the woman and blocked the second assassin's long knife with Ember. She caught his wrist, reversed her weight and pulled him over her. She landed on her back on the ground planted her foot in his gut and sent the man flying over her head to collide with Xylissa.

Amara rolled to her feet and readied herself for another attack, but none came. Xylissa's scimitar poked up through the back of the male assassin. Amara had gotten lucky, and he had fallen on her weapon.

A wet, and no doubt bloody, cough came from under the body. Xylissa was still alive.

Amara pulled the corpse off the woman and kicked away her weapons before turning her over.

Xylissa held her side as blood welled up around her fingers. Noticing Amara, she tried to spit blood at her but only succeeded in causing another painful coughing fit.

Amara knelt next to her. She lifted the woman's hands and studied the wound. She wouldn't last much longer.

"I'm sorry it had to be this way." Amara guided Xylissa's weakening hands back to the wound.

"Witch," Xylissa coughed. She reached a shaky hand out, trying to grasp Amara's throat even as her life blood pooled around her.

Amara backed up, shaking her head. She wanted to turn away from the woman. She didn't want to watch her life ebb away, but she couldn't. A tear slipped from her eye, and she wiped those behind it away. She stood bearing witness to Xylissa's last breath.

I don't understand. Blaze sounded confused. *She was your enemy. And yet you shed tears for her.*

Just because they fight against us doesn't mean their life isn't precious. Amara replied.

Part of her had hoped Xylissa would change her ways when Amara had first brought her to be tried after the attempted assassination of the city guard. However, that had been a naive dream of an innocent girl. She had seen so much death in the last few weeks. Why did this one affect her so much?

You cry because you knew her? Ember asked.

Not really, Amara replied. *At least not any more than an acquaintance.*

Why *was* she crying? Because she could have been Xylissa? If she had been raised by Lilith, she would most likely be an assassin as well. Maybe not much different from the woman she had killed. Or maybe it was just more personal than the soldiers she had killed.

She took a deep breath and calmed her mind. She needed to hide the bodies. Then she needed to find a way to make contact with the remaining Shadows. That would be easier now that she was anonymous.

She rolled the bodies over the side of the chasm and shuddered. Is that how her body would be treated when she died? Would she be discarded like debris, or would she be honored and missed? Only time would tell, but either way, she needed to leave before she was caught.

She turned just as two men in black clothing walked out of a tunnel.

"I'm telling you. We need to go in and get them." One said to the other. "There aren't many of them left and we outnumber them."

There was nowhere to run. She could fight them, but she was already tired, and she wasn't sure if she could win another fight.

"No, both the master of the chapter in Caister and the chapter in Newaught are still in there and you saw how that other man fought. He had the strength of ten men..." The second man's voice trailed off as they noticed Amara.

"What are you doing down here?" The first asked angrily.

Amara fingered Ember's hilt, ready to pull the blade if they attacked.

"You should be up at a barricade." The second assassin pointed back the way they had come. "Just because you want to see the Devil's prison doesn't negate your duty to the Dark Hallow."

"Oh," Amara moved her hand off her hilt. "Yes, sorry, I just wanted to see it for myself. I'll head back now."

"Wait," the first assassin stopped her. "What do you think we should do?"

"What?" Amara's head was spinning, trying to figure out what he was asking. "What do you mean?"

"Do you think we should charge in, or wait them out?" He explained.

"Oh, um, I think we should wait." She said, thinking fast. "They will run out of food and as they grow weaker, we will kill them easier and risk less."

"See," the second said triumphantly. "And I don't fancy going against those left, even outnumbering them as we do."

"At least those who escaped haven't returned to free their masters." The first mumbled. "Or we wouldn't outnumber them anymore."

"Some escaped?" Amara asked.

"Where were you for the attack?" The first assassin asked. "We took them by surprise but only got a few of them before the alarm was sounded. Most of the shadow's members escaped up to Newaught. The Demon forces left in the city have been searching for them, but there are barely enough of them to keep the peace amongst the common folk."

Amara had a plan now. There was a meeting house where they were supposed to go if there was heat on them after a job. Maybe if she went there, she could find the rest of the Shadow's members and come back with a force to free those in the meeting hall. She needed to make contact with them first, though.

"I'm new to the Dark Hallow." Amara lied. "I wasn't here for the first attack. I just got down here."

"A recruit?" the second asked, but before Amara could reply, he continued. "Report to Grent for your assignment, then. And no more sightseeing."

"Yes, sir," Amara saluted and ran off toward the meeting hall. She was happy to get out of that situation.

Why was the hunchback in charge of the troop assignments? Maybe she underestimated Grent and his part in all of this. She had to stay away from him, or he would recognize her as Xylissa had. He would also be looking for revenge, and she didn't want to have to deal with him yet.

She would make contact with the masters. Then bring the surviving shadows down on the Dark Hallow and take back their home.

Chapter 15

Kragen sensed Azazel's mind probing and responded without opening his eyes or moving a muscle. He didn't want to tip off his captors that he was in contact with their enemies. He was ready to kill these pitiful guards. They thought they were keeping him in this cell. They thought they were protecting their puny army from a dangerous spy. In reality, he had already secured his escape and he would snap their necks with one hand on the way out. The only thing keeping him here now was the fact that it was easier to stay here instead of being on the run. As long as he was here, they thought they were safe. His explosives remained hidden, or they would have questioned him about them. Now everything was ready. He was just biding his time until Azazel arrived with the Army. And that time was now upon him.

My master, Kragen addressed the mind touching his.

Kragen, is everything ready for the Devil's arrival?

Lucifer and Satan have been released?

Yes, Azazel sounded annoyed. *Are the explosives in place?*

Yes, master. There will be many holes in their defenses by which you and the army can enter. I have been here long enough that the explosives should do most of the work for you.

Good, we will catch the fools unaware. The army is setting up across the field from the stronghold. We have already caught them by surprise. They no doubt thought we would wait until we could move the siege engines over the mountains. Kragen, you've done well. Be patient and wait until I give you the signal and then light the fuses. Azazel cut the line of communication off before he could reply.

Kragen was trembling with anticipation. His hard work would soon pay off. He would have his reward not long after that.

"Good morning, Kragen,"

He opened his eyes to see Emmeline standing at his cell door with a tray of food and a genuine smile on her face. She had been the only one who had shown him kindness since they caught him. The only one to smile at him and the only one to talk to him other than to interrogate him. It made him sick. This girl had no idea that kindness didn't get you anywhere but dead. It was nothing but a way for someone to manipulate others. This girl would be fodder for a battle. Nothing but a body to throw at the enemy. Kragen would soon have the pleasure of running his blade through her chest. Or maybe he would rip her throat out with his bare hands.

"I brought you breakfast," Emmeline continued, breaking Kragen out of his twisted fantasy. "Cook made eggs and bacon this morning. I'm afraid it's a little cold, but it tastes good all the same." She slid the tray through a slot in the bars.

He decided he wouldn't kill the guards first. He picked up the tray as Emmeline smiled at him. No, he would kill this dumb, naive girl first. He would enjoy slowly stealing the life from her as they watch helplessly. Only a matter of time now until he could kill again.

Ariel, Skie, and Malach lay on their bellies on an outcropping of cliff overlooking the valley. Skie's hot breath warmed Malach's arm and hand. It was a comforting reminder of the wolf's presence, even though he hadn't had time to spend with her recently. Her loyalty struck him, not for the first time, as something rare and something he took for granted far too often.

The Demon army lay quietly below them on the valley floor. No one had guessed they would have arrived this soon. The army apparently had left their heavy siege engines behind to make the trek through the mountains sooner.

From their vantage point on the cliff, they could see the valley the army had marched through and now camped in. The underbrush trampled so thoroughly it would take it more than a month to grow back and there were still more troops filing in. On the opposite side of the valley, a sloping hill slowly formed the ridge once again. If they were on that side, they might be able to mount a hit and run or diversionary tactic to give the bulk of their force a chance to make a run for it. Unfortunately, the sheer cliff on this side made that all but impossible. They would have to move down the mountain on an indirect and exposed route. One, maybe two people, could move down unseen, but a force able to do any serious damage would be spotted and routed.

Maybe they wanted to catch the angel army out in the open? Malach mused.

That makes little sense, Reckoning chimed in. *When the Demon army arrived, they made camp well away from the stronghold. The angel army was allowed to pack up tents and equipment and retreat into the mountain. If they were hoping to catch us off guard, they would have attacked immediately.*

Reckoning was right. It had taken almost a full twenty-four hours for the angel army to shut the doors behind them. Plenty of time for the demon army to attack. No, they were planning something else.

Maybe a long-term siege? Wait until we are starving and ask for our surrender? That doesn't seem like something Lucifer and Satan have the patients for.

Don't underestimate their patients. Reckoning warned. *Remember, they've spent hundreds of this world's years planning to overthrow God and take the throne of heaven.*

Malach nodded slowly, still mulling over what the enemy could be planning.

Ariel interrupted Malach's thoughts by holding up a hand. He motioned for them to make their way back to their camp.

Malach scooted back on his belly even as his father did the same. He didn't think anyone would spot them this far up, but why take any chances with that many eyes below? They quickly made their way back to report what they had found.

Gabriel, Leviathan, Ana, Honora, and Daziar awaited their return in a large tent. There would have been a small fire if they weren't worried about being seen. Although simply being inside the tent was enough to warm them from the bite of the wind outside.

"What's the word?" Gabriel stood as they entered.

"Thousands." Ariel frowned and crossed his arms. "And more pouring in from the trail to Fairdenn."

"Why are they here early?" Daziar frowned. "Or rather, *how* are they here early? No one expected them until the passes were more accessible. Why didn't we see this coming?"

"Because we expected them to bring the war machines through the passes, not leave them behind." Gabriel explained. "It's unfortunate they're here. Our forces will have to stay behind the stronghold walls, but we're still on a similar timetable. They will be forced to build their war machines here to breach the stronghold walls. The more pressing matter at hand is, how do *we* get into the stronghold?"

Ariel stepped forward. "Before we answer that question, I think we should decide *if* we should get into the stronghold."

"What are you saying?" Ana narrowed her eyes at him.

"We could slow their progress in building their war machines out here with some careful sabotage." Ariel gave her a half smile. "While you've been stuck inside the stronghold for nearly two millennia, I've been out in the field. Espionage is second nature to me. With the small force and a well thought out plan, we could do a lot of damage. Not only to gain time for our forces, but to weaken the enemy's resolve and maybe weaken their numbers."

"What do you have in mind?" Gabriel crossed her arms.

"They will have brought their black powder with them." Ariel's half grin spread fully across his face. "That amount of powder could do some substantial damage. And they would have to bring more from Fairdenn, or wherever they have it stockpiled."

Gabriel nodded slowly. "That could work well. Ariel, you and Malach continue reconnaissance. Find the stockpile of powder and determine a low-risk plan to destroy it with a high chance of casualties. Ana, you and Daziar find me a path to the stronghold now that ours is blocked. I want a way out if things go sideways. If we can be a thorn in their sides, we will, but I don't want to be caught out in the cold when the real war starts."

Ariel nodded and walked out of the tent.

Malach turned and fell in behind him as they started out of the camp.

"Ariel!" Ana called.

Malach turned as the female angel and Daziar caught up with them.

"I didn't appreciate your comment in there," Ana said through gritted teeth.

Malach glanced at Daziar, who wore a scowl and crossed his arms.

"I meant nothing by it," Ariel said coolly. "I only meant you haven't been out in the field in a while and that we might want to take stock of our possible opportunities. I have extensive experience with sabotage and sticking to the shadow."

"And I don't?" Ana said accusingly.

Ariel's eyes betrayed his thoughts as he glanced at her wings.

Malach looked at them as well. They *were* quite conspicuous. They glowed and appeared like undulating whips if light rather than feathers. At night, they would be a beacon in the darkness.

"Just because my wings glow now does not mean they glow in the dark." Ana replied.

"Ana," Ariel deflated a little and took more of a mentorial tone with her. "I genuinely didn't mean anything negative, but you don't have the experience some of us do."

"But I shouldn't be counted out." Ana's expression softened a little. "I understand you were the right person for the job. I just don't think I should be dismissed so readily."

"Fair point. I apologize for offending you. I *do* think we have the correct jobs, however."

"*Do* your wings glow in the dark?" Malach asked, still perplexed at the how her wings could glow now but not during the night. He had never paid enough attention to her wings at night to know if they did or not. "For that fact, how do your wings work? I mean, I've seen many styles of wings, but I don't know how they got that way. Obviously, you can't just change them at will."

"Yeah, how *does* that work?" Daziar piped up from behind Ana before either angel could speak.

"If you're quiet for a moment, I'm sure Ariel would love to tell you." Ana shot Daziar a look that withered him where he stood.

"Ana is right." Ariel appeared to stifle a chuckle. "Wings are very important to us. We change them when some life event happens, like when our role in the war changes, or our station within the hierarchy is affected. My wings were not always black. Once all our wings looked like the white feathers Gabriel wears. Although unlike her four wings, most of us still only had two. When Satan and Lucifer led the revolt, those who fell were cursed to look as they do now. As far as I can tell, the majority of them cannot change their appearance. However, for those of us who were sent to earth were given wings to fit our roles and station. My wings were originally armored like Camael and Cathetel's. When my role changed and I needed a less conspicuous look, my wings followed suit. I didn't choose the black feathers; they just became black. They also folded down farther and easier so I could hide them better."

"We believe," Ana cut in, continuing Ariel's line of thought. "God designed them to change according to our needs."

"Why are yours light?" Daziar's brow furrowed.

"Don't hurt yourself thinking so hard," Ana laughed. "I was a scout and messenger for most of my time on earth. My wings are meant for speed and long-distance flights. They don't drag the wind or tire as quickly as others, but they are much more vulnerable."

"So, back to Malach's original question. Do your wings glow in the dark?" Daziar asked.

"Does snow?" Ana grinned at him.

"No, it just reflects the light." Daziar replied, not understanding the meaning behind her question.

Ana gestured for him to continue with that line of thinking.

It took Daziar an embarrassing amount of time to put it together and Malach finally blurted, "Just like the snow, her wings don't emit light but reflect it."

"Oh," Daziar drew out the word as realization finally dawned on him.

Malach just shook his head at his friend. "Good thing you're strong."

"And good looking." Daziar added.

"Jury's still out on that one." Ana nudged Daziar in the ribs.

"Hey!"

"We need to get moving," Ariel brought their attention back to the matters at hand. "Ana, you and Daziar have the more important job. You need to secure our path out of the mountains and to the stronghold. We will need it whether Malach and I find a way to strike at the demon army or not."

Ana's face turned serious. "Yes, we won't let you or Gabriel down. Oh, this might be of some use to you." Ana handed Ariel a tube-like object.

"What is it?" Malach asked.

"A spy glass," Daziar stepped up, taking it from Ariel, his chest puffed out with pride. "You open it like this." He extended the spy glass to three times its previous length. "And then you look through this end."

Ariel gave Daziar a withering look, but Daziar didn't seem to notice.

"I feel you are missing a key piece of information here." Malach crossed his arms.

"Huh?"

"What does it do?" Malach asked.

Ariel laughed hard and deep at the look of dejection on Daziar's face.

Ana could barely contain her laugher as well but managed to say. "You were doing so well too, Daz. Malach, the spyglass, helps you see long distance by magnifying the objects you are looking at. The farther you telescope it, the more it magnifies."

Malach glanced over at his father, who was still working to contain his outburst, and took the spyglass from his friend. "Thanks Daz, I appreciate it. And thank you, Ana. I'm sure it will come in handy."

"Sorry, I haven't had that good of a laugh in a while," Ariel replied, wiping a tear from his left eye. "Thank you two. May God give you wisdom and illuminate your path."

Malach and Ariel turned and headed back toward the cliff outcropping overlooking the Demon camp.

Not far from the cliff, Ariel pushed Malach into the underbrush suddenly and dove next to him, landing hard on his shoulder.

"Dad-"

Ariel cut him off with a harsh shush, searching the sky.

Nothing happened. Nothing Changed.

"Maybe just my imaginat-" Ariel cut himself off as a shadow passed over them, proceeding the monster by only a few seconds.

The two-headed Dragon passed just over the treetops, wind buffeting the pair from its passing. Malach shielded his eyes from the dust and detritus it stirred. When he looked up again, the dragon had disappeared from view.

Without a word, they crawled from their hiding spot and crept cautiously toward their original destination. It took them much longer to reach the cliff than the first time, but neither wanted to take any chances. They didn't have a hope in heaven against the dragon and the dual being's combined power. They reached the cliff in time to witness the behemoth disappear into the largest tent in the growing army camp.

"He didn't have anyone with him this time." Ariel said under his breath.

Malach glanced at Ariel. "Are you referring to the woman who was with the beast when it attacked us at sea?"

"Yes, Lilith." Ariel replied. "I'd know that witch anywhere. We've clashed a few times over the years, and she was the one who ordered my wings clipped, even though Azazel carried out the deed."

"Who is Lilith, really?" Malach asked, remembering Amara's heritage. He didn't feel like he should tell his father since it wasn't really his secret to tell.

"There are a lot of rumors and myths about her, but she was cursed by God for her disobedience. She was cursed to wander the earth and never have children. She is as ageless and cunning as the devil himself. Although, she is still only human in most ways."

"Then, she can be killed?"

"Not easily."

"But she's not here?"

"She didn't arrive with the Devil. I don't think we can safely assume she isn't here, however." Ariel warned. "If we work on the assumption she is here, and turn out to be wrong, there will be a lot fewer consequences than if we assume the other way."

Malach took a moment to digest that.

Ariel pulled the spyglass out and started scanning the camp. "Azazel is here."

"You see him?"

"No, but I see his spawn in one corner of the camp."

"What?"

"Nephilim. Every one." Ariel didn't take his eye off the camp but explained. "He tends to breed his own army. Training them from the time they walk to be his soldiers."

Malach shuddered involuntarily. "The Nephilim we encountered at Fairdenn?"

"Was most likely one of his soldiers." Ariel finished the thought for him. "No doubt he is in the tent with most or all of the remaining Seven."

"The Seven Lords of Hell, right?"

"Correct, although I doubt Asmodeus has arrived yet. His pride is as legendary as his power, and he rarely conforms to any constraints of time put on him."

"Even if it's the devil putting those constraints on him?"

"It would seem. He was more powerful than either Satan or Lucifer until the two of them became one. Now his power still rivals the dragon, although he seems to care less about conquest than the others, barring Belfagor."

"What do you mean? Belfagor doesn't want to fight?"

"Yes, and no. Belfagor is slothful." Ariel explained. "Speak of the devil." Ariel handed the spyglass over to Malach. "To the right of the large tent and a little way behind it."

Malach scanned the tents where his father had indicated and spotted one of the most grotesque scenes he had laid sight on to date. Atop a litter, carried by a group of humans, was a demon who appeared to have melted onto the platform on which he....sat? He couldn't tell if the demon was sitting or laying but he surely wasn't standing. Malach sincerely doubted he could.

"That's Belfagor," Ariel told him. "He's looking rather thin these days, comparatively."

"Thin?"

"If you had seen him at the height of the time of peace, you would understand. Most likely, with Asmodeus and Azazel running things, they put an end to him stealing from every caravan traveling through Demon Territory. He would have had to go on a diet. As I said, Belfagor is lazy. He is most likely only here because otherwise the other surviving seven would kill him after the war if he didn't show his malformed face. As you can guess, he himself can't fight, but he wants to win the war if only to not be inconvenienced by it. He is who we have to thank for the invention of black powder."

"He invented that?"

"Most likely. He is a quite accomplished alchemist and inventor. He is also who thought up many of the war machines and chemicals used on the battlefield. As well as many other things like the running water and sewage ways in the big cities."

"Really?"

"Yep, he lives to make his life easier, even if that means making other's lives easier in the process. However, if he *is* here, I wouldn't put it past them to have a new invention in the coming battle. We will need to watch him closely to see if we can surmise any surprises that might be coming."

"So much for eating anything, then."

Ariel gave him a confused look.

"As soon as I catch sight of him, it will all come back up."

Ariel smiled ruefully. "Yes, well, your sacrifice will be noted."

"So why don't we strike now while we have all the leaders in one place? One well place explosive would kill or injure every one of them."

"Study your surroundings before you get too excited, Malach. We would have to either sneak through the whole of the demon army or drop something from the sky. That would require killing many of the surviving demons and subsequently sounding the alarm, defeating the propose or the mission in the first place."

Malach nodded, his understanding scanning the camp of any better ideas. He almost missed it. Scanning the spy glass past it in a blur, but then snapping it back as the view registered in his mind. A small pile of barrels. "Is that what I think it is?" He handed the spyglass to his father and pointed to one close to the edge of the camp.

"I believe it is. There are a few piles of them scattered around the area where they are building their war machines." Ariel smiled at him over the spyglass. "I think we just found the best way to hurt them."

After leaving Malach and Ariel, Ana and Daziar didn't immediately head out of the camp as Daziar had hoped. Instead, they went back to the command tent, which was now empty of beings. The map of the region was laid out on a rock serving as a makeshift table. They studied it intently, as they had been for more than an hour.

"One more time, why can't we walk around the lake on the opposite side of the demon camp?" Daziar pointed to the far side of the lake. "I mean, they might attack us, but it would only be a few demons and we would be able to fend them off with little to no losses."

"Do you see where these mountains butt up against the lake?" Ana pointed to the mountains and explained it to him again. "Most of these points are impassable without wading up to your neck in the lake, and it is still too cold for that. We would lose men to exposure before the demons ever got to us."

"And we can't go around the other way or we would be vulnerable to attack from the main army," Daziar stated the obvious. "Could we build rafts and float across?"

"That's an idea, but we would be sitting ducks for any bombardment from either arrows or dropped explosives."

"Ugh," Daziar scratched his head vigorously. "Dawn doesn't have any ideas."

"Nor does Hope."

"Then we are Hope-less," Daziar grinned at his pun.

Ana just gave him a withering look.

"We might have a solution to your dilemma," Ariel stepped through the opening in the tent.

"Where's Malach?" Daziar asked.

"Still on the ridge overlooking the enemy camp." Ariel walked over to the map. "We are going to walk right by the enemy camp. Here." He pointed to the south side of the emerald lake.

"How do you propose we do that without getting utterly destroyed?" Ana asked.

"Because no one will be looking our direction." Ariel grinned, as if he knew a secret they didn't.

Ana sighed. "Spit it out. What's your master plan?"

Malach, Daziar, and Ana lay on the cliff overlooking the camp. The sun was low in the sky, darkness would soon fall. The rest of the army was waiting for their signal to move. Ana was looking through the spyglass, following Ariel's progress.

"Is this really a good idea?" Daziar asked.

"It's a bit too late to be asking that now." Ana took her eye off the glass to give him an incredulous look.

"I *did* bring up this point earlier. When Ariel was pitching his plan to Gabriel."

"That's fair, he did." Malach pointed out. "And he was shot down then, too."

"I still think this is a bad idea." Daziar grumbled. "What if he gets caught?"

"He won't." Ana once again took her eyes form the spyglass to give him a withering look. "He's been doing this for a few thousand years at this point. He won't get caught. Here, watch a master at work." She handed Daziar the spyglass.

He took it from her and found Ariel on the outskirts of the camp. It almost seemed like he wasn't trying to hide. He walked out of the bushes and directly into the camp like he owned the place. No one even gave him a second look. Daziar realized his mouth was open, and he shut it. *Shouldn't he at least be hiding from some of the soldiers? Wouldn't someone recognize him as a person who shouldn't be there?* He passed soldier after soldier, even walking through crowds of them, and no one stopped him.

"Sometimes the best camouflage is confidence." Ana smiled at his bewilderment.

Ariel walked almost all the way to the stores of black powder and siege engines before being challenged. He talked heatedly with the soldier who stopped him, making anger gestures, and he was let through in the space of a few moments. He walked past the barrels of black powder, stopping momentarily to pick one up. Ariel stabbed a hole in the barrel, letting the powder spill onto the ground as he walked away toward the Belfagor's tent.

That wasn't the plan we agreed on. Daziar thought, shaking his head. *There's no stopping him now. Is he hoping to kill the demon lord?*

Ariel approached the tent from behind, stooping to leave the barrel. He opened the barrel and took a handful of the powder out. Retracing his steps, he dropped the powder in his hands to leave a smaller trail. He saluted toward the cliff, which was the signal for their group to start moving.

"Malach go," Daziar commanded, not taking his eyes off Ariel. He heard Malach race off into the woods.

Ariel's movement alerted a couple of guards close to him and they turned his direction.

"Uh oh," Daziar said. "Ariel has been spotted."

Ariel was waiting the few minutes as planned when the two soldiers came up on him, lowering their spears. Ariel held up his hands and slowly turned to face the pair. They talked for a minute, but it was clear to Daziar the guards were not buying his story.

"We need to go help him." Daziar handed the spyglass to Ana's waiting hand.

"How do you propose we do that?" Ana asked. "Fight our way through a few hundred soldiers?"

"No, fly us down there and we can cover him while he lights the explosives." Daziar explained. "You can fly us out in the confusion and Ariel can stealth his way out, just like we planned."

"That's...well that's not a bad idea. You know we will raise the alarm when we get close."

"The alarm is about to be raised, anyway."

"Ariel's drawn storm. You're right, let's go."

"Wait, you just said I'm righ-" Daziar didn't get to finish his gloating as Ana lifted him up, her arms under his ribs stealing his breath.

She dove off the cliff and for a second Daziar thought they were destined for a bloody end on the rocks below. Just before he was totally sure his life was over, she pulled up, stealing the breath he was just fighting to get back. She was much stronger than she looked. They glided just over the treetops, coming in low. She was no doubt hoping to not be spotted until the last moment. It would seem her plan worked. The trees fell away, and they were over the top of the camp before the first shouts reached their ears.

"Get ready!" Ana shouted over the sound of angry voices and the rushing wind.

Daziar lifted his feet, preparing for the imminent drop.

"Now!" Ana let him go.

Her aim was precise. His booted feet slammed into the chest of one of the two soldiers fighting Ariel, and he drove them down as hard as he dared, crushing the man's ribs with a crunch. He felt the solid ground beneath his feet and knew the man would never rise again. Daziar tucked and rolled, using the momentum to rise to his feet and pull Dawnbreaker, his blade in the form of a sickle sword. His one arm was tied to his chest. He still couldn't feel it, and he found it tended to wander when he wasn't paying attention. With it tied down, he had less to worry about during a fight. However, he must have landed badly on it. His elbow was sticking out at an odd angle. He would have to deal with that later. He ducked under a raise axe and rammed his shoulder into the chest of his attacker, stabbing down at the same time skewing the man's foot. The soldier howled and collapsed as Daziar bowled through him and into the next enemy.

Ana had been right. He had been a skilled fighter with his great grandfather's sword, but now that he had one which complimented his size and balance; he was a force to be reckoned with. If only he had been more mindful before, he might not have lost the feeling in his arm, but it was too late to change that now. He cut his way through two more unfortunate souls and then retreated to Ariel's back. He grinned grimly. Ana landed next to them and they formed a barrier around Ariel to give him the moments he needed to light the powder.

Not like Daziar and Ana did much. None of the soldiers were keen to take them on until a beast of a man pushed his way through the growing crowd. He was no doubt a nephilim. Hefting a two-handed sword into a ready stance before charging at Daziar. He was not going to be able to block that sword with his one arm and protect Ariel this close to him, so he charged, leaving Ana and Ariel to defend against the soldiers emboldened enough to attack. Daziar ducked under the sword as it whistled through the air and ran full tilt into a solid wall made of muscle and sinew. Daziar's own muscles in his neck and chest screamed in pain. Although, his shoulder was mostly numb to anything. He fell onto his butt.

"Well, that wasn't supposed to happen." Daziar rolled as the two-handed sword came down on top of him.

He kept rolling, building enough momentum to rise to his feet again. The nephilim had stuck with him, however. He immediately had to retreat as the hulk of a man came barreling after him, giving him no reprieve. Ducking the sword again, he heard it scrape against metal as it went over. Daziar was sure he had been hit. Instead, half of a body fell next to him. He recognized the colors of the enemy. He ducked left, trying to get back around to Ariel and Ana. This man didn't care who was in his way, friend or foe, they fell all the same. Daziar fended off attacks from other enemies, but they were each killed by the huge two-handed sword cleaving them in some semblance of half. Soon the soldier stayed well out of the way of the nephilim.

"Daz it's lit!" Ana called.

"Time to go!" Ariel agreed.

Daziar's back was to the stack of black powder, and he tried to duck left. The Nephilim dropped the tip of his blade to the ground, pushing him back with his other hand. He tried to fain left again and then run right but caught a fist across his jaw for his efforts. He glanced behind him. The flame spat and sputtered toward the stack.

"You will have a front-row seat to the explosion you seek." The nephilim grinned. "If I don't survive, I'll gain a seat of honor in the life to come."

"Or you will just die." Daziar shouted, but his words did no good.

There was only one option left, and he took it. He charged the man, batting the sword away as it was leveled for him to run onto. However, instead of trying to tackle the nephilim, he let go of Dawnbreaker, letting her slide between the behemoths legs. Drawing his hunting knife, the one with the redwood handle, he rammed it home in the man's hip. It stuck fast and Daziar angled his body, using his momentum once again to swing himself behind the Nephilim just as the stacks of powder exploded.

The Nephilim's body slammed into him before he had time to set his feet and he was carried along with it. The heat of the explosion singed his hair and blistered his exposed skin. Having been through an explosion once before, he was prepared for the burning pain that came with it and the hearing loss as well. But he wasn't ready for the nephilim to land on top of him. The behemoth of a man crushed the wind out of him as they bounced along and Daziar lost his grip on his knife. He was vaguely aware his body had come to a stop on the cool ground, but the fog that swirled through his mind refused to clear. He open his eyes, the tears streaming from them blurred his vision but the bright flames were impossible to miss.

He needed to get up.

He needed to retrieve Dawnbreaker.

He needed to get out of the enemy camp.

A secondary, much smaller explosion lit up the night to his right. The barrel Ariel had left at Belfagor's tent. Then a third explosion? Maybe some of the powder hadn't been ignited in the initial explosion? It didn't matter.

"Daz, on your feet." Ana sounded far away. She lifted him onto his shaky legs and slapping a familiar hilt into his hand.

Daz! Thank the Lord almighty you're alive! Dawn shouted in his mind. *We need to leave!*

He fumbled the weapon slightly but managed to get it into the sheath. He felt Ana's arms once again below his ribs and braced himself, and she launched them into the air.

"Ariel?" Daziar's vision cleared a little, and he saw the carnage below. Bodies and body parts lay scatter on the ground with the two points of the explosions at the center of it all. Many more men were running to put out the flame before they spread to the rest of the camp. They had killed hundreds of soldiers and injured hundreds more.

"He is already out of the camp and to safety. I only hope we gave everyone enough time to sneak by."

"My knife." Daziar realized he had left it in the hip of the nephilim.

"Too late to go back for it now, but I'll get you a hundred like it for what you just pulled off. I thought for sure the explosion would kill you. Quick thinking using the Nephilim as a shield."

Darkness was creeping in on the edges of his vision and he fought to stay conscious.

"You've done good Daz. Maybe you *are* a worthy student."

He could hear the smile in her voice and let the darkness take him. He was safe in her arms.

Chapter 16

Amara had worked her way into the next guard rotation on the far side of the main hall without talking with Grent. There were only two Dark Hallow members with her, and she planned to overpower them. Guard duty was exhaustively boring.

Even though they were Dark Hallows, she didn't think she could bring herself to stab them in the backs. But that didn't mean she couldn't knock them out. They were supposed to walk sections of the tunnels every half hour. When her turn came, she got up and walked out into the tunnel. She quickly doubled back and got behind the two guards. Now to knock them out.

A strong arm wrapped around her waist from behind and she was pulled back. A hand covered her mouth and muffled her shout. Not that her shout would have brought any help for her since everyone around was her enemy, but the reflex was there none the less.

"Shhh, it's me." A familiar voice said from behind her.

She stopped struggling, turned, and gave Demien a hug.

"What are you doing?" He whispered, brow furrowed, and a disapproving scowl plastered on his face.

"I was about to try to knock those guards out and get the Masters out of the main hall." She explained.

"By yourself?" Demien raised an eyebrow, scowl deepening.

"I was working out how to do that, yes."

"You have a bit of a death wish, don't you?"

"No, I-"

"No matter, I'm here now. Let me take the one on the left and you, the one on the right."

She shut her mouth and nodded. They moved back to the mouth of the tunnel. Demien continued across the tunnel and took cover behind a stalagmite mound. He held up three fingers and counted down silently. When his final finger dropped, they moved as one. Amara had to jump up onto the man's back, but she wrapped her arm around his neck and rode him till he collapsed to the ground. Demien had his man tied up in no time, and she started with her knots as well. It wasn't pretty, but it would hold him. Demien checked her knot to confirm it would suffice, and they dragged the two men toward the barricade.

"What you lack in stature, you make up for in ferocity." Demien quipped.

"I had to reach him somehow." Amara grinned. "Where did you come from, anyway?"

"I followed you down, actually. During the attack, I was able to slip out of the main entrance and circle around. I couldn't get past the guard at the entrance, but after contemplating it for a bit, I came back with a plan, only to find you had already taken care of them."

"So why didn't you help me in the fight? I was outnumbered."

"I lost you in the tunnels. You've gotten faster since you were last here. I ended up circling back and subduing the guard who replaced the woman you faced. I will give you that your opponent was far smarter and more skilled than mine."

"All the running for my life has helped with that." Amara was happy to quip with Demien once again. She had missed her old mentor.

"I imagine that would be a fine motivator. Now, let's get through this barricade and release our allies."

They turned. Before they could get close to the barricade, however, a call came from the other side and a volley of arrow shot forth from the small openings. Amara pushed Demien out of the way and they fell to one side of the tunnel. They crawled back into cover on all fours and quick as they could, while arrows pinged off the floor and walls.

"Hey, we are friends!" Amara shouted.

"No friends of ours!" Came the reply.

"Is that Declan? It's Demien," Demien identified himself and added. "And my compatriot is Amara."

"How do I know that?"

"By the sound of my voice, ya numpty."

"Oh, well, I guess that's fair. I'll go get the Master."

They shared a look and Demien rolled his eyes, which made Amara smile despite almost becoming a pincushion.

It wasn't long before Declan came back, and Raza's voice rang out. "Demien, Amara, is that you?"

"Yes!" They replied simultaneously.

"And would you please tell Declan to stand down Raza," Demien added. "I don't feel like being filled with holes today."

"Please come out where I can see you. Is there anyone with you?" The Master from Caister called.

They did as they were bidden.

"No, Master, just us and the two Dark Hallow guards we knocked out." Amara glanced at the two forms. To her shock, one had two arrows in him, and she was certain he was no longer breathing. The other was be-hind his companion and hadn't received any visible injuries.

"Make that one guard." Demien amended. "It seems you fellows *can* hit the broad side of a still target."

"Then get in here before more arrive," Raza motioned for them to come toward her. "Bring the surviving Dark Hallow. Maybe he will be of some use."

Demien went to collect the prisoner while Amara headed straight for the barricade. She climbed the stack of furniture, which made up the makeshift defense, and spilled over the other side. The main hall had been all but emptied of chairs and tables, but they had allocated much of the floor space. One area held the wounded, another, beds for those not watching the barricades, and still another for weapons, what little they had.

Demien crawled carefully over the top of the stack behind her.

"Where are Lawdel and Raziel?" Amara turned to Raza.

"They are here. Raziel is guarding and entrance and I believe Lawdel is taking his turn resting, although no one has been getting much sleep as of late." Raza pointed as she said each of the men's names, and Amara headed off to confirm they were alive and well.

"Amara, I need information." Raza demanded of her as she walked away.

"Demien will have all the information you need and more than I." Amara waved a hand toward Demien. Her old mentor wouldn't have come to help without doing his research and recon. Besides, he was much more thorough than she was. She wanted to, no, she needed to check on her fathers.

"Amara!" Lawdel called just before he wrapped her in a bear hug. "You're alive, girly! Thank the dark lord himself." He stopped and seemed to realize what he said. "Well, I guess it was his fault you were in danger in the first place. I'm going to have to get a new saying now that I know he's real. Never mind that, I'm glad to see you well. You don't seem to be overly maimed from your flight with the Devil."

"Lawdel," Amara stopped his ramblings. "It's good to see you well. When I found the Dark Hallows in the caves, I feared the worst."

"Yes, well, it takes a bit more than a few assassins to kill me. You should know that."

Amara smiled. "Yes, I suppose I should."

"Come, you need to speak with Raziel." Lawdel continued to lead her toward one of the barricades. "

Raziel is regaining some of his mind and he will hopefully be happy to see you. He seems to remember more about you and who you and your mother are, although his memory still comes and goes.

Each of the barricade was maned by several Shadows, but at Raziel's there was only him and two other men. Maybe they thought since he was an angel, he didn't need much help. Raziel turned to great them, and tears were already in his eyes when they arrived.

"You are a Blade Bearer." He moved forward and swept her from her feet. "My daughter, my only daughter, is a Blade Bearer. Chosen by God and blessed with twin blades."

Amara couldn't help but smile, tears forming in her own eyes. Her father's joy was infectious.

He set her down and held her out at arm's length. "It would seem my mind is returning. I'm not sure if that is your doing or simply a blessing from God, but I'm not willing to question it lest it be snatched away again. I need to tell you how sorry I am for leaving you on the streets of Caister, how terribly, utterly, regretful I am for not being a better father to you all these years."

"Raziel, I...you didn't have a choice...you did the best you could...I've forgiven you and understand why things happened the way they did. You're not responsible for being absent all those years." She meant what she said, but she couldn't help but feel a twinge of hurt still. The pain of her father abandoning her regardless of his state of mind. She pushed those thoughts away and smiled at him.

"My mind is clearer than it's been in a thousand years. I can't promise how long that will last, but I can promise I will protect you for as long as I can." He smiled back at her. It was a warm, genuine smile. He was truly happy.

"You've been locked up for a thousand years?"

"No," Raziel chuckled. "I've been locked up for hundreds, but I didn't go insane at the hands of the demons. I worked to break an angel out of a trance state and failed. Many other angels were lost. I was the only one to make it back alive. So that's a blessing, I guess."

"What do you mean, a trance state?" Amara wasn't understanding what he was saying at all.

Raziel sighed. "Don't worry too much about it. It's a story for a more peaceful time. Why did you not contact me the moment you arrived? I could have relayed information quickly without you having to risk your life."

Amara's cheeks burn with embarrassment. "I didn't even think about it. I guess this is still all so new to me it didn't even cross my mind.

"No matter, you are here and safe and that's what counts." Raziel Smiled again. "Right now, we must find a way of out of this predicament."

"We *have* a way out!" Amara exclaimed. "Demien is explaining to the master's right now and we should be leaving soon."

"We ought to head over there. I think there are some extenuating circumstances you should know about before you get your hopes up too high."

Raziel told the other two guards to call if there was any activity and they hurried over to Demien, Lawdel and the masters. They were deep in conversation when they arrived, and Amara listened into their conversation, hoping to find out more about these circumstances.

"I won't leave our people to die," Raza was saying.

"I understand that, and I'm not suggesting we do." Demien held out his hands, and Amara could tell he was exasperated. "I'm only suggesting we leave the main hall and regroup before mounting a rescue."

"If we leave, we may never be able to get back in." The Master of Caister cut in. "You have made the entrances rather defensible. A commendable thing if they were manned before this attack."

Amara winced, and the thinly veiled insult.

Raza's fist clenched, but she held back any retort. "We need to hold here until we can mount a full-scale takeover of the tunnels once again. Then we can get our people out of the prison and leave this place to the Dark Hallow."

With that last piece of knowledge, Amara connected the dots. Some of their people were being held as prisoners. She had assumed the Dark Hallow had taken no prisoners.

"Where will we go after that?" Lawdel asked.

Amara stepped forward, seizing her chance. "To the Angel army."

"Why would we help them?" Raza asked.

"If the Shadows are to survive, then we have no choice." She pressed.

"How do you figure that?" Lawdel gave her a look like she had just sprouted a second head.

"The Shadows have never taken a side in this war." Raza crossed her arms.

"And we need to focus on defeating the Dark Hallow and taking back our rightful places in the major cities." The Caister Master agreed.

"I understand wanting no part in the war." Amara held up her hands in surrender. "Until just a few days ago, I could have cared less who really won as long as those I cared about survived. But the Dark Hallow is run by Lilith."

All eyes were on her now, most giving her a blank stare, not comprehending her point.

"My mother," Amara continued. "She is in league with the devil himself."

"You believe if the demons win this war, we will have no place in the new world?" Raza raised an eyebrow at her.

"Unless you want to join the Dark Hallow." Amara motioned with her hand to the Enemy outside the room. "They will not let any oppose to the Dark Hallow survive if the demons claim victory. Our only hope of survival is for the angels to win, and we can't just sit around hoping that happens. We need to take action; move against the demon army with the might of all the chapters."

"You have changed since you left us." Raza stared at Amara. "I, however, do see the logic in your argument."

"Except the Angel army will seek to wipe us out as well." The Caister Master accentuated his point with a stab of his finger in Amara's direction. "They will not suffer us to go back to our thieving peacefully."

"I believe they will." Amara argued. "I believe they will let us go for two reasons. One, because we fought by their side, they will not mind pardoning us of our past crimes against our respective cities. And two, they will be so busy hunting the last of the demons and trying to rebuild society to bother with us. We will be able to go back to our lives as they were. At least for a few hundred years. That's better than being hunted to extinction."

"Fine, but this is all conjecture until we decided what to do about our people." The Caister Master conceded. "If we leave now, we can regroup and come back to free them when we've gained a better position. But on the other hand, we will have to fight our way back in, regaining the ground we currently hold. Both options have the opportunity to be the wiser choice, but both have a large margin for failure. However, one plan gets our wounded out of the tunnels and to safety while the other leaves them here to be killed if a wayward Dark Hallow were to slip past our lines."

"If we leave now, we'll never get back in." Raza stood firm. "We will be forfeiting their lives."

"We need to get the wounded out." Raziel stepped forward. "Amara and Demien have given us a chance to do so. Raza, if you truly believe they will kill the prisoners, then those of us who can fight will stay and fight to free them. If we play our cards right, we can push through the enemy and rescue them, but the Master is right. We cannot do that with the wounded still here."

Everyone paused, seeming to take in the wisdom of Raziel's words, and both Masters nodded their agreement.

"I will scout the path out, so we don't run into any undesirables." Demien turned to leave. "Amara, I could use your help."

She followed him quickly, glancing back at Raziel. He was already moving to get the injury ready to leave. She turned back and followed Demien over the barricade. She followed him through a series of tunnels. He wound through them, sometimes taking a tunnel that led them in a roundabout path out.

"Do you think they post a second guard after you took care of Xylissa's replacement?" Amara asked as they went.

"I don't believe so, since I took care of him quietly. Unlike someone else I know." Demien gave her a knowing look.

"Hey even *you* admitted I had the tougher opponent." Amara restored.

Demien chuckled softly.

They made it to the surface without encountering any members of the Dark Hallow. The trap door was still open, and they searched the surrounding trees for any surprises. They found nothing that wasn't there when they had entered.

"Demien, we don't have enough time for this," Amara rolled her eyes after Demien insisted on a third look around. "Let's get back and lead them out."

"There was a twofold reason for scouting." Demien replied. "One to confirm the path was still open, but two. I need to make contact with the other half of our force. If we can make contact and bolster our forces, the Dark Hallow should be taken by surprise. Plus, we will need people to take care of the wounded. I recommend you head back in and give the all clear while I make contact with our people."

"Other half? You found the others who made it out." Amara spun, expecting to see people among the trees.

"Yes!" Demien's eyebrows shot up. "I guess you weren't there for the first half of our conversation. Many of our people made it out. They are waiting for us out toward the cliffs. That's why I wanted to bring everyone up, to regroup before mounting a rescue."

"That's great!" Amara's anxiety lowered with that information.

"Yep. Now you need to get going before our scouting goes to waste."

"Sounds good. We will be back out shortly." Amara whirled and headed back down.

She followed the path they had taken to the surface, and it was still clear of Dark Hallow Members. She arrived back at the main hall in short order and found the wounded ready to go. Most had to be carried on makeshift litters, but there were a few able to walk.

"It's clear for now." She reported to Lawdel. "Demien is waiting for us with the rest of the Shadows who escaped. He has a force to send back down to help fight."

"That's great news, girl." Lawdel smiled. "We might just make it out of this alive."

She smiled back at him and then quickly got ahead of the group, leading them out, following the path Demien had shown her. It took them longer to get to the surface. They had to move slower with the wounded, but also Amara was much more cautious. Making sure the area really was clear before moving the group forward. The last thing she wanted was to get them all killed.

They arrive at the surface all the same and with no incidents. Amara searched around for Demien, but he wasn't anywhere in sight. The sun was lower in the sky, casting shadows over the forest floor. She could have sworn it was closer to midday when they had first made the journey up. She must be losing her sense of time in the tunnels. It really hadn't been that long since she had lived down in the tunnels or in the sewers of Caister, but so much had happened.

"Amara, over here." Demien's voice came from just out of sight in the woods surrounding them.

She moved toward his voice and the others followed as they could. Suddenly, hooded and robes figures moved in around them cutting off all escape. Lilith materialized out of the shadows, holding a knife to Demien's throat.

Malach watched as their soldiers marched out from the mountain pass toward open ground. All was quiet except for the click of armor and crunch of boots on the rocky ground. Had something gone wrong? Was his father captured? It took all his discipline not to go running back to the cliff to find out what was happening. Instead, he replaced that compulsion with action. He fell into line with the rest of the soldiers, moving with them as quietly as possible. He trusted they would complete their part of the plan so he and the rest of the soldiers could make it past the enemy camp. If they could get some distance between them and the enemy camp without being seen, they would have a fighting chance of surviving this insane plan. Malach hated that he wasn't part of the infiltration. He wasn't used to being on the outside of the plan. Was this how everyone else felt? Waiting, trusting that he would do his part? He had a greater respect for those he left behind.

He hadn't frozen through it all. Maybe the meditation and mental centering his father was showing him was helping. Even when the dragon surprised them on the ridge, his muscles hadn't frozen on him. Maybe this was all he needed and some time to heal.

They arrived at the Pangor river and marched right across it using an old, dilapidated bridge. Malach wondered how many more winters it would hold firm and how much weight it would take tonight. Still no explosions racked the night air and still they moved. Soon they would be forced to stop, or they would march right into view of the enemy. However, no matter how close they got, Gabriel kept them moving.

Malach heard a distant shout. At first, he thought they were spotted, but he fought to keep his legs from locking up. He fought to keep in step with those around him. He managed to stay in line and trust his commander. The shouting, he realized as he emerged from the tree line, was not directed toward them. All the enemy soldiers he could make out at this distance were headed into the camp, not out. His father had been spotted. He started toward the camp, but before he got more than a few hundred feet, a fireball blasted into the sky. The shockwave hit him a moment later, and he felt it vibrate his chest.

He stopped where he was, chest tightening, legs locking in place. Fear gripped him where he stood. There was nothing he could do to help, yet he couldn't make his feet move in either direction. He watched as silhouettes ran hither and thither in the camp, not one glancing in their direction as the flames ran rampant through the tents. Malach couldn't tare his gaze away from the carnage before him.

"Malach!" Honora's voice called from behind him.

He didn't turn her way, but her voice seemed to break the spell the flames had on him, and he continued searching for his father.

"Malach!" she called again. This time, she was closer.

He felt her hand slip into his and attempted to pull him away from the camp.

"No, I need to make sure Ariel is ok," he told her, easily countering the force she exerted to move him.

His excuse was true, but the fear still held him in place as well. He didn't want to admit that to her, however. What would she think if she knew? What would they all think?

"We need to go. If you're spotted, you could put us all at risk."

Her words made sense, but he wouldn't leave without his father. His limbs regained their vigor, and he flexed his fingers slowly. A figure shot up through the billowing smoke and zipped toward them. His first thought was a demon had come through the blast and he drew Reckoning. However, he noticed the wings on the figure reflected the red and orange of the blaze below.

It was Ana, and she was carrying a figure. She flew overhead and Malach gave chase, pumping his legs as hard as he could. He heard Honora call again from behind him, but he didn't pay her any attention. His father must be hurt, and Ana had flown down to save him. Honora would catch up and they would be able to help his father, provided it wasn't too late already.

He glanced behind him and realized what he was doing. He slowed to let Honora catch up and motioned her to climb onto his back. She gave him a skeptical look, but did as he asked. He felt her warmth press up against him and he took off as fast as he could, using his extra strength to propel them through the night.

"Was Ana carrying Daziar?" Honora asked in his ear, uncomfortably loud.

"I assumed it was my father."

"It looked like Daz." Honora pressed.

"We will find out soon." Malach ended their exchange, concentrating on his breathing.

Malach watched Ana land not far in front of them, not able to fly far with her heavy burden. They caught up quickly and, sure enough, Honora was right. Daziar's unconscious form lay on the ground in front of Ana. Malach let Honora down and they ran to their friend. He was relieved to see Daziar was still breathing, but had no idea what condition he was in. Honora dropped down beside Ana and the two women went to work.

"Dislocated elbow on his bad arm." Ana pointed to his limp arm tied to his side.

"You brace, I'll untie."

"He was in the blast. Need to check and make sure he's not bleeding internally. No major external wounds."

"Elbow looks fine other than the dislocation. I doubt he even felt it."

And that's how their conversation went back and forth while they check Daziar's body for injuries. Malach kept a trained eye out for any pursuit by the enemy camp, but the night still echoed with shouts of panic and orders. Malach tried his best to wait for the two to finish with Daziar before he asked what happened and busied himself with scanning his surroundings. He spotted movement from the direction of the Pangor. A singularly wet figure pulled themselves from the water and flopped onto the bank.

Malach ran toward the prone figure. They would need help or they would soon freeze to death. He recognized his father laying there already shivering.

"Dad," Malach pulled him up into a sitting position as his father continued to catch his breath. "What possessed you to take a midnight swim in this weather?"

"Only Asmodeus trying to separate my head from my shoulders." Ariel gave him a wry grin.

"I guess that's a pretty good reason." Malach grinned back. "And he didn't want to join you?"

"Apparently, he's too used to the heat of hell to take a dip in the freezing water."

"Huh, might do him good." Malach helped his father to his feet, and they started moving. The water streaming off the man soaked into Malach's clothes and made him shiver. "You mind keeping that water to yourself?"

"Ha, I'll try, but it seems to have a mind of its own."

They stumbled up to the two women who had Daziar stable by this point.

"I'm going to have to give him a firm reprimanding." Ariel shook his head, frowning. "First, you two go against my orders and fly into the demon camp, and now he's sleeping on the job. Then I guess I'll have to thank him for saving my life. And thank you, Ana, I might not have survived the night without your interference."

"It was Daz's idea." Ana replied. "Honora, help me get him up and I'll carry him. We need a little more distance from the demon camp."

"Asmodeus might be headed this way." Ariel frowned. "He caught sight of us, and I might have thrown a few verbal jabs to get him to chase me instead of the two of you. I might have hurt his feelings a bit."

"Then we need to double time it." Ana hefted Daziar up onto her shoulders. Much like Malach would have carried a deer he had just killed. "We won't have any support unless we catch up with the main group and even then, we are all vulnerable until we are safe behind the stronghold walls."

They all started off at a jog. Ariel straightened and moved out of Malach's support as they went, his strength returning slowly. It wasn't long before they spotted the group of soldiers marching across the open expanse toward the stronghold. They were gaining quickly. Malach had kept an eye out behind them, but no pursuit was evident. As they can, within hailing distance, the group ahead of them stopped and cheered as they approach.

Daziar stirred and Ana quickly set him down, even as his eyes fluttered open. "What- what happened?"

"You got blown up," Malach grinned down at his friend.

"Again," Honora added, reminding them of the last time a bomb had gone off. They were in Fairdenn the first time they had encountered explosives and Daziar was caught in the blast there as well.

They all laughed, and Malach helped Daziar to his feet. "These two patched you up." Malach motioned to Ana and Honora.

"Of course they did." Daziar smiled at them. "They always do. Thank you both. I don't feel overly pained, though."

"The biggest injury was on the arm you can't feel," Honora explained.

"You will feel worse in the morning," Ana chuckled. "But good job using that brute as a shield. I thought you were dead for sure this time. It would have been the shortest career as a Blade Bearer."

They continued their short walk into the midst of the soldiers and were greeted by Gabriel. "Good job, Ariel, Ana, and Daziar. We don't have time to waste. The demon army will regroup and could send a force to chase us down. Let's get moving."

She called for the group to continue their march, and they moved toward safety. The gates of the stronghold rose up before them in the growing light and gave them renewed hope. No signs of pursuit were spotted, and they all breathed easier to know they were almost to safety. Gabriel sent a message ahead to have the gates opened in preparation for their return.

They passed under the giant archway and into the relative warmth of the stronghold. Medics were waiting in case there were wounded, and they rushed over to offer their services. One woman walked up to Daziar, who still had his arm tied to his side.

"Where are you injured?" She asked, searching his arm for visible injury.

"I'm not, not really." Daziar gently lifted her hand from his arm. "This is something that cannot be fixed."

She nodded solemnly and moved away.

"You've accepted it then?" Malach stated more than asked.

"Yeah, that injury back in the Demon camp I didn't feel. I fully dislocated my elbow and only found out when I saw it. No pain, no sensation, nothing."

Malach nodded. "I'm sorry."

"Not your fault." Daziar smiled at him, but it was a sad smile. "The only one to blame is me. Ana tried to warn me, but I was too hotheaded to listen. I can't even say it was fully Azazel's fault. However, I won't let this slow me down. I can't feel it, but I can still fight."

Malach nodded. "I'm glad you feel that way. Wouldn't want a useless lump sitting around in the coming battle." He winked at Daziar.

"Who are you calling a useless lump? I just saved your father." But Daziar was chuckling,

"You should also talk to your family about it. They should know of your injury."

Daziar nodded solemnly. "I'm going to go see them now and I don't want them hearing about it from anyone else."

"I'll go with you." Malach clapped him on the shoulder. "No reason you should go talk with them alone.

"Thanks Mal."

They walked into the stronghold together, the new day dawning behind them as the doors of the massive gates closed behind them.

Chapter 17

Amara couldn't understand what she was seeing. Lilith had left riding on the dragon's back. How could she be here now?

"Awe, you fell for my little ruse." Lilith cooed at her. "Poor little thing, you thought you were going to save your friends and defeat my Dark Hallow. You're so pathetic. Although, you could be of some use. You *did* kill Xylissa. I might have to take you back to my tower and train you correctly. Although we would have to beat out that stubborn streak."

Hooded figures moved out of the trees in a ring around the group. Silently, they herded the Shadows away from the trapdoor. That would have proved a poor escape route as more hooded figures emerged from the tunnels. They were outnumbered at least two to one, and the odds only worsened with every new hooded assassin who appeared.

Amara found her voice once again. "You witch! If I last thing I do, I'll kill you!"

"There that. That stubbornness we will have to focus it and aim it like a weapon."

"Let Demien go!"

"Hmmm, no." Lilith made a pouting face at Amara. "I think I'll keep him for a plaything."

A blur shot past Amara, and before she could register what was happening, Lawdel was halfway to Lilith. She pushed Demien toward the man, but Demien acted just as quick throwing his body to the side and out of Lawdel's path. Lilith extended her knife, ready to take the charge but Lawdel batted it aside and tackled her to the ground. The contact between the two seemed to snap everyone out of their stupor. The hooded men around them drew weapons while the Shadows lowered litters and reached for their own. One injured man who could walk charged the circle of Dark Hallow members and shouldered his way through, taking another knife wound as he did. He didn't slow, however, but ran off into the night.

"Coward!" Amara heard someone shout, but she didn't know who said it.

She pulled Ember and Blaze, lengthening them slightly to give her better reach. Then they fought. They fought for their very lives, for they knew they would be slaughtered to a man if they lost.

All dressed in black, it was hard to tell the difference between Shadows and Dark Hallow, though the robes certainly helped. She cut at a robed figure moving past her in his fight with Demien, gouging a deep furrow in his side. He grunted, falling to one knee, and Demin ended his life with a thrust through his eye into his brain.

Amara and Demien found themselves back-to-back fending off an assassin each. They parried and attacked, each following the ebb and flow of the other.

"More are flanking." Damien shouted at Amara. "We are losing this fight."

"Just keep fighting." Amara shouted back. "It's not over til it's over."

They did, but as the fight went on, Amara watched as more and more Dark Hallows came against her and Demien. Their tactics turned from and balanced stance to pure defense. They couldn't keep this up for forever. They were already slowing. She couldn't see Lilith or Lawdel anywhere and most of the shadow's members lay on the ground unmoving. They would soon join them in their cold sleep.

A shout sounded from the woods to their right and all heads turned to see what was happening. Many voices quickly joined the single shout. A group, fifty strong, charged out of the woods into the clearing overwhelming the Dark Hallow. Something about a war hammer held high in the group looked familiar. However, it was swept away in the crowd before she could get a good look. Like water hitting a sculpture of sand, the Dark Hallow was washed away in a violent and bloody torrent.

Amara and Demien collapsed, backs still pressed together, holding each other in a sitting position.

"And you thought all that running wouldn't come in handy." Demien chuckled.

"We weren't running," she replied, puzzled.

"But your stamina kept you going throughout the fight."

"Fine," she conceded. She didn't have the energy to argue with him. "Where's Lawdel and Lilith?"

"Last I saw, they were on the edge of the fight and Lawdel was winning." Demien got up and helped her to her feet.

She searched the bodies and people around them but couldn't find either Lawdel or the witch.

"Amara," Demien called. "I found something."

She rushed over to him and knelt next to him. Two sets of footprints headed into the woods. She caught her breath as she spotted the blood that littered the forest floor following the trail. She locked eyes with Demien.

"They must have gone this way and one of them is injured." Demien set his jaw muscles working furiously.

"Let's go, Lawdel might need help."

Demien nodded, but she got the feeling he thought this *wasn't* a good plan.

They followed the trail as fast as they could in the dark; the blood lessening as they went. The clash of weapons reached their ears, and they sped up, not bothering with the trail anymore. They walked into a clearing in time to watch Lilith plunge a knife up to the hilt in Lawdel's chest.

"No!" Amara shouted.

Lilith twisted the knife, grinning wildly at Amara, and ripped it from the man. Lawdel sank to the ground, holding his chest weakly. The lithe woman strode forward gracefully, licking the blood from the knife. The two motions in stark contrast to each other. Lilith was a graceful monster, to be sure. Amara planned to end the monster's reign over her evil horde.

Amara charged. She was vaguely aware of Demien circling around Lilith, heading for Lawdel. She hit the woman who had birthed her, both knives extended. However, neither tasted the blood of the evil creature. Lilith had ducked her attack, putting a shoulder under Amaras ribs and hefting her up and over. Amara tried to twist in the air but only managed to land on her side, sliding on the detritus decaying on the ground. She quickly rolled to regain her feet and pulled her knives up, ready to defend herself. No attack was forthcoming; Lilith was nowhere to be seen.

Amara glanced at Demien, and he shook his head, a grave expression on his face.

"Can you move him?" Amara asked.

"No, not unless you want to lose all hope of saving him." Demien had his hands pressed down on Lawdel's chest, but Amara noticed blood welling out around his fingers.

Lilith seemed to materialize as she sailed through the air, her robe flapping out behind her like the wings of a demon. She had murder in her black eyes and Demien was her target. Amara charged to intercept her, but she would arrive too late. Demien took one hand off Lawdel's chest and deflected her knife at the last second with his own. Amara was upon them before Lilith could strike a second time. She attacked wildly, having no goal in mind except to keep Lilith off of Demien and Lawdel.

Slow down, Ember said calmly. *Think about your stance, you too easily thrown off balance right now.*

Also, set us alight! Blaze shouted.

Amara didn't know how to accomplish the second task, but she slowed her racing mind and brought her body into alignment. Widening her narrow stance and striking with more confident and stronger blows. She slowly and methodically took ground, pushing Lilith back toward the edge of the clearing, away from Demien. Blaze nudged at her consciousness.

I don't know how. Amara told her.

Another nudge, but this time Amara felt something instinctively. She let it happen, whatever it was, and she felt heat on her hands. Not uncomfortable heat, more like the warmth of a fire on a cold night. She saw the blue flames shooting up her blades and watched Lilith's expression turn from one of surprise to that of disgust.

"You had so much potential, but I see that you have chosen your path." Lilith then turned and ran toward the woods.

What was she doing? Running away? Not on her watch. Not after she stabbed Lawdel. She sheathed her blades, extinguishing the flames, and threw knife after knife as fast as she could. Most missed the fleeing woman, but two disappeared into her robes and she let out a grunt but didn't slow or fall. Amara started to run after.

"Amara," Demien called. "Let her go. I need you here."

She changed directions, sprinting toward the fallen man. She fell to her knees on the other side of Lawdel to Demien. He didn't look good. The knife had gone in deep, and it had done a lot of damage.

"He's dying," Demien said softly.

"No!" Amara jerked her head up. "Save him!"

"I doubt any healer could save him now." Damien shook his head. "I'm only slowing the inevitable. You need to say your goodbyes."

She turned to look at the man who had been her father most of her life. "Why...why did you have to attack her?" Tears blurred her vision.

"I knew you were something special the first time I saw you on that stoop. You pulled at my heart even then. I never told you..." he coughed again, turning his head to spit blood.

"I know, and you were...are...my father, in all the ways that matter." She took his hand and felt his strength waning.

"I'm proud of you. Proud of what you've become and the woman you are. I only wish I could have been around to see more of your life and your magnificent accomplishments to come. I love you, my daughter."

"I… I Love you too."

Lawdel's hand went limp and the dam holding back her anguish broke. She wailed, shouting her grief to anything within earshot until her throat was raw and her tears were spent. She lay down next to Lawdel's body and pulled her knees to her chest exhaustion, mercifully taking her into unconsciousness.

Amara awoke in a soft bed in the cave system. At first, she thought she must have been captured by the Dark Hallow but then the horrible memory of Lawdel's death hit her like a cave-in threatening to crush her. She curled up on the bed, knowing somewhere in the back of her mind she was safe, and cried bitterly. She didn't know how long she stayed like that, but she slipped back into the darkness once again.

The next time she woke, someone was in the room with her. She felt the presence more than anything. If someone was here to kill her, she just hoped they did it quickly.

"It's time to get up." Demien sat in a chair in the corner of her room. "It's time for us to pay our respects to the dead."

"I'm not going." She mumbled and turned over, pulling the covers over her head. She felt like crying again, but her tears were spent.

"You won't want Lawdel to depart without a proper goodbye, would you?"

"He's already gone. What good will it do to burn an empty shell?"

"It will help give you closure."

"You're not leaving until I get up, are you?"

"No,"

"Fine, I'll go." She rolled over and gave Demien her best death glare. "It won't do any good, though."

"I wouldn't insist on it if I didn't think it would help." He shook his head. "I missed Viessa's funeral, so wracked with grief as I was. I still regret it."

"Does the pain go away?"

"Never."

"Then what's the point?"

"The point is to honor those who have fallen. To live for those who have given everything. To remember their life and be changed by it."

Amara didn't know what to say. The pain would never heal, but maybe, just maybe, Demien was right.

She dragged her body out of bed. First one leg, then the other. It felt like they were filled with lead. The act of leaving the bed was monumental in that moment. Heaving her mind from the pit of despair she had sunk in to was just as taxing.

She had been cleaned of the grime and gore of the last few days' events and dressed in clean clothes. Her armor had been cleaned and polished and it hung on a mannequin, her knives sheathed with in the armor. The angel blades were also in their sheaths, the belt firmly placed around the lifeless things waste. Maybe the mannequin was really her lifeless body, already dressed in armor ready for her inevitable death. Could she even survive this? She had already laid the groundwork to send the rest of her friends to their deaths. Would any of the Shadows survive if they marched to war?

She put on her leather armor, remembering when Lawdel had given it to her for her first job. She had never thought it would have come to this. Her first job was supposed to be just the start. It was one of the last times she had seen him happy. How had it all gone so wrong?

Demien lead the way through the tunnels, Amara following automatically. She felt numb. She felt like the reality she was living was not reality at all. Only a dream and soon she would wake to see Lawdel again. That was only wishful thinking. He was never coming back. They climbed up into the forest. Darkness had fully fallen, but it didn't seem to matter to Demien. He walked toward the tree line as confidently as if the sun had been shining. They would be on the side of the forest facing away from Newaught. It wouldn't do to have the city guard catch them during their time of morning. A row of wooden alters were setup each holding a fallen friend or comrade. Some bored the weight of two bodies, couples who had died side by side.

Demien stopped in front of her, and she stopped with him. She didn't want to look at the body on this pier. She didn't want to acknowledge Lawdel was gone. Tears started rolling down her cheeks again, and she forced her head up. This would be the last time she would see him. She wanted his face burned into her memory forever, so she would never forget him.

"Fellow Shadows." Raza called, standing off to one side of the pyres. Her voice carried across the gathering, but the soft, strained tone betrayed her own grief. "We gather today to honor those who lost their lives in the recent Dark Hallow attacks. Not only the one here in Newaught, but in Caister, Ragewood, and Yargate as well. We have been targeted and systematically attacked in the efforts to wipe out our organization, our family. Thanks to these and many other brave men and women, we have survived these attacks. Their sacrifice has allowed us a second chance. Even now, the final Shadow's chapter is converging on Newaught, where we will make our stand against this threat. These who have lost their lives defending us will not be forgotten, but nor will they go unavenged. Tonight, however, we honor their passing and say our goodbyes to friends, lovers, and family."

The Master of Caister moved to the first pier and reverently lowered the torch in his hand, holding it until the wood supporting the body was lit. He drifted to the next and repeated the motions like some silent specter, taking the dead to their final rest. Then the next, and then the next. He moved down the rows of bodies until he was standing in front of Amara. She jumped, startling at the realization that he was waiting for her. He had stopped next to the pyre that held Lawdel's body and was offering her the torch in his outstretched hand.

She stepped forward reluctantly. She didn't want to take the torch. She didn't want to light the fire. She didn't want to say goodbye. That would make Lawdel's death final. She would have to admit to herself this was not a dream, this was not something that could be reversed. Tears once again blurred her vision.

"He would want you to light it," the master said softly.

"I can't," she mumbled.

Demien stepped up and put a hand on her shoulder. "I can help you if you would like."

She turned and looked up at him. She slowly nodded, still doubting that she had the strength to do it. Demien guided her hand gently until it was holding the torch. Then he moved with her to the pyre and lowered her hand until the flames were licking the wood but not close enough to set them ablaze. "The rest is up to you." He took a step back from her and nodded as she peered at him over her shoulder.

She let the torch's weight lower it the rest of the way and the flame sprang into the night, taking the only father she had known with them. She fell to her knees, vaguely aware of the torch being taken out of her hand and letting the awful heat of the fire grow on her exposed skin. She almost wanted to jump on the pyre with him. A part of her died with him. Why not burn it in the same way? Demien's muscular arms pulled her gently away from the fire, removing that temptation from her reach. The cool night air kissed her skin, comforting the burning sensation that lingered. Tears carved their way down her cheeks, and she sobbed.

She didn't know how long she stayed at the pyre, but it had long since burned out when fatigue finally overtook her. Demien, the Master, and Raziel stood by until she could no longer keep her eyes open. Her head never touched the ground.

Amara spent the next two days in her room. She hadn't wanted to leave. She had laid in her bed for most of that time, staring at the cave ceiling. Demien and Raziel had brought food to her every day, taking turns sitting with her when she allowed and leaving when she didn't want them.

She had grieved.

Her adopted father's death leaving a void in her life. One that would be hard pressed to be filled. She had decided she may never fill it, carrying this loss with her for the rest of her life. She would never forget him that way.

After two days, she was done grieving. She had a task to do, and resolve had taken hold in her heart. Demien and Raziel had given her updates on what was going on in the world around her. The other Shadows chapters had arrived in Newaught, bolstering their numbers and filling the cave system. The leaders would be meeting today. She had things she needed them to hear, and she wouldn't leave their meeting chamber without an answer.

The Dark Hallow had left Newaught, she was told. Their remaining members limping their way north. No doubt, to join the demon army at the angel's stronghold. They would most likely be used to wreak havoc, assassinating key leaders, possibly even angels. She suspected Lilith would be with them, and she planned to follow. To thwart Lilith at every turn. Her mother had been wounded. She would find safety and healing with her Dark Lord. The Dark Hallow would be accepted among such monsters as he.

She would have to convince the Shadow leaders to follow her. To take the fight to the Dark Hallow and, subsequently, the demon army. They would take their revenge for the death of their members. Every chapter from every city had lost people to Lilith. She hoped the masters would want to take the fight to them and not hide to lick their wounds. She hoped to march north to provide support for the angel army. Ember and Blaze approved of her plan and believe it would prove a deciding factor in the last battle. They hoped to use the Shadows as the proverbial knife in the back of the demon army. It was fitting in a morbid way.

She didn't know if she could kill her mother. She had thrown the dagger in anger and rage after Lilith had wounded Lawdel. However, on an even footing without the emotion fueling her fire, could she actually kill her mother? Could she take the life of the one who *gave* her life? She didn't know, but she would stop her. She would stop the Dark Hallow. She would bring help to that angel army where she could. After all, she was a Blade Bearer now.

Blaze and Ember had been quiet for the last few days, keeping her company when she asked for them and only giving her counsel when she sought it out. Now she would need them to convince the council. They were young but so full of wisdom, as if, in their creation, they had been imbued the knowledge of all the blades who came before. She thought she would have to teach *them*, however, they seemed to be teaching her.

She walked out of her room and into the tunnel that would lead her to the leaders and ran right into Raziel. She thumped against his broad, powerful chest, and he grabbed her reflexively. Their eyes met as she glanced up.

He pulled her into an embrace. "I'm so happy you are out and about, little one."

"I have things to do and duties to perform." She stated.

He pulled her out to arm's length, stared directly into her soul, and asked pointedly. "How are you?"

"Fine," she turned away from his piercing gaze. "Really, I'm fine. Lawdel...his death still hurts. I don't think that will ever change." She sighed. "But I need to do this. I need to talk to the leaders. They *will* listen to me, and they *will* send help to the Angel Army."

"Don't be so sure. They will do what is in their best interest and taking their members into an all-out war is not in their best interest. If you convince them, it will be because they want revenge." Raziel shook his head. "They are not soldiers; they are not assassins. They will only follow you if they have good reason to. As soon as Lilith is dead or the Dark Hallow is defeated, do you think they will stay the course? Do you think they will throw themselves at a war that would be no longer theirs?"

"I don't know," she admitted. "But I have to try. I was sent here for this reason. I was chosen as a Blade Bearer to convince them to help our cause."

Raziel nodded and stepped to the side of the tunnel, allowing her passage. "I will be with you during this as well. I pray you can convince them. They would be a strategic advantage and one, I think, could sway the war to our side."

They walked down the tunnel together toward the chamber the leaders would be meeting in. Amara didn't know how they would take her intrusion, but at least two of the master owed her a favor so she didn't think they would bar her entry.

A thought hit her as they walked. "You have all your memories back! How are you doing?"

Raziel smiled at her. "It's a lot better than not having them, but I don't have *all* my memories back. There are still large gaps."

"Do you remember how you were captured?"

"Most of my recovered memories are before that time. However, I do remember how my mind became lost." He turned forward and seems to be lost in thought.

"You told me that already." A stab of fear that he was losing more recent memories hit her heart and in her fragile state, it almost buckled her knees. "Remember, in the main hall? You said the story of how you lost your mind had to do with a trance state."

"Oh," Raziel looked down for a moment. "So I did."

"Raziel?"

"It would seem we don't have time for this at the moment." Raziel motioned ahead of them.

Amara hadn't realized they were already at the opening to the meeting room. "After this then?"

"Sure," Raziel smiled. "After you."

Amara took a deep breath, squared her shoulders and marched into the chamber before she could talk herself out of it. As she entered the room, all eyes turned to her, and all voices went silent. It took all her willpower to stay rooted to the spot.

"Amara?" The Master of Caister calmly asked. "Is there something you needed?"

"Yes, what is so important that you barged into our meeting room?" Another Master who she didn't know asked.

"Gresham, calm yourself." Raza stepped forward. "Like Dror, I want to know what Amara has to say."

Was that his name? Amara thought. *That's why he kept his name a secret. I might too. Or change it.*

"Amara?" Dror broke her from her thoughts. He was looking at her expectantly.

"Right!" Amara moved forward slightly, trying to look more confident than she was feeling. "I have something to talk with you all about. I want to go after the Dark Hallow and their leader Lilith."

Silence hung heavy in the air as each of the leaders peered at her as if she had sprouted a second head. Then all but Dror broke out into shouting. Each turn to a different person to accuse or attack one another. Amara had no idea what was happening. Dror sat in his seat heavily, pinching the bridge of his nose and looking as if he might be fighting a headache.

"Silence!" Raziel boomed in the small meeting room.

Amara was certain her heart skipped a few beats.

"My daughter has something to tell you and she has not been sent by any one of you, nor has she been influenced by any of your ranks. You will hear what she has to say, or you will meet my wrath."

Amara stared at Raziel. Just ask quickly as his anger arrived, it abated. He smiled at her and motioned for her to continue.

"Uh, yes, I have *not* been told to say this by anyone here in this room, but the one who sends me is much more powerful than any other being. I understand the Dark Hallow as a whole has fled north. I aim to go after them with a force and wipe out their number. We've all lost people to their rank and they *will* pay for what they did to us. Then I plan to continue on and fight by the Angels in a battle that will decide the fate of our world. I would ask each of you to pledge your support for as long as your feel is wise for your people. Raza, Dror, I ask you do not follow me out of any feeling that you owe me anything, but that you decide what you believe is best for each of your chapters. I pray you all see that rule under the angels will be far more prosperous than under the demons." Amara believed in the war, in the angels, and even in God. She understood she was doing the right thing, but she didn't think those motivations would sway the minds of the masters. Instead, Blaze, Ember, and she had decided to appeal to their desire for prosperity and revenge. If she could get them to follow her to destroy the Dark Hallow, she hoped she could persuade at least half of them to fight in the final battle.

All was silent.

Amara turned and walked out of the meeting chamber, leaving them to discuss her proposition. Raziel followed, his footsteps heavy behind her. When they were out of earshot of the masters, Amara stopped.

"Well spoken," Raziel beamed at her.

"Do you think they'll listen to me? Do you think any of them will send their people to war?"

"I don't know. What I do know is you have done what you were called to do, and you have done it to the best of your ability. It's all up to the one who sent you now."

Amara and Raziel sat on a stone bench to wait for what felt like ages to Amara. Only about two hours later, Dror glided out of the chamber. He spotted Amara and angled toward them.

"I should have had you in contract negotiations in Caister, my dear." He smiled. "You have a certain way with words, and the fire to back it up."

Did he hear the same speech I just did? I didn't think it was anything special, Amara thought, then said. "Does that mean they will follow me?"

The master's delay made her heart drop.

"Most of the masters have pledged to follow you until the Dark Hallow is destroyed."

"And the others?" she leaned forward.

"The others, you have their full support, including myself and Raza."

A weight lifted off Amara's chest. All the worries of the masters not listening, all the fear of looking like a fool, all of those dissolved.

"We need to make preparation." He motioned them back to the chamber. "The Shadows are going to war."

Togan gaped at the enormous cave around him where he sat on the ledge. The stonework was that of a master and the designs were ancient. He couldn't believe this had been under Newaught when he had lived here a few hundred years ago. All of this was under his feet that whole time. The sizeable gap in the wall stood out like a gaping wound in the otherwise masterful work around him. How long would it be until this place was discovered once again?

"Togan!" a voice from behind him snapped him out of his revery.

How long had he been sitting there? He turned to see Marena hurrying over to him, and his heart jumped in alarm. "Is somethin' wrong?"

"No, but the Shadows are preparing to march."

"March?" He climbed to his feet, careful not to lose his balance this close to the edge. "What's happenin'?"

"Don't worry, dear. Someone has convinced them to fight on our side." She stopped several feet from the edge of the cliff. "We march in two days for the north. They are hoping to overtake the group of assassins who attacked them just before we arrived. They plan to destroy them before the assassins can join the demon army. Then there are some of their numbers who will most likely march back, but many of them will continue on to provide support to the angel army."

"How'd you know all this?" Togan asked.

"I listen." She winked at him. "Instead of spending all my time staring at the past."

"I don't think that's a fair assumption, but I'm glad ya know what's goin' on. We need t' get ready t' march then, not that we have much t' take."

The couple strolled arm in arm toward the cave they were given when they arrived.

Togan thought about their journey so far and a part of him didn't want to march north to the war. He wanted to stay here and keep Marena where it was safe. Maybe even start their family right here in the tunnels. But no, that was only a dream. The reality of the situation was they would never be safe if the Angels didn't win. No one would be.

He had lost so much already. He didn't think he would survive another. His heart had broken in half when he had lost his wife and son all those years ago. It had finally stitched back together when that little whelp of a boy had entered his shop. He had convinced everyone, including himself, that he was older and wiser than his years, but Togan had seen the fear, anger, and determination in the boy. But much more than that, he spotted the pain hidden behind the fire in those black eyes. Togan had seen himself there as well.

He spent days away from the forge after that. Following Malach, just out of sight. Bartering with the shop keeps making sure Malach got the very best prices for his supplies. Doing anything, he could to help this boy survive. Malach would have never taken his help outright. He was too proud, too much like Togan. Those years they had healed together. Every time Malach walked into the forge and spent time with him was another stitch pulling the two halves of Togan's heart back together.

The night Malach was attacked by a demon, Togan had donned his battle hammer for this first time since that fateful night of the fire. Malach was in the healer's hands and Togan was going to make sure this demon would die for bring this pain back to him. For hurting his boy. Togan spent the better part of that night tracking the beast. Malach had made his job easy. Large drops of blood evenly spaced as far apart as they were clearly marked the trail to the fallen demon.

Togan crept up on the monster when he was tending to his wound with his back up against a large oak. He charged out of the brush, a war cry springing to his lips as he brought the hammer down. But it hadn't been that easy. The demon had fight in him yet. It hit him in the chest and sent him flying. His hammer slipped from his hands and the wind was knocked from his chest. He regained his feet, still gasping for air as the demon tackled him. Togan latched onto its spiked head using the horns to bring the creature down. Getting around behind the demon, he grasped the two biggest horns. And he pulled. Every muscle in his body screamed with the strain, but he didn't stop. He couldn't stop. This monster would never hurt his boy. He would never touch another person Togan loved. A loud pop reached Togan's ears, but he didn't stop even then. Malach's face clearly pictured in his mind. His wife's face flitted into his mind's eye, and then his first son.

"Isaac!" With that final scream to the heavens and tears streaming down his face, Togan stood. His powerful arms and legs bracing until the demon's head ripped free from its shoulders.

Togan had collapsed, his entire being spent. At dawn the next day, Marena had found him. She had been out looking for berries for a pie, hoping there would still be enough this late in the season. She had helped him back to town. With the threat of a demon still gripping the people, no one had even glanced out of their shutters. When they reached his shop, she helped him into his room in the back, where he had a passable bed. She had watched over him while he slept for the next day and had a slightly smaller pie than she had intended, waiting for him with supper. However, that pie was glorious.

They had agreed to keep his kill a secret for the time being, and he had almost told Malach, but he stopped when Malach had shown him the blade the demon was wielding. He didn't know what to make of it. Then, of course, Malach had left. Marena kept him company through those few months of worry. Togan couldn't do anything about it since the snows had come and the mountain passes were closed to them. But the next time he had a chance to go with Malach on his journey to save his mother, he had jumped at the chance. No more waiting around, hoping the boy he had grown into a young man survived. This time, he would make sure of it or die alongside him.

Then Marena had been lost. He had been torn between the two of them, but Malach was with his real father and the rest of the group. Marena didn't have anyone.

And so Togan left the party to find Marena. Instead, *she* had found *him*. He had worked his way along the coast, hoping to find where she had washed ashore. Some brigands had seen him moving along during the day and had started following him. Their mistake had been waiting. He had caught sight of them on the second day and was ready for them that night, although no attack came. The third day through tired from a sleepless night, he pressed on. He had hoped they would attack the night of the third day, and he got his wish. They had fallen on him from three different directions. He had fought them off, but not without some minor injuries. Those who he hadn't sent to their final rest with his war hammer had followed just behind him the next day. He was again ready for them that night, but they didn't attack. And after his third sleepless night, he was exhausted.

That afternoon, knowing he wouldn't survive another sleepless night, he had slipped off the coastline. He used a rocky outcropping to break the line of sight between him and his pursuers. When they rounded the rock, he fell upon them. Nine in all, he intended to take as many with him to the afterlife as he could and let God sort out the rest. As he set to his grim work, arrows had flown from atop the rock, and he knew his life was over. However, the arrows hadn't been aimed at him. Three of the enemy fell, two of them dead before they hit the ground, the other injured enough he was no longer in the fight. Togan swung his hammer with renewed strength and hope. He had seized his chance at survival. His hammer crushed the chest of the first man within reach, breaking through his sword as if it wasn't there. It didn't take them long to destroy the group with the support from above.

He turned to see who his savior was and caught a figure flying at him from the top of the rock. Relief flooded his heart. He dropped his hammer to crush Marena in his embrace, never wanting to let go of her as long as they both lived. He had finally set her on her feet and kissed her deeply.

Someone cleared their throat from behind Marena, but they ignored them. It overwhelmed Togan with joy, knowing Marena was safe. He imagined she felt the same way.

When they broke off their embrace, Togan held her at arm's length and drank in the sight of her, checking for any injuries.

"I'm OK, Togan, but we need to see to your wounds." Her eyes were filled with worry.

"None of them are life threatening." He finally looked at her two companions. Both had been sailors on the ship.

One of the sailors introduced them as Orson and Naylor. As Togan had said, his wounds were all minor, but Marena cleaned and bandaged them. They got a few more miles away by nightfall and setup a camp with no fire, just in case.

"What happened to you three?" Togan asked. "How did you end up getting separated from the rest of us?"

"I was knocked unconscious during the destruction of the ship." Orson said. "Luckily, I seemed to have landed on a piece of the ship still floating and the current sent me to shore. When I came to, I picked a direction and started walking, hoping to find any other survivors. I apparently picked the wrong direction." He shrugged.

"I was drug down with the ship." Marena spoke next. "I thought it was my end. A rope had wrapped around my ankle and was pulling me deeper and deeper. Naylor here had his wits about him and spotted me sinking. He grabbed the tail of the rope and pulled himself down to me. He gave the rope slack enough to free my foot and get me to safety. When we breached, we didn't see anyone. I think an underwater current carried us away. At least far enough away, we couldn't catch sight of you. We worked our way to shore and once we recovered, we noticed Orson's footprints leading away from some of the wreckage and we followed."

Togan nodded to Naylor. "Thank you for saving her. I don't know what I would have done if I'd lost her."

The man nodded but didn't say anything. In fact, Togan had noticed he hadn't said anything the entire time they had been traveling.

"Naylor is a mute." Marena explained.

"Oh, sorry to hear that." Togan replied. "But I'm in your debt all the same. If there is anything we can do to help you someday, please grunt in our direction."

Naylor let out a muted chuffing sound, and they all laughed with him.

They had ended up in Newaught not long after. It had been a stroke of luck they had found the Shadows. They had skirted around Newaught to the small forest, hoping to spy on the town and find a way in to get the supplies they needed, but instead they came across a camp of wounded and weary people. Most of the uninjured pulled weapons and advanced on them.

"Wait," Marena called. "I'm a healer. I can help."

They all turned to one man, who was obviously their leader.

He nodded slowly and allowed them to pass into the camp.

Marena got to work immediately and helped wherever she could. Shortly after she finished with the last person, a messenger arrived and conferred with the leader. He then, in turn, moved to his people, and they started gathering weapons.

Togan walked up to the man. "Looks like your people are preparing for a war."

"We are taking our home back." The man told him. "Any help would be appreciated."

"I will do what I can, but I have prior obligations I must stay alive for."

"I understand. I wouldn't ask for you to give your life for our home." The man replied. "However, if we survive this, we are in your debt."

Togan nodded, hefting his hammer. It was only after they hit the wall of black cloak figures, Togan realized he was with the Shadows. With his war hammer in the lead, they had far fewer casualties that day. Afterward, he had talked to the master about his debt; the Master had agreed to pledge his support to their war effort, but he would only go so far.

Now, after the dust had settled, it seemed like he was following through with that promise. They were to march north to aid in the war effort. Unfortunately, they weren't taking a large army. With the recent hardships the Shadows had been through, they were only a few hundred strong. Togan hoped they could take the enemy by surprise and do more damage than would otherwise be possible with their small numbers. He followed Marena through the tunnels. He had to catch her after she stopped, and he toppled her with his bulk.

"Marena?" He glanced up to see what had stopped her in her tracks.

Amara was standing in the hall with a tall, slightly emaciated man behind her.

"I thought you went with Malach and the others?" Togan hadn't meant it as an accusation, but that's how it came out.

Amara didn't meet his eyes but stared at the floor.

The man behind her stepped forward, locking eyes with Togan. "She has done what our Lord has commanded her. She has secured reinforcements for his army."

Togan studied Amara. She had two new long knives strapped to her belt and if the hilts were any indication; they were of the best make money could buy. In fact, He had only seen they're like a few times in the past. His eyes widened. "You're a Blade Bearer?"

She raised her head and met his eyes. "Yes, I was called on the road north and led here to aid the Shadows, my family, and bring their forces to bear against the Demon Army."

Togan pushed past the skinny man suddenly and wrapped Amara in a bear hug, lifting her off her feet. "I'm happy to have you back on the correct side. You must have the noon meal with us and tell us everything."

He set her down and Marena moved forward to give her a much gentler, although just as enthusiastic, embrace. "We are proud of you Amara."

"You two aren't angry?" Amara asked. "I betrayed you."

"Yes," Togan frowned. "That was unfortunate. But God turned it around and now you are a Blade Bearer with, I presume, your father by your side?"

"Oh, yes!" Amara beamed. "This is Raziel. My father. He is the Angel of secrets."

Togan's eyes widened further and glanced between the two. "You must tell us everything."

She did just that as they moved to the mess hall, recently put back together from its time as a defensible base. They laughed and reminisced late into the afternoon until Raziel reminded them they all needed to be ready to march in the morning. They side their goodbyes for the day and split to their respective rooms. Togan's heart was light, despite the hard road that lay ahead of them.

Chapter 18

Malach wrenched the man's wrist to bring him to his knees. He had to defend himself. He brought Reckoning up from under his pillow and put it under the man's chin.

Malach, no! Reckoning's voice snapped him back to the present.

He wasn't in danger. He wasn't on the road being attacked by some faceless assailant. Before him knelt an innocent man in tears. Reckoning clattered to the floor, and he released the man falling back, appalled at his own actions.

The man fled from the room before Malach could say anything.

What was wrong with him? Why did this keep happening? This was the fifth person he had attacked in two weeks. Each had been bringing him food or the like. Every time he woke, his mind was still stuck in the prison, on the road, or in the spider caves. Each of these people would unwittingly play the part of some villain or terror Malach had lived through. Reckoning had been able to bring him back to the present in time, but what happened if he couldn't? What happened when Reckoning was too slow or couldn't shock his mind back in time? He would kill the person who was only trying to help.

There had only been a few nights where he was still in his bed when they bought his food. Most nights, his dreams would wake him long before sunrise. He was certain the servants were always hoping he wouldn't be in his room when they brought his tray around, so they didn't have to risk their life. He preferred those days as well, even if he was bone weary. At least he hadn't hurt anyone.

He sighed and righted the items that had fallen over on the tray. He snatched the loaf of bread from it and walked the familiar path to the top of the wall. This walk had become so common in the last two weeks a part of him was surprised there wasn't a rut in the floor.

He needed to be out in the open. Out of the claustrophobic rooms of the stronghold. The ramparts were the closest wide-open space. He found himself here at least once a day to clear his mind, trying to make sense of what was happening to him. Was he going insane? Was his mind breaking from the strain of all he had been through? The elders had said that could happen when he was attacked by the demon in Brightwood. It seemed like ages ago that he had been there hunting with Skie. It had its hardships, but what he wouldn't give to be back there. Back to the way it was.

He sighed again and stopped, leaning on the wall overlooking the field below. It wouldn't be long and this field would be littered with bodies and stained with gore. He had heard the reports of the damage his father had done to the enemy camp. The explosion had killed Sloth, one of the seven lords, destroyed most of the war engines they had already put together, and damages the rest. It had set the enemy's preparations back for weeks. Initial reports from the spies stated none of the cannons were affected by the blast, which was unfortunate. The troop numbers the demons had brought to bear against them alone made the outcome of the battle bleak. If they still had cannons, it would have been all but decided.

The Angel Army wasn't without their own shiny new weapons, though. Sitting to Malach's left and a little removed from the edge of the ramparts was an odd-looking weapon. It reminded Malach of the cannons at its base with only two wheels to allow it to be aimed up at an angle. However, the top was far from cannon shaped. Resting on the two wheels was a large box with slats which made a grid of square openings. Each of these openings contained an arrow with a small device attached to it. These little devices were filled with a less volatile version of the black powder he himself had used to escape a few scrapes. When lit, they would take their arrow into the sky, as if shot from a bow, and drop them into the enemy ranks. He was told they were not accurate and not effective against a small group of enemies, but should do nicely to thin out the ranks of an army.

There were two more of these large boxes sitting next to the first. He had seen the soldiers drilling with the weapons and as one was being reloaded, the next would fire, and then the next. Each would be reloaded and fired again until they ran out of ammunition.

Malach? Reckoning broke through his thoughts. *You need to talk to your father about your dreams. You need to seek help. This isn't something that goes away.*

I appreciate the concern, but I'm fine. Malach thought back. *Ariel has already been spending an hour plus with me every day to help me meditate. He doesn't need to worry more than he is. They are just dreams.*

No, you're not fine. The nightmares are getting worse. You haven't slept for a full night since arriving at the stronghold and you have tried to kill a total of five different people. You need to tell him.

Malach signed. *Fine, I'll talk to my father about them, but I won't talk to him until after the battle.*

Malach-

No, I won't have him more distracted during the battle. I won't be the cause of his, or anyone else's, death. I've been healing. I haven't frozen while sparring in more than a week. It's a process but I'm getting better.

Reckoning sighed, but didn't say anything else.

"Malach?" Honora's voice came from behind him.

He turned to see her climbing a set of stairs to the ramparts.

"Couldn't sleep again?" She asked.

Malach shook his head and turn back to the field.

"I heard the servants talking." She leaned on the wall next to him and when he didn't respond, add. "Do you want to talk about it?"

"Not really." Malach replied.

"Malach, you're not alone."

"I know," but he didn't feel that. Even though he was surrounded by friends and family now, he felt more alone than he had when he lived in the cottage with Skie. He felt hollow. The thought of the wolf made him search her out. He didn't have to look any farther than by his own side. She had followed him up here and was standing at one of the kill windows. He wondered if she felt things like he did. How was she handling all of this?

She locked eyes with him, and he could swear he saw his own sadness reflected in them.

Maybe he was just projecting. He wished he could talk with her like Michael had the last time they were at the stronghold. He had told him she was a dire wolf. One of the last of her kind. What would happen when she passed from the world? Was she the very last dire wolf, or were there others? He thought he would enjoy searching with her for more of her kind if they survived.

"I have nightmares too, Malach." Honora's voice was small and quiet. "I... They've kept me from sleeping since we got here. I've spent more time with my horse, Celwyn, in the stables than I have since we left Newaught."

"They're worse when you're in a safe place." Malach turned to look at her. "You find solace with your horse. I find it under the open sky."

She nodded, and her eyes told him she really *did* have nightmares. "I haven't been through near the amount you have and yet I'm haunted by what's happened. I can only imagine what you're going through."

"I'm done after this battle." He studies the dimly lit horizon just visible over the distant mountain range. "No matter what happens, I can't take it anymore."

"What will you do?" Honora asked. "I mean, if it goes badly, or even if it goes well, but the war isn't over, where will you go?"

"It will be over one way or another." Malach frowned. "We have our back to the proverbial wall. If we don't win, none of us will survive. They will keep driving at us until one of us is destroyed. Some of the Angels or demons will survive the destruction. If the angels win, the humans on the demon side will most likely be shown mercy, but do you think the demons will spare any of us?"

"I hadn't thought of that."

Malach watched a tear slide down Honora's cheek.

"I'm sorry. My melancholy leads me to a dark place."

"You're right though. We will need to fight hard to keep those we love protected."

Movement drew Malach's eye to a shadow under the mountain range. He squinted, studying, watching for the movement again. *Reckoning?*

No, your eyes aren't playing tricks on you. I saw it too.

"Malach?" Honora asked. "Something wrong?"

He held up his hand, all sense on high alert. His muscles wound as tight as a spring. He spotted the dragon then. Much closer than it had been skimming along the ground at inhuman speeds. Both heads stretched out ahead of it. Fire blossomed in the two mouths, illuminating rows of teeth and spilling out each side to trail behind them.

"SOUND THE ALARM!" Malach shouted, pulling Honora down as the first fireball splashed again the stone wall. He could feel the intense heat coming from around the wall, searing his skin. His chest tightened and his limbs seized. Fear gripped him as it had so often lately. But the sensation passed this time, his locked muscles melting after the initial shock.

Bells sounded throughout the stronghold, and soldiers started spilling out onto the wall. The first set of soldiers who arrived at the top of the stairs spotted Malach and Honora and ran toward them to give them support. The men were met with the second large fireball, sending many flying off the wall and setting others ablaze.

Malach and Honora huddled against the wall until the beast shot past them over head reigning death down on the courtyard below.

"Go!" Honora pulled Malach to his feet and pushed him into movement. His feet obeyed, but only by habit. The movement sparked the release of Malach's mind, however, and he started regaining his faculties.

They ran with their heads down, imaging an oncoming assault of either arrows or a blast of fire from the devil himself. They made it to the stairs leading down and into the stronghold. Skie ran past the pair and turned down another hall, away from the battle. Malach and Honora glanced at each other, confused.

Malach shrugged, besides it got him away from the coming battle so he could recover. "Let's go."

Kragen knelt in his cell, eyes closed in meditation. With the demon army drawing near, the guards had taken stations within the prison. It didn't matter. He had already weakened the hinges as much as he dared. Anymore and they would fall off with their own weight. Now he prepared his mind and body for the call. It would come at any time, and he would finally be able to leave this prison. He was only upset that he wouldn't be able to kill the little mouse of a girl.

Emmeline.

He grinned at the thought of her name. The fear he would have inflicted on her innocent mind would have been delicious. The smell of her fear would have only heightened his pleasure as he ran her through. But unfortunately, it would seem his blood lust would have to wait until after he finished his mission. Maybe he would find her after the wall was down.

He chuckled to himself. Yes, that's what he would do. Hunt her like the mouse she was.

"What are you laughing at, scum?" One of the guards asked gruffly.

Kragen, it's time. Lord Azazel spoke into his mind.

Kragen stood, eyes still closed, and flexed his muscles. "Come and find out meat."

"What did you call me?" The guard took a challenging step forward.

That's right, you have all the power. Kragen thought, amused. *Until you don't.*

"Sit down, hell spawn, or I will teach you a lesson." The guard took another step forward, his boot crunching as it ground the dust into the stone.

Kragen opened his eyes. The guard had his hand on the hilt of his sword. Fear and excitement making the man's chest rise and fall quickly.

He spit toward the guard. It fell short, but it was the reaction he was seeking. He wasn't disappointed.

The guard snatched the keys to the cell from the belt of his fellow guard and started forward.

"Don't," the other guard grabbed the first wrist. "We'll get in trouble."

The first guard twisted his wrist free. "Coward, I'm going to teach the prisoner a lesson, and you will keep your mouth shut if you know what's good for you." He turned back to Kragen and crossed the small space in a couple more steps.

Kragen burst into action, kicking the cell door. The weakened latched buckled under the assault and took the guard off his feet. He leapt forward, both feet landing directly on the bars over the man's head. Gore shot through the bars and he bathed in the first blood he had spilled in weeks. The second guard screamed, and the smell of urine reached his senses. He sprinted forward and seized the man by his breast plate pulling him away from the door. He tossed the guard through the cell entrance and intended to follow him through, but his head had landed squarely on the bench, breaking his neck cleanly.

Kragen sighed. He wanted to have a little more fun with his prey, but things happened when you tossed around the weak. They tended to break too quickly.

The noise of a tray clattering to the floor drew his attention, and a smile returned to his face. There she was, hands still outstretched, as if holding the tray of food that was now scattered on the floor.

"Little mouse." Kragen cooed. "I was so looking forward to our time together. Now be a good little thing and play along."

She didn't move an inch.

Kragen frowned. "I did hope for more from you, but alas I don't have much time for games." He retrieved the sword from the guard in the cell and turned. Emmeline was gone, the patter of her foot falls retreating quickly down the hall.

Kragen laughed. The hunt was on.

It didn't take him long to catch up with her. He could have almost followed her by the stench of her fear left in her wake. However, her heavy breathing and the sound of her panicked running directed him better. He slowed, not wanting the chase to end so soon.

Kragen! Azazel's voice sounded in his head, and he reined in his thoughts so the demon wouldn't know what he was doing. *When will the wall be down? Lords Lucifer and Satan need that wall down now!*

"Little mouse," Kragen ignored Azazel's call, letting Emmeline gain a little ground. "All I want to do is play before I break your neck."

Her squeak of a gasp barely reached his ears, but he cackled in response. Yes, he would enjoy this kill. She ducked around a corner, breaking his line of sight, but he wasn't worried. There wasn't much down this far. He had scouted these halls prior to his incarceration, and no one came down here unless they were lost.

She ran through a door and slammed it behind her. He could hear the nails on her fingers scratching frantically, searching for some kind of lock, no doubt. These doors required a key to lock them. He reached the door and kicked it.

It didn't budge.

He frowned and kicked it again. Nothing. "Clever little mouse," He called. "You found something to the block the door."

"Leave me alone,"

He could hear her tears. She was sobbing. Maybe he would hold her for a few minutes before he killed her. The fact that she hadn't run from this room meant she was trapped. She would be his. There was no doubt in his mind.

So, when the first of the bricks fell, he was shocked. The walls shook from the impact of something large and stone fell all around him. He dove out of the way and jumped up in a panic.

Did Emmeline survive? She was his! If a falling stone had killed her before he could... He didn't know what he would do. He ran to the door and hit it with all his might. The door moved in by a few inches and ground to a halt.

Kragen! Azazel shouted in his head.

He pushed the door again. Another inch, but there was no way he would make it through. He searched the room as best he could through the crack, but there was no sign of her dead or alive.

Kragen!

Then she came into his view. Relief flooded through him. Blood trickled down her forehead, but she otherwise appeared uninjured. Sweet terror played across her face as she noticed him in the doorway. He would still have her.

Kragen! If you don't answer me, I will kill you myself!

Another impact shook the stronghold, and more rubble came down around them. This time Kragen didn't leave but shoved the door, hoping for just another few inches. He would be able to squeeze through soon.

Emmeline, however, ran to one of the walls and, with a glance his way, disappeared through it. The shaking of the stronghold had collapsed part of that wall. There was no telling when she would end up.

"No!" Kragen shouted. "Little mouse, come back here! Your mine!"

But she didn't reappear. He pushed again, letting out a frustrated growl that turned into a roar of anger. He backed out and tried to find a way around, but couldn't.

Kragen!

"I'm coming!" Kragen shouted back, both mentally and physically. And turned to go. He would have to hurry, but he could still retrieve his sword on the way to the first explosive. He would still complete his mission. Then hunt his little mouse once again.

Malach and Honora ran after Skie. They met many men along the way headed toward the wall, and whereas they glanced quizzically at the two, none stopped or questioned them.

"Did you notice something wrong with the assault?" Malach asked, catching sight of Skie disappearing around another corridor.

Honora gave him a puzzled look. "You mean other than the fiery balls of death raining down from the sky?"

No enemy troops were anywhere close to the wall. This is a distraction, not an assault. Reckoning replied, and Malach repeated his words to Honora.

"That must be where Skie is taking us." Malach spoke out loud for Honora's benefit. "Reckoning, send a message to any angel close enough to hear. They need to redirect troops from the wall to our location. Tell them what we know and-" Malach stopped short as he skidded to a halt around the next corner.

Skie stood, hair standing on end, hackles raised, and a low growl emanating from deep in her throat.

On the other side of the enormous wolf was a nephilim. One whom Malach knew. Kragen stood with a torch in one hand and a two-handed wavy-edged blade in the other. He didn't seem to have a problem holding the heavy sword with one hand, but Malach didn't know how skilled he would be with such a large blade. Malach did his best to shove down the growing fear in him.

"Your companion does you justice," Kragen growled, a smile playing across his lips. "To bad I will have to kill her." He tossed the torch to the side, took his sword in two hands, and charged.

Malach drew Reckoning, changing him into his standard pole weapon with the blade at each end, and prepared for the assault. His movements slow the methodical. He tried to take solace and comfort in the familiar movements to fight back the panic tightening his chest once again. Then Kragen was upon him, and his survival instincts kicked in.

Malach the torch has lit a fuse! Reckoning noted.

Malach deflected the downward strike of his opponent and followed up with a reverse slash, causing Kragen to retreat. *Not sure if you noticed, but I'm a little busy.*

There is an explosive and, if I'm not mistaken, this is a load-bearing wall for a section of the ramparts.

"Honora!" Malach shouted, not daring to take his eyes off Kragen. "The fuse." He pointed with his weapon, hoping she would understand.

Kragen started forward again, stabbing at him. He dodged, bringing the center of his pole up to catch Kragen's nose.

Kragen's hand came up faster and caught the pole, but instead of trying to pull it out of his grasp, he pushed, causing Malach to stumble and lose his balance.

Luckily, Skie chose that time to hit him broadside with her bulk or the nephilim would have easily finished him. Malach regained his feet and glanced over to see Honora kicking the torch away and cutting the fuse. At least that was taken care of. He returned his attention to see Skie in the air over Kragen's head just before he hefted her toward him. He turned Reckoning intime not to stab her but took her fully weight to his chest, bowling him over backward. They fell in a tangled heap, but it only took a few seconds for them to regain their footing. It was too late. Kragen was in full stride, headed for Honora's back.

"Honora!" Malach called in warning.

Honora turned, pulling a knife too small for be effective against Kragen. She stood her ground, determination in her eyes.

Time slowed as Malach and Skie charged to catch Kragen. They would not make it in time. Kragen was closing the distance too fast for even Skie to save her. Malach watched in horror as the wicked wavy two-handed sword disappeared to the hilt in Honora's abdomen. His mind didn't want to believe what his eyes were telling him. He must have seen it wrong. Honora must have gotten out of the way at the last second. The look that spread across her face told Malach the terrible truth. Kragen leered, leading her around with the sword so Malach could see the blade protruding from her back. His heart stopped, his knees buckled, and he couldn't think, couldn't move.

Skie continued her charge, but it almost didn't matter to Malach in that moment. He watched as Kragen tried to pull the sword free of Honora, but couldn't. Her hand was on his hilt, holding it in place. Skie lunged, missing Honora by only inches and digging her teeth into Kragen's throat.

He let go of the sword and Honora collapsed, his hold on the sword the only thing keeping her on her feet. Kragen flailed, trying to defend himself in vain against Skie's assault. He would be dead shortly.

Malach slide to a stop at Honora's side. She was struggling to breathe and trying to pull the blade free of her ribs. Malach put a hand on hers, stopping her. "The healers say to leave it in." He breathed. "They will be here soon."

She smiled at him sadly. "They...won't... be able... to fix... this." She wheezed out. Her body convulsed with pain.

"Don't talk," Tears started spilling down his cheeks. He frantically looked around them. No one had shown up yet. Not even the soldiers.

"Malach." She reached a hand up to touch his cheek. "It's my time."

"No!" He shouted, grief twisting his face as he sobbed. "No, you'll be ok. You have to be ok."

"This isn't your fault." She said, as if reading his mind. "You did everything you could."

Skie plodded over and lay down her snout inches from Honora's face.

"You were magnificent, as always." She smiled at the wolf. "I was just too slow this time. Protect him. He needs you."

"Honora, the healer will fix this." Malach remembered to put pressure on the wound and Honora grimaced.

"Nothing short of an act of God could fix this, Malach." She pushed his hand down gently, and of course, he knew she was right.

"I failed you."

"No, I told you it was not your fault. You are my best friend. You have stood with me through everything, you who had it much harder than the rest of us, still took time to make sure we were alright. You protected me time and again."

"But not this time. I failed."

She coughed, blood spurting out of her mouth, and she spat it out. "You can't save everyone. And you can't hold yourself responsible for everyone's death. Remember me when it's all done and take care of Daziar. This will hurt him. You know how he loved me all these years. Tell my parents I died protecting the stronghold." She had another coughing fit. "And... take...care...of Celewyn."

"Honora, please don't go." He pulled her up to him and sobbed into her shoulder, holding her close. "Please don't leave me."

"Malach, I love you," she whispered into his ear and her body fell slack.

He sobbed, rocking back and forth, cradling her in his arms. Somewhere along the way, he pulled the sword out of her lifeless body and threw the cursed thing as far away as possible.

He didn't know how long he stayed that way, but no one had arrived yet. Muffled screams and shouts still sounded from outside, but a much more curious sound perked Skie's ear and pricked at Malach's mind. A fizzing was coming from behind him.

Skie growled and rose to her feet.

Malach whirled to see Kragen holding his neck, grinning through bloody teeth. The lit fuse disappearing into the wall. Malach picked up Honora's body and sprinted away as the explosion rocked the stronghold and lifted him off his feet.

He landed in a heap, protecting Honora's body as best he could as rock and dust rained down on him. Coughing as he attempted to fill his lungs, he glanced around him. He couldn't see anything through the particles in the air, but as they cleared, he could see daylight filtering through them, and his heart dropped. He'd failed not only Honora but the whole of the angel army.

The stronghold had been breached.

"Malach! Honora!" Daziar's voice called through the dust.

"Over..." Malach caught another lungful of grit and was sent into another coughing fit.

Skie appeared, with Daziar following close behind. "Malach, are you two alright?" He spotted Honora and fell to his knees next to them. "What happened? We need to get the healers."

Malach shook his head, unable to talk through his grief. He felt tears burning their way down his face, carving through the accumulated grime.

Tears formed in Daziar's eyes as well, no doubt having guessed what Malach meant. "No, she can't be...we need the healers. They can help her."

"She's gone, Daz." Malach choked out.

"No!" Daziar pulled Honora's body into his lap and out of Malach's grasp. He cradled her and rocked back and forth. "She can't...She's not supposed to be....YOU WHERE SUPPOSED TO PROTECT HER!" He roared at Malach.

His words cut deep, echoing Malach's own thoughts and set him back on his heels.

As the dust settled slowly, he noticed the army filing down the hall and into the slightly larger room that was fully open to the field outside. Angels and men alike stood gaping at the hole and the staring at the three on the ground. No one said a word.

Ana and Ariel pushed their way through the crowd, Ana rushing to Daziar's side and Ariel to Malach's.

"What happen?" Ariel asked in hushed tones, kneeling and putting a hand on Malach's shoulder.

Malach just shook his head, shaking the tears loose. A series of wet coughs sounded behind Malach and Ariel and Ana stepped around them, pulling weapons.

Malach turned around, searching for the source of the coughing. He spotted the nephilim half buried by rubble, and badly burned. "How did that monster survive?" He heard himself ask.

The coughing turned into gurgling laughter as a smile crossed the man's face. His eyes were wide and wild, and he looked like something out of a nightmare.

Anger boiled in Malach, and he took up Reckoning.

Send this piece of excrement to his judgement. Reckoning's voice was heavy with hate.

"I have fulfilled my duty to the great dragon." Kragen spat blood with every word. "I will gain my reward in the next-"

His words cut off as the two-headed dragon dove through the opening and a clawed hand crushed the nephilim's face. The impact sent gore flying, and the two angels shielded their faces from the ichor. Malach was too busy retreating to block any of it and Daziar, too numb to care. The dragon lifted his paw, and one head lick the remnants of the man from its claws.

"Deluded fool," the second head grumbled.

"Nephilim blood is always the best." The first head said through a grinning maw of teeth.

"Angel is better." The second replied, turning to the crowd of angels and soldiers.

A ripple of fear moved through the crowd behind Malach, but all stood their ground against the beast that stood before them.

"Pitiful," the first mumbled, then louder. "Listen and cower!"

"Your stronghold has been breached!" The second head continued.

"You wall crumbled!"

The two heads of the dragon continued switching off, apparently knowing what the other was thinking. They never stilled through the speech, each snaking out, up, back, and down while they spoke.

"You will die on the dawn of the 'morrow."

"We give you one day to bury your dead,"

"Abandon the stronghold,"

"or shore up your meager defenses and entomb yourself."

"Hear our words and despair,"

"For death rides on the wind of our wings,"

"And will spare none who stand here at the rising of the next sun."

The dragon launched its bulk into the air and vaulted off the rubble that remained of the wall, leaving gouges in the fallen stone. The Devil was gone almost as fast as he had appeared. A collective sigh moved through the troops.

Despair descended on Malach as heavy as if the wall had buried him alive. He collapsed to the floor, curling up. Sobs racking his prone body.

The Masters of the Shadows had driven them hard. None of the members complained, however, the promise of revenge propelling them as much as the continued calls of those in charge. They wanted to catch up to the Dark Hallow as much as the masters and send them to their dark demise.

Amara marched with Togan and Marena, not saying much after the first day where they recounted the stories of their respective roads to Newaught. They didn't have much breath to talk now with the higher elevation. Togan and Marena were more used to the elevation, but even *they* were breathing hard.

The Shadows had followed the Dark Hallow, picking up their trail shortly out of the woods outside of Newaught. Raza didn't believe anyone was leading them, though, as they followed the main road. Amara wondered if she wounded her mother more than she had initially thought. Or had she taken a different path than the rest of the Dark Hallow? They would find out soon enough. They had been gaining on the assassins and would come upon them within the next day or two.

The scouts estimated the group was forty strong, and the Masters thought they would have no problems wiping them from this life. Their own numbers were more than triple that, and Raziel alone counted as ten men.

They had passed the burned-out husk of Whiteshade a few days back and it surprised her how much the wilderness had taken it back in such a short time. It wouldn't be long before they reached Brightwood. Togan had relayed to the masters they were worried the Dark Hallow would try to take refuge there. The walls would give them a defensible location to hold out in.

Amara didn't think it would be as big of a problem as they anticipated. Not long ago, she and Malach had snuck into the town and took it back from a band of mercenaries. She imagined they could do that again without issue. They weren't assassins, but they were skilled in the art of the shadows.

The biggest thing she was worried about was the killing. Sure, she had killed before, but she hadn't been able to assassinate anyone. The only times she had killed were face-to-face fights. Taking a life from the shadows had always been against what she believed, but she expected she would be called to do just that soon.

Amara searched for Raziel. Maybe he would have some wisdom for her dilemma. She spotted him walking with Raza a little way ahead of her and took her leave of Togan and Marena. She quickened her pace, her muscles burning with the extra strain. When she caught up with Raziel, her heart was pounding out of her chest and she was breathing so hard she couldn't even greet him and Raza.

"Breath, little one," Raziel chuckled. "We will wait until your breath is, once again, under control."

It didn't take her long to recover enough to request to speak to Raziel alone.

Raza nodded her consent, and Raziel and Amara stopped for a minute, falling back toward the end of the group.

"What did you want to talk to me about, my daughter?" Raziel smiled down at her.

Amara blinked at him for a moment. She still hadn't gotten used to being called his daughter. She liked it, though. Her father hadn't turned out to be a bad person, as she had feared all of her life.

A smile played involuntarily at the corners of her lips.

"Are you ok?" He asked.

She shook her head to clear her errant thoughts. "Yes...well no..."

"Which is it?" Raziel raised an eyebrow at her. "Yes, or no?"

"I'm fine right now, but I have a dilemma and want to get your opinion."

He nodded, and they started walking again so they wouldn't get too far behind the group.

"I'm afraid I will be asked to do something I don't know if I can do."

He nodded, slow and thoughtful.

"I think in the next few days, I will have to become an assassin. I don't believe in killing someone in cold blood."

This caused Raziel's eyebrows to lift. "You believe assassinations are cold-blooded killing?"

"Aren't they?" Her brow knitted together in a scowl. "If you take a life before they have a chance to defend themselves, that seems pretty cold-blooded to me."

"Let me ask it this way. Do you think any of the people you'll have to kill in the next few weeks will be innocent?"

Amara thought about that before speaking. "Certainly not any of the Dark Hallow. They are the worst of the worst. But what of the soldiers? How many of them are just following orders, unaware of what they are really fighting for?"

"Very good," He nodded approvingly. "and a worthy question to ponder. But let's start with the Dark Hallow, since they are more black and white. None of them are innocent. Given the chance everyone of them would stab you in the back unawares, correct?"

"Of course they would, and have, to too many of our people."

"Then it's not a cold-blooded kill. Their own actions have brought the consequences upon them. What would you gain by killing them in a fight instead of slitting their throats in their sleep?"

"It would be a fair fight at least." Amara shrugged.

Raziel's laughter caught her off guard and was a little out of place for the serious conversation. "I am sorry." He got his mirth under control, noticing her scowl. "There is rarely ever a fair fight. And if two warriors come together with equal skill, strength, and speed, each will look to gain the upper hand for neither want to die. Take me, for instance. If I waited for a fair fight, I would be no use to anyone against mere mortals. Or worse, I would put my own life at risk trying to fight so many men in the hopes of evening out the fight. No, there is rarely a truly fair fight."

Amara could see the wisdom in his words, but it tore at a long-held conviction, making her confront the possibility she was wrong.

"Then, if you don't believe the Dark Hallow are innocent, and you agree there are no fair fights; what would stop you from killing someone without endangering your life? Why would you seek a fight which you could avoid?"

"I...I don't know," she admitted. "I have believed for a long time assassination was wrong. An absolute."

"There are few absolutes in this world. Most times, you will find things to be one shade of gray or another."

"I'll need to think about this more. I'm not sure what I believe anymore."

"Doubts are a good thing, young Amara. They push us to find the truth and that is never a bad thing."

"What about the soldiers?"

"What about them?"

"Many of them might be innocent. I don't know if I can assassinate them knowing that."

"Are you going to ask each one if they truly believe what they are fighting for?"

"No," Her brow knitted again. "Besides being impossible, I wouldn't be able to trust their answer."

"Then we are forced to make a generalization, however erroneous we know it to be. We fight, because to stand by would mean seeing the end of all that is good in the world. There are good men on each side of this war, but many have chosen to follow evil. They are therefore lumped into the same group. We have to assume they are just as evil as the masters they serve. If you follow that logic to its inevitable end, you will see none of them are innocent. Those who are innately good and have made the wrong decision are no longer innocent."

Amara nodded again. "I see your point. Thank you Raziel. You have given me a lot to think about."

"Of course," Raziel smiled. "I'm always available if you need to talk."

She smiled back and nodded.

Raziel paused for a moment, as if unsure of what to do next. Then he walked a bit faster and left Amara to her contemplation.

He had systematically dismantled her argument against assassinations, but he did it in such a way she couldn't even be mad at him. He presented logic to her and then left her to reconcile it with her own beliefs.

The Keeper of Secrets indeed, she thought with a rueful smile.

She spent the rest of the day wrestling with her feelings and beliefs on the subject. In the end, she was no closer to knowing what to do.

As the sun was sinking behind the mountains, the scouts reported the Dark Hallow had set up camp. They marched for another hour or so and made camp in the last dregs of daylight. Amara contemplated their options, and she lay on her bed roll. If they didn't catch up with the Assassins tomorrow, they would be facing the possibility of assaulting the town. Or they would have to wait even longer until the Dark Hallow left to join the demon army. From her experience, they would only have a few days between Brightwood and the angel's stronghold to strike. If they didn't take their chance at that point, they would face the whole of the demon army. The more reserved masters had already stated they would not support all-out war.

No, now was the best time to strike.

She couldn't sleep. The anxiety of the coming battle and the struggle with her own beliefs keeping her awake. She needed to take a walk to clear her head. Blaze and Ember sheathed at her sides. She made her way out of the tents, feeling more and more claustrophobic the longer she was within the camp.

She reached the edge of the camp, and the feeling of claustrophobia turned to paranoia. The hair on the back of her neck rose, and a shudder coursed down her spine. She shook her head at her own irrational fear of what was in the dark woods. She walked through the trees and left the light of the camp behind her. Her eyes slowly adjusted, and she could walk more confidently through the underbrush.

Your feeling of being watched is no irrational paranoia, Blaze stated.

Assassins are about this night, Ember agreed.

Where? Amara asked, fighting to keep her breath even as she turned back toward the camp. Everything in her body screamed for her to run, but experience told her this was a time to keep calm.

The trees, Blaze responded. *These assassins are used to urban environments and can't hide as easily in the trees as they think they can.*

I've seen three so far through your eyes, Ember added. *The whole of the Dark Hallow might be here hoping to kill and melt back into the forest. No doubt they hope to pick at your group until you retreat. They don't have the numbers for anything else.*

She hadn't noticed a single assassin yet. Maybe *she* was too used to an 'urban environment' as well. *Malach would have seen them.* The thought sprang unbidden to her thoughts and a stab of guilt cut at her heart. He must think her a traitor twice over now.

Clear your head of these thoughts Amara. Ember cut in before she could spiral farther. *They are best left for a time when you're not being hunted.*

We need to warn the camp, Amara replied, forcing her thoughts to the problem at hand. Ember was right She could figure out what to tell Malach later. If they survived.

I doubt they will let you back into camp uncontested, Blaze stated.

The hair on the back of her neck prickled suddenly, and she pulled only Blaze, turning to deflect the knife plunging toward her back. To her surprise, it was lower than expected and a hand was still grasping the hilt. The knife scraped against her blade, slipped off, and bit into her leather armor. She spun away, sheading her cloak and wrapping her assailant's arm in it. She pulled on the arm and shoved Blaze into his eye with the other. He dropped like a pile of rocks, taking her cloak with him.

The attack will have started. Hurry, Ember implored.

She didn't have to say any more. Amara was already running back toward the camp, shouting to raise the alarm. She burst out of the forest to find war on a scale she hadn't seen since Fairdenn. The Dark Hallow had reinforcements.

She ran at the first enemy she found stabbing him in the back before he could turn from the man he was fighting.

"Amara?" Demien asked, a smile spreading across his face. "I thought you didn't stab people in the back."

"Shut up and fight." Amara growled back.

They put their back to each other, fighting off enemy after enemy. These men weren't trained well. They were either fodder for the army or they were hired hands the Dark Hallow had stumbled upon. A man barreled in from the side and slammed into the one advancing on Amara. She turned, expecting to see Raziel. Instead, Togan came rampaging through the enemy lines, oblivious to the cuts and scratches the enemy inflicted. He was unstoppable, smashing ribs, arms, legs, and even heads with his war hammer. She was very glad he was on their side. Marena skated through in his wake, loosing arrows almost point blank into those who survived the blacksmith's charge.

"Demien," she called behind her. "Our ticket out of here has arrived."

They broke off from the enemy and followed Togan, helping Marena mop up the carnage. He finally slowed halfway through the camp. The Shadows, who he had saved, surrounded him, allowing him to rest while they fought any attackers off.

She spotted Raziel weaving his deadly dance through the enemy soldiers. He had found a light blade to his liking and his blade now tasted blood. He stabbed, dodged, cut, and retreated, leaving many alive but unable to continue the fight. The back of the knees and ankles seemed to be his favorite target, a trail of writhing bodies left in his wake. Most would never walk again.

Amara wondered if their conversation and an effect on him as much as it had on her. Maybe he was trying his best to minimize the body count while still maximizing the loss of fighting men of the enemy. He danced out of her view and her break was over. She replaced one of the men at the edge of their small force, allowing him a breather.

They fought well into the night, doing all they could to survive. They kept moving as Togan could, using him as a battering ram when needed and protecting him when he was too tired to fight. Finally, as quick as it had started, the battle ended. The remaining enemies retreated, but Amara didn't see a Dark Hallow among them.

The surviving Shadows cheered and took up chase.

"Wait!" Amara called, but no one was listening.

The front runners were cut down before they stepped a single foot into the forest.

"The Dark Hallow are in the trees!" She warned.

All eyes, and any shields among them, turned up, which saved many of the second line from facing the same end as the first. The archers among them loosed arrows into the trees and many cloaked figures fell. Those who had shields moved forward cautiously, ready for another attack. None came. They worked their way into the trees, but it seemed the Dark Hallow were either all dead or had fled.

They returned to the camp to start picking up what was left of it. After a few hours, they had an idea of their numbers and damage. Amara wanted nothing more than to fall into her bedroll and get a few hours of sleep before the first light of morning.

Raziel walked up with a few of the masters. "Amara, please join us."

She sighed and trudged over to them.

"I'm sorry, daughter, but sleep will have to wait." Raziel put a hand on her shoulder.

He led them to the meeting tent where the rest of the masters we already in a heated debate. Amara couldn't help but wonder what she was walking into. She had led them here. The death of so many sat squarely on her shoulders.

"We need to return to the safety of Newaught!" One man shouted.

Amara didn't recognize him.

Raziel leaned over as if reading her mind. "His master was killed. He is now the master of the Ragewood chapter. He also holds the most surviving members of the Shadows now."

She nodded, then stepped forward. "I understand how you feel."

He spun to see who was addressing him. "How would you know? I need to protect my people. More than half of them were slaughtered tonight."

Amara winced but pushed through the pain and embarrassment. "I know because of who I've lost. But I also know who and what we stand to lose if we turn back now."

"Let the angels rot and the demons take power. We will survive as we always have. In the shadows." He spat at her feet before turning to face many who were nodding along with him.

"And what happens when those shadows start to disappear?" Amara continued, undaunted. "What happens when the demons hunt you and slaughter you in your homes as they did using the Dark Hallow?"

"The Dark Hallow is no more. We have seen to that tonight. They were not a part of the demon army."

"Who do you think those soldiers were?" Raziel stepped forward. "Those were not assassins or rouges for hire. They were part of the demon army. I know not how they came to be here tonight, but I know those who survived will tell their master. If the demons are victorious, you *will* be hunted."

"Raziel is right," Amara motioned his direction. "Lilith led the Dark Hallow. I witnessed her bring back the devil himself. She was in league with him for many, many years. To say the Dark Hallow weren't pawns of the demon army is to say clouds don't float. We must see this to the end or it will be the end of the Shadows."

Many of the masters who were nodding along with the new master were now nodding with her. That was an encouraging sight. The Man was having a hard time ordering his thoughts to rebut her argument, and she didn't want to give him the chance.

"If the angels do not win this war, I truly believe it will be the beginning of the end for mankind." Amara pressed. "It might be years, but the eventual extinction would come. The demons don't care about any human. If they don't send their forces to kill you in your hiding places, the poverty of the people who survive their regime will starve you from them. We cannot stop now."

"I will follow Amara to the death if need be. Who else is with me?" Raza stepped forward.

To her shock, each of the Masters stepped forward and pledged their support to her until the only one left was the Ragewood Master. He crossed his arms, and his scowl deepened every time each of them stepped forward. All eyes turned to him now to see what he would do.

His jaw tightened, and he didn't say anything for a long time. Finally, he said, "I need to protect the rest of my people. I don't wish for there to be any hard feeling between our factions. However, now the Dark Hallow has been delt with, I'm going to take my people back to Ragewood and rebuild. When this goes badly for you, if any of you survive and need shelter, we will be happy to supply it. For now, this is where our paths diverge."

Amara felt a spike of anger. He was taking over half of the remaining Shadows with him. They would be less than a hundred strong after he left. How could he turn his back on them now?

Raziel put his hand on her shoulder and spoke in her ear under his breath. "He has been thrust into leadership and faced with an impossible choice. Don't judge him for wanting to protect what remains of his people."

She disagreed with Raziel's assessment. He was a coward, and he would have no place in the new Shadows if she had anything to say about it.

To her surprise, though, each of the masters clasped arms with him and wish them good luck on their journey back. How could they do that? He was leaving them in fear. He was very possibly leaving them to die. Their numbers had been halved and now were being halved again. Didn't they understand he was undermining their chance for survival?

The Ragewood Master turned to her. "Girl, I hope you know what you are doing and wish you the best."

She didn't trust herself to say anything to him, so she just stayed silent.

He took the hint and moved out of the tent.

The rest of the masters turned to her, and panic rose in her instantly. She fought it back and took a deep breath. Raziel's hand came to rest on her shoulder, and she took strength from him. She wanted nothing more than to go lay down, but they needed a plan.

"Amara," Raza stepped forward. "You fought well tonight, and your actions saved many lives. We have been talking, and we have decided to make you an equal."

"A master?" Amara asked.

"Per se." Dror stepped forward. "You wouldn't be a master of any chapter, but you would be a master in title and be afforded the authority."

Amara was profoundly honored. Here, at what might be their final days, they would treat her as an equal. "Thank you. I'm honored to accept this title."

"Let's get some sleep," Raza suggested.

Everyone agreed wholeheartedly, reasoning there wouldn't be another attack for the rest of the night.

She trudged back to her tent and didn't even care that her tent was half collapsed. The part over the head of her bedroll was propped up well enough it would most likely continue standing for the next few hours. She slid in and was out before her head hit her pack.

When Amara awoke, the sun was far into the sky. Her tent stood, repaired and in place. Her back ached when she moved. She must have twisted it in the battle the night before. She fought through the discomfort and exited her tent.

Raziel was waiting.

"How long have you been waiting there?" She asked.

"Since sunrise."

"Really?" She raised an eyebrow at him.

"Sure, I spent hundreds of years in a cell, away from any light save a candle when permitted. What's a few hours, sitting in the light of a new day watching the sunrise and the birds sing?"

"I guess when you put it that way." Amara shrugged.

"Your presence was requested in the meeting tent, but we thought it best if you got some rest."

"Lead the way."

She followed him to the meeting tent and for the first time she entered as an equal of the masters. Conversations stopped, and they turned to see who had entered.

"Ah, Amara," Raza step forward to greet her. "I hope you were able to sleep after last night's battle. The other masters and I have refrained from making any major decisions until you awoke."

"Um...Thanks," Amara didn't know what to say. She had never had a group of people so important wait on her out of respect. "I guess...we can start now." She meant it as a statement, but it came out as more of a question.

"Yes," Raza led her over to the others and they all gathered.

They quickly decided it was time to break camp and leave. They hoped to arrive at Brightwood and take shelter there before marching to the stronghold. While the Shadows packed up camp, the masters and Amara worked through how to get past the demon army. They would be camped outside the stronghold presently.

"If they haven't crossed blades yet, we have a chance to get to the stronghold unseen." Dror said. "If they have, the army will be on much higher alert. From Amara's and Raziel's description of the terrain, I see no way of moving past them at that point."

"Then we hit them where we can." Amara couldn't believe the words came out of *her* mouth, but there was no stopping now. "We become a thorn in their side. Quick hits. In and out. We show them what our name really means."

She caught Raziel's eye, and he nodded almost imperceptibly. She turned back to the rest of the masters, who were all nodding as well.

"I like it," Raza praised. "We can always reevaluate when we get there."

They broke to finish packing up camp and start the march toward Brightwood. Everyone said their goodbyes to the Ragewood Chapter and the two groups parted ways. Their group was now just over sixty strong with the wounded being sent back with the other group. She hefted her pack onto her shoulders and peered up the road as it wound its way through the mountains.

Only an hour later, they ran into the Pangor River. The bridge had been destroyed the last time Amara had come through with Malach. It had been rebuilt, but she could see hinge points where it could be scuttled quickly if needed. They crossed cautiously, not fully trusting the bridge with so many failure points built into it. However, everyone arrived on the other side without any issues, and they continued.

Dusk had started to fall when Togan approached the masters. "It's not far to Brightwood. We have passed the most dangerous parts of the mountain pass. If we continue instead of breaking for camp, we should be able to take shelter in Brightwood. Even if the gates are closed for the night, I doubt those left would bar myself and Marena's entrance."

They all agreed quickly and spread word to keep marching.

Shortly after darkness had fallen, they crested a hill, and the valley spread out before them. Amara could just make out the faint outline of the small mountain village in the darkness. She smiled despite her aching legs.

With renewed vigor, they all headed down into the valley, excited to lie in a real bed tonight. They weren't far from the front gates when Raza held up a hand to halt. They obeyed, but many grumbled about having to wait.

"The gates are down," Raza whispered.

"That's not unexpected if they abandoned the town," Amara pointed out. "Would you take the time to close the gates if you were fleeing?"

"They aren't just open," Raza clarified. "They are off their hinges and laying on the ground."

Amara only then understood the woman's caution.

Raza motioned two scouts forward in the silent hand code of the Shadows.

They moved ahead and off the road, disappearing into the darkness as if they were apparitions.

Amara shivered as the cool mountain air moved down into the valley.

It wasn't long before the scouts came back along the road. They hadn't found anything or they would be sneaking back. Instead, they were walking upright and at ease.

Raza stood to greet them. "What's the word?"

"Town's empty," One of them stated.

"It's been abandoned." The other agreed.

Raza nodded. "We should move into the town then. Get some rest."

The other masters agreed, and the group started moving again.

It didn't take them long to reach the town, and Amara glanced around her as they moved through the archway. An eerie feeling hit her like a ton of bricks and the hair stood up on the back of her neck. They were being watched. She found Raziel and caught his eyes.

He nodded. He felt it too.

They moved through the seemingly abandoned town. Doors hung open, windows boarded, and grass was already pushing through the packed earth on the sides of the streets. How long had it been since they abandoned the town? And who was here now watching them?

She caught movement out of the corner of her eye and whipped her head around to peer into an open doorway. The darkness was too complete to see anything, but Amara could swear the shadows swirled slowly as if something had moved through them. Although, she couldn't see anymore than a foot inside. She kept walking. Maybe her mind was playing tricks on her. She was tired.

Trust your instincts, Ember said softly.

They didn't fail you when the Dark Hallow attacked. They won't fail you now, Blaze reminded her.

She nodded and kept an eye on the doorways. Whatever was going on, it wasn't a trick of her mind.

They arrived at the town's center without Amara seeing anything else in the town. The feeling of being watched lessened as well. Or maybe she was just getting used to it. They set the supplies down and teams were sent into the building to see what they could find.

It wasn't long before the rest of the Shadows were filing into the buildings and setting up bed rolls. No one talked more than to communicate needs and no one lit fires. They were all too exhausted.

Amara ate some of her rations and laid down to sleep. But sleep didn't come easily. She tossed and turned for a while, the unease she felt since arriving growing once again. Frustrated, she flopped her head on her pack and stared up at the rafters of the building.

Directly above her was the face of a girl staring down.

Amara froze, her eyes going wide.

The girl continued to stare at her. Then cocked her head to the side as if she had never seen another human being. Suddenly, she darted away as fast as if she were on solid ground.

Amara got to her feet to give chase, but by the time she had, the girl was gone. Disappeared into the shadows of the building. She had no idea where the girl had gone.

She sat back down, questions flitting through her head. Who was this girl? Where had she come from? Why had she been left behind? What did she want? Was she dangerous? She seemed so young Amara didn't think she could hurt anyone. Maybe she should go look around herself.

She stood up again, deciding she wouldn't be able to sleep as long as this mystery wasn't solved. Leaving the building, she spotted a foot disappearing into an alley down the road. She sprinted to catch up with the girl and turned the corner. It was a dead end. She glanced up and saw the girl pulling herself over the lip of the roof. Taking a running leap, she grabbed the same storm drain the girl had climbed and pulled herself onto the slanted surface. There was no sign of her. She had vanished. Amara searched around, but besides a smokestack, there was nowhere to hide. She peered down the soot covered hole just in case, but the opening was too small for anyone to fit down.

She searched for another half hour and finally forced herself to give up. She had no clue where the girl had vanished to and didn't know if she would see her again. However, she needed to get some sleep for the next day's march. Leaping from the roof, she caught the drain and slid down it, landing expertly. She felt some pride in still being able to do that. It had been a while, but she hadn't lost her skill. She glanced back up at the roof and could swear she caught a brush of the girl's hair disappearing past the edge of the roof.

Amara shook her head and trudged back to the building her bedroll was in. She stopped by the watch and warned them to keep an eye out for the girl, if only to help her if she needed help. Only moments later, she collapsed into bed. Nothing could keep her awake this time. Not even the mysterious girl in the rafters.

Chapter 19

Amara awoke early the next morning despite her fatigue. She pulled Blaze from her sheath and sat up, ready to fight. What had woken her, she did not know, but she wasn't about to let it take her by surprise. She fumbled with Ember at her waist, trying to retrieve her second blade. Peering around her, nothing other than sleeping bodies was apparent. She glanced up at the rafters and started.

The girl was up there, staring down at her again.

How long had she been there? All night? Amara put Blaze back in her sheath and strapped the blade to her belt. She slowly stood, monitoring the girl in case she bolted again. The girl did not move. Instead, motioned her to be quiet with one finger over her mouth and pointed outside.

Amara didn't know where this was going, but she wanted answers to who this girl was. She picked her way through the sleeping bodies and out onto the street. The light of the sun was just starting to show on the horizon.

The girl appeared in an opening of the building's wall where the boards were old and cracked. She swung herself down, landing nimbly on the road only a few feet away from Amara.

"Hello," Amara smiled at her. She couldn't be more than ten years old. How did she get left behind? "What's your name?"

The girl didn't say anything.

"Where are your parents?" Amara tried again.

The girl shrugged.

"Did they leave you here?"

She shook her head.

"Are you all alone?"

She nodded.

"Can you talk?"

She shook her head again.

"Are you hungry?"

She nodded emphatically.

"Come with me and we will get you something." Amara reached out her hand towards the girl.

She hesitated but reach out her hand tentatively and took Amara's.

Amara squeezed her small hand gently and led her back to the building. The girl stopped at the doorway, pulling out of Amara's grip.

Amara turned to her. "It's ok, no one is going to hurt you."

The girl shook her head.

"If I go get food, will you be here when I come back?"

The girl thought about it for a few seconds and then nodded slowly.

"Ok, stay right here. I will only be a few minutes."

The girl gave her a blank look.

It occurred to Amara she probably didn't have a concept of time like she did. "Umm, I'll be right back. Don't go anywhere." She hurried to her pack, pulled rations out, and almost sprinted back to the little girl.

She was still standing in the same spot, waiting on Amara, just like she promised. She slowed, not wanting to scare the girl, and walked out to her.

She smiled up at Amara and took the proffered food. She studied it for a second as if making sure it wasn't poisonous and then tore into it ravenously.

"How long has it been since you ate?" Amara asked.

The girl paused long enough to put up three fingers.

"Three hours? What have you been eating?"

She shook her head.

"No? No what?"

She held up three fingers again.

"Three days?"

She nodded.

"I'll go get you more."

The girl glanced up at her and smiled.

Amara went back, grabbed another bit of rations, and sat down with the girl. They shared the morning meal and Amara asked questions while they did. The girl nodded or shook her head as they went along and used hand motions for anything else. Amara deduced she had been on her own for a long time. Living on the street of Whiteshade until it was attacked. She had been able to escape the city but live in the woods for many days until stumbling across Brightwood. She must have been there when the mercenaries attacked and took Brightwood. The sights she must have witnessed during that time would have been awful. Amara didn't blame the girl for hiding when they arrived. She must have been hiding ever since, assuming terrible things would happen to her if she was caught.

The girl laid her head down on Amara's lap, and Amara's heart melted. She would take care of this child until a guardian could be found for her. She put her hand on the girl's head and she felt her stiffen for a moment until Amara started stroking her hair softly. Soon, the girl fell asleep.

Amara waited there until the other Shadows' member started to stir.

Raza walked out and sat beside her. "Who's your little friend?"

"I found her, well, more accurately she found me," Amara studied the slight frame of the girl laying on her. "She doesn't have anyone. She needs a home."

"And you plan to bring her with us?"

"I plan to take care of her until I can find someone else to care for her."

"Amara, war is no place for a child." Raza frowned. "She would be better off staying here."

"She hasn't eaten in days Raza," Amara protested. "If we leave her here, she will starve before the war is over."

Raza sighed.

"I'm not saying it's a good situation, but at least she has a chance if she comes with us."

Raza stood, keeping her eyes on Amara. "You don't need anyone's permission to do this, but make sure you have thought through all the possibilities first. It would have been best if she went to Ragewood, but that isn't an option anymore. This is a lot of responsibility, Amara. If you aren't ready for that, the girl will suffer for it."

Amara nodded solemnly. "I hope to find a more permanent solution for her once we're at the stronghold."

"Then she is your responsibility until then," Raza turned to walk inside. "We leave as soon as everyone is packed. Make sure she is ready to go."

"Yes, Ma'am," Amara smiled up at her. "We will be ready."

Two days later, they crested the top of the mountain overlooking the stronghold and the valley that stretched out before it. There was no sign of the Demon army. They must have beaten them to the stronghold.

A terrible thought struck her. Maybe instead of being ahead of the demon army, they were too late. Maybe the war was already over, and the angels had lost.

Raziel stepped up beside her. The girl from Brightwood was on his back with her head laying on his shoulder, asleep. He must have guessed her thoughts. "There are no bodies, no carrion birds. If the battle had begun, there would be many dead on the field."

She let out a breath she hadn't known she was holding. "Then where is the demon army?"

"Most likely camped on the other side of this mountain range where they're well out of range of any attacks. At least until they are ready to start the battle."

"Why have they waited so long?"

"I don't know, but don't question a blessing."

"'Don't look a gift horse in the mouth' is the saying you're searching for." Demien said, walking up next to them. "How's the stray holding up?"

"Fine," Amara replied, smiling at him. "She still hasn't said a word."

"So, no name yet?"

Amara shook her head. "No, I hope she will tell us soon."

"How do you know she *can* talk?" Demien asked.

"What do you mean?"

"I mean, maybe she hasn't said a word because she *can't* say anything,"

"I hadn't thought of that." Amara replied. "Maybe I'll ask her next time we have a conversation."

It turned out Demien was correct. When they made camp that night at the base of the ridge, Amara asked the girl and the girl nodded and opened her mouth to show Amara a missing tongue.

"Who did this to you?" Amara wanted to murder whoever had done this to a child. Slowly.

The girl shrugged.

"You don't know?"

She made a motion with her hand, holding it just above the ground.

"You were too small to remember?"

The girl nodded, grinning.

It obviously didn't bother her. She seemed more happy that Amara was understanding her, than sad about her lack of speech. Being alone for so long, and most likely an outcast for her disability, must have been hard. To find someone who actually tried to understand her must be exciting.

They stayed up late working on their communication and a name for the girl. Amara threw out a bunch she like but the girl shook her head at all of them. Finally, Amara gave up for the night. She needed to get some sleep. Their march across the field in the morning may turn into a run if they were spotted.

Amara awoke to thunder crackling over the field. She hadn't expected rain, there had been no signed of it at dusk. Then a roar filled the silence, and she knew it wasn't a storm. She jumped out of her bed, rolled and was out of the tent in an instant. She had a final thought of the little girl who had curled up beside her and turned to find her still fast asleep. Amara would protect this tent with her life but if the girl slept through the whole thing that wouldn't be the worst outcome. She closed the tent flap and secured it. She assumed they would be under attack soon and she wouldn't be the one to be caught unawares.

However, as she turned to fight, she realized no one was running around or preparing for a battle. Instead, they were all lined up at the edge of the cliff, looking toward the stronghold. She ran to join them, wondering what was happening. She stopped short as she saw the two-headed dragon dive into the stronghold.

Into the stronghold.

Through a massive crater in the wall at the base of the mountain. How had that happened? How had the enemy breached the wall so easily before the battle had started? Nothing made sense.

Shortly after the devil had entered the stronghold, it reemerged and started flying toward them. Amara and the others scrambled for cover. Many grabbed bows and readied themselves to ward off the dragon but it soon became clear it wasn't headed for them. It turned west toward the Emerald Basin and was soon lost to sight behind the mountain range. A collective sigh ran through the group as they relaxed slightly.

"If we have any chance of getting to the stronghold, we need to leave now." Raziel stood from behind his cover.

Raza nodded and then started shouting orders.

"Wait!" Amara shouted before she could second guess her instincts. "We aren't soldiers. We would do little good from behind the stronghold walls."

"You are the one who wanted to join the angel army." Raza stared at her. "Have you lost your nerve?"

"No," Amara shook her head. "I'm suggesting we stay where we can be most effective. Which isn't on the front lines. It's in the shadows. At least for now."

Dror nodded. "Very good idea. I like it better than the thought of all-out battle."

"Sabotage and Assassinations?" Raziel lifted an eyebrow at her. "Will you be able to stomach such savagery?"

"I will be in charge of the sabotage." Amara smiled. "The other masters can plan and carry out the assassinations."

Raziel nodded. "You *do* know many times the two go hand in hand."

Amara grimaced and nodded once. "I will deal with that if it happens."

"Once the Demon Army crosses the open field we will be of little use outside the wall." Raziel warned. "We would have to cross the field unseen to carry out any action against the enemy. Then there's the added difficulties of getting back without being killed by the demons themselves. Men, we can out pace, it's the beings with wings that will end our endeavors."

"Are you saying we should go now?" Amara asked.

"No, I'm saying we need to be careful. If we wait too long, our best intentions will mean little to nothing. Then we will be no more than observers for the duration of this war."

Amara mulled his words over in her head realizing he was right. They could do a considerable amount of damage over the next few days if the demon army didn't march. Which was growing ever unlikely.

"Let's get under cover then and setup a camp farther into the trees." Raza suggested. "I don't want that dragon seeing us or all our decisions will be taken from us. Forcibly."

It didn't take them long to pull down camp and start hiking back into the forested mountain range. Amara turned to look at the stronghold. She genuinely hoped her friends were alright. She wanted to run across the field and find Malach to make sure he was alive. The realization she still loved Malach hit her suddenly. She vowed to herself then, if they both made it through this war alive, she would do all she could to show him she still loved him. If he rejected her, then she would know he didn't feel the same way.

She continued up the hill, following the group. They came upon an outcropping which was more or less flat, jutting out over the valley below. It was heavily forested, so it would hide them from any demons flying overhead, and the cliff would hide them from anyone below. They setup camp and camouflage the tents as best as possible. The masters sent some members out into the mountains to hunt, while Amara took a group to scout. She hoped to find out what they might do to sabotage the enemy war effort.

It took them most of the morning to traverse the unfamiliar terrain, but after following a winding game trail, they got their first sight of the enemy camp. Amara's stomach dropped, and she felt sick. The vast number of troops was unbelievable. She couldn't even start to count their numbers. The angel army only had a chance because they were defending an extremely fortified position. Now that the wall had been breached, they had lost that advantage. They didn't have a chance.

Amara noticed a large, blackened area within the camp. There must have been some kind of fire recently. Maybe something the angels had done. She would have to be careful. If they had already been attacked once, they would be more vigilant. She noticed there were no towers or other war machines for scaling the wall. They had *planned* for the wall to be destroyed. How had they known? And they were so sure it would happen that they hadn't even built anything in case it wasn't.

She scanned her eyes over the camp again. This time, her eyes were drawn to another area of the camp. Cannons were lined up just on the outskirts of the camp, waiting to be rolled into battle. The wheels would be the key to moving them. However, getting the wheels off wouldn't do much but delay their march. Amara realized she had no idea how the cannons actually worked. She had only been on the receiving end of the weapons, not the sending end. She would have to examine them before she knew how to sabotage them. Maybe Raziel would have some insight.

The one thing that was suspiciously unaccounted for was the amount of gunpowder needed to fire the cannons continuously. Could that be the source of the scorched earth? If so, would they march to the wall without the cannons? Now that it had been breached, would they even need them? There was a small stack of four barrels outside the camp, not far from the cannons. She hoped that was gunpowder. However, it was a paltry amount for a full-scale assault. They would have to check those barrels.

The last thing she noticed was there were guards everywhere. The highest concentration of them was around a singularly large tent. With no dragon in sight, she assumed he would be in there, maybe even with the other surviving lords of hell. If only she could find enough of the black powder to send that tent sky high, the war would be over before it started. Although, she doubted any of them would get within bow range of that tent.

A thought struck her. She smiled, an idea forming in her head. She had little time, but it would be enough.

Malach was numb. His mind refused to think, refused to feel, refused to function. Men worked around him, trying to patch the gap in the wall. They wouldn't even get close to fixing it by the next morning. He didn't know why they even tried. They were all dead. It was over.

Daziar had taken Honora away, but Malach couldn't move. He wanted to cry. He wanted to crawl under a rock and die. But he couldn't do anything.

"Malach," Ariel knelt next to him. "It's not your fault."

His father's words broke the spell that held him, and his sobs finally escaped.

Ariel pulled him close, and Malach was vaguely aware of being picked up.

He woke up in his own bed and, for one brief, glorious second, he forgot what had happened. It hit him like a ton of bricks. He curled into a ball and the pain radiated through his chest. The deep ache of loss, physically manifesting. He had felt it often as of late.

Skie jumped up on the bed and curled around him, laying her head on his shoulder.

Sobs racked him, but no tears came. He had none left. Would he ever be the same? Could he go on? He was in no shape to fight, but somewhere in the back of his mind, he knew he would need to soon. Except, he had no willpower to get up. No energy to lift his limbs.

Honora was gone. It was his fault. He would *never* forgive himself.

Malach, it isn't your fault, Reckoning said. *You did your best and so did Honora.*

"I couldn't protect her," Malach almost screamed in his pain. "I wasn't good enough."

Ariel rushed in. "Malach." His father moved to his bed and pulled him into his lap.

"It's my fault." Malach sobbed into Ariel's shoulder.

"No, it's the *enemy's* fault. They did this. Don't assign the blame to yourself."

"*I* was supposed to protect her. *I* promise Arjun I would protect her. *I* couldn't protect her."

Ariel pulled Malach closer and held him tight, long into the night.

Daziar kneeled beside the bed that held Honora's body. His body felt numb. Not numb like his arm but numb emotionally. Every ounce of the passion and drive he had was gone. Ana was there with him and normally he would have enjoyed her presence. But now...now he didn't care if she was there. He didn't care if they won the war. He didn't even really care if he died.

Honora wasn't supposed to die. She was supposed to make it through the war with them. The three of them. They had started this journey together and she would never see the end. Malach hadn't protected her. He had been there. He should have stopped that hell spawn.

Anger welled up in him. He knew Malach wasn't to blame, somewhere deep down inside, but the anger didn't care. It was all he felt. It was all-consuming. He latched onto the anger as if it were his last lifeline.

"I'll avenge you," Daziar whispered and stood.

Daziar set his jaw and his mind and turned to leave. He had something that needed to happen. Someone he never thought would be his enemy was about to become just that. His brother for so many years was the reason Honora was dead.

"Daz?" Ana stood as he started moving out of the room.

He didn't respond as he turned down the hall that would lead him to Malach's room. She would stop him if he told her his plans. He had no doubt he wouldn't be able to get past her, and Malach had to pay.

"Daz! Come back!"

He marched down the hall.

"Daz, where are you going?"

He didn't respond. She wouldn't understand. He turned the corner to the hall, which housed Malach's room.

"Daz." Ana moved in front of him and stopped him with a hand on his chest. "This won't help anyone."

"Move out of my way," Daziar surprised himself by the venom in his voice but didn't let it show.

"Daz, you're grieving, and anger is a part of that. But letting that anger control you and drive you to do something you will regret is not healthy."

He pushed against her hand, and she gave way, letting him fall into her embrace. Tears flowed freely now, and she held him close until he collapsed with exhaustion. He vaguely remembered her carrying him to his room and laying him in bed. He fell asleep feeling completely empty.

Amara led her group down the cliff side. She had outlined the plan, and the other Masters agreed it was best to wait until nightfall. However, when they arrived at the camp at dusk, it was alive with activity. That gave Amara pause. There should be less activity at this time of the day.

Unless...

"They're getting ready to march," Raziel stated.

"Should we hold?" Amara asked.

"Should we?"

She wondered for a split second if he was backsliding into the condition, she had first found him in, but one glance into his clear eyes told her otherwise. "I'm not sure. It would be more dangerous."

"But with the possibility of a higher reward."

"How so?" Amara glanced between him and the busy camp.

"If one were to, say, set off a line of cannons pointed at a busy camp, one might cause more casualties than a concentrated attack on a singular tent." Raziel mused.

"And the more casualties we can cause, the longer it will delay them." Amara stated, catching on.

Raziel nodded.

"Then we just need to decide whether possibly killing the dragon is worth more than delaying the army or not." Amara didn't take her eyes off the dragon's tent.

Raziel took a breath to speak, but Amara stopped him with an upraised hand. She pointed to the tent.

The dragon slowly lumbered out of the tent as soldiers started to take it down.

"That answers that question." Amara felt the need to whisper, even though there was no possible way her voice would carry down to the camp.

"Let's get moving then, before they start to wheel the cannons away."

The group moved as fast as they could down the hill, sticking to as much cover as possible to lessen the chance of being spotted on their descent. They arrived on the valley floor just after nightfall and moved under the cover of darkness to the cannons. They were lined up facing away from the camp. They had to get them turned around. There were only twelve in all and if Amara hadn't seen the devastation they could cause first hand, she wouldn't believe these twelve cylinders would do anything to delay the army.

They started to turn the cannons painstakingly slow. Raziel could manage one on his own, but the others had to work in teams. Amara couldn't really help, since Raziel didn't need a partner, so she started searching for the supplies they would need to fire the weapons. She spotted metal balls stacked in a pyramid near the cannons and started moving them one at a time to each cannon. They were heavier than she thought they would be, and it took her a bit to get them in place.

The last two cannons were being moved, and Raziel moved off to the four barrels Amara had noted previously. He returned with one and pulled the stopped set into the side of it. Powder flowed like water from the opening, and he put the stopper back quickly.

He grinned up at Amara, excitement dancing in his eyes. "This is going to be loud."

He demonstrated to the group how to load and prime the cannon and quickly poured powder for each cannon, allowing the others to come behind him and finish loading each one. He then poured a line of powder from a spot behind the cannons all the way to the small barrels.

Amara grinned, understanding what he had in mind.

"Hey!"

They all turned toward the camp where the call had come from and froze.

"Get those cannons ready to move!"

Amara didn't know what to say or do.

"Sir, yes sir!" Raziel replied with little delay. Then quieter, "Move quick. We have little time,"

They all redoubled their efforts and quickly finished loading the cannons, while Raziel lit a torch. They moved behind the cannons, and Raziel finished priming the weapons.

"Time to leave," Amara told the group with a grin. She turned to Raziel. "Let's return some of the pain they've caused."

Raziel lit each cannon in order, but before he even lit the third cannon, the first exploded. Amara had forgotten the amount of noise these weapons generated. Her hands shot up to her ear to protect them, but the noise still reached her as the second explosion rattled her ribcage. Raziel lit the last one and dropped the torch on the trail of powder leading to the barrels.

He pushed her toward the mountain range, but she was already moving. Neither wanted to be anywhere close to the barrels when the fire reached them.

Amara glanced back at the camp for a moment but could only see silhouettes in the failing light. There must have been screams and cries of terror, but she could only hear ringing in her ears. They reached the overlook they had watched the camp from earlier just as the final series of explosions rang out over the valley.

"We can't stay." Raziel still had a silly grin plastered on his face. "They will be searching for us. We need to get back to base camp and be ready to leave in the morning."

Amara wanted to see if they were successful, to see if they had accomplished their goal. Had they possibly killed one of the seven? Raziel wouldn't let her stop, however. She would have to wait to find out the next morning when they would either see the army marching or not.

She had a hard time sleeping that night with the anticipation of war on the horizon. She tossed and turned until she finally drifted off into a fitful sleep.

When she woke, the sun was just starting the light up the sky. She jumped out of her bedroll and ran for the cliff overlooking the valley, fearing to see the two armies already locked in battle. As the valley came into view, there was no sign of the demon army. The large hole blasted from the side of the stronghold was half covered, but with what, Amara couldn't tell. She seriously doubted it was stone, but maybe it would be strong enough to repel the army for long enough if they could finish the repairs.

She moved much more carefully down the ridge to the overlook above the demon camp. They hadn't moved. She breathed a sigh of relief. She continued to study the camp and noticed signs of the damage they had caused. Tents lay, ripped and flattened, and although no bodies were visible, dark stains pockmarked the ground throughout the camp.

Two of the cannons closest to where the barrels of black powder used to be, were ruined. The rest were turned back around. She smiled as she spotted the guards watching the cannons just at the edge of the camp. There would be more guards out of sight.

The main tent that housed the dragon and other demons was still standing. A part of her wished they would have aimed the cannons toward that tent. Maybe they could have killed the demons who were truly responsible for this war. She had to take comfort in the fact they accomplished their goal. They delayed the army and gave the Angels a fighting chance.

"Looks like that will be the last time we get close to the cannons." A voice said from behind her.

Amara almost fell off the cliff, she jumped so high. She whirled on Raziel. "Are you trying to scare me to death?"

"Sorry, my dear, I didn't mean to startle you." Raziel chuckled. "I saw you leave the camp this morning and decided to follow you. It would seem we succeeded, however, I'm not sure we will get another chance like that."

"It might be time to join the angels in the stronghold if we can't be of any use out here."

"Are you willing to die for this cause?" Raziel asked.

"What?"

"If we join the army now, there is a large chance we will not survive. Are you prepared to make that sacrifice?"

Amara paused, reflecting on the events of the past few months that had led her to this point. She remembered her betrayal and the events that led her to accept the commission of Blade Bearer. She stared Raziel directly in the eye. "Yes, I am."

He nodded. "Then it's time to march before our window of opportunity closes."

"Malach, wake up!" Ariel pounded on his door.

Malach jumped out or bed snagging Reckoning and hit the door prepared to fight. "What's wrong?"

"Woah," Ariel held up his hands. "The enemy isn't here yet, despite what the dragon stated. There is someone else here who I think you will be interested to see."

With his heart rate going down, the pain and grief set in. Could he have really done anything significant if the enemy was there? His shoulders sagged, and he sheathed Reckoning. He would just get people killed.

He followed his father down the corridors, not bothering to keep track of where they were going. The thought struck him that at least Amara was smart enough to get away from the war while she could. She had been wise to leave. He hoped she would have a good life. She didn't need him, anyway.

"Malach?"

He could almost still hear her voice.

"Malach!"

He lifted his head, and his heart hit the floor. "Why are you here?"

Amara stopped, visibly deflating. "I understand. I'm here to help, but I will leave you alone."

Malach moved forward and pulled her into an embrace. "You need to leave. You need to be somewhere safe. I can't protect you....I can't protect anyone."

She pushed him to arm's length. "Malach? What happened?"

"Honora...." His voice choked off and tears started to flow again.

Amara pulled him back in. "I don't know what happened, but I'm here and I'm not going anywhere. You don't have to protect me. Malach, I'm a Blade Bearer."

It was his turn to push her to arm's length. "Is that why you left?"

"Yes, I was tasked with bringing the Shadows here to help. What happened to Honora?"

"She's dead."

Amara knees failed her, her face a picture of shock.

Malach held her up. "Amara, I need to you leave. I can't lose anyone else."

"Malach...I'm so sorry. How?"

Malach guided her to a bench not far from them and they sat. With difficulty, he recounted the events leading up to Honora's death. When he got to the moment of her death, he couldn't continue. His voice cracked and tears came again.

Amara hugged him. She knew the pain he was feeling. Or at least something very similar. "Lawdel died." She told him softly. Not to compare her pain to his, but to let him know she understood.

He met her eyes. "I'm so sorry."

"My mother killed him."

It was Malach's turn to look shocked. "Lilith?"

"Unfortunately," she gave him a half-hearted smile. "Not really the family reunion I had always pictured."

She filled him in on everything that she had learned and her journey until they arrived at the stronghold.

"Togan and Marena are here?" Malach asked.

"Yes! I'm not sure where, but they're here. They found their way to the Shadows and journeyed with us."

"You need to get them and have them take you back to Brightwood, or somewhere safe."

"Malach, Honora's death wasn't your fault. You can't blame yourself for everyone who dies in this war."

"Everyone dies around me, and I continue on." Malach turned away from her. "I can't keep anyone safe. In fact, you need to take Skie with you."

"Malach. You're right."

His head spun to stare at her.

"You can't protect everyone. But that's not your job. You can't make people's choices for them either. Honora understood the risk, and she came here anyway. Your mother fought for years against the demons and she suffered to keep you and the angels safe. You couldn't protect either of them, but their deaths also weren't your fault. You can't push everyone away and make their decisions for them. I'm staying to help, to fight. That's my decision and if I don't make it through, *I* made that decision."

Malach nodded, but his melancholy didn't subside.

"Malach, you are not the cause of these terrible things. The demons are. You can only do your best."

"My best isn't good enough. *My* best brought us to my mom too late to save her. *My* best allowed Honora to be killed. I'm having nightmares. Waking up thinking I'm being attacked. I've almost killed people who were just there to help me. Something is *wrong* with me."

Amara didn't know why Malach was telling her all of this, but once he started, it was like a dam had opened.

"I'm broken, and I'm not sure I can be fixed."

"Malach, what we have seen and experienced has been a lot. I would be more concerned if you weren't affected by it all." She put a hand on his arm. "I'm here. We *can* get through this and then we can help each other pick up the pieces afterward."

"I'm glad to have you here." He smiled at her. "Thank you."

Silence ensued. Amara wanted to ask about how he felt about her betrayal. Last time they had gotten a chance to talk, he had forgiven her, but he hadn't wanted much to do with her. Now he seemed like he needed her. Would that fade after he picked up the pieces of his life? His mental state seemed to be teetering on the edge of sanity. Which gave her an idea.

She smiled back. "Come on, I want you to meet my father, my biological father."

They stood and for the next hour she introduced Malach to many more people than just Raziel. He seemed to be more like his old self the more they talked with people. They spent some time on the top of the wall together. They didn't say much, but they could see the demon army starting their march toward them as the midday sun reached its apex.

"You and Raziel gave us a fighting chance." Malach broke the silence.

"We only delayed them by a day, at best. Not really long enough."

"But that gave us enough time to fortify the wall where it was breached. It won't be back to full strength, but it will hopefully repel the army long enough for us to wear them down."

"I guess, I wish we could have killed a demon or two along the way. Especially one of the seven."

"Do you think we even have a chance?"

The sudden change in topic and demeanor almost gave Amara whiplash.

"I mean, we're outnumbered by a hefty margin." Malach didn't take his eyes off the marching army. "I thought we could do it while the wall was still intact but now..." His voice trailed off.

"Malach, there are a lot of people who wouldn't be here if they didn't believe we could win. In fact, about half of the Shadows didn't complete the journey with us because they didn't believe we could win. The other half believe wholehearted-"

A heavy vibration hit Amara and made her chest reverberate. It felt the same as when the cannons had fired. She turned back to the marching army, alarmed at the sensation. Was something wrong? She didn't feel any dread.

A demon has died. Blaze spoke, soft and assured and Amara felt Ember's agreement.

What demon? Amara thought back.

"Reckoning just told me a demon died?" Malach asked, finally pulling his eyes away from the valley below.

"Ember and Blaze just told me that's what I felt," Amara admitted. "I'm not sure how to know whether it's a demon or angel, though. Is this what you feel every time?"

"I've never felt it. I bear a blade, but I'm not ordained as a Blade Bearer." Malach smiled at her. "But I assume what you felt is normal. You might seek out an angel and ask them."

They heard footsteps, and both turned to see Daziar and Ana taking the stairs two at a time. Daziar slowed as he spotted the pair, but Ana continued forward to them. She grinned at them as she arrived. "Did you feel that?"

Amara nodded.

"Looks like you might have done more damage in your raid than you realized."

"How did you know it was a demon?" Amara asked.

"You felt the vibration in your chest, right?"

Amara nodded again.

"Obviously, that's what it feels like when a demon dies." Ana's grin faded. "When an Angel dies, you will feel it in your heart."

Daziar finally joined them. He pointedly didn't look at either of them but addressed Ana. "Do we know what demon died?"

"In the past we could learn that by the intensity of the feeling and our intel of which demons were in the area. However..." Ana's voice trailed off.

"Since all the demons are presumably here, we have no way of knowing." Malach finished for her.

"Either way, its good news." Ana shrugged.

"What about the dragon?" Daziar asked.

"What about him?"

"If you killed one head, would you get the same feeling, or would you have to kill both?"

"Seeing as that has never been done, I have no answer for that."

"Oh, yeah, that makes sense." Daziar glanced down at his feet and then out to the valley. "Umm, Malach, can I talk with you?"

Malach nodded, and they walked away.

"Daziar blames Malach?" Amara asked after they were out of earshot.

"He has. Daz *should* be apologizing to him now. Hopefully, they can start the healing process together."

Amara nodded. "Do *you* think we have a chance?"

"Don't count us out just yet." Ana's smile made her feel more confident. "We still have a few tricks left."

"We will need more than just tricks."

"We have right on our side. We have God on our side. No one can stand against us." Ana frowned. "However, I hate this part."

"What part?" Amara asked.

"The calm before a battle. Waiting for the storm wall to hit."

"I'm learning to hate it, too." Amara agreed.

They stood in silence as the sun slowly burned its way across the sky. It wasn't long before Malach and Daziar came walking back. The streaks on their faces told Amara they had been crying together. And who could blame them? They lost one of their closest friends. Amara's heart went out for them. She knew that pain all too well. She tried to give them a supportive smile, but she was afraid it came across as pity.

"You two will need to fight as brothers before the day is over." Ana told them. "Come, we need to rest before the enemy arrives. I fear it will be a long night and we'll need all the strength we can muster."

They all retired to their rooms, but Amara had no chance of sleeping. Her nerves were wound too tight. She laid in her bed staring at the ceiling, thinking. Malach and her seemed to be on the mend and for the first time, she thought they might be able to patch their relationship.

The little girl, who Amara still hadn't found a name for, crawled up into bed with her and snuggled in under the covers.

"Don't worry," Amara whispered. "You'll be safe in the stronghold. I won't let anything happen to you."

Amara had made sure the girl was settled before finding Malach earlier. She had been told there were hidden tunnels which let out behind the mountain. If they were overrun, they would have to hold the enemy off long enough for the innocents to escape. Hopefully, they would be able to disappear into the mountains and eventually make their life somewhere free of the demons.

She prayed fervently she wasn't lying to the girl. That even if she herself didn't survive the next few days, this girl would. She hugged her close and closed her eyes, holding her until she heard the horns signaling the enemy was at their doorstep.

Chapter 20

Malach Should have been resting or preparing for the coming battle. He just felt so empty. He sat on the end of his bed, lost in thought. After talking with Amara, he had felt better. She made him feel sane again. However, shortly after leaving her company, he once again spiraled into the darkness of his mind. He was so useless he couldn't even keep his own thoughts safe. He couldn't even pick himself up off this bed. How would he fight in this state? How would he continue living?

Malach, Reckonings voice cut through the darkness in his mind. *You must seek help for this. This will not go away on its own. You need to talk to someone who has experience in matters of the mind. Raziel, Keeper of Secrets. He has many millennia of experiences in mental issues even before he entered a sleeper's mind and lost his own. He can help you.*

Malach was vaguely aware of the horns blowing somewhere above him.

I'll seek help when this is over. Malach thought back. *I promise. Right now, everyone needs to focus on the enemy. Focus on keeping themselves alive.* He needed to pull himself out of this slump and prepare for war. With effort, he forced himself to stand. Forced himself to don the new spotless steel armor he was given and set Reckoning as his pole weapon on to the holder on his back. He stopped at the door, his muscles freezing stopping him from opening the door.

The horns blew again, calling him out to war, calling him the horrors of the battlefield. Calling him to the loss of friends, family, and innocents. Calling him to give up his life for the cause of others.

"Malach!" a female voice sounded from behind him.

Malach whirled toward the voice, pulling Reckoning from his back and swinging before he could fully process what was happening.

A dagger met Reckonings blade and stopped it cold. Malach gaped at the slim arm holding the dagger in place. There was not a chance in heaven or hell that small arm had stopped his strike. He then realized who the arm was attached to and ran forward to embrace her.

"Mom," Tears spilled freely from his eyes, and he held onto her as if she were his last lifeline.

"Malach, I don't have much time."

"No, mom," Malach held on to her even tighter. "You can't go."

"Malach, listen to me." She pushed him out to arm's length as easily as if he was a small child. "You are the next generation of Blade-Bearers, the same as Daziar and Amara. Your time of service may be short, but it will be the most important of us all."

"I don't want it." Malach hung his head. "I want *you* back. I want us to be a family. I want to live in the cottage with you and dad again."

"I know, son." She pulled him into her embrace. "I want that too. But that is no longer a possibility. Right now, I get the honor and absolute pleasure of naming you a Blade Bearer. You've been carrying Reckoning for some time now, but now I, on God's behalf, am imparting to you all the honor and power deserving of your station."

"Mom, how to I go on? How do I deal with the darkness, the night-mares?"

"You have everything, and everyone, you need to overcome this." She squeezed him tight, her hand gliding over his back. "Malach, you are strong, stronger than I ever thought you would need to be. I'm proud of who you have become. You can overcome this. You can do anything you set your mind to. But don't forget to use the tools you've been given, and there is no shame in seeking help from those who have experience. It doesn't make you a burden, it makes you human."

Malach had closed his eyes, enjoying the embrace of his mother, but as she spoke the last few words, her warmth and touch faded to noth-ing. He fell to his knees, fighting back the tears. He missed his mom so much. But he had to get up. He had to be strong. He had to fight. If they survived this battle, he would talk with Raziel and Ariel about his condi-tion. Until then, he just needed to push the darkness aside and carry on.

Pain lanced his back sharply. He reached back, but there was noth-ing there. He shrugged. *Must have been laying in the wrong position for too long.*

Skie walked up to him and stared directly into his eyes. Her blue eyes burned into his and she growled, low and dangerous. He could swear she was smiling as she did.

He understood. "Let's go kill some demons."

Amara scanned the valley. It was just past midday, and they still have many hours of sunlight. The enemy would surely press their attack today.

Just out of bow range, the enemy army stood and, for what seemed like miles, the ground wasn't visible. Behind the army, the two-headed dragon prowled like a caged beast. Several colossal figures stood in the back near the dragon, but they were too far away to make out any details. Those would be the remaining Seven Lords and the other surviving Demons. There weren't as many as Amara had thought, but there weren't many Angels left either.

Amara wondered, not for the first time, if Lilith was out there. She had to be. Unless Amara had done more damage than she thought. However, she was all but certain Azazel was out there. He had been defeated, and she was told Ariel had removed his wing. However, his stump would have healed by now and he would seek revenge. Even though she wouldn't be his target, he would be hers. She had a vendetta against him for what he had forced her to choose.

"What are they waiting for?" Daziar asked.

Several more minutes went by in silence. The enemy didn't make any move, and the defenders waited. Amara had noticed the lack of cannons. She smiled at that. It seemed between the sabotage Ariel had committed and then Amara and Raziel's actions; they didn't have enough black powder left. Or at least that's what she reasoned. Not that they needed them with the enormous crater in the wall, only partially rebuilt.

They built the stone and mortar up just above an angel's head. Althhough, there was no telling how well the fresh construction would hold, even reenforced with heavy wooden beams. Above the stone, they had built up the wall farther with wooden beams and there was a team working, even now, to strengthen it.

She caught sight of Malach out of the corner of her eye, making his way toward them. He was very late. The horns had already stopped blowing. Maybe he was actually getting some sleep.

Lord knows he needs it, she thought.

"Your late," Daziar grumbled at him.

"I know," Malach replied. He opened his mouth and closed it several times, as if wanting to say something.

"Well, out with it Mal," Daziar prompted.

"It's unbelievable." Malach replied.

"Look in the last few weeks alone we've communed with a sea monster, attacked by a two-headed dragon, watched that sea monster transform into an angel, and my, very dead, ancestor appeared to me to tell me I'm a Blade Bearer." Daziar gave Malach an incredulous look. "Anything you have to say, I'm probably going to believe off-hand."

Amara chuckled. Daz was right. The lists of absurdities and impossibilities they had seen only lengthened as the war progressed. What could top what they had already seen?

"My mother came to me in my room."

Amara and Daziar's mouths dropped simultaneously.

"I'm officially ordained as a Blade Bearer," Malach continued.

"Hold on," Daziar shook his head. "Go back a second. Your mother came to you? Like your mother that just died?"

"Daz," Amara elbowed him, which was much less effective when he had on a full complement of armor.

Malach smiled. "Yes, Daz, the same. My *only* mother. She came to deliver God's message and to see me again."

Both heads of the dragon let out a terrible bellow, causing them all to jump. Every eye turned to watch the front line of soldiers start marching. Their time of sharing was over, and Amara prepared her mind for the battle. They would celebrate later. Now they had to fight. Only a few moments into their march and the front lines were well within bow range. She pulled her bow off her shoulder, even as everyone else did.

"Hold!" Ariel called to them.

Ariel's shout reminded her of the plan. The teams of men with the fire propelled arrows were to fire first, thinning out the charge. The rest of the archers would wait for the easier shots as the survivors approached the wall. She readied an arrow anyway as the first of the arrows shot from their housings and the box was wheeled back to be reloaded.

Screams returned from the field as the arrows found their victims. A few of the arrows popped as they impacted plate armor or the stone ground. The explosions sending fragments of shrapnel into those unfortunate enough to be close or blowing holes into men's chests.

Malach tensed next to her, and she reached out a hand to let him know she was with him. She could see he was struggling with more than physical demons. She pulled her hand back after squeezing his to ready her bow once again.

Hundreds lay on the field after the first volley, but thousands more continued forward. It wouldn't be long before they were called to take their first lives of the day. The second volley of arrows fired out of their housing and more men fell, but the survivors of the front line were already past the danger zone of the rocket propelled arrows.

"Ready!" Ariel called.

Every man and woman on the wall drew arrows and notched them.

"Aim!"

Amara brought her focus to the arrow set in her own bow, picking out a woman charging at the wall directly in front of her.

"Fire!"

She let her arrow fly. The sounds of war faded from her ears as if the arrow streaking away from her had taken the noise with it. Her chest tightened as everything else faded from her mind except the woman on the field and her arrow. Both the arrow and the woman slowed as she watched the trajectory. She knew it would strike true and almost wished it wouldn't.

Everything came screaming back as the arrow struck the woman in the throat. Amara could all but hear the gurgle as the woman dropped to the field and never got up. She gasped for air, realizing she had stopped breathing.

"Take cover!"

The enemy finally responded with their own arrows and even though there were far fewer of them than the volley from the wall, they had less of an area to cover. Most ducked down behind the parapets before the arrows reached them, but a few were not fast enough. One man on the team reloading the rocket propelled arrows was hit high in his chest and lost his balance. He screamed, falling off the inside of the wall and it wasn't long before his shout was cut short for good.

"Fire at will!" Ariel shouted just as the third volley from the fire propelled arrows shot out overhead.

Amara pulled an arrow, stood, and fired at the first soldier she saw. This time she didn't watch the arrow, fearing the possibility of becoming a target herself. She lifted and fired two more times before dropping and realizing Malach hadn't moved from his first position on the wall. His eyes were bulging, and he seemed frozen in place. It was a miracle he hadn't already been hit.

"Malach!" Amara shouted at him.

He didn't respond.

"Malach, get down!" She reached out and pulled him down next to her. He still seemed stunned, but she didn't have time to figure out how to help him. He was safe for the moment. She needed to turn her attention back to the battle.

Something wasn't right. Her pause to help Malach had pulled her mind out of the battle long enough to realize that. She scanned the battlefield as best she could from her position.

"Daz," Amara shouted over Malach's head.

He loosed an arrow and glanced her way.

"How come they haven't brought things to scale the walls like in Fairdenn?"

"How should I know?" He shouted back. "Just count your lucky stars and keep shooting. The more we kill now, the less try to kill us tomorrow."

She couldn't argue with his sound, albeit simple, logic. However, it still nagged at her. They weren't even attempting to bring ladders or hooks and ropes. They stopped close enough to fire arrows back at the soldiers on the wall and didn't advance any farther. Large shield walls advanced slowly and would soon be in place but there was still no sign of any siege engines. All the while, the enemy was dying in droves. Why would they do that?

Then it dawned on her.

She glanced toward the weakest part of the wall. There was little to no fighting in that direction. It was all directed to either side of that section. Pulling everyone's attention from that area. Soldiers on top of the wall had already started moving away from their posts to lend aid to those already engaged with the enemy.

Amara sent a mental message to Ariel. She hadn't fully got the hang of sending those messages, but she thought she got her point across to him. She stood and fired another arrow.

Malach still hadn't moved. He sat where Amara had put him. She couldn't help him now. There was too much happening.

"Malach!" she shouted at him mentally as loud as she did physically, trying to snap him out of whatever this was. She stood and fired another arrow off, not bothering to aim.

Skie moved forward and bit him on the ankle hard enough that Amara saw blood.

Malach seemed to come back to himself, but it didn't help. His eyes widened so much she thought they might pop out of their socket. He then curled his knees up to his chest and laid on his side sobbing. Something was very wrong with him.

Men ran past Amara toward the half-repaired part of the wall, and she grabbed one. "Help me with him."

He all but slid to a stop and helped Malach to the stairs off the wall. A healer appeared as if from nowhere, taking Malach from them and finishing the descent. Amara took one last look at Malach, then turned, taking the stairs two at a time. Skie followed her up, taking her place behind Amara and to her right. The same position she always took with Malach. Amara followed a group of men heading for the break in the wall. She surveyed the battlefield as best as she could as they went. Most of the enemy troops still only attacked either side of the break in the wall. However, there was a small group of heavily armored soldiers moving slowly but steadily forward. They looked like a slow-moving turtle or some kind of armored bug the way they held their shields at all angles. Only the perfect placed shot would even have a chance of penetrating the shields.

One of the large rocket propelled arrow machines rolled up behind her, Ariel peering from behind it beaming like a child just told he could eat all the candy he wanted.

She returned his wild grin, understanding his plan. She scrambled out of his way and then fell in behind him, pumping her legs to keep up. Even with the bulky machine in front of him, he was almost running.

He pulled up about even with the advancing 'turtle' and turned the machine toward the battlefield. Instead of aiming up, however, he used some stray stone debris to prop the device up, aimed slightly down at the field well in front of the advancing shields.

They waited. Amara barely breathed, but every one of her muscles tensed. She watched as arrow after arrow deflected off the shields of the enemy. Somewhere in the back of her mind, she thought she should be shooting, even though she felt it was pointless. She moved just behind the machine and gaged the distanced.

"Do these arrows have explosive ends?" She asked, not taking her eyes off the battlefield.

"That has been more of a happy accident." Ariel replied. "Raphael speculates that if the charge isn't spent by the time of impact, it forces the rest of the powder to ignite. I'm hoping he's right."

Amara had to think about that for only a moment. "That's why you are waiting for them to get close!"

"Correct," Ariel replied. "Now, if you don't mind, please ready yourself to fire upon any left standing."

"Oh, yes." She moved forward and readied her bow. It was only a few moments later she heard the fuse light, and she drew the arrow back.

The sound of the first arrow flying from the machine assaulted her ears, and the smoke stung her eyes. She wiped the tears and drew her bow again. Time seemed to slow as the line of explosive arrows streaked toward the field. Many arrows were already well wide of their target, but as the first struck a shield, it blew apart, wrenching the shield up and exposing the men in the middle. A shield shifting to fill the gap covered a flash of something burning in the middle of the group. However, another arrow struck, then another, and another. A dark rain from the archers on the wall followed their explosive counterparts, cutting down any of the men exposed.

Ana appeared in the sky, attacking the group from above. It appeared as if one of their men was down there as well. He recklessly waded into the middle of the formation and was lost to her view. Amara would do her best not to hit them, but there was no way to guarantee that. She prayed God would guide her arrows.

Amara didn't know why, but she had held her arrow when the others had loosed theirs. Something didn't feel right. These soldiers were protecting something. As soon as the first volley landed two nephilim burst from the group, one of them crushing a dying man's head beneath his boot. She took aim and loosed her arrow at the front running man before she had even fully taken in the scene and what it meant.

The arrow struck him in the eye, dropping him only a few steps from the group. The second nephilim lit a fuse with the torch he held and threw it to the side, bellowing as he surged forward. An explosion rattled her ribcage. Causing her to fumble her second arrow and she had to pull a third from her quiver. It came from behind and above the enemy formation, but she didn't have time to even glance that direction. The nephilim had a barrel on his back and her eyes widened. She notched the arrow and fired. It ripped down into the man's neck and was surely a killing blow, but he only stumbled slightly, continuing his charge. Another arrow struck him just above his knee. He stumbled and did not get back up. Amara held her breath as she watched the barrel strapped to the nephilim's back fall loose of its bindings and tumble toward the wall. Time froze, and the battle seemed to pause as they all watched the barrel continue its slow roll.

"Get down!" Ariel's command broke the spell holding them all in place, and men and women scrambled to get out of the way.

Amara was pushed to the ground and managed to not get trampled as she tried to struggle to her feet. She felt hot breath on the back of her neck and then she was being drug forward by her armor. Through the tumult of bodies and feet, she caught glimpses of grey, fur-covered paws.

Then the world exploded. She landed, a flash of light, and then darkness took her.

Daziar was no good with the bow. He never had been and his lack of feeling in his arm didn't improve his shot in the least. After the first few volleys, where it was about the number of arrows they could rain down and less about accuracy, he fell back and readied his sickle-sword for the enemy to climb the wall, but that never came. Amara voiced the questions he had, shortly after he thought them. He was just about to go find the reason for the lack of enemies when he heard the call for warriors to move to the partially repaired section. Was this just a distraction? It didn't matter. The order was all he needed to hustle to the wooden makeshift ramparts.

Amara and another man were helping Malach off the wall as he passed. He prayed Malach wasn't badly injured, but that would be the healer's job. He couldn't do anything for his friend now. He turned back to the task at hand. The ramparts resembled more of a heavy-duty scaffolding rather than proper battlements and they were packed to capacity before he even got close. Archers lined either side.

He found a ladder, sheathed his weapon, and slid down it to the ground where a host of other soldiers waited. If he was needed, he would be ready. He watched Ariel roll the large arrow firing machine through the crowd as they parted for him, many using the same ladder he had to make room. Daziar had no clue what was going on or why Ariel had pulled one of the machines from its post. He would have to trust the angel knew what he was doing.

"Daz," Ana alit next to him. "I need you to come."

She lifted off again and flew toward the stronghold proper not waiting to see if he could keep up with her.

He sprinted after her, calling for men and women alike to, "Make a hole!"

He managed to keep her in sight and watched as she landed on top of the wall. Taking two stairs at a time his helmet rattling on his head, he finally caught up with the angel. He sucked in a breath as hard and as fast as he could, resting his hands on his knees. This part of the wall was receiving little to no attention from the enemy, and only a handful of archers fired down at the edges of the throng below.

"Daz." Ana didn't wait for him to acknowledge her. "We need to get onto the field and break up the enemy's ploy."

Daziar nodded, still breathing too hard to speak. He took the time to strap his helmet down a little tighter.

Ana wasted no time. She wrapped her arms around his waist and beat her powerful wings, lifting him off the wall and stealing what little breath he had regained. She more fell than flew at first and Daziar thought their endeavor would end before it even began, but she leveled out quickly. "You need to lay off the second helpings!"

It was all Daziar could do to breathe. As such, he was unable to defend himself from the verbal onslaught. He planned to return the insult tenfold once they were back on solid ground, but he soon realized that would not be an option. Ana aimed them at a clear patch of land not far from the slow-moving shield formation, but it wouldn't be clear for long. The enemy was advancing not far behind the shield formation. Daziar didn't understand what was going on or the strategies behind the enemy's formation, but it didn't matter. Their mission was to stop the formation. They would deal with the rest later.

"May the Lord protect and deliver us from those who would do us harm." Ana prayed just loud enough for Daziar to hear and then let out an ear-splitting, undulating war cry.

Daziar joined the cry as best he could before Ana released him. He hit the ground and rolled into a charge. The explosive arrows hit the formation, the blasts deafening him. One explosive arrow hit the ground close enough to push him off balance. Then came the rain of arrows. He dove behind an enemy who soon resembled more of a pincushion than a man. Daz scavenged a shield from his corpse and held it up toward the wall just in time to catch a few more of the deadly missiles. He didn't blame the men on the wall. As far as they were concerned, only the enemy was down here.

Ana hit the shields on the opposite side of the formation seconds before Daziar plowed into them, using his newly acquired shield as a ram. Together, they sent men flying into those behind them. Daziar dropped his shield and used his gauntleted fists to pump pain into anyone within reach. He was too close for his sword to be effective, so he grappled with the enemy. Most only realized he was there once he had hit them, if they didn't simply crumple from the blow.

One man stood a foot taller than him with no weapon to see but a torch in one hand and a barrel strapped to his back. He lit the fuse just as Daziar realized what was happening. He tackled the man, taking him to the ground and reaching to snuff out the fuse before the explosion took him, Ana, and everyone else with the nephilim.

Daziar almost succeeded.

The nephilim pumped a fist into Daziar's face hard enough a burst of light filled his vision even with the helmet taking most of the impact. Then he was under the man. He threw up his arms, absorbing most of the punches thrown his way. Daziar pulled his knee up and caught the man between his legs. He crumpled with a whimper. Daziar threw him off and pulled at the barrel, trying to find the fuse. He couldn't, but he managed to pull the barrel free of its binding and hefted it as far up and out to the field as his considerable strength could manage. It wouldn't be far enough, but at least it wouldn't do any damage to the wall.

To his horror, Ana caught it as it followed its trajectory toward the ground. She lifted the barrel into the sky and threw it out toward the demon army. An explosion deafened him and knocked him from his feet.

"No!"

Leviathan flew high over the battlefield as the demon army charge the wall. They fell against it like water against a dam. Yet, Leviathan watched. The demon Lords were smarter than this. They had something up their sleeves. They would spend lives like copper but not without a plan in place. She hoped to see that plan before it happened.

"Sister!"

She knew that voice, although she hadn't heard it in ages. Asmodeus flew up in front of her, arms spread wide, a grin on his face. He was the most human in appearance of all the demons, although, two small horns poked out of his hair. His incisors were larger than normal, and he had the telltale bat wings but everything else about his features were human.

"You join us for the final battle to send these God lovers to their graves!"

His joy broke Leviathan's heart. He had once been as close as a brother. They had both been created on the same day. Practically the same minute. They experienced all the God had given them at the same time. Yet he followed Lucifer willingly from the beginning. *She* had been tricked.

"How did you shed your fins?"

"Lucifer has not brought you into his confidence?" Leviathan asked.

"What do you mean?"

"I'm no longer a Lord of Hell. God has redeemed me. Given me a second chance."

"No!" Asmodeus shouted. "You are still one of us. You are wrong and I won't accept anything less. Sister, join me once again and you and I will reign glorious destruction on those who would stand again Lord Lucifer."

Leviathan could only shake her head. Tears streamed down her cheeks and her heart broke anew for her brother. She knew what had to be done but didn't know if she had the strength to do it.

"Sister…" Asmodeus' voice trailed off, and he shed a tear, just one before he wiped it away and steal hardened his gaze. "So be it. Next time we meet, we meet not as siblings but as enemies."

"Asmodeus," Leviathan cried. "It doesn't have to be this way. God redeemed me. He isn't without mercy to those to turn from their ways."

"It is far too late for me my sis-" He bit the word off. "Leviathan. It is far too late for me. I will see my actions through. And reap the consequences. Good or ill."

Leviathan dropped her head. "Them we have nothing more to talk about. Goodbye my brother, for I still love you as one. I will grieve your loss."

"And I yours." Asmodeus spun and folded his wings plummeting toward the earth, only to level out and angle toward the back of the army.

And explosion sounded down at the wall and Leviathan knew she had been distracted for too long.

Malach fought the darkness and demons in his head. The healers had left him. Amara had left him. Skie had left him.

He was alone.

He was useless.

Pain burned through his back.

He had mounted the stairs and watched the proceedings, ready to fight, ready to defend his friends and family.

However, as soon as the first arrows started flying, he froze. He couldn't move, not even to save his own life. Fear gripped his heart and rooted his legs to the spot. Amara had done her best to help him and had eventually gotten him to the healers. However, they were so busy with the wounded they had set him down on a bench and left.

His mind was now his prison.

Malach, Reckoning pushed through the fog of Malach's mind, his voice calm and soft. *Slow your breathing.*

He slowed his breath with effort, and the feeling started returning to his extremities. His mind started to process what was happening to him. He flexed his muscles slowly, focusing on each one until he could move all of them on command. He didn't know how long this process had taken him. However long it was, it was too long. His friends were out there fighting without him. The panic started to rise again, tightening his chest.

Continue to breathe slow and deep. Reckoning instructed. *You're suffering from mental wounds caused by everything you've been through over the last few months. You cannot fight in this condition. Retreat to safety. When there is a break in the fighting, we will seek help from Raziel.*

Can you keep my mind sharp? Malach asked. *I can't leave my friends to fight without me.*

I can try to suppress it, but it is a reflex, the same as your fight response or what tells you to run when you are in danger. There is only so much I can do. Reckoning replied. *There is no telling how much or how long I can keep it at bay. You need to retreat until we have a better handle on this.*

No. Do what you can, but I need to help. I need to protect my friends.

Malach, this is not a good idea.

But Malach wasn't listening. He stood, stretching and flexing his back muscles to ease the pain, and set off for the wall. Men ran by, headed for the newly repaired and weak part of the wall. He turned that direction as well. He would still be able to assist there and not be in the direct war.

Reckoning would be happier with that, He thought and felt some measure of relief from the blade.

As he arrived, a muffled explosion sounded well outside the wall, but Malach didn't pay it much mind. Only seconds after, he heard shouting and all the men standing around the area started scrambling for safety. A second explosion pushed the wall in at the base. Malach turned and pumped his legs to get away from the collapsing wall. He lost his footing and as he hit the ground; he clawed his way forward on all fours.

The dust choked and blinded him at the same time. He had managed to avoid most of the falling rubble, although he had cuts and bruises from the splinters and shards of debris. Standing, he coughed. His eyes burned and watered uncontrollably, but he could hear the moaning of the dying. He stumbled toward where he thought the wall should be, climbing over boulders and trying to stay clear of the burning timbers that lay strewn across the field.

The surrounding noise changed. It sounded less hollow, more open. His brain took a minute to catch up with his senses. A brisk mountain breeze cleared the air of dust, and he was finally able to make sense of where he was. He had passed the boundary of the wall without realizing it and he was now on the battlefield.

His mind numbed and his muscles froze him in place as a demon dived out of the air toward him.

Chapter 21

Something wet and warm wouldn't let Amara sleep. Insistently lapping against her face. All she wanted was sleep. She was comfortable in her bed and in was the middle of the night. Wasn't it? Pain was the first thing she registered in her head.

Screaming pain.

So much so she thought she might be dying. She rolled off the boulder her body was draped over, and the pain subsided for a split second before her body landed on the ground with a thud.

Again, the warm tongue started licking her face and a high-pitched whining sound seemed to pierce her aching head like a spike being driven into it. She brushed it away this time. Why couldn't she sleep longer? Was there really anything more pressing at the moment? The tongue was back, however, insisting that she wake up. She opened her eyes and stared directly into the eyes of a wolf. She jumped back, her ribs protesting every movement. She lowered herself to the ground gingerly.

The memories that flooded her mind brought her back to full consciousness. It didn't take her long to orient herself to her dire situation. She was on the ground. She had no idea if it was in front or behind the now damaged wall. The explosion had blown her clear off the wall and she was lucky to be alive. Her ribs were hurt, most likely broken. Every breath, every movement sent shoots of pain through her chest and back. The boulder she woke up on was flat, rough, and at least twice her height in both directions. She was thankful she ended up on top of it instead of under it.

Skie nudged her insistently, pushing her to get up and move. She struggled to her hands and knees. Her chest felt like it was being pulled apart. She got to her feet unsteadily. Skie nudged her in a direction and even though Amara couldn't see anything, she trusted Skie and staggered off in that direction. It wasn't until she pasted the ruins of the wall she realized where she was and that Skie was no longer with her. She was met by soldiers who all but picked her up and carried her away from the battlefield. She was done for the moment. Even if she wanted to go back and fight, she would be a liability. She took the cot offered to her and closed her eyes, trying not to move. The pain died down to a dull throb.

The weight of what had just happened landed squarely on her and a lump formed in her throat, which had nothing to do with her injuries. How would they survive this? They had been counting on the wall holding longer. She tried to get up. Injured or not, she was needed. Her ribs screamed in protest, but she growled through the pain.

"Don't get up." A healer walked in.

"I'm needed."

"Your breastplate is in need of repair and your rib is most likely broken." He stood in her way. "Not to mention you hit your head heard enough to draw blood. You could black out on the field and then you won't be useful to anyone."

Amara glanced down at her breastplate for the first time. It was indeed heavily dented just below her left breast. Flat would be the best way to describe it. though it had pits and dents in it from the rough stone she had landed on. She touched her head and winced. Her hand came away bloody.

She ground her teeth together but lowered herself back down to the cot.

The healer helped her out of her breastplate and started cleaning her head wound.

"Didn't I leave Malach with you?" Amara asked, immediately feeling stupid since he obviously wouldn't know who Malach was. "I mean the tall man who froze on top of the wall during the first charge."

"I had one man during that time, yes." The healer frowned. "I sat him down on a bench and haven't been able to get back to check on him." He pulled a roll of bandages from his bag. "He wasn't injured, so I had to leave him to keep others alive."

"When you're finished, please show me where you left him." Amara held still for him to wrap her head.

"Yes, I can. Then you need to rest. However, you can't sleep tonight."

She stared at him quizzically.

"If people with head wounds fall asleep the night after the injury is sustained, some never wake up." He said it as if he was repeating it for the umpteenth time today.

He probably was. Amara thought. She just nodded as he moved to her rib. She winced when he touched it.

"Hard to say, but you might have fractured a rib. I don't feel anything overly substantial, but you'll be feeling this for a while to come. Your breastplate saved you from having your whole ribcage caved in." He shook his head and pulled out another roll of bandages. "Not much you can do until it heals."

Once he was finished, he handed her the breastplate and started to hurry away.

"Wait, aren't you going to show me where you left my friend?"

"Oh, um, I left him sitting on a bench just over there. I have too many people to take care of to take you myself." And with that, he was gone.

Amara followed the direction he had pointed and found an empty bench. Screams echoed from the direction of the wall, reminding her there was still a war raging. She hoped Malach had gone back to his room, but deep down, she knew he was at the wall.

She only hoped he hadn't frozen again.

Malach was frozen again. This time, instead of arrows, a demon was bearing down on him. He wanted to pull Reckoning. He wanted to jump to the side. He wanted to duck. Anything but stand there and get demolished by the behemoth about to rip him apart.

The weight hit him as hard as a tree falling. He hit the ground; the pain jarring him loose of whatever trance held him. An ear-splitting roar deafened him, and he understood it was all over. He was going to die. He had failed once again. Curling into a ball, he waited for the end to come.

A wet nose nuzzled his face, shocking him just as much as the demon tackling him had. He stared up into the eyes of his oldest and dearest companion. True understanding dawned on him. Skie had tackled him out of the way of the demon. But what then had stopped the demon from turning about and attacking him?

He turned just in time to roll out of the way of a body landing hard next to him. On instinct he used the momentum of the roll to get to his feet and Reckoning all but sprung to his hand. His father lay on the ground, regaining his breath. Ariel had fought off the demon.

Steel entered Malach's heart and fire ran through his veins. He didn't know why he had frozen, but no longer. It was time to fight. He let out a battle cry and charged the demon, fending off the outstretched sword, letting the blade's collision spin Reckoning and running the blade on the other side of the pole through its chest. It wasn't a killing blow, but it would have been a mortal wound on a human.

The demon jumped back, holding his chest. He took to the sky and hovered for a moment. Ariel joined Malach, and the demon seemed to realize he was outnumbered and outmatched. He retreated, making way for enemy soldiers to move in on the trio.

"Are you ok?" Ariel asked, keeping his focus trained on the demon.

Malach understood what he meant and knew he had to tell the truth. "I'm not sure. Reckoning is helping, but it's like I can't control my own body anymore. I have no idea how long this will last." And there it was. He was now a liability. "And my back has been killing me." He threw in, since he was now being completely honest.

"Then we fight to retreat." Ariel engaged the first man to reach them, giving away ground until he found an opening in the man's defense.

Malach followed his lead, giving ground just as quickly as his father. They stayed in sync until the rubble of the ruined wall caused them to split off from each other. However, the rubble provided him with a similar cover, keeping his enemies from flanking him. Skie mostly remained behind Malach but darted out here and there, ripping a chunk of flesh from unprotected shins or to latching onto armor, pulling the soldier off balance. A death pulse hit him while he was retreating. The first he had ever felt. He truly was a Blade Bearer. However, he didn't have time to analyze the feeling to determine whether it was a demon or an angel who had died.

Malach felt hands on his shoulders pulling him back. He instinctively fought them off without taking his attention off the next enemy soldier in line. Two men pushed past him, filling the space between Malach and the enemy. He realized he was safe. At least for the moment. Fatigue hit him and he let the strong hands help him back behind even more men shuffling forward. There would soon be bodies stacked in every opening in the wall, and Malach only hoped the majority of them would be wearing the colors of the demon army.

Daziar landed hard, but he was back on his feet quickly. He was getting used to being blown up. The second shock wave hit him square in the back. This time, he didn't get up as quickly. Many parts of his body screamed in pain while his one arm was still absent of any feeling. He climbed to his feet again, struggling to find which way was which.

Ana, he had to find Ana.

He turned in a circle, orienting himself with the sight of the wall. He spun back to where he had last seen Ana and ran forward, searching for the angel. Fear gripped him and he prepared himself for the sight of her smoking corpse. However, there was no sign of her anywhere.

Enemy soldiers moved in on him. Apparently, they had realized he wasn't a part of their number. No matter what he wanted, he needed to retreat, or he wouldn't do anyone any good. He prayed Ana was alive as he turned back toward the wall. He ran as fast as his armor would allow, but the gap between the two flanks of the enemy was closing swiftly. It didn't take him long to realize he wasn't going to make it back. Slowing, he readied himself to fight.

Dawn, I know we haven't been together long, but this might be our last stand. Daziar thought.

Oh, no. We are not having the "This is my last stand speech". Dawn replied. *I intend to have many, many more years with my first bearer.*

Daziar was about to reply, but he needed to concentrate on the fight at hand. It wouldn't be a fair fight and he would need to keep moving to have any chance of survival. He used every ounce of training Ana had imparted to him to dance around the soldiers and keep one step ahead of them. Several times, his quick movements cause collisions between them, giving him a moment's reprieve from the onslaught. These were not well-trained soldiers. These were most likely former farmers and merchants conscripted for this war. He lost count of how many men he killed or mortally wounded. Faces and armor blended together in this dance of death he weaved.

A death pulse hit him like a blow to the gut, causing him to flinch and stumble. A sword caught his shoulder. His pauldrons took the worst of it, but the impact spun him off his feet. He rolled out of the way of the first sword, but many more plunged toward him. This was it. This was his end. He would join Honora and possibly Ana soon.

Against the wishes of the healer, she headed back to the wall in only her black leather armor sporting her throwing knives. She had dropped her ruined breastplate at a blacksmith's stand, but he had no spare armor to give her as a replacement. She would have to be careful.

Arriving at the break in the wall where the worst of the fighting was, she surveyed the area. Despite the cover of the large chunks of ruined wall, the Angel Army was stretched thin. Arches on the top of the wall killed the enemy by the score. However, there seemed to be an endless number of soldiers willing to replace them.

Amara spotted a group of female soldiers being pushed back in the middle of the chaos. Two throwing knives left her hands as she started forward. The women were slightly taken aback as the two front enemies screamed, holding their necks. But as Amara pushed past them to intercept the next soldier, two of the women moved forward to cover her to either side. Her ribs protested, but much less than they had before the healer wrapped them.

Amara used Blaze and Ember to take the man apart. Stabbing the knives over and over into different seams of his armor until he collapsed from sheer blood loss. Then worked her way through the next soldier's defenses until she slid Ember across his throat. On they went, pushing the enemy back farther and farther until they had solidified their position. Then they stack the bodies up in front of them, killing soldier after soldier until the flood slowed then stopped all together.

Had they won?

"Hold!"

Amara heard the command before she spotted where it originated from.

The arch-angel Michael descended. He was bloody and his armor dented. One of his four wings hung useless at an odd angle. Amara hadn't seen him at all during the fighting, but he had obviously taken his fair share of the battle. Come to think of it, she hadn't seen a single demon in the entire battle. Was he the reason no demons had joined the fray?

"Half of you hold the wall." His voice boomed larger than he appeared. "Half of you gather supplies. Food, water, stone and mortar. Take this reprieve to rest and regain your strength, for you will need it in the coming days, but do not become complacent. The enemy will return shortly."

They did as he bid them. Amara held her position while others brought her food and drink. Healers moved in and out of the troops, doing what they could to help and taking the more gravely injured away to be worked on or to die in peace.

How long had they been fighting? It seemed like only an hour, but the position of the sun told her otherwise. They had been fighting for most of the day. She was exhausted.

She wanted to leave and find Malach, but she didn't know where to start searching for him and she didn't want to make anyone take her place at the breach. Instead, she ate the bread and dried meat she was given and tried to rest. Fighting was the most tiring thing she had ever done. It could wear you out in less than an hour, and that was just against one opponent. Fighting multiple opponents was worse.

"Healers!"

Amara jumped up and looked out to the killing field where the voice had come from. Dusk was settling and she couldn't make out who was out there through the gloom and dust. She drew Blaze and took a step forward, readying herself in case it was a trick.

Ana stumbled into her view, barely able to hold the body in her arms.

Amara almost didn't recognize the angel. Burns covered most of the visible skin and her once shining armor was bent and blackened. One wing hung behind her, a burned husk of the splendor it used to be. The man in her arms was limp and Amara thought for sure he was dead or too far gone to survive for long.

"Daziar, needs help." Ana stumbled forward.

Amara rushed to steady her, and Togan appeared as if out of nowhere to relieve her of Daziar.

"He's alive." Ana insisted. "He was struck on the head, but he's alive."

"What I'm more concerned about is you." Amara got under the angel's arm, lifting her as best as her small frame could. "You look like you stood too close to one of those black powder barrels when it went off."

"I was flying, but that sums it up rather well." Ana smiled weakly.

"Really?"

"I took one away from the wall and released it only moments before it exploded. A demon tried to take advantage of my injury, but he overestimated his position. He didn't live to regret that mistake."

Amara shook her head and let out a low whistle. Even in this state, the angel was a force to be reckoned with. "Was Daziar with you?"

"Up until the barrel exploded." Ana confirmed. "After that, we got separated. I found him just after killing the demon surrounded by the bodies of those he had slain. No doubt he knew the danger he was in and was attempting to make it back to the stronghold. I was able to hold out until the enemy called a retreat."

Amara sat her down in a healer's tent and waited until she was in good hands before leaving her. The pain in her ribs had been slowly getting worse as the day had gone by and she needed to rest. She made her to a relatively safe place under an overhang, intending just to rest for a few moments to give her ribs a break. Instead, her eyes closed, and she drifted off into a fitful sleep.

Malach sat on the edge of his bed, feeling absolutely useless. His friends and family were out there fighting for their lives and the best he could do was sit on a bed and try to stay out of danger. The feeling overwhelmed him again, just as it had on the bench. He didn't know if he wanted to cry or put his fist through something.

A faint knock came at the door. "Malach?"

"Come in." He wiped his face quickly and stood.

Raziel walked in. "Malach, we need to talk."

"I'm not sure I want to right now." Malach sat back down. "Aren't you needed at the wall?"

"We've won a reprieve for the moment, but you need my help. Michael believes you have an integral role to play in this war. That being said, you seem to have developed a freeze response to danger."

"A what?"

"A freeze response." Raziel replied, as if that explained everything.

"So how do I fix this?"

Raziel brows knitted together. "Malach, you're not broken."

"I almost got myself killed. Several times today alone. Something is obviously wrong." Malach crossed his arms.

Raziel smiled warmly. "The trauma you've recently endured has caused your body and mind to use a new tactic for survival. No one quite knows why this happens, but it sometimes does. There isn't anything broken in you. Your body is just trying to survive."

"How to I stop it from happening then?" Malach asked.

"To put it simply, you can't." Raziel shrugged. "Reckoning can help keep the instinct at bay for only so long. That can give you a chance to time the freeze and get through it. But you will have to get through it. I can teach you how to ground yourself."

Malach nodded. "This freeze response. Could it cause pain in my back?"

"Theoretically, it could cause all sorts of muscle problems. Soreness, spasms, shooting pains; All of those could be caused by long term tensing of your body. Especially since you haven't been sleeping well."

"Then let's work on this. The pain hasn't been getting worse and I'm ready to be finished with the whole thing."

Raziel smiled. "Then let's get started."

Amara awoke to horns warning of an imminent attack. She rolled onto her side, her ribs screaming in protest. Darkness was falling and the light of the sun was almost gone. She had slept for an hour or so, but it felt like only minutes. Everything ached and her limbs felt like lead. Non the less she forced her body to move, fighting the pain and getting to her feet. Once standing, the pain in her ribs lessened to a dull ache. She didn't know how long she could fight, but she would do her best to support their efforts however she could. She worked her way to the wall, dodging soldiers running towards the same goal. The enemy would be here soon, and they would make them pay dearly for every step.

She arrived behind what felt like half the army. In this position, she might not even have to fight. She glanced up at either side of the wall that remained. Archers were lining the parapets as far to each side as she could see. There would be no room up there for her.

She heard the twang of the bows from the top of the wall. The enemy would be there soon. She waited. A sharp crack sounded, then another, and a third after that. A man fell from the wall, landing in a heap, but no arrow could be seen protruding from him. Amara shifted her gaze to the wall, looking for new cracks that might be forming but couldn't see anything.

What had made that sound? Then she remembered the small cannon like weapons that could be held in someone's hand. They were using them against the archers on the wall. She would have to be careful when it came time for her to fight. Those weapons could be hidden and used to end a fight before it even begun. Malach had done that in the demon compound.

The sound of blade against blade reached her ears, bouncing off the stone. It grated on her nerves. If she didn't know better, she would think the fighting was already inside the walls. Still, she resisted the urge to pull her weapons. They wouldn't server her standing in the middle of this crowd. She would wait her turn to fight on the front. When it came, she would need every ounce of strength she had.

Dawn was just starting to light the sky when she received her chance. Many had fallen on both sides, and the ground was slick with blood. Footing would be treacherous. She had seen many leave wounded and many simply needing a break, but none had left the front unscathed. She readied her blades, preparing her mind and body for battle.

The soldier in front of her moved forward to attack as the next enemy drew a pistol and fired the projectile into the man's head. The enemy soldier shed the pistol as fast as his victim fell and drew another, leveling it at Amara's head. A massive, scaly body crashed down, crushing the man before he could fire and end her life. Amara pushed back against those who were behind her. All she could think about was not getting crushed by the writhing mass. The beast righted itself and took off, headed toward Michael and Leviathan. Both heads swiveled independently, striking out at each of the angels. One head caught Leviathan's leg, pulling her from Amara's view.

She turned her attention to the battlefield once again. Just in time to get her blades up to deflect and downward chop of an axe. She spun to the side, slamming her back against a rock and sending stabs of debilitating pain through her ribs. She fought for air and tried to get her blades up once again. Too late. The axe was already whistling through the air to split her skull. She prepared herself for the end.

Malach stood as the horns blew their warning. He and Raziel had been practicing grounding techniques to snap him out of his next freeze.

Reckoning was more prepared to fend off the response, but they were still unsure of how long they would have when the real thing happened.

"Where are you going?"

Malach's hand paused on the door latch. The tone in Raziel's voice had his senses on alert. He spun in time to block a right hook. Out of reflex, he brought his fist up into the angel's gut, pushing the wind from his lungs. Pain shot through his back once again at the sudden twisting of his body, but it subsided quickly.

Malach, the freeze response. Reckoning warned as they had practiced.

Hold it off as long as you can. Malach pushed Raziel back, but the angel recovered and came on quickly, pulling a dagger this time. Malach knew Raziel had his struggle with mental stability, but this was ridiculous.

Malach it's getting more intense. Reckoning warned.

Malach grunted in response, pulling Reckoning as a bow staff, twisting it around to deflect and send the dagger clattering to the floor. *Let it come.*

Malach's muscles tighten involuntarily and he focused on the cool touch of Reckoning in his hand. The smooth metal that ran the entire length of the shaft. How it warmed as he held it. How familiar it felt in his hand.

He brought the staff up in front of him just in time to clip the blade out of the way a second time. Then he spun Reckoning, bringing the end across under Raziel's guard. He pulled his blow at the last second, understanding dawning on him. The staff connected solidly non-the-less and Raziel grunted, dropping to a knee.

He was grinning up at Malach despite the obvious pain. *Well done. Both of you.* The angel had made him think he was in danger, to test his response and how well they handled it in a crisis.

Malach bowed to the angel slightly. "Thank you Raziel, I couldn't have learned this on my own. And it most likely would have gotten me killed if I had tried."

"You're a fast learner, Malach. But remember, the more intense the reaction, the longer it will take for you to ground yourself." Raziel put both hands on Malach's shoulders. "If you were anyone else or someone without a blade of such caliber as Reckoning, I would have told you to stand down. I would have told you not to fight but to run with the elderly and children. However, I truly believe between the two of you, you will still fulfill whatever purpose God has for you in this war."

"Thank you." Malach nodded solemnly. "I will do my best."

They ran through the halls and Malach worked on keeping his mind grounded in the moment. They entered the courtyard behind a sea of soldiers. The Archers were already firing from atop the wall and men and women fought in the maze of corridors among the large stone debris. Malach started forward toward the front of the line. He pushed his way through, and most didn't have any problem letting him pass. He saw many scared faces, many resigned looks, and a few angry ones. Most would die fighting; some would lose their nerve once their turn came up. That was the truths of war. Malach felt his muscle tense, and he stopped to work though the reflex. He wasn't in danger yet. He had time.

He spotted Amara up to his left. Her face was a picture of calm and serenity. If her expression was your only indication, you would think it any other day. She might have been waiting in line for the morning meal. He wished he had her calm. Instead, anger boiled inside of him. Anger against those who would ally themselves with the demons. Anger against the demons who would bring such an army against them to utterly destroy their way of life. But most of all, anger…at himself.

That realization stopped him in his tracks. Not frozen like he normally was, but shocked into stillness. He was angry at himself. Angry he had never searched for his parents all those years in Brightwood. Angry that he had failed to understand Amara's predicament and subsequent betrayal. Angry he had been too late to save his mother. And angry he had failed, not only Honora, but everyone he had ever known growing up.

His legs gave out, and the tears flowed again. He understood those things were not his fault, or at least not his fault alone, but he wept all the same. Grieving for all those he had lost, all those he knew would be lost here. He let it all out, holding none of it back. Soldiers shuffled around him, not paying him more than a cursory glance. Once his emotions were spent, he stood feeling empty, but somehow right. Like a dam being let loose, allowing his emptiness to flow out to be filled by something else. He allowed himself to forgive himself for the first time since he could remember.

Reckoning,

Yes Malach?

Are you ready to kill the devil?

Pride radiated through Malach's consciousness from the blade. He was back, and he would fight to the last breath. Raziel warned him he would always have to deal with the freezing, but he was armed against it, and he would only get better at conquering it. He pushed forward once again, this time with more purpose and with a goal in mind.

Slay the two-headed dragon.

Satan and Lucifer needed to die. He had no idea how he was going to manage that, but he planned to find a way. He glanced up in time to spot the very thing he had just purposed to kill. The devil descended, pursued by several angels, Michael, Gabriel, and Leviathan among them. His bulk hit the ground just in front of the breaking the wall and lifted almost as quickly. Malach snapped his attention forward, hoping Amara hadn't been in the landing area. He spotted her recovering from the shock of almost being crushed as an enemy soldier ran forward with an axe.

Malach pushed soldiers out of his way, pressing forward.

Amara got her knives up in time to deflect the first strike.

Malach fought through the crowd, so close to saving her, but, he feared, still too far away.

She spun to gain room but hit one of the stone boulders littering the area. All the fight left her. She had no chance to defend herself.

Malach all but trampled those in front of him, pulled Reckoning and reached forward. He was too late. Too slow once again. He was more than a few spear lengths away as the axe fell. Malach locked eyes with her for only a moment. She knew it was the end. She knew nothing he or she could do would save her life. In that moment, Malach understood two truths he couldn't deny. One, he loved the woman in front of him with all his heart. Two, he had lost everything he held dear in this world.

The axe fell, striking flesh and rending bone beneath its deadly blade. Malach carried his momentum forward, screaming in rage and terror. Reckoning ran the man through, and Malach kicked him off the blade, turning to catch Amara before she hit the ground. Instead, he found himself staring into her eyes. Not a mark blemished her face, no blood or ichor streamed down her forehead. She was unharmed.

"How..." Malach whispered.

They both stared down at the form on the ground, and Malach's freshly mended heart broke once again. Skie lay on the ground between them. He dropped to her side, holding pressure on the wound. The part of her hind, right leg below her knee was missing, cleaved off by the enemy axe. She needed help right away or she would bleed out. Malach clutched at her, pulling her into his arms and lifting her from the battlefield. He was vaguely aware of their troops filing past him to fill the gap left by the dragon. He pushed past the same men he had on his journey out. Only one thing mattered. He had to get his oldest friend to a healer.

He reached the healer's tents and entered the first one, pushing past those waiting with more minor injuries. He laid Skie on a cot in the tent and held pressure on her leg. The blood was coming in spurts. And her eyes had rolled back into her head. He was losing her.

"I need help!" He shouted.

Chapter 22

Daziar awoke on a cot in a tent. His head throbbed worse than he ever could remember. He was slightly surprised he woke up at all. His last memory was being buried under a pile of enemies. How he arrived here was a mystery, but he needed to get up and fight. There was no chance the war was over. He would be needed on the front lines.

Daz, Dawn chided, but he could tell she was relieved. *Take a breath and give yourself time to heal. You nearly died out there.*

I can't rest. I will be needed.

He sat up and swung his legs over the side of the cot. He had been stripped of his armor and all but his underclothes. Glancing around, he found his clothes cleaned and folded off to the side and his boots were next to it. Although, his armor was nowhere to be found. He didn't relish the thought of going into battle without it.

He chuckled to himself. Only a week ago, he had never donned anything more than hard leather and in that short time, he already felt naked without it. He shook his head. He would need to find where it had been taken. Standing, he almost toppled over again, but he gained his footing and propelled himself forward through a flap in the tent. He nearly ran into Ana and a healer.

"Ana?" Daziar's eyes grew wide, and tear started to form. He all but smothered her with a big bear hug. "Your alive! I thought...well the explosion. I assumed...I'm so happy to see you!" He sputtered.

"It's good to see you too, Daz." Ana's tinkling laugher filled his ears. "I managed to escape death by inferno, however, not unscathed."

Daziar pulled back and notice her wing for the first time. It was half covered in bandages. The half that wasn't covered was slathered with a paste but he could see the burns underneath. He winced. "That looks like it hurts."

"Ha!" Ana laughed mirthlessly. "No, it's so much fun having a wing burned almost off. Of course it hurts."

Daziar held up his hands in surrender. "Sorry, I'm just happy you're alive. Did *you* get me back here?"

"Yes, and you're heavier than you look." Ana cracked a genuine smile but winced as the healer got back to work. "I had to drag your sorry butt all the way back to the wall. Next time, do me a favor and get knocked out in a safer place, huh?"

Daziar grinned. "I'll keep that in mind next time. What now? I mean, the war is obviously not over. What's going on?"

"We've had a small reprieve. The enemy breached the wall and retreated temporarily to regroup. They'll be back and the lords won't hold back this time. They will press the breach until either we break, or we push them back." Ana explained.

"Then I need my armor. I need to get to the breach to fight." Daziar turned and looked around. "Where did you put my armor?"

"You and I will be sitting this battle out." Ana replied.

"What? No! I need to be out there helping." Daziar replied.

The healer spoke up from behind Ana, never taking his eyes off his work. "We've seen people with head wounds as bad as yours black out within the first few hours of returning to consciousness. You are more of a liability at this point."

"I'm not going to sit around while people die for me just 'cause I might black out." Daziar shot back. "Where's my armor?"

"I sent your armor for repair. It took several major hits while you were out there," Ana replied. "Several of the pieces needed repair, and I knew you would need them later. We can pick them up in the morning. Until then, you need to get some rest, so you are fresh. Then you can relieve those who have been fighting through the night. Don't worry, the fighting will be going on for days. You won't miss your chance."

"Fine, which black smith has my armor?" Daziar asked. "Togan?"

"Togan and Marena decided to serve in the army rather than blacksmith." Ana replied. "You didn't know?"

"No." Daziar paused for a second. "That means they could be out there fighting right now. I need to get back out there."

"Daziar." Ana shook her head. "You can't protect everyone. You're starting to sound like Malach. Togan and Marena can take care of themselves and each other."

"Fine," Daziar conceded. "Where is my armor, though, so I can pick it up in the morning?"

"Go to your room," Ana smiled. "I will come get you when I have it."

Daziar sighed. "Fine, I'll leave it for now. But if I'm needed, I will go to the breach with or without my armor."

Ana rolled her eyes at him. "You and I both know you won't last long out there. It's not a small skirmish or a fight with untrained bandits. This is all out war."

Daziar nodded his consent and wished her well as he left. She was right. He would need his armor before he fought again. He had no choice but to rest or check with every blacksmith in the stronghold. Shaking his head, he started for his room but decided to clear his mind first. He passed out of the throngs of soldiers into a more open part of the courtyard. His nerves needed some time to settle.

Daz, hit the deck! Dawn shouted in his mind.

He did.

A demon shot over head, his sword at such an angle to separate Daziar's head from his shoulders. Rolling to his feet, he readied Dawn for the follow up attack. So much for resting.

The demon angled around just as he predicted, diving at him. He set his stance and held his ground. He would have to time his strike. Instead of going for the attack, however, the demon dropped at the last second, his clawed hand scrabbling at the ground to keep his momentum and launched himself directly at Daziar.

The Impact jarred him so badly that Dawn was ripped from his hand. He felt a rib pop, and he had a hard time gaining his breath. Opening his eyes, he glanced down to see the ground was already falling away from him. The demon was already at a dizzying height and climbing, too far to survive the fall. He pulled his knife, luckily, he had replaced his last one already, and slammed it into the demon's side up to the handle and it stuck fast. As it had, no doubt, planned all along, the demon released him, causing him to slip down, hanging by the one hand still grasping the knife. He flailed the rest of his limbs, trying to gain some hand or foothold to pull himself up. The demon rolled in the air, trying to throw him but only succeeding in giving him a chance to get a hold of one of the spikes protruding from the monster's shoulder.

He hosted himself up onto its back, pulling his knife and plunging it down again. It never connected. The demon rolled the other way and dove, throwing Daziar off balance and making him concentrate on not plummeting to his death. He noticed the twist the demon had wretched his numb arm into. Had he been able to feel it, he might be screaming in pain at this point. Something might even be broken or dislocated. But his hand held firm. Not having feeling might have its perks after all. The demon righted and Daziar noticed they were headed back toward to wall. Below, the armies collided at the breach. Their reprieve was over.

The demon angled up, wings beating hard to climb. It was all Daziar could do to hold on, and he prayed the spike he held onto was stronger than it felt. They reached the angels' council room at the top of the stronghold and the demon turned, folded his wings and landed directly on top of Daziar. The table they landed on collapsed under the impact and they collided and crushed several chairs as well.

His hand let go involuntarily, the demon bounced off his body, and Daziar skidded to a stop among the wreckage, chest heaving. He had to get up, or he was dead. He was probably dead anyway, without a proper weapon to defend himself, but he wouldn't die without a fight. Rolling over, he pushed himself to his feet. Before he could ready himself, the demon was on him. He threw his knife up, desperately trying to defend against the onslaught the demon brought to bear. Backpedaling to try to get space between him and the demon, a terrible thought struck him. He was backing toward the opening of the council room. There were no barriers between him and the open space beyond.

Daziar reversed directions, suddenly ducking under the swipe of the demon's sword and rolling forward, coming back up in a ready stance.

The amount of floor between him and the drop off made his stomach twist. A couple more feet and he would have been praying for wings.

The demon spun, grinning wildly.

Daziar set his jaw and pressed the attack, pushing the demon back. He had to be perfect with his timing and angle of his blade. If he was off by an inch, he would lose a hand, or worse, his life. He pushed the demon toward the remaining chairs, hoping to trip him. It didn't work. Just when Daziar thought the demon would trip over one of the intact ornate chairs, the thing simply climbed it, using it as a springboard to launch itself into the air. He was headed for open air and Daziar gave chase. There wasn't a chance in Heaven or Hell he would catch the demon.

An angel hit the monster from the side as soon as he passed the opening, taking him from Daziar's view faster than he could blink. He couldn't tell which angel it was, but he was grateful all the same. He ran to the edge and peered over to see the two-headed dragon dive toward the breach. The behemoth landed for an instant, then took off again, leaving many broken bodies in his wake. This far up, Daziar couldn't tell who was on what side, but he prayed none of his friends were there. He turned and ran for the door. Many flights of stairs stood between him and the ground floor. Having not been to this part of the stronghold, which corridors would lead him where, was a mystery to him. It might take him all night to traverse them.

Amara ran through the tent entrance, followed closely by an irate-looking man. They made their way to Malach, and the man gave Skie a cursory glance.

"She's a wolf." The man sputtered. "I have men in need of treatment. I can't spend time on an animal."

Malach rushed the hapless man and picked him up by his collar. "If you let her die, I will flay you alive and leave what's left of you for the crows!" He roared inches from his face.

"What he means in this is no mere wolf, and she has saved many lives on the battlefield. She is just as worthy of your care as any war hero." Amara pleaded. She didn't need to, however. The man was already moving to work on Skie. His eyes were wide and breathing heavy when he chanced a glance back at Malach.

He shewed Malach and Amara away and started working on Skie's ruined leg. Malach watched as close as the healer would allow. Constantly moving around the cot to get better vantage points. He worked meticulously, tying off the leg to slow the blood and pulling bone shards out. Finally he pulled a metal rod out of the fire at the center of the tent. At the end of the rod was a flat circle, red hot from the fire.

Malach caught the hand with the metal rod in it and stopped the healer in his tracks.

"This is how I stop the bleeding." The healer explained. "Without this she will bleed out soon. We might already be too late."

Amara walked over to Malach and gently pulled him away from the healer. "It's ok, let him do this. You don't have to watch if you don't want to."

Malach didn't say a word but also didn't turn away.

The healer pressed the hot metal against the stump of Skie's leg. The wolf didn't stir which scared Amara more than if she had jumped up and attacked the healer. He pulled the rod away from the wound and sure enough the bleeding had stopped. He applied a salve to the burned flesh and finally wrapped it with bandages.

He turned to Malach. "I've done all I can. Whether she lives or dies is up to her at this point."

Malach nodded and moved quickly to Skie's side.

Amara made a point to thank the healer, but he was already fleeing in case the madman tried to follow through with his threat.

Skie had remained unconscious for the whole procedure and hadn't woken up yet. However, Malach still stroked her ichor laden fur, picking out flecks of dried blood and dirt. He stared at her face, and it seemed like he would stay there until either the wolf passed or pulled through.

Amara had never seen him like this. She knelt next to him and put a hand on his shoulder. "She's strong. She'll pull through this."

"But what kind of life will she have?" Malach asked.

"She will still have a good life. We will make sure of it."

Malach turned to her. "There's still a chance at a 'we'?"

"Of course," Amara smiled, genuinely happy. "If you want, that is."

"I do want that." Malach smiled back. "I'm sorry it's taken me this long to realize. I saw you on the battlefield and the thought of losing you along with..." His voice trailed off.

"You won't lose me. I'm hard to get rid of, remember?"

He chuckled despite himself. "That you are." He pulled her close, and they laid their hands together on Skie's chest, praying she would awaken.

The fighting stopped sometime after midnight, but the healers still bustled around the tents tending to the wounded. Rested soldiers replaced the exhausted ones to stand watch for any attack. Amara laid on the same cot as Skie, sleeping next to the big she-wolf. Malach had sent someone to find her breast plate after hearing it had been damaged in the fighting and they had delivered it to him shortly after she had fallen asleep.

He should probably sleep, but no matter how tired he was, his mind wouldn't slow down to let him. Nor did he want to miss Skie waking up. She could be disoriented, and he didn't want her feeling threated and hurting herself or any of the healers. Lord knew they didn't need any additional injuries. Instead, he sat, practicing his grounding techniques.

"Malach?" A deep, resonating voice hailed him from behind.

He turned to see Togan and Marena walking up and he stood to greet them. "I'm happy to see you two alive and unharmed through all of this. Many haven't been as fortunate."

"We heard about Skie and we came as soon as we could." Marena moved forward and hugged Malach. "I'm so sorry."

Malach Smiled despite himself and embraced the woman. "The healer said if she wakes up, she should pull through it. But she hasn't woken yet."

"I see young Amara has found her way back into your life." Togan grinned at him. "A young man wise beyond his years once told me, 'You better make a move before someone else does.' I think that applies in this situation."

Malach chuckled, glancing over at Amara sleeping with Skie. Those were the words he had spoken to Togan in Brightwood before all of this. Togan had been too shy to ask Marena to court him back then.

Togan pulled Marena close, and they shared a look. Then Togan turned back to Malach. "If you need anything, just ask."

"And Malach, you couldn't have stopped this. It's not your fault." Marena added.

He smiled at her and didn't have the energy to contradict her sentiment. "Thank you."

Togan and Marena left, and Malach sat through the rest of the night and into the morning with Skie. Amara woke up sometime after sunrise as one of the kitchen staff brought around breakfast for the wounded. They ate mostly in silence before Amara dismissed herself to relieve someone at the wall. The enemy would be back soon. He was surprised the enemy hadn't attacked at first light.

Malach would have to leave Skie's side if the fighting started again. He didn't want to, but he had a duty to uphold, and now that he had learned to deal with his mental disarray, he needed to make up for lost time. He also needed to find a way to kill that dragon once and for all. Michael and Gabriel had sealed him away, but Malach was set on killing the beast. It was the only thing that felt right.

He sighed and leaned forward, burying his head in Skies side. Her warmth was comforting and familiar. He ran his fingers along her sides and through her fur.

He woke up some time later. He didn't remember falling asleep. Warm, moist breath wafted across his face and when he opened his eyes, a gapping maw of teeth was all he could see. He jerked back as Skie finished yawning and felt a little foolish, but the joy he felt overran it completely. He fell forward onto Skie, hugging her tightly.

"I'm so glad you are awake!" Malach cried.

Skie licked him weakly and then fell back again, her energy spent.

"Rest, my friend. I will find you something to eat." Malach stood and search around him. Not finding any food, stood and exited the tent. He headed directly for the kitchen and it didn't take him long to find a freshly butchered slab of pig. He ran back and proffered it to the wolf.

She took it feebly and picked at it.

"Come on, girl, you need to eat," Malach prompted. "You need your strength."

Skie turned and nosed the bandaged stump and then looked pointedly at Malach.

"I know, but you're not dead. I will take care of you, just like when we first met." Tears welled up in his eyes for her. "You're going to be around for a long time to come. I need you, and missing leg or not, I can't lose you too."

Skie seemed to understand and took a larger bite out of the meat, holding it with her front two paws.

"Good! That's good." Malach smiled at her. "It's always going to be me and you, girl. We'll always be there for each other."

Amara spotted Togan and Marena up on the wall from where she was in the courtyard. She hiked down the wall and climbed the first set of stairs she found to join them. They weren't alone when she arrived. Daziar and Ana had joined them. Ana's wing was bandaged and folded behind her. They were deep in conversation, and no one seemed to notice her. She didn't mind though, and sat down behind the group.

"If we could get him to the council room and trap him there, we could make a stand against him." Daziar was saying. "After my involuntary trip, I took stock of the room. I think it's just the right size for it."

She didn't say anything, not wanting to interrupt.

"One problem, *we* would then be trapped up there with him as well." Togan pointed out. "I don't fancy standing that close for that long. It wouldn't take much for him to just step on us like bugs. You saw him when he landed. He killed a half dozen soldiers without even realizing it."

"That's the beauty of the idea." Ana shrugged. "He's so big once we are in close quarters like that, it will disable a lot of his weaponry. The most we'll have to do is not get stepped on. His wings, tail, and claws will be pretty well useless, and his fire could only reach us if we were out in front of him. He wouldn't be able to turn well either."

"Are you talking about the Dragon?" Amara asked.

All heads turned to her, and she realized none of them had known she was there.

"Maybe," Daziar narrowed his eyes.

"Daziar," Ana scolded. "Yes, Amara we are. You're good with a bow, aren't you?"

"Malach taught me a lot of what I know, so he would be better." Amara replied.

"That being said, I think he would want to be fighting the dragon on the ground." Togan said.

"We need to pose this plan to Michael and get him involved. We will need any angel that can be spared to fight the dragon. Also, we need a way to guaranty none of the other surviving seven try to join the fray." Ana nodded slowly. "Yes, I think this could work. Amara, go get Malach and Ariel and meet us at the council room. Ariel will know the way if you don't." Ana took a step to the edge of the wall and spread her good wing, but winced and folded it again. She didn't say anything, but swung herself around and headed for the stairs.

It must be like losing a limb. Amara thought. *You would try to use it by reflex before realizing it wasn't there.*

Amara followed the group down, leaving Togan and Marena to their post. She went by the tent she had left Malach in and found Skie awake and eating. She grinned and knelt next to the wolf.

She wrapped her arms around Skie and whispered. "Thank you for saving me. I'm so sorry you have to endure this on my behalf. I will do everything I can to help you."

Skie pulled back and stared directly into Amara's eyes. She could swear the wolf understood every word. Skie bobbed her head slowly and then gingerly went back to her meal.

Amara turned to Malach. "You have been requested in the council room."

"I can't leave Skie just yet." Malach shook his head.

"Malach, there are healers to look after her and we are planning on taking down the dragon." Amara replied tentatively, watching Malach's response to her words.

His eyes grew hard and cold. He turned to Skie. "I have to go. You'll be safe here for the time being, but I need to do this."

This time, she held his gaze and blinked slowly at him.

He nodded and stood.

Before they left the tent, Skie growled and barked, drawing both of their attention. She had raised herself up on her front two paws and growled again when she locked eyes with Malach.

"I will make sure to send your regards when I slay the dragon." Malach told her and she laid back down on the cot.

They exited the tent. "We need to get my father." Malach stated and started toward the stronghold before Amara could tell him that was already the plan.

She ran to catch up. "You and your long legs are always making me run!" She shouted.

He threw her a grin over his shoulder but didn't slow his pace.

"Ugh, you're the worst." but she smiled despite her words.

Ariel was already waiting for them outside his chamber, dressed in his armor and ready for battle.

Ariel nodded in greeting and addressed Amara. "Malach already told me. Ana and Daziar have come up with a plan to get the Devil alone?"

"Yes," Amara replied. "It seems like a pretty solid plan, but as with anything, when you are facing a powerful foe, there are many potential points for things to go awry."

Ariel pursed his lips and nodded. "I think any plan regarding the Devil will be the same. We will need to mitigate any possible risk and trust God for the rest."

They followed Ariel up to the council room. Malach had been there before, but he let his father lead. However, with so many twists and turns, Amara seriously wondered if Malach would have been able to find his way.

They entered the council room and Amara almost ran into the back of Malach. She was about to protest when she saw what had stopped him. The room was a complete mess. Chairs, broken and strewn across the floor, and the large table was flattened in the middle of the floor.

"What happened here?" Amara asked.

"Um, well, I fought a demon up here." Daziar shrugged. "He didn't seem to care about the furnishings."

"Everyone's a critic," Malach shrugged and grinned over at Amara.

He was joking. She grinned back at him. She couldn't remember the last time he had joked. It had to have been before the spiders attacked them in Ragewood. Maybe he was starting to heal.

Before anyone could say anything else, Michael stepped onto the edge of the council room as if he had simply walked down a flight of stairs. As before, one of his four wings didn't seem to function correctly, and it had been bandaged and tied down to his side. He walked forward, taking stock of the ruined room. "Its seems we will need to replace the furniture again."

"Again?" Daziar asked.

"Surely you don't think this is the first time war has ruined this room." Ana chuckled. "It's not even the *second* time."

"Oh, well, I guess that makes sense," Daziar shrugged. "I just thought he would be more upset when he saw it."

Gabriel alit next to Michael and her shoulders slumped. "I told you we should have struck first."

Michael closed his eyes and sighed. "If roles were reversed, we would be routed already."

Amara had the feeling they had had this conversation many times.

"I see our new Blade-Bearers have been getting their hands dirty." Gabriel ignored Michael's comment.

"You have no idea," Daziar replied.

"Oh, but I think I do. We have been able to keep most of the demons occupied, allowing you and those angels lacking wings to take care of the defense of the wall, mostly unmolested."

"Tell that to the demon who carried me up here and tried to kill me," Daziar mumbled just loud enough for the group to hear him.

Amara was a little impressed he had survived, but then again, Malach had survived something similar not long ago.

Gabriel just shook her head and dropped the conversation.

"We were called up here to listen to a plan, however unlikely, to defeat the devil." Michael folded his arms. "Let's hear it before the enemy strikes at us again."

Togan stepped forward and presented the plan. Most of it Amara had overheard, but something she hadn't, was the plan to contain the dragon. Togan had a plan to drive anchors into the floor with heavy steel rings attached, allowing for ropes to be run through them. Once the dragon was in the correct position, archers would fire arrows over the top with ropes attached. Soldiers on the opposite side would run the ropes through and draw them down, pinning the dragon to the ground. Once done, the angels would attack the dragon, hopefully ending him once and for all.

Michael had listened in silence through Togan's explanation, but when he was finished, Michael was frowning. Amara didn't know if he was frowning because he didn't like the plan or because he was thinking. They all waited for the archangel to say something. Instead, he slowly nodded.

"This might just do it, Michael." Gabriel spoke first, turning toward him. "This plan has a good chance to succeed and I, for one, would be willing to help."

Michael opened his mouth to answer but didn't get the chance.

"If you don't want to, I won't be surprised, but I think this plan has a real shot and I'm tired of sitting around waiting for him to attack again." Gabriel cut him off.

Michael raised an eyebrow at her and took a breath to reply.

Gabriel cut him off a second time. "At least let us try this. It's better than imprisoning him for another two thousand years just to start this war over again."

"Are you finished?" Michael spoke as soon as Gabriel stopped talking.

"Fine, but if you are going to try to stop us, you better lock me in a cell for the duration of the war."

Michael closed his eyes and shook his head. "I was going to say it sounded like a solid plan and that we should start the preparations immediately. I agree with you, our last plan of imprisonment was not a solution. It was a stopgap to allow us to fight another day. That day has come. It's time to end this if we can."

Gabriel just stood there, her mouth slightly agape.

Ariel stepped forward. "Malach and I will take a rope. Ana and Daziar should take one as well. Soldiers should man the others leaving the Archangels to deliver the killing blows."

They all agreed, but Michael insisted on more soldiers on all the ropes just in case things didn't go as planned. They all got to work. Togan found a forge he could use and started fashioning the anchors and rings while the rest of them cleared the council room and found places where that archers could lie low until they lured the dragon in. The rest of the soldiers would be out in the open and would have to fend for themselves until they were needed. Michael and Gabriel agreed the Devil would pay the commons soldiers little notice focusing on the angels in the room. A horn sounded down at the wall. The enemy was attacking again.

Michael and Gabriel sprinted for the edge of the plateau. "Finish preparations. We will hold the devil at bay," Michael ordered as the two disappeared over the edge.

They redoubled their efforts. Malach and Ariel were able to work the fastest, driving the holes in the floor quickly with their superior strength. Ana and Daziar were a close second and the normal humans followed them. Another hour and they were ready for the anchors. It wasn't long and Togan arrived with the crudely forged metal. He was still handling them with gloved hands, and no one questioned his caution. Heat still radiated off the metal.

"Hot off the forge!" Togan shouted as if he was serving them breakfast instead of the implements for the devil's demise.

It didn't take them long to finish securing the rings down, and it was a good thing. Not a minute after the final anchor was placed, Amara spotted the two archangels speeding their way to the council room with the fearsome two-headed dragon hard on their heels.

She quickly prayed for them all and that the metal had cooled enough to not burn through the ropes.

Everyone scrambled to their places, tossing tools to the side and hefting weapons. Amara glanced around the group, knowing not all the faces she was looking at would survive this encounter. For the first time, she realized Togan only had a breastplate on, and his arms were bare. She took a moment to admire the rippling muscles on them as he shouldered his heavy war hammer. Marena caught her eye and smiled knowingly, winking at her. She felt heat on her cheeks and shook her head to clear her thoughts. She needed to be ready to fight.

Chapter 23

Fury and Oathbreaker had been left somewhere deep in the stronghold and had been in contact with the nephilim until he had been killed. Then Lord Azazel had contacted them. Oathbreaker informed him of Fury's insubordination and as Fury had predicted, he didn't care. This gave Fury an immense amount of satisfaction and he lorded it over Oathbreaker. After the first day of fighting, Azazel had let them know he was within the stronghold walls to retrieve them. They provided him with as much information about their location as they could, working together out of necessity. It wasn't long before the demon lord strode through the door. With everyone at the wall, there were no guards and no one this deep in the stronghold other than women and children.

Azazel picked Fury up first, then Oathbreaker. Both blades were changed to short swords and placed, one on each hip. *Now what madness and mayhem should we cause first?*

My Lord, if I may suggest, there are women and children gathered ready to leave when their wall and army fail. Fury informed him. *Many of those children would serve you well if molded by your hand.*

Fury, you presume I would need any assassins but my nephilim after this war is won. Azazel replied.

My Lord, I would never presume-

If I might suggest, Oathbreaker interjected. *If my Lord doesn't need assassins, maybe these children would serve you better as slaves and concubines?*

Hmmm, now that's an idea.

Azazel strode casually down the stronghold corridors, unchecked and unchallenged. He soon arrived at the door leading to the large, cavernous room the elderly and children had gathered in. He kicked it in, breaking the latch. The sudden violence cause Fury and Oathbreaker to feel satisfaction, while those in the room scrambled away in fear. Some were pushing children ahead of them, but all were moving toward the exit. Azazel leaped and, even though he was missing a wing, his remaining appendage aided his trajectory so that he landed ahead of the group.

Screams of terror filled the silence echoing off the ceiling and walls, along with the wails of the infants and children. A small group of elderly warriors armed with makeshift weapons gathered in front of him. Azazel brandished Fury and Oathbreaker and the weapons reveled in the blood the demon spilled as he carved his way through their meager defense.

Panic and pandemonium filled the space as the final warrior fell. Bodies ran in every direction, screams, whimpers, grunts, and cries combined in a cacophony of fear and desperation. Azazel caught a woman by her head and lifted her from the floor, plucking the small child from her arms as she screamed. He shoved her to the side, not caring what damage he did to her. The child was the prize here. The little girl would be old enough to wean from her mother's teat, but young enough she wouldn't remember this night and despise him.

A rock bounce off Azazel's head. Fury felt the sensation of warm blood flowing down his temples if it were his own, so in tuned with the demon as he was. Azazels' gazed fell on a girl standing not far away. Her stance loose and ready. She was a practiced fighter.

"Ciarán," Azazel smiled at the girl.

Fury didn't know who this girl was to the demon, but he seemed to know her well. And the name was the same name he had given that traitor Serilda. Was he trying to replace her? She *had* been his favorite.

"I've been looking for you, little one. Why don't you come back with me and we will finish your training?"

He set the small child back in the unconscious mother's arms and advanced on Ciarán.

She shook her head emphatically and bared her teeth. She set her feet and leveled a glaive from one of the fallen warriors. The haft had been broken, but it seemed to fit her better with the short handle. She wouldn't go willingly.

"Little one," Azazel cooed, "We were going to find a remedy for your speech problem. You just needed to complete that last mission."

Fury recognized that false promise for what it was. Azazel would string the girl along until he had something else to control her with. He would then break the bad news that her *ailment* couldn't be fixed. At which point she would be totally under his control. She would have done so many unspeakable things she would never be anything but a monster.

The girl saw through his ruse as well, shaking her head once again.

Azazel charged, stabbing at the girl with both blades. His speed was considerable, but she managed to slap the blades to the side and spin in close, spitting in his face. She then dropped, pulled a knife from her boot, and stabbed it into his foot. Azazel sprung back, taking the knife with him. He ground his teeth together in frustration as much as pain.

Azazel! Satan's mental shout pulled all three from the concentration of the girl. *Get up to the council room now!*

Sire, you will remember that I can't fly?

Figure it out or I will eat your offspring and then flay you alive and leave your body for the crows.

Azazel rolled his eyes. "Always so dramatic." Then to the girl. "It would seem I'm needed elsewhere. We will have to finish this dance later, my dear. Watch over your shoulder, for I will always be just behind you."

He strode past her, the rest of the humans scrambling out of the way. The girl never once took her eyes off Azazel. She never once let her guard down. Fury could respect that. She did not know he had been summoned by the one being you did *not* keep waiting. Azazel walked out of the room, giving off the air of indifference, not glancing in any direction, but Fury understood his senses were on high alert.

As soon as he was out of sight of the humans, his wound caused him to limp. The pain would be with him for a few days, and his boot squelched with each step from the blood seeping from around the blade. He reached down and pulled it free. She would pay for that insult when this war was ended. Fury hoped he would be the tool of her suffering.

Leviathan had been appraised on the plan to trap and kill the devil. She had joined Michael and Gabriel to lure the dragon in. He seemed to want to kill her all the more now that she had betrayed him *and* survived his assault. She should be able to goad him into the trap easily enough. She spotted the Devil flying over the battlefield and the three angels angled toward him as one. As they got closer, she almost cursed, old habits die hard. Asmodeus flew with him. She knew she would be the one to face him, but every fiber of her being didn't want to. In fact, she had hoped he would be killed by some other angel so she would be spared the deed.

As they drew close, the dragon angled toward them, maws opening, and spewing fire forth. He was too far away for the flame to reach them, but the heat burned the cold air around them none the less. They banked and beat their wings hard to regain their speed. Despite the bulk of the dragon, they were fast.

Asmodeus was faster.

The blow hit leviathan directly between her wings. The impact folding them and causing her to plummet toward the army below. They had assumed the devil would want her over the other two since they had only imprisoned them. It would seem Asmodeus had arranged for something different.

She righted herself in the air with and swipe of her wings and started after Michael and Gabriel, but Asmodeus cut her off. The two heads of the dragon snapped at the two angels and none of them, friend or foe, glanced their direction. It was just her and Asmodeus.

"Brother," She turned to him. "I will give you one final chance to turn from you wicked ways. Join the God who created you, who created us!"

Asmodeus' mouth twisted in disgust. "I told you we would be enemies when next we meet. Defend yourself or die sister."

A spear grew as if from air in his hand and he plunged it down toward her. She batted it away with her sword. Understandably, the angels hadn't trusted her with an angel blade, but Asmodeus had no such problems in procuring one of the sentient blades, no doubt one who had swapped sides. She tried to get a better look at it, but she couldn't recognize which it was while defending herself.

She batted away thrust after thrust of the spear with her sword waiting for her chance to close the gap between them. She seized the haft of the spear as it hummed between her side and arm, drawing first blood on both. Curse this clumsy body of hers. For the first time since her redemption, she missed her serpentine body. Her speed in the water and razor-sharp teeth would have made short work of Asmodeus.

She pulled on the spear bringing him in and plunged her sword toward his chest. In the blink of an eye the half of the spear changed to the curved edge of the sword again drawing blood, this time from her hand.

Asmodeus' forehead slammed into her nose, and she tumbled backward. Her nose was bloodied and most likely broken. Tears blurred her vision, but she knew on instinct Asmodeus wouldn't let up for her to recover so she struck out blindly. Her sword connected with his and she felt its weight disappear.

She fled.

So disoriented was she that she didn't know which way she was flying but she needed space between them. She dropped the hilt of her ruined blade and wiped her eyes to clear her vision. She had lost this fight and if she wished to live, she had to get away from Asmodeus. Regroup and re-arm herself.

To her shock he wasn't following her. As she took stock of her surroundings, she spotted the devil retreating and Asmodeus followed. He had her dead to rights, but he chose to leave her. A death pulse hit her, and she faltered in the air. Someone was dead. It was one of the few she had felt from this close to the source. She had been flying mostly away from the stronghold and she banked to correct her course. She might still be needed.

Malach watched from the side of the opening as the angels led the devil into the trap. He heaved a sigh as he prepared once again to do what everyone said was impossible. It seemed like the more he tried to end the fighting, the more he was targeted or looked to for salvation. Even Michael and Gabriel looked at him as if he was going to be the one to end things once and for all. That didn't seem fair to him. After all, how many years had Michael and Gabriel fought against the demons? For as powerful as they were, they were unable to end the war, to end the Devil. How was he supposed to do it?

At least the pain in his back had subsided. It must have truly been caused by the long periods of time his muscles had locked up. However, now his armor felt a couple sizes too small, and he couldn't understand why. Nothing had changed over the last few days, and he hadn't tightened the leather straps. Although, he hadn't taken the armor off in the past few days, either. Not even when he had slept. Maybe the feeling of it being tighter was all in his head? An effect of wearing it so long?

He brought his thoughts back to the present as Michael and Gabriel shot past him, landing hard and sliding to a halt. The two-headed dragon landed harder than the angels, shattering stone and shaking the entire mountain. Malach felt like a bug compared to the behemoth. Its legs were larger than many of the great trees near his mountain cottage. He's legs froze, rooting him in place.

Malach, I can't do anything to help you with this one. Reckoning said. *You will need to manage this on your own.*

Malach worked through his grounding techniques as one of the dragon's head turned their slitted eyes on him. He closed his eyes and worked on his breathing, feeling the stone beneath his feet. The stone shook. He worked to keep his breath under control. He tried to focus on the sound of the wind outside. A low growl cut through the air, shattering the calm Malach was just starting to feel. The stone shook again. Malach could feel the panic rising, but instead of pushing it down, he made the decision to feel it and breathe through it. He opened his eyes in time to see the claw headed his direction.

He jumped back, breaking his paralysis and dodging just in time.

Several men ran forward, but the dragon swatted them away with his tail as if they were just an afterthought. "You are God's chosen?" The two heads gazed down at Malach from either side, sizing him up. "You, a meager human, are to destroy me? Your paltry existence will be snuffed from the earth with as infinitesimal thought as you smash a bug."

Malach didn't know how to respond. "You've heard of me?" He immediately regretted his words.

Both heads of the behemoth bellowed laughter buffeting him with their foul, moist breath. "We had been told you were God's chosen."

"We were told you had killed many of our lesser demons and led the only successful raid on our castle."

"We were told you were a warrior."

"To find you at the insect that stands before us now only shows how far our captains have fallen in our absence."

"You, who will soon be only a scrape of flesh caught in our teeth, you are the one God calls to kill us."

Malach interjected. "I have killed many of your demons-"

The dragon's claw shot out and sent Malach across the room. "You're not worthy enough to let speak in our presence."

Togan and Ariel ran forward to help. Ariel raised Storm and caught the next swipe of the enormous claw. He dug in as best he could, but the force of the blow still sent him flying. However, he slowed the claw down enough for Togan to bring his hammer down on the talons, shattering the first two at the base.

Both heads of the dragon roared in pain.

Malach regained his feet, gasping for air, but pressed forward anyway.

The devil twisted, battering its shoulder against one of the walls to bring its tail to bear. Malach and Ariel dropped to the ground, but Togan was off balanced from his heavy strike and the tail caught him in the chest. One of the tail spikes sunk in deep before lifting him off his feet and throwing him across the room. He slammed against a wall close to the opening and flopped to the floor. Malach wanted to run to him, but Ariel was already picking him up off the ground by his armor and carrying him in the opposite direction. A claw split the stone where they had been only moments before, obscuring Malach's view of Togan.

Malach got his feet under him and matched his father's pace. The dragon crashed after them, claws scraping on stone. He didn't dare look back. They just angered, arguably the most powerful being on the planet, and now it was intent on killing them. He had to trust the others would execute their part of the plan and save them from whatever gruesome machinations the dragon now held for them.

The first arrow flew from Marena's bow. Instead of sailing over the dragon as planned, the arrow streaked its way toward the closest head. It struck its eye, sinking in almost to the fletching. Malach wondered how it hadn't killed it. Marena and the soldiers with her grabbed the rope and pulled. Malach shuddered at the wet sucking noise the arrow made as it slid free, but it was quickly drowned out by the bellow of pain from the head that had been struck. More arrows flew. All aimed well over the dragon, carrying their payload to the other side, where men and angels alike grasped the ropes. They were threaded through the metal loops and, simultaneously, all were pulled taught.

The dragon roared in protest and kept its feet under it despite their advantage of surprise. Malach and Ariel ran to lend their strength to the rope Marena had retrieved and fired a second time. They pulled and brought the heads crashing down. The front legs buckled, bringing the front of the dragon to its knees, but the back half continued to struggle.

"We need more men!" Gabriel shouted from her position near the back.

"We have none to spare." Michael replied through gritted teeth as his muscles bulged with the strain of keeping the dragon on its knees.

Malach caught movement from the direction of the opening. He turned as much attention as he dared in that direction, fearing the worst. A strange sight met Malach's eyes. A demon beat its wings furiously, working with all its might to keep himself and the one who dangled below him in the air. The one being carried had only one wing protruding from behind him, but Malach recognized him instantly.

Azazel.

He dropped from the demon's grasp, landing on the edge of the platform, and rolled with practiced ease. As Azazel drew himself up to his full height, Malach noted his boot was leaking blood. He drew not one, but two blades. Malach would know those two anywhere in any form they took. Fury and Oathbreaker had been liberated.

They couldn't spare anyone on the ropes to stop this new threat, but neither could they safely ignore it. The Lord of Hell strode forward casually, as if the trapped dragon was an everyday encounter. He grinned at those straining on the ropes until his gaze found Amara. His grin turned to a smirk.

"Little thief," He cooed. "Good to see you once again. I see you have done your job well. You will be rewarded."

A stab of fear and pain shot through Malach. Had he been betrayed once again? Amara's response only moments later put his mind at ease.

"Go back to hell, snake," Amara spat in his general direction.

Azazel made a 'tsk tsk,' noise. "One day very soon you will beg to be in my employ, and on that day, I will show you no mercy."

Azazel's hand shot out, losing a knife. However, instead of striking out at any person, the knife cleanly cut one of ropes holding the dragon in place. Those holding the rope collapsed with the sudden release of tension. The dragon clawed its way to its feet, dragging any who refused to release the ropes along with him. He shook himself free of those as well, sending men flying. More than one man met his fate off the side of the cliff, but most skidded to a stop on the floor or hit a wall.

Azazel laughed. "Amara, come, let's see what God's newest Blade Bearer can do."

A hammer crunched into the side of Azazel's knee. "Amara!" Togan bellowed from the ground where he had mounted his assault. "Kill this snake before he can slither away."

To Azazel's credit, he didn't make a noise. He took the pain in stride and was able to shift his weight quick enough to his right leg before he collapsed. He turned and laid Togan out with a single punch. The dragon turned to look at what was unfolding behind him, and Malach spotted his chance.

He sprinted forward, changing Reckoning into a large ax. He brought the weapon down with every ounce of strength he could muster and landed his blow directly in the middle of the serpentine neck of the right head. The impact rattled his teeth. The dragon writhed and the left head reacted. It snapped out as quick as a viper and snatched Malach, picking him up and hurtling him away. It was several moments of freefall before Malach realized he was no longer in the council room. Instead, he was careening toward the battlefield below.

"No!"

Amara heard herself shout as if she wasn't the one screaming at the sight of the man she loved being tossed off a cliff. She ran forward toward the edge, not having the slightest clue of what she would do when she got there.

A sword cut a shallow furrow across the back of her shoulder, separating the armor and her skin as if it was warm butter on a hot day. She spun out of instinct, batting the sword away from her with her vambrace. She noticed Ariel disappear over the edge of the landing. What was he thinking? He had no wings. How would he do Malach any good?

Azazel stood with all his weight on his good knee. Togan lay not far from him, unconscious, but breathing for now. Blood seeped from his wound. He wouldn't last long without a healer.

Azazel stepped forward, wincing as his knee barely held his weight. Did he plan to fight her? His one wing unfurled, helping him balance, and he sheathed one sword. "Little thief," He smiled at her. "Little traitor. How have you made it back here? I thought you were finished with the war once you took your father away. Now I find you here fighting alongside my enemies."

She pulled her blades and readied herself for anything Keeping one eye on the battle with the dragon. "I only worked for you because you had something precious to me. They understood and have forgiven me."

"More than that, I see."

The Dragon roared, spewing flames at Gabriel as she flew past and drawing their attention.

"God has forgiven me and given me purpose again." Amara turned back to Azazel. She realized something and smiled back at him. "Now, enough stalling. I have a wrong to right, and I plan to do that by killing you."

Simply put, she was wrong. Azazel wasn't stalling. He leapt toward her, using his good leg and wing to propel himself. She parried the thrust of his sword and spun, using her shoulder to deflect his body. He landed on his good leg and free hand. Apparently, he wasn't as helpless with only one leg as she had thought. This would still be a tough fight.

Daziar had seen Malach get tossed over the edge, but there wasn't much he could do about it now. Malach had also shattered a large swath of the armored scales on the side of the head he had struck. Daziar thought that head was Satan, but it was hard to keep the two apart. Of course, no real damage had been done yet, but it gave them a strike point. Marena was making her way around the dragon toward Togan, and Daziar spotted Amara engaging with Azazel.

He glanced over at Ana. "You go high, I'll go low. Aim for the place where Malach struck."

Ana nodded, and they entered the fray. Daziar immediately took a blow from one of the dragon's claws and before he knew it, he was on his back, sliding across the stone floor. Ana reached him and pulled him to his feet.

"Watch the pattern of battle." She admonished. "It will give you a clue as to where the next strike will come and give you a better chance of not becoming the next stain on the wall."

He grunted an affirmative, and they charged again.

This time, he ducked under the swipe of a massive claw, drawing the attention of Satan. He slid under the bulk of the giant beast but continued his momentum back to his feet, hot breath prickled at the back of his neck. He spun, striking out with Dawn. His sword connected with one of the long, fang-like teeth and shattered it, making its whole head turn and recoil. As the neck uncurled back through its legs, Ana brought her spear down on the weak point of its neck.

Daziar kept moving until he was out of range of the dragon's thrashing, before turning around. Ana still had her spear in hand and was still backpedaling, dodging attacks from the angered beast. Daziar turned and, taking a running start, ran up the dragon's leg, vaulting off it. He raked Dawn across the dragon's wings. It cut the membrane easy enough but bounced off the bones that ribbed the wings. The wings unfurled directly into Daziar's face. When in flight they appeared delicate, but the impact tossed Daziar off the dragon's back. It turned and charged toward him.

Daziar scrabbled out of the way. One of the enormous feet missed him by only inches, but at least he wasn't trampled. He recovered just in time to watch the back half of the dragon drop out of sight over the edge of the cliff. Michael, Gabriel, and a couple other angels jumped after it, but the fight was now out of his hands.

Ana ran up to him. "Are you ok?"

"I'm going to feel that one in the morning, but otherwise, I'm fine." He stood, allowing her to help him up, blood leaking from his nose. He wiped at it and searched the area. Amara and Azazel were nowhere in sight and Malach and Ariel had fallen off the cliff.

Ana must have seen the panic set in. "Let's go find out what happened and see if we can help."

He nodded, and they ran for the stairs.

Azazel was winning. Amara had no delusions about that. Even with his handicaps, he had maneuvered her away from the main fighting and into the confines of the stronghold's halls and corridors. Here, he didn't have to pivot and turn as much to keep her at bay. He masterfully parried and blocked any attacks she threw at him and turned her attacks back on her. She continued to give ground to stay alive. The demon blade aided his speed and skill, but Amara had a feeling he wouldn't necessarily need them. All she could do was continue to stay alive and hope someone would reach her before Azazel killed her.

The noise of the battle with the dragon receded the farther they moved away from it. She blocked and parried, somehow able to keep ahead of Azazel's blade. Fury came across and she reached up to block it, only realizing at the last moment the blade wasn't aimed at her, but at her blade. She pulled her block but managed to keep a hold of the blade as Azazel batted it away and reversed his attack. She pulled her other blade up to block and he batted that one away, leaving her completely exposed. His boot came forward and caught her in the chest, taking her off her feet and causing her injured ribs to scream in agony. The wall at an intersection of two corridors arrested her momentum suddenly. She almost blacked out. As she came back to her senses, she had to duck a thrust that would have taken her through her neck.

Instead, Azazel drove his sword into the stone, the metal screeching in her ears. Her reflexes pulled her hand up to cover her ears, but she caught herself and redirecting her left hand. She drove Blaze into his thigh up to the hilt. Simultaneously, she plunged Ember up into his gut.

Their eyes met. Both were equally surprised. Then Azazel crumpled and both her blades slid free, just as both the demon's blades slid from his grip. Amara knelt there for a second, unsure of what to do next.

"You know, little thief." Azazel smiled at her. "You-"

But he never got to finish his final words. Amara rammed both blades into his withered heart. She didn't want to hear what lies he had to say. She had a feeling they would only bring her pain.

The death pulse hit her like the shock wave of one of the explosives. She fell back, leaving both Blaze and Ember in the dead demon's chest. She had done it. He was dead, and she was free of him forever. He had haunted her ever since she left Caister, and he was dead.

Relief flooded her, and she sighed, resting her back against the wall.

A small form ran around the corner and stopped at the sight laying before her. The little girl she had found in Brightwood stood there, staring at the demon on the ground. Tears formed in her eyes.

Amara stood and ran over and pulling her into a hug. "It's ok, don't look. He was a monster."

The little girl pulled free of her, and Amara expected her to be afraid of the demon, or of Amara herself. Instead, she pulled a blade of her own and rushed the demon's body, plunging the blade again and again into the corpse. Amara rushed and pulled her away. Tears spilled from her eyes, and this time she buried her head in Amara's shoulder.

"You're ok, I'm here and he's gone. I'm not sure what he's done to you, but he's gone now. You and I can pick up the pieces now. Together." Amara hugged her tighter.

Umm, I know you two are having a moment, but would you mind pulling us out of this monster? Ember asked.

"Oh!" Amara gently extricated herself from the girl and pulled her blades from the demon's chest. She cleaned them and slid them into their sheaths. "I can't believe it's over." She said out loud, staring down at the very dead Lord of hell.

Daziar and Ana came running up to her. Daziar whistled low and long. "Well, you took care of him."

"Well done, Amara. Many have tried to kill this beast, and you suc-ceeded where others failed." Ana grinned.

"Dumb luck really." Amara shrugged it still felt very surreal. "What about the dragon?" She pulled the girl close to her again.

"Escaped," Ana replied. "But not before Malach gave us an opening on one of the necks. I used that to injure him, but he fled, the coward. Mi-chael and Gabriel took those who could still fly to chase him down, but any surviving demon will come to his aid, and I doubt we will get another chance as we did."

"What about Malach and Ariel?" Amara asked at the mention of his name. "I saw him fall."

"We haven't heard anything about him." Daziar spoke up. "We were working our way down the stronghold to find out what happened to him and Ariel."

"What are we waiting for, then?" Amara asked.

Without another word, they set off for the bottom of the stronghold. It didn't take them as long as the climb up and they soon exited into the main courtyard. There was a crowd not far off circling around something, and Amara feared the worst. Nothing else mattered at this point. She ran forward, pushing, shouldering, clawing her way through the crowd.

She burst through the leading edge of the circle to find two bodies in a heap, black feathery wings wrapped around them.

Chapter 24

Malach flew through the air, over the edge of the council room and out into the open space. Gravity took effect, and movement changed from flying to falling. There was nothing he could do but pray an angel would catch him, but most of them were either engaged with the devil or too injured to fly. He resigned himself to a sudden end when he hit the ground. At least it would be quick. He never thought this was how it would end.

Pain radiated through his back. The dragon's teeth must have pierced his armor and cut into him. Insult to injury. At least reckoning would survive. He hoped the opening he had made on the dragon's neck was enough to make a difference.

Something hit him from behind. He craned his neck to see what was happening.

"Son!" His father's voice shouted over the rushing wind. "I'm here!"

Malach twisted to face his father, but the joy at seeing him quickly turned to fear and dread. "Why? You don't have wings."

"I won't leave you to face danger alone ever again."

"'Ever' doesn't seem like it will be a very long time."

Pain shot through his back again. Had he hit something in the air? Whatever it was, had stuck into his back and caused them to drag, slowing their descent nominally. They spun until Malach was now facing the ground.

Ariel's eyes went wide.

"I know something hit me, but that's the least of our worries right now." Malach grimaced as the wind tugged on whatever it was in his back.

Pain stabbed at him again on the other side of his back, causing them to slow even more. Malach's eyes grew wide now as well. Something hadn't *hit* him. Something had come *out* of him. He turned, trying to get a glimpse of what it was.

"You have wings!" Ariel shouted with glee.

"What? How?" Malach turned even more, causing them to spin and drop faster. "That doesn't matter now. How do I use them?"

"Umm, you... well, you... just open them up and use them." Ariel replied, shrugging.

"Really? You've had wings for thousands of years and you can't tell me how to use them?"

"No, I guess not," Ariel gave him a half grin. "Angels were created with wings and could use them immediate-"

"Fascinating, but we don't have time to get too far into the history of the angels' creation." Malach rolled his eyes. "The ground is approaching rapidly, and I need to figure this out."

"I just-"

"Shut up." Malach warned.

He consciously thought about the wings, feeling a little like he was going insane. Their connection to his bones was there, the strain was there. The pain was a bit of a sting and a burn. It must have been the tearing of his skin as they burst forth. He mentally followed the sensation of feeling up the bones of the wings and felt the wind through each individual feather, much like the sensation of the wind through his hair. He opened the wing and jolted up.

He opened his eyes, beaming from ear to ear. His father wasn't in front of him anymore and it took a couple moments to realize his father had slipped from his grasp. He folded the wings, *his* wings, that was going to take some getting used to, and dove toward his father, grabbing ahold of him and lifting with his whole body. They hit the ground with an impact hard enough to break bones. Luckily for Malach, Ariel took most of the impact.

They rolled a little way in a mass of tangled limbs and wings. Finally coming to rest somewhere in the courtyard in the shadow of the stronghold. Soldiers quickly surrounded them, but none dared to come too close. Ariel seemed unconscious but breathing, and Malach was relatively unscathed but drained of any energy or motivation to get up. He glanced up and caught sight of the dragon leaping from the council chamber. The beast spreading his wings and flew off toward the open field. He notably still had both of his heads, which meant they hadn't been able to take advantage of the opening Malach had given them.

He sent a prayer up for his friends' safety and then closed his eyes to rest. The next thing he remembered was waking up to Amara, crying over him. He reached up to comfort her and to assure her he was still alive.

"You have wings!" She pulled back a little. "Real wings!"

"Good to see you too," Malach grinned. "No, no, I'm fine. How are you?"

Amara slapped his breastplate. "You know what I mean, you half-wit. You're alive!"

The healers took him and his father to the same tent that Skie inhabited. She lifted her head to watch them carry him in on a stretcher even though he had insisted it wasn't necessary. They set him down next to the big wolf and she gave him a lick before searching him for injury. She stopped short when she noticed the wings coming from under him and sniffed them for an extended period.

"I'm fine, Skie." Malach assured her. "Although, yes, I have a couple of new appendages."

She pulled back and tilted her head slightly.

"I'll tell you everything shortly." He ruffled her ears. "You seem to be doing much better since I left you."

"Yes, she is." The healer from before came by. "Have you ever tried to keep a hundred-and-fifty-pound wolf off her feet when she doesn't want to?"

Malach chuckled. "Actually, you could say that's how we met. Thank you for taking care of her. I feel like we didn't get off to the best of starts. I'm Malach."

"What? You mean to don't kidnap and threaten all the people you first meet? I'm touched."

Malach gave him a withering look.

"Fine, my name is Silas. I'm going to be taking care of you and your father for the time being. Where do you hurt the worst?"

"What hurts the worst and what is the worst injury aren't one and the same." Malach turned to show him his back. "I think we ought to start with these."

"Woah!" Silas took a step back. "I know I've been working pretty hard, but you didn't have these last time we saw each other, right?"

Malach chuckled. "No, it seems I grew them during our descent from the council chamber."

"That was you two?" Silas asked, wide eyed. "I heard it was two angels."

"I can see where they got that from, but I'm just half angel." Malach replied. "Now, they burn like fire around the base. Can you help?"

Silas moved closer and started carefully poking around at the base of Malach's new appendages. It was a bit surreal thinking about the wings as his, even though they were attached to his back. How had this happened? Would this have always happened because of his birthright, or had it been brought on by something else? He would have to talk with his father about this when he had the chance.

"I'm going to have to cut your shirt off. We should be able to get your armor off without any issues, though." Silas said and started to cut off his shirt carefully, fully exposing Malach's back. "This is extraordinary! Your wings seem to have pushed through your skin and clothes fully formed, although a bit smaller than I think they will become when compared to the size of Angel's wings. Have you been having pain in your back?" But he didn't give Malach a chance to speak. "You had to have been. To have these growing under your skin and pushing their way to the surface. I would imagine it would hurt pretty bad. Oh, the reason for the burning is your skin, although not bleeding, has still been stretched around the base of the wings. There is quite a bit of pressure from the swelling right now, which probably stopped the bleeding. Although, you might still have some bleeding as the swelling goes down, but we will bandage it just in case and put a salve on there to make sure everything stays clean."

Malach took his chance to get a word in edge wise before Silas started rambling again. The healer was obviously excited about this. "You said they are small compared to angel's wings. Do you think I will be able to fly right away?" Then thought, *As soon as I learn how, that is.*

"Oh, I'm really not sure." Silas scratched his head. "I mean, I'm not an expert on angels' wings by any means. I just know the sizes I've seen in the past. If you are able to fly immediately, I would think long distances or a large amount of extra weight might be a problem, though."

Every touch or brush of the healer's hands burned as if Malach's back was on fire. Malach didn't have much choice be to grit his teeth and bear the pain as best as he could until the healer finished bandaging his back. The salve Silas applied was the only relief he received during the entire process, and that only stayed the pain for a few moments. The burning returned quickly until it was back to full force.

"I'm done," Silas declared.

Malach sighed with relief.

"I'll be back to check on you in a few hours."

But Malach barely registered the comment. He was looking forward to sleep. He consciously worked to fold his new wings down behind his back. Managing to get one completely folded, he started working on the other, but it just didn't want to cooperate. Finally, he was able to retract it all the way down. However, when he checked on the first, it was now half extended.

"Ugh!" Malach rubbed his face with his hands.

"You'll figure them out and they will become second nature to you." Ariel spoke from his cot. "It will be just like your arm or your leg. You don't have to think, at least most of the time, about walking. We need to work on your control and practice your flying. Especially your landings. *They* need a lot of work."

"Hey," Malach grinned. "We're alive, aren't we?"

"Yes, because you landed on me." Ariel held his back as if he was in pain.

"I knew you could handle it, old man." Malach chuckled. "And look, we both came out of this without any major injuries."

Ariel chuckled as well. "Yes, yes, we did. And you dealt a major blow to the dragon as well."

"Ha!" Malach barked a laugh. "I barely drew blood."

"Malach, what you did, no one else has been able to do since Satan and Lucifer transformed into that abomination. You have no idea the opening you have given us to defeat him once and for all. We have hypothesized if one head is killed, the other would lose much of its power. Some have even wondered if it would eventually kill the other head or if it would affect the body in other ways. However it happens, it would be more than anyone has done since the fall from heaven. It would be a monumental win."

"We will see," Malach replied. "It might not help us at all. If it's really that monumental of a feat, he's going to be more careful from here out. We might not get another shot at him."

"Let's see what Michael and Gabriel have to say before we get too far into this. We need to get a game plan together."

Malach rested his head against one of the posts holding up the tent and sighed. "I'm so tired of planning everything out. I just want this to be over."

"I know son, I feel the same way."

Amara rammed her dagger into the eye slot of her latest enemy. Before their body hit the field, she was onto the next soldier. For three days since she killed Azazel, it had been nothing but fight, sleep, and try to get some food before fighting again. No one had seen the dragon, and none of the demons had come out to fight. That was good and bad. It freed the angels to help with the defense of the stronghold, but it also meant when the demons joined the fray, they would be fresh while the angels would be all but spent.

Another soldier dropped dead at her feet. She didn't even know how she had killed him. Fighting, killing, had become automatic for her. Fatigue didn't matter. The burn in her muscles didn't matter. Stinging pain from the mirid of small cuts she had sustained didn't matter. Only the next fight. The next kill. She was only acting and reacting, letting her instincts and muscle memory preserve her life.

Amara rolled out of the way of a spear thrust just in time to not get impaled and grabbed the haft to pull the soldier in close. Ariel landed on the unwitting man, crushing his chest before laying waste to two more soldiers with his axe. She just about fell over in shock at his sudden appearance. She watched Malach soar overhead on his newly grown wings. He took to his flight training with ease and was now skilled enough to fly with the extra weight of a person. He and Ariel watched where they would be needed most, and Malach would drop his father at strategic points to help push back the enemy. As she watched him turn to double back, one of his wings got off beat and he dropped a few feet before regaining his rhythm. He still had a long way to go before he was comfortable with them.

She returned to the battle, stabbing, parrying, dodging, and inevitably killing. She had at one point taken time out of the daily grind to go check on Togan. He had saved her life when he crushed Azazel's knee. She would have never survived without the demon losing his advantage somehow.

Togan's wounds were worse than they had initially appeared in the council room. He had multiple puncture wounds across his upper chest and his left arm was shredded. So shredded, the healers had to take the limb to give him a chance to survive. When she had been able to check on him a day and a half prior, he had still been unconscious. Marena couldn't be spared to stay with him as their numbers dwindled. They needed every body they had to hold the breach. And they had held it...for a time. It had cost them dearly in numbers, but they had made the enemy pay for even inch into the stronghold wall. The builders were able to erect fortifications, and the healers were able to move the wounded out of harm's way. Now they fought within the walls and with the disappearance of the bulk of the demons, they still had a chance at victory, however slim.

A roar shook Amara to her core and the little hope she felt left instantly. The field grew all but motionless for only a few moments as all eyes turned to the sky to see what would happen. Angels took flight from the council room and other high balconies, Malach slightly behind the group. Amara couldn't see, but it seemed to her they'd just lost their advantage.

Malach soared over the courtyard turned battlefield. All but one entrances to the stronghold proper had been collapsed before the enemy had broken through the defense at the wall. This gave them only one point to defend. It also meant if any of their forces were routed, they would be cut off from any escape and put to the sword. Which was why Ariel had commissioned his new wings. Ariel was a brilliant tactician. He understood the movements well before Malach could even notice there was a difference. He would then direct Malach where to drop him, and they would push the enemy back in that area before repeating the process. It didn't take the other angels long to follow his example. It seemed; however, Ariel almost always spotted the problem areas before the rest of them.

From the air, their numbers looked depressingly small compared to the press of soldiers pouring in from outside the wall. They had lost. They would take a good number with them, but there was no scenario Malach could think of where they won. The demons knew it as well. They had pulled back and let the grunts wear them down. He was sure once they had whittled away at their numbers enough, they would attack in force, overwhelming and routing them.

Malach lost his coordination between his wings for a moment and his heart leapt into his throat. He quickly regained his altitude. Every time that happened, his brain shouted warnings of imminent death. He wondered how long it would take him to get used to his new wings. Reckoning was able to fend off the freeze response for those moments while he regained control over his flight.

Dusk was falling, and torches were being lit on both sides. It seemed the fight would go well into the night. The enemy wouldn't retreat at this point. They wouldn't lose their hard-won ground. Malach doubted they would see the next morning.

He circled around and caught sight of Raphael. She was beckoning him in to land on one of the high balconies. He hadn't realized how many of those stuck out from the stronghold. He had only ever thought of the council chamber balcony, but there were many more than that. Maybe a hundred or more. He landed, albeit a bit awkwardly, next to her.

"I have new toys!" She beamed at him, holding up a spike in one hand and an explosive in the other.

How can she be so happy at a time such as this? Malach thought. *Does she know the odds against us? Has she stuck her head outside of her workshop lately?*

"A spike is hardly new." Malach raised a brow at her. She and the other angels had treated him differently since his wings had emerged. More like they did each other. He hated it. It felt two-faced to him.

"This spike has a payload with it."

"What's a payload?" Malach asked.

"I, well, never mind," Raphael shook her head and sighed. "No one understands an inventor." She mumbled. Then louder. "This spike has an explosive set in the cone with an ignition system-built in."

Malach gave her a blank look.

"After stabby stabby, press button, enemy go boom." Raphael rolled her eyes.

Ok, maybe they don't treat me that *much differently.* Malach thought, giving Raphael a withering look.

"Can we mount these to spears and distribute them to those at the fortifications?"

"No one is ever happy," Raphael sighed. "That is being worked on right now, but I doubt that will happen before the war is over, one way or the other."

Malach nodded. "And your other weapon?"

"A similar idea to the bombs dropped from the sky, but this one has its own ignition system with it, so when it hits anything, it will detonate. It doesn't work one hundred percent of the time, so don't rely on it too heavily, but it's worth it to drop a few." She held up a satchel filled to bursting with the two new weapons. "One time use each, obviously."

Malach took the satchel and thanked her even as she turned away from him to flag down the next angel. Malach knew already where the bombs would work well. There were legions pressed into a small area just inside the wall. These would wreak havoc there.

Eye's on the horizon, Malach. Reckoning warned before Malach could take to the sky.

Malach snapped his eye to the horizon and spotted the line of demons coming toward them. His muscles locked up on him. *Let it come.* He calmed his mind and took a few moments to ground himself before opening his eyes to take stock of the situation. What stood out the most in the group flying toward them was the dragon's absence. Malach spread his wings and prepared himself for the flight. He still had to mentally run through the steps to take off and fly. Although, starting from a high point was much easier than from the ground. He stepped onto the low wall around the balcony and leapt into open space. Instincts fighting him at every step. He was already behind the main group of angels because of his pause, and he needed to catch up.

Below him, the encroaching army pressed into the breach and Malach couldn't help but drop a couple of the new explosives, almost as an afterthought.

He didn't get to watch and enjoy the explosions, however. He glanced up and notice the demons were much closer than they had been and he focused his mind on their assault. Reckoning and one of the explosive spikes in hand, he headed directly toward the line of demons. The angels collided with the front line of demons, but they were obviously out-numbered. How had they managed to keep their numbers up? Malach arrived in time to hit the second wave of demons. Engaging with one who looked more or less like the rest of them.

Other than the Seven Lords, how did demons tell each other apart? The thought popped into Malach's head unbidden, and he push that line of thinking down before it could take hold. He had to concentrate on the fight.

He batted the demon's sword away and taking a glancing blow from its claws. The claw left a small furrow in his breastplate and pushed him back in the air. Fighting in the air was very different from fighting on the ground. On the ground, it was all about footing and balance. Up here, it was about anticipation, strength, and finesse. He had to anticipate not only where the attack was coming from but how hard it would hit him.

Then he would counter that strike with a harder beat of his wings to make sure he didn't go tumbling through the air. He also had to know how he was going to block it. If he deflected the attack, it would take a different amount of strength and angle in his wing beat. He deflected another attack and rammed the spike up under the demon's armor. The demon punched him in the chest, denting his breast plate and sending him tumbling through the air before he could hit the ignition point. He righted himself as quickly as he could, but it was almost too late. The spike he had driven into the demon was plunging toward his eye. By reflex he brought Reckoning up and over, taking the demon's hand off at the wrist. The hand still holding the spike fell from view. Malach pulled a second spike from the bag and rammed it home into the demon's neck and slammed the ignition button. He pushed the demon off him and controlled his fall. Seconds later, the explosion ripped the demon apart, sending pieces in all directions. What was left of the thing plunged down toward the ground with force.

Malach didn't have time to take in the complete horror of what had just happened. Instead, he was forced to defend himself against the next demon. This one didn't make it near as easy as the first, but Malach had dispatched it not long after that, but the constant flying had taken its toll on him. He needed to land.

He was halfway back to the stronghold when the dragon roared. Craning his neck up, Scales filled his vison as clawed talons reached out to grab him. He folded his wings and dropped, angling away from the stronghold. There was no way he could outrun that monster, but he needed to stay out of its reach long enough to have some support from the other angels.

He must have circled around and come from behind the stronghold. Malach thought to Reckoning.

Help is on the way Malach, Reckoning replied, not commenting on Malach's postulation.

Good, I'm running out of steam-

Fire hit him from behind, pushing him down and singeing the feathers on his wings. He folded them instinctively and rolled right. He fell through the fire and back into the blessedly cold air. Unfurling his wings again, he worked to level out, but floundered and continued to drop, which ended up saving his life. A dragon claw narrowly missed him, and he folded his wings once again. He opened them but kept his momentum, pulling up his arch and spinning his head wildly to catch sight of the dragon. The claw hit him as he rolled and it closed around him, pressing in on him from all sides painfully.

"I'll kill you for ruining my scales." The dragon roared over the wind.

Malach struggled to get free of the claw, pushing and flexing his body. It was no use. He was stuck fast.

Explosives Malach, Reckoning said calmly. *You need to get free before you freeze up again.*

Malach did just that. He reached for the satchel at his side but couldn't get to it. He stabbed down with Reckoning but barely scratched the hard scale on the dragon's claw. With Reckoning in the form of the staff weapon, he couldn't get the correct angle to effectively do any damage. He changed him to a dagger and rammed the blade home. This time, he *did* some damage. He felt the claw twitch, and he slipped a little. With just that little extra reach, he could once again reach the satchel. He fumbled with the top strap, his fingers shaking from the cold as much as the rush of battle. He managed to open the satchel. To his horror, he felt the explosives slip past his hand. His heart jumped, and he grabbed at anything he could, juggling one of the spikes before it, too, slipped through his grasp and into open air. A series of minor explosions retorted from the ground below.

Malach had few options left to him, so he started stabbing anything he could reach and soon blood slicked the claws that held him. He pushed and contorted his body and got his second hand and wing free. Now he could use both hands and his wings to leverage his escape. He pushed with all his might, beating his wings hard until finally he popped free of the dragon's claw. He was so surprised that he almost forgot to escape. Letting go, he plummeted toward the ground. Beating his wings to right himself, he took stock of his surroundings. They had flown out across the battlefield and were close to one of the forested mountain ranges. He beat his wings furiously, heading straight toward the tree line. If he could make it there, he had a chance to survive.

Malach's wings burned from the strain, but he didn't dare let up. He didn't dare look behind him. The dragon was surely there, and any chance Malach gave him could be his last moment of life. He didn't slow his breakneck pace until after he had passed into the forest. He had to weave between the trees and he was liable to kill himself on a tree if he didn't slow. The dragon's roar reverberated through his chest and the sound of cracking timber was awful. He chanced a glance behind him and regretted it. The dragon rampaged through the trees, parting them like water and snapping the timbers like saplings.

Tree limbs reached out and grabbed at Malach, but he didn't slow down any more than was required. The dragon finally got tired of destroying the forest and took to the sky. Malach wasn't going to be able to stay ahead of him for long. He spotted a clearing to his left and banked toward it. He only hoped help was on its way. On his own, he didn't think he stood a chance at surviving, much less killing the dragon. He landed on the edge of the clearing, the dragon only a few second behind him.

Daziar fought the endless waves of enemies. Their backs were to the stone wall of the stronghold, and they had no other recourse but to keep fighting. Ana and Ariel were on either side of him and fighting just as desperately. Even though the enemies lay in piles at their feet, more pressed in. The fire light danced on their armor, making the enemy appear more ethereal and demonic. It was frightening at times when his mind forgot they were mere men, and his heart would jump into his throat at the sight.

Ariel had verbally noted the angels taking to the skies to answer the demon's charge and many death pulses hit them, but they could no more watch than retreat. He hoped they were winning, but the reality of what was happening in front of him contradicted that hope, declaring the futility of their desperate fight. Then the dragon passed over their heads, blocking the sun for only a moment. The beast attacked an angel off on their own. Daziar couldn't do anything about that, though. Fire erupted from the dragon's jaws, and it engulfed the angel.

Daziar couldn't watch any longer, turning his full attention back to surviving. There were so many death pulses happening, he had no idea which side was winning. All they could do was keep fighting. He kept an eye out for Amara, but they had been separated in the fighting while trying to retreat to the new fortifications just outside the stronghold.

They had to hold them long enough for the children and elderly to escape into the mountains. Not that Daziar, Ana, and Ariel were holding any position right now. The best they could hope for was to be a distraction from the main force.

"We need to move toward the entrance," Ariel called to them over the din of battle. "We can't hold here forever."

"You have the best chance of pushing through," Ana called back. "You lead and we will follow. Keep your backs to the wall and we will have one less flank to defend."

Ariel didn't reply, but swapped places with Ana and started methodically cut his way through enemies. They fought their way slowly toward the entrance to the stronghold proper. About halfway there, they found a pocket of resistance. Five soldiers held their ground against the press of enemies. Ariel surged forward, Ana and Daziar working to keep pace with him. They joined the small group of soldiers, allowing several of them to fall back and catch their breath or look after the worst of their wounds.

"Thank the Lord you showed up when you did." One of the soldiers, presumably the one in charge of this small band, said.

"We aren't out of this yet," Daziar warned, blocking a thrusting spear meant for that very soldier.

"We are pushing toward the stronghold entrance," Ariel told him. "Can you and you men move?"

"We are dead if we can't," the man said grimly. "We will do our best to not slow you down."

Ariel didn't say anything else, but he made his way through the group to the far end and continued their grisly march. They left a trail of dead in their wake, but it wasn't long before they lost one of their own. A few hard-won feet later, a second soldier fell to a spear that snaked its way in past Daziar and Ana.

"Ariel, pick up the pace. We are losing men," Daziar shouted.

Ariel took his command to heart and carved his way through a dense group of enemies. He burst out into the clearing made by the defenders at the stronghold entrance. Arrows streaked through the air, narrowly missing the small group. The commander shouted for them to check their fire and redirected the archers away from them. It took them only a few moments to cover the distance and dive behind what appeared to be tables upended in a semicircle.

Raziel reached out and pulled Ariel over the barricade as Amara fired arrow after arrow behind them, covering their flank and driving back the enemy. The group followed, diving over the tables and landing in a heap behind them. A hand reached down to help Daziar up. He followed it to find it was attached to Amara and, with surprising strength, she pulled him to his feet.

"The demons are making their final push," she told him.

Daziar realized only then the amount of death pulses he had felt in their push to the entrance. "Malach?"

Amara shrugged, shaking her head. "He was on the run from the two-headed dragon, but I have no idea if any of the pulses were him."

Daziar set his jaw and turned back to the barriers. "Then we keep fighting until we can't. We might not survive, but we will hold to allow the next generation to carry the banner."

Deliverance

With Dawn in spear form, he joined Ana, who was already stabbing out with Hope. Together they held their table, but looking out over the endless force, Daziar couldn't help but feel despair. His own words ringing in his ears, he realized this really was the end.

The enemy push through their barricade to his left and he was forced to defend himself from that direction. A war hammer crushed the skull of the soldier he was about to stab at and he redirected his attack. Togan waded into the fight, missing arm and all. He grinned at Daziar as Marena covered his bad side.

"Ya didn't think I'd sit around feelin' sorry for myself while you all fought and died, did ya?"

Daziar grinned at the man as Togan crushed in another helmet, sending its wearer to the gates of hell. He looked a bit white, but his fighting arm didn't waver.

Skie leapt in beside them, tearing the throat out of a man who had made it past Togan. Her movements were awkward missing a leg as she was, but it didn't slow her enough to matter. She was just as much a fighter as any soldier, and she bit and clawed at the enemy. Together they drove them back, filling the gap in the barrier with the bodies of the slain.

The largest death pulse Daziar had felt in his short time of being a Blade Bearer hit him as hard as Togan's hammer. He dropped to one knee and saw Amara, Raziel, Ana, and Ariel all affected by it. Did that mean Michael was dead? Or Gabriel? Daziar didn't know, and he wasn't sure it mattered at this time. He stood again and fought all the harder.

When he could, he dropped back to rest just behind Ariel. He was careful to stay out of the way of the angel's deadly axe but close enough to ask him the question burning in his mind.

"What was that?" Daziar asked, not giving any context.

Ariel seemed to know what he was asking. "A very powerful being has died." He shook his head. "No telling who it is, but there are only a handful of beings that could have been, and it doesn't bode well for us."

Daziar nodded slowly, but it wasn't but a minute or two later when a second, even stronger, death pulse almost put him on his butt. Hopelessness followed in its wake, but Daziar stood determined. If this were to be his final moments, he intended to go down swinging and take as many of them to the grave with him. He charged, vaulting the barrier and changing Dawn into a hand and a half sword. Using all of his strength, he laid waste to the front line and started into the next.

Explosions rang out, lighting up the battlefield. Daziar didn't stop, didn't look up, and didn't care. If the demons were dropping explosives again, he would keep fighting until something killed him. The man he was about to kill suddenly disappeared in a blur. He took a beat to understand what had happened to him and realized the enemy was in retreat. How had that happened? Had they actually won?

"You're still so headstrong," Ana laughed as she ran up beside him. "You would have been much safer if you had stayed behind the barrier."

"We won?" Daziar asked, still dumbfounded that he was still alive. "How? We were routed, defeated, dead to rights."

A shout rolled through the survivors around the courtyard. Most were dazed or confused, but with the shout of victory starting with a singular man, the rest took it up and grew more confident. There were only a few hundred left in the courtyard. How close they had come to destruction.

"It would appear we have. However, I have no more information than you do." Ana smiled at him. "Let's go get you patched up."

Daziar looked down at his arm. A deep cut ran down it. He couldn't feel it, though, and he had no idea he was losing blood. They walked inside, Ana already working to stop the flow of blood.

Chapter 25

Leviathan had fought tooth and nail killing many lesser demons even with her mundane sword. One day she would earn one of her precious blades back and wield them as they were meant to be but for now, she swung the lifeless thing with ease. All the years of not wielding a blade melted from her movements and her old skill with the weapon was starting to show again. She dispatched the demon she was fighting and spotted the devil spewing fire at Malach. She angled to aid him. She would do whatever she could to help him succeed in the mission God had given him.

The devil grabbed Malach in its claws and started flying away from the battle. She would free him if she could. She was almost on the beast, targeting a knuckle on the claw holding Malach.

A mass hit her broadside and stole the wind from her lungs. They fell, and a fist hammered her jaw and stars burst into her vision. She struck out at her assailant and felt a rib crack under the force of it. She twisted placing whichever demon this was below her. She tried to extricate herself from its grasp but to no avail. The demon rolled with her making her overcompensate and she was once again on the wrong side of this fall. If she didn't do something soon, she would be hammered into the field.

She locked eyes with her assailant and Asmodeus stared down at her teeth gritted his own blood tinting them red. She spread her wings hoping to slow their descent and fought to turn them again, but she couldn't gain the upper hand. He got his feet between them and pushed, propelling her down. This was her chance.

Pain lanced from her back down her legs and then everything went numb. Darkness enveloped her, and she fought her way to consciousness. She tried to rise even as the darkness retreated but her body wouldn't respond. She turned her head to see Asmodeus kneel and then lay next to her. His eyes softened as they locked eyes. He seemed to have fared much better than she. Although she wasn't in much pain. She couldn't feel anything in the lower half of her body. She understood the connotations of the lack of sensation.

Asmodeus rolled toward her pulling her head toward his chest. "Shhh, I'm here sister. I'm so sorry it had to turn out this way."

She didn't resist. His embrace comforting, despite the situation that brought them here. He was her brother before her enemy. The tears started to flow again, and she knew she wouldn't live through the day. He stayed with her holding her, crying with her, and comforting her. He could have left. He could have finished her off. Instead, he laid with her in her final moments.

How could one being's choices bring so much death, destruction, and heartache? Turning brothers against sisters. Sons against fathers. How could lucifer have been so wise and yet so shortsighted and prideful? She sent up a prayer for Malach. Maybe he could finish this war today.

"I love you, Brother" She breathed out her final, rattling breath.

The dragon didn't gloat, as Malach had hoped. Instead, he immediately had to dodge out of the way of the rampaging beast. The two heads went to either side of a tree, but the body stopped long before it hit. Malach could see the patch of scales that was missing or broken. That was his target area. He just had no idea how he was going to get to that. He didn't have a bow or anyone to play the role of a distraction. It was just him and the beast.

It turned toward him, slowly leveling its heads at him. Both breathed in sharply, and Malach rushed for cover. Fire erupted from the mouths and Malach scrambled behind a tall pine, making himself as small as he could as the inferno licked at the edges of the tree. The heat was intense. Malach could feel any exposed skin cooking.

Just as suddenly as the fire had arrived, it stopped. The icy wind replaced the inferno, shocking Malach's skin and making him shiver uncontrollably. The tree he had been hiding behind was still on fire and he needed to move lest it fell on him. He ran for the next tree as he heard the dragon breath in again. He slid behind the next pine, using his wings to steady him, and then pulled them in quickly. This volley of fire was much shorter than the first, and it took Malach a few seconds to realize it was over already. He ran toward the next tree and the devil's heads breathed in for a third time.

Reckoning, how long can they keep this up? Malach asked and felt something hard smack against his thigh as he took cover behind the third tree. The satchel.

Unsure, Reckoning replied.

Malach dug into the satchel, hoping against all hope there was still something in there he could use. His hand felt something metal and cylindrical, and his fingers closed around it. An explosive spike. He grinned wickedly, a plan forming in his mind.

Malach, that's less of a plan and more of a hope and a prayer. Reckoning retorted.

You have something better? Malach shot back.

Reckoning didn't respond, which gave Malach his answer.

The fourth torrent of fire hit the tree, and Malach had a somewhat alarming realization he hadn't moved since the last one. He wondered if the tree would hold up. Although the torrent stopped almost as quickly as it started.

Malach, it appears the dragon is taking longer to catch its breath and the volleys are getting significantly shorter. I believe you would be served best by charging directly after this volley.

He quickly dodged behind the next tree to make sure that it held up to the fire. No sense in tempting fate twice. He steeled himself for the charge, working through his grounding techniques as the fire licked at the edges of the tree. Then it was finished, and he spun around the side of the tree, directly into the tail of the dragon. It sent him flying, only to be stopped by another tree a few feet behind him. He hit the ground hard and fought for consciousness, darkness creeping in at the edges of his vision. If he passed out now, he would never wake up.

He pushed himself to his knees and rolled as the tail of the behemoth came down on top of him like a rope as thick as a tree. He fought for breath as he pushed his body to its limit. Staying just ahead of the next attack from the dragon. He tried to use the trees as cover as he did with the fire, but the claws of the devil made quick work of any he hid behind.

As his head cleared, he realized he was no longer holding the explosive spike. Frantically, he glanced around him, searching for his only hope of survival. The short metal cylinder stuck up out of the ground close to where the tail had hit him. He scrambled through the snow, his armor slowing him down. He reached the tree just as it exploded from the force of the massive claw. Hitting the ground hard, he slid the rest of the way, snatching the spike as he did.

He changed tactics and charge the serpentine head without the vulnerable spot. He got as close as he had up to this point. However, it wasn't good enough. The second head came around and bit at him. He dodged out of the way of the deadly teeth but as he did, the head moved sideways and the thick neck took him off his feet.

He hit the ground and rolled, sweat beaded up on his forehead. He wouldn't last much longer. This needed to end.

The dragon rumbled a laugh from deep within its chest. "Give up and die. You have no other recourse."

"*You* give up," Malach shouted back. "I have you right where we want you."

The one head roared with laughter while the other arced its neck, obviously noticing a sharp pain. Malach rushed forward, the laughing head lunged for him, and he leapt over it, assisted by his wings. He used his foot to depress the ignition button on the spike he had left in the brake in the scales. Two seconds later, the explosive ignited. The shock wave hit him in the back, helping his momentum drive him forward. His foot felt like it was on fire for one moment and then like he had plunged it into ice water the next. As Malach hit the ground and rolled, he caught his first glimpse of the damage he had done. A burning smoking crater was gouged out of the dragon's neck. Malach righted himself, changing Reckoning to an ax. One last battle cry tore from Malach's throat as he charged and, aided by his wings, he jumped, bringing Reckoning down with all the force he could muster behind his strike.

The head came free of its neck, the body and second head recoiling as the first head hit the ground, flopping and writhing. Malach scrambled back from the grisly sight, dodging gore and stomping claws alike. The dragon took to the sky, retreating away from the stronghold.

He collapsed onto the ground, ignoring the cold bite of the ice and snow and allowing his body to relax. Cold air moved across his foot. He seemed to have lost his boot. His laughter started as a mere chuckle, but quickly grew to an almost insane cackle as his body shook from the cold and what had happened. He sat up, peering down at Reckoning. The sword he had stolen from a demon not that long ago. The sword who had been a true companion through all his trials and heartache.

"We did it." He said aloud. "We actually did it."

Malach, you *did it.* Reckoning corrected. You *did what no one has been able to do since the fall.*

"How?" A gurgle came from the direction of the head still twitching.

Malach turned to regard the head, disconcerted at what his mind was telling him was impossible and his ears reported as fact.

"How did you do it?" The head spoke from the ground.

"Your pride was you undoing." Malach replied. "You didn't think you could be hurt. So when you were distracted by the attack on your other head, I placed the spike in your neck. Then it was a matter of waiting until you realized enough of what was going on that you were distracted by your disbelief."

"Lucifer will take revenge on you and your descendants." The head threatened, its eyes starting to glaze over.

Malach smiled. "So, I killed Satan. Good to know. If Lucifer shows his ugly head, I will make a matching stump on that body you shared all this time." Malach would never know if Satan had heard him as the head finally stopped twitching and made no more noise, coherent or otherwise. Moments later, the death pulse hit him and he laid his head back down on the ground. His body ached, his skin burned, and his foot throbbed in time with the beating of his heart. He didn't think his wings would carry him very far, which left him with a long walk to the stronghold. He sat up, breathed in deep and remembered the tooth Amara had pulled from the monster in the swamp.

The monster's mouth was open. And he wouldn't be using them anymore. He selected an incisor and dug it out of its place. This tooth was twice as long as hers. It would serve as proof if he needed it to help end the war and proof that his unbelievable tale was true to any naysayers in the future.

Trophy in hand, he turned the head over once more and notice something he hadn't before. In the center of the dragon's head was a small gem cut perfectly spherical. It was red and seemed to swirl in the light. He reached down and was surprised when it popped free rather easily. He pocketed the gem and thought to ask Michael or Gabriel about it later.

Malach sheathed Reckoning and started trudging through the trees in the direction he thought the stronghold lay in. Hopefully, he could get back to help finished the war. The devil might be defeated, but they still had an army to claim victory over.

Ana just finished patching Daziar up with their supplies when word came they were wanted in the council room. With Ana's wing in no shape to carry her, much less the both of them, they started their long climb, meeting Amara, Raziel, Ariel, and Skie on their way. They had heard no news on the retreat, survivors, or who the death pulses belonged to. Michael, who was apparently still alive, would hopefully explain everything.

They finally arrived at the chamber. Amara and Daziar were breathing heavily, and Skie was panting. Michael, Gabriel, and Raphael were the only angels there and Daziar wondered where the rest of the angels were.

"We are the last, Daziar." Michael bowed his head. "We have suffered severe loss today, not only in troops but friends, brothers, and sisters. Even those who were once enemies. We will search for other survivors, but I wouldn't count on many."

"Leviathan?" Ana asked, her voice cracking slightly.

Gabriel nodded. "She fought valiantly. Worthy of the redemption she was gifted."

Ana bowed her head and Daziar watched silent tears roll down her face.

"Why did they retreat?" Amara asked what they had all been wondering.

"We are unsure. The final death pulse sent Asmodeus running and his remaining demons with him. Once those on the ground realized their generals were running, their discipline failed, and they joined them, allowing for panic to reign in their troops." Michael explained.

"A few well-place explosives also helped them make up there mind," Gabriel smiled despite the gravity of the situation, but it quickly faded.

"That death pulse had to be the devil," Ariel finally spoke. "Who was the angel he attacked?"

"We believe that was Malach," Michael replied.

"Has anyone gone to search for him?" Ariel stepped forward.

"Not yet," Gabriel shook her head.

Michael held out his hand to stop Ariel's objection. "Go find your son. Amara, you no doubt will want to join him in his search. They flew east over the mountain range. Ana, Daziar, ride out and bring back the elderly and children. We will oversee the rebuilding of the wall in case one of the surviving demons rally enough support to march on us again. We are vulnerable at the moment."

Ariel nodded. "Amara and I will be back in three days' time. If we haven't found him by then, we will return. I will require one of you to search from the sky."

Skie had laid down at the start of the meeting, but now her ears perked up and she lifted her head.

"What is it Skie?" Daziar asked.

She turned her head to the open side of the room just as a winged figure landed and collapsed on the balcony. They all rushed over to them and Ariel rolled the person over to reveal it was Malach. He had burns, cuts, and bruises across his body and one of his feet was exposed, although it seemed to be mostly intact.

He smiled up at them. "It would appear we survived."

The after math of the war was grim. The stronghold was ruined, the wounded still needing tended to, and the threat of an attack was ever present, looming over them like some monster just outside of their view.

They took it an hour at a time, starting the process of rebuilding their defenses and taking a full count of the survivors. Thousands were dead on both sides of the conflict and this war would be felt for generations.

Malach recounted his tale, including the survival of Lucifer after Satan was severed from the body and killed. Lilith was also nowhere to be found, and accounts of Asmodeus' survival left little doubt he was still at large. Other than those three, there were several demons and nephilim reported having fled and survive the last moments of the war. They would put a team together to hunt for the surviving leaders of the demon army and kill them if they could. However, that would have to wait. Right now, they would need to rebuild their infrastructure.

Riders were sent to all major cities to discover the state of each. Most were in ruins, but Fairdenn seemed to be the most viable of the cities to send the refugees. Those from Brightwood who survived, of course, left for their little town. Malach, Skie, Amara, Ciarán, Daziar, and Ana traveled with them, with plans for Daziar and Ana to continue on to Fairdenn afterward. Ciarán had taken to Malach and Amara, and they decided they would be best to look after her. She learned the shadow's silent hand code quickly and told Amara her story, including the name she had kept despite the monster who had given it to her. For Malach and Ariel, that name reminded them of Serilda, not Azazel, and Malach was happy for the namesake to continue on.

Arjun and Zahra had survived, and they carried Honora's body with them to lay her to rest at their farm. They had a pyre for her the first night back in Brightwood. A veritable army of people attended and stood vigil including Michael, Gabriel, and Raphael. Most didn't stay more than a few hours, but Daziar and Malach stood with Arjun and Zahra until the sun crested the mountain tops.

Daniel, Jennari, Emiline, and Marletta returned to their house to find it standing, but most of their possessions were stolen or destroyed. Daziar and Ana planned to stay and help them rebuild along with the rest of the town.

Jecrym and Kath stepped up to lead the rebuilding of the town. The first order from them was to rebuild Togan's forge and to erect a sawmill. Togan and Marena would be integral to provide any metal works needed by the town and the sawmill would see to the wood needed. With Togan missing an arm, Marena had a lot to learn in a short time, but Malach trusted they would enjoy the work together.

Finally, on the third day after arriving at Brightwood, Malach, Skie, Amara, and Ariel started up the path to his parents' cottage. Ciarán had stayed with the Wervine family for the day. The path was already overgrown and in disrepair, and Malach hoped against hope that mercenaries had totally missed it, allowing it to stand undisturbed. It wasn't to be. Where the cottage had once stood. Only a blacked husk remained. The remaining beams collapsed in a haphazard pile. Malach dropped to his knees and grieved the loss almost as heavily as the loss of his mother. His best memories of her had gone up in smoke without a fight.

They picked through the wreckage, but it was clear there was nothing left to be salvaged. Anything that hadn't been burned had been ruined by the weather. They returned to the town with nothing to show for their day, but Malach decided he wouldn't rebuild there.

Days passed. Weeks turned into months, months into years, and not one demon was seen. Cities started to be rebuilt, people started picking up their lives again, and Malach and Amara were summoned back to the stronghold. With Skie and Ciarán in tow, they made their way over the mountain range.

The wall had been rebuilt, but the stone used was obviously not as weathered and old. A scar, a reminder of the terror of the past. Malach shuddered as they approached the stronghold. The large doors were open wide and inviting, but the ghosts that lingered in the halls followed them up to the council room.

A new set of table and chairs sat in the center of the room. However, it was much smaller than its predecessor. That hit Malach as profound. This room was designed for a much larger host.

How many times over the years had the table been replaced with a smaller one, as the occupants left and never returned? Michael, Gabriel, Ariel, Daziar, and Ana all sat around the table waiting for them. With only two chairs vacant, Michael rushed, half flying, across the room to bring up another chair for Ciarán and they all took their spot at the table.

They talked and caught up with what each had been doing over the past couple of years until Michael called the meeting to order and told them why they were there. "A demon has been sighted in Caister," Michael said without any preamble. "We need a team to go find if he is still there and if there are more."

"No," Malach replied, shaking his head. "I'm done. I've lost too much to continue this fight. Amara and I have decided to settle down and start our family. We are to be married at the year's end and we will start building as soon as the snow has melted in the spring."

Michael nodded his understanding. "I cannot begrudge you two your happiness. Gabriel and I would be happy to attend your festivities if you will have us."

"We would be honored," Amara smiled. "Everything will be done in Brightwood. Most of the Shadows are going to be there. They will travel up from Newaught. I hope that doesn't pose an issue for you."

"We would be happy to break bread with those who stood by us in the war." Gabriel assured her.

"No matter how many crimes they have committed since then." Michael added.

At first, Amara thought he might have been mad at them, but she noticed the amused grin on his face and knew he was giving her a little jibe. She smiled back at him. His demeanor had changed since they last saw him.

"This is joyous news to be sure," Ariel smiled. He, of course, already knew. Malach and he had corresponded over the last few years. Even though they had been busy with their own effort to rebuild and hadn't been able to visit each other. "As much as I would like to continue on this subject, we have an important matter at hand. If the demons are rallying, we could be in trouble once again. We need to find out if this is an isolated incident or if there are more demons around that city. We also need to search the old demon compound and make sure there has been no activity there. I will take Daziar and Ana and do a reconnaissance of the city and compound and see what we can find out. We will be back before the wedding and report our findings."

"Very good," Michael agreed. "I don't have to tell you to be careful. Lucifer and Asmodeus are still at large, not to mention Lilith is a very accomplished assassin. Since she has never been found, we must assume she is alive and well. If any of the three of them are behind this, it could be extremely dangerous."

Once the details were talked through, they all stayed at the stronghold. They talked late into the night, telling stories new and old. At first, it was a little awkward with Michael and Gabriel there, but as stiff as they had been at the height of war, they were equally laid back now. They joked laughed and told stories from better, happier times.

Ciarán fell asleep with her head on Skie, and the wolf was content to stay half curled around her slight frame.

The next day, as they prepared for their separate journeys. Michael walked up to Malach's group. "Malach, I truly desire for the two of you to have an amazing life together. A relationship to last your extended lifetimes. I will warn you that this will not be easy, more so than most. You will have at least three lifetimes together and you will watch many friends

and your descendants come and go in that time. You will know the life and
death of your children and grandchildren. You two need to prepare your-
selves for this. On the other side of that same coin, you will have a companion for just as long. Learn about each other. Learn how each other thinks,
functions, down to your inner cores. Then you can face the world without
fear, leaning whole heartedly on each other."

He knelt down to be eye level with Skie.

It was odd and felt out of place for one such as Michael to humble
himself, and it spoke volumes to his character. "You will find your companion. There are still dire wolves in this world. They aren't easy to find, and
you will have a much harder time with your injury, but I have no doubt
you will find them. It would break my heart you see your noble line end
with you. You are truly a wolf with no equal. Please bring more like you
into this world, for we truly need companions of such beauty and loyalty
and to lose such a gift would be a tragedy all its own. Also, make sure these
two survive, please."

Skie rubbed her head against his hand, then back up and looked
him directly in the eyes.

"Good girl," Michael smiled, and then turned to Ciarán, not getting
off his knees but instead bowing farther in front of the young girl. "I heard
what happened in the escape tunnels with the demon Azazel, from the bottom of my heart. Thank you. You are a shining beacon of hope for your
generation, and your courage is unmatched. Although you are not the biological child of these two, you fit with them more than you could ever
know."

Malach and Amara shared a confused and slightly shocked looked
between them at the Archangels' words. What had happened with Azazel?
And was she really *their* child? They were taking care of her, sure, but to
call her their daughter was a big step. They would have to talk about it, but
they both loved her and intended for her to live with them, so why not?

They left, Malach and company working their way back toward Brightwood with big plans in mind. Ariel, Ana, and Daziar off on another harrowing adventure. With as weary as Ariel had been after the war, Malach was surprised he went along at all, but His father needed something to keep himself busy. Even for all the possible danger, this trip would be good for him mentally.

Epilogue

100 years after the war.

--

Malach paced the floor of his home. Amara was facing something he could never have prepared for. Something he couldn't help her with or do anything about. He felt helpless and useless.

"Malach," Togan stood in his way. "You're going to wear a rut in the floor. Sit down."

He did, but he wasn't happy about it.

"Marena and Ana are in there with her, as well as Silas." Daziar assured him. "They won't let anything happen to her or the baby."

"I know, but I feel like I'm useless." Malach stood again and continued his pacing.

"Come, son, let's go get some air." Ariel guided him out the back door and out onto the deck overlooking the valley below.

Raziel was already out there and turned to regard them as they walked out. "Sorry, I couldn't stand being inside any longer. Listening to her in there brought back some bad memories."

"At least it brought back *any* memories old friend." Ariel clapped his hand on Raziel's shoulder.

"No need to apologize." Malach added and joined the two angels at the railing.

Malach and Amara had built their house over the cliff side where they had shared a very important moment for their relationship. It was next to the flume of water that had almost killed them. Since then, they had enhanced the flume and made it much safer for canoes to traverse. They also played a large role in the rebuilding of Whiteshade. After the burning of the city, much of the surrounding forest had also caught fire and new saplings were just starting to grow when they started the rebuilding process.

The now booming city had rebuilt using timber they sent down the Pangor river. In exchange, they provided Malach and Amara with anything they needed. Malach had also built a lift that helped those without wings to traverse the cliff side.

After Ciarán had grown into a young lady, they had tried for many years to have a child of their own, but for a long time, they were unable to. They had finally faced the fact that they couldn't have children. Amara being the daughter of an angel and a cursed woman, and Malach, the son of an angel and Blade Bearer. They were in uncharted waters.

Only a couple years after that, Skie had left for a few weeks and had come back, her belly bulging with a litter of her own. The father was nowhere to be found, but as the puppies grew, it was clear he had to have been a dire wolf. The four puppies were huge and were more than enough of a handful for Malach and Amara.

Togan and Marena had become pregnant with their first child only a few months after that, and Malach and Amara had made the journey to help them when the time came. The five wolves had caused a stir in the city of Brightwood that had more than doubled in size. Rumors of "the mountain angel and his pack" circulated with very little truth to any of the tales. They stayed for nearly two months helping where they could with anything Togan and Marena needed.

Arjun and Demien had gone into a business that was completely legitimate. They now ran a caravan, or more accurately a *fleet* of caravans. Demien did more of the management, but Arjun had provided the funds. Amara was able to visit with Demien during their time in Brightwood. Malach knew that was a special treat for her.

On their return journey, Amara had come down with a mild sickness that seemed to hold on for almost a month. It was worst in the morning and smells seemed to really affect her stomach. Then her belly started growing and their miracle had slowly formed in her womb. Now the day had arrived for the baby to come.

Malach glanced at Marena and Togan. If Malach wasn't wrong, Marena was starting to show once again with their second little one. He would let them share their news, however.

"Malach, your wife is in excellent hands." Ariel peered out of the valley.

"I know. I just can't help but feel I should do something more."

"I know how you feel." Ariel smiled at him. "I felt the same way when you were born. We are men of action. But what do you do when there is no action to be taken?"

"What did you do?" Malach asked.

"Found something constructive to keep me busy." Ariel replied. "I started a project that would eventually become your room. Of course, you seem to have thought well ahead on that front."

It was true. Malach had added several rooms already for guests and he had turned one of them into the nursery. He had also already built all the things they would need for the baby; a crib, a padded table, even a place to put the little clothes acquired for their tiny miracle. There was nothing he could think of that he needed to do that was constructive.

Ariel laughed at his plight. "Have you given any thought to toys?"

"What?" Malach couldn't believe he had overlooked that.

"Come on, let's go to your workshop and we will make some toys for your new little one."

They did just that. When they left the house, they were immediately accosted by the pack of wolves. Ciarán was with them, and Skie trailed behind her. The she-wolf greeted Malach by putting her head under his hand.

He kneeled and looked her in the eyes. "We will soon have a little one to protect. I know your pups will be just as loyal companions as you have been over the years."

He swore she smiled at him, and he set his forehead against hers.

A tap on his shoulder brought his head up to look at Ciarán. She signed to him, "Dad, there's something in the woods tonight."

Malach sighed.

Having been practically raised with horrors everywhere she turned, Ciarán tended to be jumpy. It served her well in a few choice situations, but for most, it turned out to be something benign. He tried not to hold it against her, but after the hundredth time or so, it was hard to be concerned about her warnings.

"There's always something in the woods, darling." Malach replied as kindly as he could.

She gave him a withering look and signed, "Don't treat me like a child. Something big is stalking around out there."

Malach nodded. "We will keep an eye out tonight for anything out of the ordinary. For now, take the pack into the house. If there really is some predator out there, I don't want you and the wolves to get in its path."

She nodded, and the wolves followed her inside.

"Do you think she saw something?" Ariel asked. "She's not a child, hasn't been for a long time."

Malach shook his head, not knowing what to think. "She still sees demons where there are only shadows. Sure, she doesn't wake up shaking in the corner dripping sweat like she used to, but for all I know, it's a bear that will soon leave the area."

"Then keep her warning in the back of your mind and watch for signs yourself." Ariel advised. "Until then, let's get to making toys."

It was late into the night when Malach got word Amara had birthed their baby. A storm had blown in by this time, and he and Ariel fought through the driving rain to reach the house. He rushed into the room he and Amara shared, not bothering to dry off.

"Your sopping," Silas said. "Get out, you'll make her sick."

Malach was shooed out of the room, and he quickly found a towel, dried himself, and changed into dry clothes. This time, when he entered the room, he was allowed over to Amara's side. The amount of blood that was still present alarmed him, but she appeared fine, if a little pale. And the most beautiful little creature lay on her chest already partaking in its first meal on earth. Malach couldn't breathe and he felt like a young boy again, his heart and stomach a flutter.

Amara beckoned him over to her side, and he obliged. "Meet your daughter, little Nasiyah. Our miracle."

Tear sprung up in Malach's eyes as he looked at this tiny human being in front of him. His knees just about gave out when she peered up at him and smiled. He understood at that moment how Ariel could jump off a balcony for him without having a clue how they would survive. He would do the same and more for this perfect angel. Hell couldn't send anyone against him that he wouldn't slay to keep her safe.

"Nasiyah," He whispered, testing the name on his tongue. This was his greatest legacy. Nothing he had done or would do was as important.

"Malach, you need to let them rest now." Ana put a hand on his shoulder.

"I love you," Malach kissed Amara on the forehead and then did the same to his daughter, who had closed her eyes and was sleeping contently.

Ana guided him back out to the common room and closed the door behind him.

"It's a girl!" Malach shouted, and the room erupted in congratulations.

Once the excitement had died down, they all sat around the common room talking and laughing until Marena and Ana came out, leaving Amara and Nasiyah to sleep. Marena moved to Togan and sat on his lap, giving him a quick peck on the lips. Ana sat next to Daziar, and they shared a look that Malach had seen before. He smiled, knowing they would never admit it.

"We have an announcement of our own," Marena said and smiled down at her husband. "Not to take away from the joy of Malach and Amara, but to add to it. We are having our second baby."

A second round of congratulations went around the room and the couple shared another kiss and grinned as large and Malach had ever seen. Their first child, a son, was asleep in the room they were staying in even now. He was just starting to walk and say a few words.

"What about you two?" Marena asked, looking at Daziar and Ana.

Panic spread across Daziar's face and Malach suspected that reaction was the reason Marena ask her question in that manner.

"Well, everyone knows what we've been up to, but what have you two been doing this whole time?" Marena clarified and grinned at them.

"Oh, well, we've been hunting demons, of course." Daziar's cheeks burned red.

"Daz," Ana replied in a warning tone.

"They asked," Daziar objected .

"What's wrong Ana?" Malach asked. "It's not like any of us here have any love for demons. How many have you found?"

"We promised each other no talk of demons while we were visiting." Ana shook her head. "This is a time for joy and celebration. Talk of such negative topics would only steal that joy."

"We've killed three, just to answer your question." Daziar replied.

Ana shot him a look that said, in no uncertain terms, to shut up.

"Sorry," He mumbled, studying his feet.

"I would like to hear more about it personally," Malach stated. "But maybe at a later time. Now I believe I will retire to my room with my wife and daughter. Thank you all for coming and being a part of this wonderful time in our lives."

Everyone said their goodnights and most moved to retire to their respective rooms. Daziar was the only one who didn't move, as his bed was the floor of the common room.

Malach entered their room as quietly as he could not want to disturb either mother or daughter. Instead of crawling into bed, however, he walked over to the window. Something drew him to peer out into the storm. Lightning flashed and the silhouette of a man hovering on bat-like wings appeared for that split second. Malach clutched Reckoning's hilt and stared more intently out the window, searching for signs that what he had seen was real, but the next time the sky lit up, there was nothing there.

Skie pushed her way into the room, and Malach moved to close the door. The she-wolf growled, low and threatening. Malach sighed heavily, knowing better than to doubt his oldest friend.

Malach, I will communicate what you've seen to the others, Reckoning told him. *With everyone ready, any demon would have to be insane to attack this house.*

Thank you Reckoning, Malach crawled into bed with Amara and little Nasiyah. Reckoning was within arm's reach, and he would sleep with one eye open tonight. Despite his joy at his new baby girl, he had a bad feeling his family's part in this conflict was far from over.

Appendix A

Akila: uh – k EE – l uh

Amara: uh - m AH r - uh

Anahita: ah n – uh - h EE – t uh

Anauel: AH n - oo - eh l

Angelcross: AY n - g eh l - cr ah s

Ariel: Ah r - eebe - uh l

Arjun: uh r - j UU n

Auron: AW - r ah n

Azazel: uh – z AI – z uh l

Barclay: b AH r - k l AI

Bartholemu: b ah r - th AH L - uh - m oo

Bray: b r AI

Brightwood: b r IY t - w uu d

Caister: c AY - s t eh r

Camael: c AA m - ay eh l

Cathetel: c AA th - eh - t eh l

Celewen: s EH l - eh - w eh n

Daniel: d AA - n ih - y uh l

Darhian: d AH r - ee - eh n

Daziar: d ah - Z EE - ah r

Deadpost: d EH d - p oh st

Demien: d eh m - EE - eh n

Dros: d r AH s

Durvain: d R - v ay n

Dyeling: d IY - l ih n g

Elzrod: EH l - z r - ah d

Emmeline: eh m - ee - l EE n

Enziarel: eh n - z IY - ah r - eh l

Fairdenn: f AY r - d eh n

Fang: f AI ng

Fury: f UU ry

Gabriel: g AA – b r ee – eh l

Honora: h aw - N OH - r ah

Jarsar: j AH r - s AH r

Jecrym: j EH - c r ih m

Jennari: j eh n - ah r - ee

Johm: j AH m

Kargod: k AH r - g ah d

Kath: k AA th

Lanifair: l AA n - ih - f ay r

Lawdel: l AW - d eh l

Lindow: l IH n - d ow

Malach: M AH L - ah k

Marena: m ah - r EE - n uh

Maria: m ah - r EE - uh

Marletta: m AH r - l eh t – uh

Michael: m IY – k uh l

Newaught: n OO - aw t

Oathbreaker: OH th – b r AY - eh r

Pangor: p AY n g - oi r

Prinna: p r EE - n uh

Raphael: r AH – f ay - eh l

Ragewood: r AY j - w oo d

Ravenbard: r AY - v uh n - b AH r d

Raza: r AH - z AH

Raziel: r AH – z ee – eh l

Reckoning: r EH - k uh - n ih n g

Reybella: r ay - B EH L - uh

Reymold: r AY - m oh ld

Rose: r OH s

Serilda: s eh r - IH l - d aa

Shasta: sh AA - s t uh

Skie: s k IY

Storm: s t OH r m

Tresch: t r EH sh

Togan: T OH - g eh n

Vadis: v AY – d ih s

Viessa: v EE - eh s - uh

Wervine: w R - v IY n

Westbay: W EH - st b ay

Whiteshade: w IY t - sh ay d

Yargate: y AH r - g ay t

Zahra: z AH - r uh

Acknowledgments

First, I would like to thank God, since he has given me the dream and ability to write this trilogy. This has been a nine year journey since the idea for this series came to me. I was sitting through a Sunday morning sermon. My pastor mentioned what it might be like if we had to physically fight the spiritual battle that is waged every day. As the idea for this book blossomed in my mind, I have to admit I didn't listen to a word, he said after that.

I want to thank all the people in my life that have encouraged me through this process. Whether it was just listening to an idea that I was working on or simply an encouraging word. Also, I would like to thank my parents for instilling in me the love for a good story.

There are several people who have really done a lot to help me through the writing, editing, and publishing process. First, I would like to say thank you to my beta readers; Chantelle, Lisa, and Jasyn. The beta readers slogged through my writing that was not as well polished as the story you just finished and help me iron out my plot. Their reactions and comments made sure the correct feelings were felt throughout the book and they were absolutely brutal pointing out my mistakes and I thank them for every bit of their hard truth.

The final and probably most important person would be my wife. She has done so much for my writing career. She has listened to my endless rantings about ideas for this and many books to come. She has patiently, and sometimes not so patiently, endured me waking her up in the middle of the night as I write down things that have come to me mid-dream. She has taken care of our children while I've gone away on weekend to sit as comicons and other events and the list could go on and on. I love her more and more each day and I know that she will continue to be there for me as I continue my writing career.